The Thin Place

a novel by

Bob Lively

TREATY OAK PUBLISHERS

Publisher's Note

Printed and published in the United States of America

Treaty Oak Publishers

ISBN-13: 978-1-943658-00-8

DEDICATION

Dedicated to my grandson,
Henry Fontaine Hill,
whose light shines brightly.

The Thin Place

Blessed are the peacemakers,
for they will be called children of God.

Matthew 5:9

CHAPTER ONE

As Jan Love approached the churning water, the muddy river twisted and turned in the desert of the Big Bend like a diamondback whose head had been severed by a grubbing hoe. Her trembling knees compelled her to settle upon a rock only a few feet above the swirling currents. The first of a torrent of tears flooded her eyes, and she rubbed them with the sleeve of her denim shirt until they cleared.

A thin, coffee-bean brown, and shirtless man perched in the center of an aluminum boat. The man rowed vigorously toward the Texas side of the river and called, "I take you to Mexico, señora. Only uno dollar, señora. I take you all the way. You will like Boquillas. *Mucho cerveza. Muy frio, señora.*"

Standing to amplify her voice, Jan hollered, "Go back please. Go back! I don't want to cross the river."

Undeterred, the emaciated boatman continued to pull his craft through the swift currents.

Jan grimaced, then cupped her hands to her mouth, and, hoping she sounded angry, screamed, "No, señor, NO! NO! NO! I can't cross the river. You go back now and get the hell out of here."

"I take you to Mexico," yelled the boatman as the bow of his boat remained anchored in a thick bank of Texas mud.

Jan launched one last refusal in the direction of the boatman. When the man bowed his head, she reached into the right front pocket of her red capri pants until her fingers located a five-dollar bill. Gripping the bill, she jumped off the big rock and slid toward the river.

The boatman lifted his head to present a grin void of all teeth. She thought the sight disgusting, yet guilt pushed her to step and slide toward him.

Raising his hands toward the sky, the boatman yelled, "*Bueno, señora.* I take you to Mexico."

"No!" screamed Jan much louder than she intended. "I do not want to go to Mexico. But I do want you to have this." She gripped the bill between her index and middle fingers and extended her trembling arm toward the old man.

"Oh yeah, that old man is familiar with gringo guilt," Jan muttered.

The ancient man accepted the bill with the same toothless smile he offered only minutes before. With a joyful bow, he pulled his tiny boat back toward the Mexican side.

Struggling to keep her balance as she ascended the slippery bank, Jan stretched out her hand. A tall stranger towered above her, standing on the very rock she had only moments before abandoned.

His smile rattled her entire being so much she feared she might faint. She was certain this man, whoever he was, meant to do her harm.

Beads of cold sweat formed on her forehead, and her stomach tightened into a knot. She did her best to appear confident by stuffing her shaking hands in the front pockets of her capri pants.

His presence blocked her escape route to the new red Porsche convertible she had parked only yards away. His unfashionably long salt and pepper hair belied a smooth youthful face, and she estimated him to be about fifty. His teeth were picket fence straight and alabaster white. Although wiry strong, he stood stooped at the shoulders as though it had long been his plight to haul about heavy burdens. His sad eyes mocked a broad grin.

The man spoke her full name in the rich, resonant tone of a voice well trained for radio. "Janet Marie Macdonald-Love," he crooned. His delivery was slow as though each name was a distinct musical note.

Jan yanked her hands from her pockets and folded her arms. Stamping her feet, she did her best to demonstrate the kind of anger that refuses all attempts at intimidation. She felt like crying and collapsing, yet she whispered, "I must not appear weak. I can't do that."

She clinched her fists and waved them at the man as she screamed, "I don't know who the hell you are, but I do know you were sent here by the pompous ass I married. You're either with the FBI or you're a private detective he hired to keep tabs on me. Either way, I won't be intimidated, so you can go back to wherever it is you came from and leave me the hell alone."

Through the determined smile, the stranger spoke in a much softer tone, "Janet, I knew you would be frightened, but I mean absolutely no harm. I'm not with law enforcement. I'm nothing more than a priest who serves the poor of Boquillas."

"So how do you know my name?"

"A sweet fellow named Juan Diego visited me recently in a prayer and instructed me to find you today on this stretch of the river. I am to take you to meet him and he, in turn, is to take you to meet the very Mother of God, known as Our

Lady of Guadalupe in this part of the world. You have been most blessed, Janet, in that the very Mother of God wishes to speak directly to you. This is likely the greatest blessing any human being can receive. Oh, Janet, you must surely be a very special woman."

"I'm nothing but a miserable drunk who is married to a hypocrite the entire world views as a living saint. And you, sir—priest or no priest—are crazy. I'm not going anywhere with you! Not today! Not tomorrow! Not any day! But I am going to climb up this muddy river bank, and then get in that brand new red Porsche convertible parked up there, and I'm driving as fast as those wheels will take me to the first land line I can locate, and I'm calling the Highway Patrol to report you and this attempted abduction. In a day or so, I'll be back in my comfortable University Park mansion and you will be languishing in some hot, miserable West Texas jail."

She unclenched her fist. "What did you say your name was?"

"I didn't, but my name is Royal."

"Well, Royal, you'd best step aside and let me pass. You don't look like the kind of man who would enjoy jail."

The stranger presented a smile. "I mean no harm, Janet. You are free to leave here and do as you wish. I will not bother you. I knew you would be afraid. Who wouldn't be? But someday, you must come to trust me. Otherwise you will never know the truth I suspect you have searched for throughout your life. Once you come to trust me, I am to take you to meet Juan Diego and he will introduce you to Our Blessed Mother at the Thin Place. And then, you will be blessed beyond your wildest dreams. I promise."

Taking one cautious, slippery, step toward the parking lot,

Jan inhaled a gulp of desert air in the hope of strengthening her resolve. "Don't you dare touch me, or I'll add attempted rape to the charges."

"I won't dare touch you, Janet, I promise."

As she kept her gaze fixed on the tall stranger, she crept toward the Porsche until her fingers gripped the door handle. After popping open the door, she more fell into the front seat than sat. Following a minute of fumbling with her keys, she managed to switch on the ignition. The cougar-like growl of the engine so reassured her she dared to turn her head one last time.

The tall stranger was nowhere to be found.

"What the hell just happened?" Jan screamed. "I'm getting out of here!"

Pressing the accelerator until the tires gained traction, she drove toward the west without any certainty of her destination. She hoped to be as far away from this ghost, hallucination, or whatever it was, as soon as she could possibly manage on a road with more twists and switchbacks than a state fair rollercoaster.

Maybe I'll go somewhere and buy a bottle and get drunk enough to wander in the desert until I die of snake bite or mountain lion attack or dehydration or whatever comes first. I think I'd much rather die than feel this fear much longer.

CHAPTER TWO

Behind the wheel of her Porsche, Jan averaged a hundred miles an hour until she reached the little resort town of Lajitas. There she discovered a saloon still open and staggered in.

The surly bartender, who at first only grunted like a Neanderthal in response to her simplest questions, suddenly abandoned the bar he tended and sauntered across the room until he reached a big picture window overlooking the desert. He stayed there for a moment or so before dropping to his knees.

As he knelt, he began to whimper. Jan remained very still at the bar and nursed her Sprite, refusing to look at this idiot making a spectacle.

Within moments, another fellow, this one a Mexican she judged could not have been more than five feet tall, entered the saloon through the door. Dressed in snow-white linen, he clutched a straw hat that appeared to be half eaten by a horse. This strange little man floated across the floor in the direction of the whimpering bartender, still on his knees. As best Jan could tell, he remained silent while he appeared to levitate only a few inches above the kneeling bartender near the big window.

Without warning, the bartender rose to his feet and shuffled straight to Jan. "Lady, I have no idea whatsoever why I'm telling you this, but you must go back to the river immediately across from Boquillas and find a man named Royal. A great deal depends on it, maybe even life or death. But ma'am, you absolutely must go back to the river."

Jan jumped off the barstool, ran to the Porsche, and drove straight to her cheap motel room. She gave serious consideration to walking a few feet to the motel office where Jack Daniels was sold. She figured a fifth of "old Jack" would kill her as painlessly as possible.

Instead, just as Jan managed to shove the second dead bolt into its hole, the phone rang louder she imagined than any phone had ever rung before. She shrieked as she staggered toward the unmade bed where she fell face first before covering her ears with two small throw pillows.

A deafening second ring signaled the kind of danger that might easily culminate in her death. The old black telephone was now the enemy as it threatened her from its place on a crude, unpainted nightstand adjacent to the kind of broken gooseneck lamp that is indigenous to flea markets and yard sales.

Through a veil of tears, she witnessed the telephone morph into a tightly coiled cottonmouth. She knew she must answer even if she was to be subjected to the horrifying voice she had encountered hours earlier on the river. A courage she had no idea she possessed drew her trembling hand to the receiver where she lifted the thing to her face. Drawing a deep breath, she managed "Hello" in a voice as hoarse as it was weak. She imagined the pause that ensued required at least an hour.

Two distinct clicks preceded the warm, if overly solicitous, voice of her friend and AA sponsor, Emily Sands. "Jan, Jan, is that you, sweetheart?"

"Thank the God I don't believe in that it's you," said Jan, still trembling upon the cheap bed's dingy sheets. "I'm so glad it is you."

"Jan, are you okay?"

"I'm scared shitless, that's all."

"Who or what's scaring you, baby?"

"You wouldn't believe me if I told you, Em. Hey, how did you find me all the way down here?"

"Wasn't all that hard. You mentioned you would be staying in Study Butte, and since there is only one motel in the whole area, at least according to Google, I figured you had probably landed there."

Still prone on the sheets, her head braced by a hard pillow, Jan fumbled in her big Prada bag for a pack of cigarettes she had purchased that morning at a service station. She pried open the cellophane wrapper and withdrew a long unfiltered cigarette which she wedged between chapped lips. She was grateful and a little surprised her two-dollar lighter ignited on the second flick of her thumb against the flint. Lighting the cigarette with her still-trembling hand, she drew hard as she waited for the tobacco to calm her jangled nerves with a small dose of counterfeit comfort. As she released a steady stream of smoke through her nostrils, she wedged the phone's black receiver between her shoulder and her ear.

Emily rattled on. "What's got you so spooked, honey? And don't say I wouldn't believe it. Just tell me what's going on or I'm coming down there myself to bring you home."

"Just a few hours ago I was down on the river, on the

Texas side, of course, doing my best to commune with nature. I've told you about this special spot before. It's where I used to go as a girl when I was in desperate need of solace. Each fall my father brought me to Big Bend to this very same place and dropped me off. For the better part of a full day, I would remain very still beneath the Sierra del Carmen Mountains and do my best to pray even, though I had no idea whatsoever how to pray. I would just sit there for the longest time, close my eyes and whisper, 'God help me... God, help me... God, help me.'"

Jan rose from the bed. "Hold on for a second, will you?"

After laying the receiver on the pillow, she stepped into a bathroom covered from floor to ceiling in tiny squares of tile the color of a freshly picked cucumber. She tossed the cigarette into the toilet and stood above it to watch the remains of the smolder sizzle before dying. Flushing the toilet, she studied what little remained of a pleasant smoke swirl about until it disappeared.

She returned to the bed, picked up the phone, and continued where she hoped she had left the story. "After I did that for maybe an hour, I would feel a fleeting touch of serenity. The sensation really never lasted very long, but I considered the fact that it came to me at all as a miracle. The Sierra del Carmen is a magical place, and in its presence is the only place I've ever really felt truly alive and safe."

"Isn't it dangerous down there on the border, sweetie?"

"I've never thought so until today."

"Good God, tell me what the hell happened."

"I was at the very spot where I always tried to pray as a girl, and all at once I heard a man's deep voice call me by my full name. Nobody has ever called me by my full name except my crazy old mother, and that sick bitch has been gone now for more than twenty years."

"Who was he?"

"I have no idea."

"What did he look like?"

"He may have been seven feet tall, for all I know. His face was brown and leathery, but not Hispanic in that his eyes were pale blue. He was large and imposing, but lean, strong in the way a laborer can look fit. A head full of salt and pepper hair that fell to his shoulder in one of those ridiculous pony tails the Austin hippies down on The Drag wore forty years ago."

"Have you called the police?"

"He didn't break any law. He just scared the holy shit out of me."

"Harassing another person is against the law."

"He simply called me by my full name, which means only one thing. Chuck put him up to it. That's the only logical explanation. I swear I hate that son of a bitch."

"So come back to Dallas and divorce the bastard."

"It's not that simple. I hate him, but I don't want to live without his money. In fact, I can't live without the big bucks he makes. Chuck may be the biggest hypocrite ever, but the man does make real good money."

"Why don't you hire a good divorce lawyer and go after his money?"

"On what grounds? The whole world thinks of him as the perfect man, the man with all the answers. Hell, even the President kisses his ass."

"Sue him for cruelty."

"I can't really prove it. He's as narcissistic as they come and he treats me as his concubine, but actual cruelty is not a part of his game."

"He sent a man to follow you and to scare you. If that is not cruelty, I don't know what the hell is."

"I'd have to prove he sent him in order to prove cruelty, and I can't do that. But listen, there is more to this story."

"Tell me, sweetie."

"After the tall stranger terrified me, I jumped into the Porsche and drove to a saloon in the resort town of Lajitas."

"Oh my God, Jan, please say you didn't drink."

"Calm down. I only drank a Diet Sprite over ice."

"Promise me you're telling the truth."

"Chill right now, or I swear, I'm hanging up."

"I'm composing myself, and I desperately want believe you. What happened in the saloon?"

"A little Mexican dressed in glowing white linen came into the bar and appeared to float across the floor until he reached the bartender, who knelt on the floor near the big window. The little Mexican hovered above the bartender for what seemed like a full minute, and then the bartender crawled across the room until he reached my place on the stool"

Jan paused. "He stared a hole in my soul and said, 'Lady, I have no idea why I'm telling you this, but you must go back to Boquillas and find the man named Royal.' I'm okay now, but after that incident, I wanted to kill myself with a fifth of Jack."

"Jan, don't talk like that. Stop it this minute. Do you hear me?"

"Yes, Mother, I hear you."

"I'm not your mother, so stop the sarcasm or whatever it is, and swear to me you are not going to harm yourself. I've devoted countless hours caring for you this past year, and at the very least, you owe me that one, solemn promise."

"You've been a fine AA sponsor. And you've also been a very good friend, but I do know this about myself—once we hang up, I will definitely be tempted."

"Just don't act on the temptation. Come back to 'Big D' and we'll figure this thing out together."

"Oh, I've got it all figured out. Chuck had me followed down here, and he hired a troupe of professional actors to terrify me. It's just that simple and that mean."

"Come home and my Harvey will help you find a divorce attorney who will take that SOB to the old proverbial cleaners."

"First things first. Tonight I need to eat something. I'm not up to driving, so I'll walk a few feet over to the little café attached to this motel and buy me a big greasy cheeseburger. I'll wash it down with my second Sprite of the evening, and then come back here, unplug the phone, and get me a good night's sleep. By first light, I'll grab some breakfast and drive straight to Midland to catch the first flight back to Dallas. I should be home well before dark."

"Sweetheart, promise me you won't speed."

"My car is probably three-times faster than any county-owned vehicle in all of West Texas and at least two times faster than the Highway Patrol. The real problem is that my little sweet Porsche has a mind of her own. I will, however,

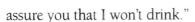

assure you that I won't drink."

"Fair enough. Now, you will call me when you get home?"

"I promise."

"I love you, Jan."

"Thank you, Em. Right now you must be the only person on this planet who does."

"Good night, Jan."

"Good night."

After she hung up, Jan wondered what Emily would think if she decided to stay in Lajitas. Not that she cared, but... What if the little man who floated through the bar wasn't her hallucination? Or the tall stranger wasn't an actor?

CHAPTER THREE

As the pastor of the University Park Presbyterian Church stepped into her workspace on his way to his study, Margaret Baxter lifted her gaze above the computer's wide screen monitor to offer her standard greeting. "Morning, Dr. Love," she said.

"Good morning, Margaret."

"Sir, you had three messages, all from your wife, waiting for you when I arrived. Her first call came in at 5:30, the next at 6:01, and the final one at 6:20." She handed him a sticky note. "She said it was urgent."

"Thank you, Margaret." Dr. Love frowned. "It's never as serious as she makes it sound. The tendency toward histrionics runs like sap throughout her entire family tree."

"Yes, sir. Will there be anything else?"

"Please contact Harry Singleton's office. Ask him to call me as soon as possible. And convey to his girl that my need to talk to him is urgent."

"Yes, sir, right away."

"Thank you, and be so kind as to hold any other calls. At the moment, I'm not up to being all that pastoral."

"Dr. Love, are you okay?"

"Oh, I'm dandy," he muttered over his shoulder, fumbling with a ring of brass keys as he stood before the locked door of his study, a spacious multi-windowed room that more resem-

bled a library reading room than a pastor's office.

Except where the windows bathed the room in the new morning's brightness, the walls were lined from floor to ceiling with bookshelves containing tomes neatly arranged by subject and alphabetized by the authors' names. On walnut paneling between hung oil landscapes of Scotland, highlighted by frames gilded in gold leaf. A Persian rug hugged the maple wood floor immediately before an antique roll top desk, once belonging to Aaron Burr, which the church had purchased as a gift upon his installation. Two leather wingback chairs faced the desk, and behind it, a high, upholstered executive chair awaited the weight of the taut, athletic frame he worked assiduously to maintain. A crystal chandelier lit the desk area dimly, leaving the opportunity for an antique desk lamp and two pole lamps to provide more light.

The desk chair welcomed him with a familiar hospitable sigh. He squeezed his eyes so hard his head ached and he wondered if he might rest soundly some day, but he rejected the idea of sleep medication. He'd not slept, at least not more than a couple of hours a night, for a full week.

Since Jan had ventured to the Big Bend, he had lain awake each night expecting a call either from her or some law enforcement agency reporting a scenario that would no doubt cost thousands. After all, her ventures were always costly.

This was the one thing about his wife he could count on. Once more, he considered praying but rejected the idea of entering into any experience over which he did not have full control. Again he sighed as he worked to convince himself that he could keep up the charade that his life had become. At the moment, he could see no other alternative.

He rose from his desk and walked across the spacious room to study a spider descending from the ceiling on an invisible thread. He wondered why a man *Time Magazine* only the year before had named the most influential preacher in America would be called upon to endure the indignity of a creature dangling in this study from a lengthy strand of silky spit. The church had invested a half million dollars renovating this space to suit his spiteful wife's exquisitely demanding taste. Spending a fortune on this study had embarrassed him to the bone, which of course, was her purpose. Nevertheless, he could not deny Jan the opportunity to harass him and still maintain her willingness to pretend theirs was a happy home.

As he stood before the dangling spider, his legs trembled so much he wondered if he would be able to return to his comfortable desk chair without collapsing.

Oh God, I'm burning up, my head is on fire. I'm so dizzy I think I'm going to faint. I can't faint. I can't do this. Oh my God, what is happening to me?

Turning slowly toward his desk that now appeared to be a mile away he muttered, "Oh please, God, help me make it to my chair. Please, God, help me. God, I must be dying."

As he ripped open his dress shirt, his legs buckled and he landed full force upon the surface of his desk. With his left hand, he managed to hit the button that activated the office inter-com. Now flat on his back, he untied the knot in his silk tie and slung the slender red fabric as far from him as he could manage.

He yelled as loudly as his constricted lungs would permit, "Margaret, would you come in here, please?"

The static from the intercom reassured him enough him

to lift his head from the rug. Immediately he dropped his head to the floor.

I'm going to throw up. I've never been so nauseated. My hands are wringing wet and I can't breathe. God, my chest feels like a mule just kicked it. I can't breathe. I can't breathe. I can't breathe.

He closed his eyes and opened them. Margaret leaned toward him, her face tormented by anguish.

"Dr. Love, what is happening? I've never seen anyone look so pale."

"I don't know what's wrong with me."

"I'm calling 911."

"It's probably nothing, but let's err on the side of caution, if we must."

"I'll make the call and be right back."

He awakened again to find Margaret once more hovering above him. She laid a damp paper towel upon his brow.

"That feels nice. Remind me to recommend you for a raise next year."

"Oh, Dr. Love, you don't have to do that. The honor of working with you is payment enough."

Chuck smiled as the first of several sirens disturbed the morning tranquility for which University Park was both notorious and highly valued. He closed his eyes tightly and attempted to draw a deep breath. His lungs were every bit as tight as the blood pressure cuff now squeezing his right bicep. He opened his eyes. Two uniformed young men hurriedly taped electrodes to his bare chest.

"Morning, gentlemen," he said with a weak voice.

"Morning, sir. How do you feel?" one said.

"Not great, but I'm sure I'll be fine. I have too much important work to complete not to be fine."

"Dr. Love, have you ever been told you have cardio-vascular disease?"

"No, I have a physical once a year and my last one was only last summer, just three months ago. My internist, Dr. Henry Stands, pronounced me as fit as a brand new fiddle. I can't imagine my arteries clogging up between July and October. It could be stress."

"Well, we'll find out in a minute or so after we run an EKG."

"You men are good to come so soon." Chuck raised his head. Margaret stood in the door now appearing more determined than worried. "Yes, Margaret, what is it?"

"Dr. Singleton is here."

"Why?"

"When I told his receptionist about you passing out, Dr. Singleton got on the line and said he'd be right over."

"Tell him to come right in." When he opened his eyes, Dr. Singleton stood next to him. "Oh my, what a pleasant surprise," said Chuck.

"Chuck, what in the world are you doing down there flat on your back? Are you seeking attention again? I just read the EKG these boys ran on you, and I can tell you, it's not your heart."

"Are you a physician?" one of the uniformed men said.

"Board certified psychiatrist," said Dr. Singleton with a wink and a smile. "But before that, I was a real doctor."

"He's a doctor, all right," said Chuck, still on his back. "He reminds me of the fact every time I beat him at golf."

"I thought preachers were supposed to be truth-tellers."

"I'm a scratch golfer and your game stinks worse than a dead carp. That, my friend, is the truth!"

"Whatever you say. After all, you are the man of God."

"I am, indeed."

"Chuck, I pronounce you well enough to get off that floor and to sit in your chair and to act like you are busy, even if you're doing nothing more productive than simply daydreaming." Dr. Singleton turned to the two paramedics. "Will you two gentlemen be so kind as to help me return this over-paid preacher to his chair?"

The younger of the two men said, "Sir, we have to get permission from our supervisor before we can release him to your care."

"Fine," said Singleton, "Get your supervisor on the line and let me talk to him."

The older paramedic placed the call and handed the phone to Singleton.

The doctor took the receiver. "My name is Dr. Harry Singleton and I am a board-certified psychiatrist licensed to practice in Texas, and, yes, I am willing to take full responsibility for the well being of the Rev. Dr. Charles Love. I will sign the appropriate forms so your crew can return to the station."

Singleton returned the receiver to the paramedic, scribbled his name on two documents without bothering to read so much as a word on either one, and handed them to the exiting paramedics.

Margaret entered the office as silently as a seraph. Seeing her boss behind his desk, she sighed her relief. "Oh, Dr. Love. The color is returning to your face, thank God. You scared the daylights out of me, sir. I thought you were dying."

"I'm fine, Margaret. You've been most helpful, as always, and I've put you through quite a lot. Why don't you take the rest of today off, and we'll start over tomorrow?"

"Are you sure, Dr. Love?"

"Go home and rest. You've earned it."

Margaret Baxter disappeared, and within seconds the outer office door wheezed shut.

"She's a good woman," Harry Singleton said.

"Yes, but in many ways she's also a tragic woman." Chuck couldn't stop a protracted yawn. "Her husband of forty-something years lost both legs in a helicopter crash in Vietnam, and he's never worked. Consequently, Margaret has always been their sole support. This rich church barely pays the woman a living wage. I've advocated for her at least a dozen times over the ten years she worked for me, but the personnel committee will only give her a small cost of living bump every other year or so."

"Ouch," said Singleton.

"Ouch is right. Dallas' top businessmen run this church, and to a man, they're real misers. Consequently, my administrative assistant and her disabled husband live in a slum in a run-down apartment in Oak Cliff. And guess what? The owner of the apartment complex is none other than the chairman of this church's personnel committee. Ironic, is it not?"

"I see it as sad more than ironic," said Singleton.

"I see our treatment of her as sinful, and that's what troubles my soul when I choose to think about it, which I can assure you, is not very often. I can't afford to feel guilty, so I don't."

As Chuck lifted his feet to his desk in an attempt to

appear relaxed, he said, "So Harry, if it wasn't my heart, what was it?"

"We psychiatrists call it a panic attack."

"I'm familiar with the term, but I've never been certain as to the real definition."

"Overloading of all the body's circuits with acute and intense anxiety. Of course, the body reacts through distinct signals we call symptoms. For example, the heart races, blood pressure peaks, the patient experiences a severe tightening of the chest, making it difficult to breathe thus causing dizziness, nausea and even vomiting. These attacks are very scary. The patient feels as though he is suffering a heart attack and is, therefore, dying. But, in truth they are not lethal and only mimic a myocardial infarction. And fortunately, they never last long. But they are most uncomfortable, to say the least."

"Is there a cure?

"There is no cure because a panic attack is not a disease, and only a disease can have a cure."

"What I mean is, can this thing be fixed?"

"It can be treated very effectively."

"What must I do so it never happens again?"

"The typical treatment involves talk therapy combined with medication."

"Whoa, Harry, you know I can't do that! In my best selling book, *Living to Win*, I rather boldly proclaim that if anyone practices my program of cognitive correctness and daily prayer, he or she will experience the kind of success that fulfills life-long dreams."

Chuck shook his head. "I can't go into therapy and take some kind of mind-altering drug, and hope to remain on national television every Thursday night raking in the kind of dough only rock stars and major sports figures ever realize."

"No one needs to know."

"Harry, you don't get it. I'm famous! The minute I walk into some shrink's waiting room, I'm recognized. All it takes is one anonymous call to the media and I'm finished."

Chuck wadded a sheet of church stationery into a ball and tossed it squarely into a brass trashcan next to the doctor's right foot. "But if you and I could visit by telephone occasionally—and if you give me some samples of the medication—I could definitely do that. But otherwise, I can't go for help. My image simply can't afford it."

"I can't be your therapist for two reasons. One, we're friends, and two, telephone therapy is notoriously ineffective."

"So what do I do?"

"You swallow some of your neurotic pride and you take my suggestion to heart and seek professional help immediately."

Chuck bobbed his head from side to side, as if weighing possibilities. "Can you recommend a good doctor?

"Several. But before I do that I want to ask you some questions. And if I am going to make a good referral, you must answer truthfully. You cannot hedge or dodge. Do you understand?"

"Let's get this thing over with."

"So now let's get on with the questions. What is the greatest stressor in your life at this very minute?"

"That's easy. It's my wife, Jan."

"How is she a stressor?"

"First of all, she hates me and is hell bent on destroying me."

"Short of killing you, how can she possibly destroy you?"

"The President's people have hinted to me that he, assuming his re-election next year, wants a trained, born-again Christian theologian to serve on his cabinet as Secretary for Our National Spirituality. He wants very much to demonstrate to the world, especially the Muslim world, that a man of the One True Christian God informs this President's every decision. Harry, you may recall that I made what many claim was an audacious speech at the Republican Convention four years ago. Of course, the liberal media panned it, but this President loved it. In fact, he claimed it blew him away."

"How could I forget it? You all but proclaimed that God was a Republican."

"I merely proclaimed that the Republican agenda is wholly consistent with the Kingdom Jesus proclaimed and that no one who votes for a Democrat can possibly claim to be a Christian."

"I remember the firestorm it launched, too. Your mug was on every cable show for a week."

"And now President Billy Jack Rush, our former governor, wants me on his cabinet, and this, my insufferable friend, is the fulfillment of my lifelong dream."

Feeling stronger, Chuck rose to his feet in a gesture of feigned triumph. "From my earliest days, my mother told me God had chosen me to lead the world for Christ, and this is my one great chance to fulfill my saintly mother's prophecy."

"This is all very heady stuff. So what's the problem? Is Jan not all for this?"

"Jan hates the Republican Party and everyone in it, including the President and me. My wife is a drunk, which means she is a loose canon. Every other month or so, she takes off on some spiritual adventure in search of her myopic, not to mention pathological, version of the truth. And far more often than not, she ends up in trouble."

"What kind of trouble?"

"DWI or public intoxication. Typically, I send one of my high-dollar lawyers to her jail cell, and they pay the exorbitant fine along with an even more exorbitant bribe to the local sheriff to keep my name out of the papers."

Chuck fell gently into the comfort of his chair. "If the President's people discover this, I'm history. Never in my life have I wanted anything so much, but I can't have it because I made the mistake of marrying an insane bitch who is also a drunk."

"You're in what we psychiatrist's call a real crazy-making bind."

"So what do I do?"

"Go see my colleague, Dr. Dan Waters. Forget the anonymity issue, screw up your courage, and go see him and do exactly as he tells you."

"And if I don't?"

"Your panic attacks will return with a real vengeance."

"Oh, I don't want that."

"Call Dan and go see the man." Harry rose from his chair and turned to face the door. Looking over his shoulder, he said, "And now, I'm going home. I've had enough excitement for one day. My wife is in Key Biscayne for the week at a cosmetics convention, so I have a quiet house all to myself, and I feel a nap coming on. Chuck, how do you feel?"

"Better, thanks to you. And thank you for being such a wonderful friend. The next time we play golf, I just might let you win."

"I'll believe it when I see it, preacher." He closed the door behind him.

Sitting alone in his spacious empty office, Chuck lifted his gaze toward the ceiling and whispered, "God, if you want me to do this thing for you, you will have to fix my wife, because I have no idea how to get her in line. Help me, God. Amen."

He lifted the Yellow Pages from an adjacent shelf. Turning to the section marked psychiatrists, he slammed the book shut before dropping it to the floor. "I can't do it, God. The risk just is too great! There is simply too much to lose! Help me not hate her, God. Help me not want to kill her, because I swear I honestly want to murder her."

Chuck dropped his head to his desk and sobbed.

CHAPTER FOUR

As Jan ambled down the tree lined Dallas sidewalk two blocks from her psychiatrist's office, she mumbled, "I pray to God, but then I don't believe in God. So forget it, girl, you don't do prayer. Remember? Well then, how about if I beg fate for Ken to be in and available to see me right away?"

She stopped and studied her reflection in a window. "But who exactly am I'm begging to make this little miracle happen? I have no idea. Nevertheless, I beg! What choice do I have?"

Jan shuddered and resumed her walk. "Oh please! Oh, forget it. God, I am so confused I don't know what I think about you, about me, about my life, or about what happened on that river yesterday."

Arriving at the physician's office, she climbed the steps and yanked on the door handle, but the thing resisted what force she could bring to bear. "Why in God's name would this door be locked at this hour?" she mumbled. "The man can't be gone today! This is a weekday, for God's sake! I swear I'll kill myself if the man is not in!"

Through tears, she fixed her gaze upon the nameplate bolted to the brick and framed in neatly cropped English ivy. As though this brass rectangle was a holy icon worthy of reverence, she whispered, "Kenneth J. Coughman, M.D."

Even before she finished sounding out his name, she

recognized her thinking was all too frequently magical. Still she knew it would be difficult, even impossible, to give up the idea that her sanity, if not her very survival, might be attached to this doctor's name. She knew she desperately needed to believe that some power beyond herself could buoy her plummeting spirits by signaling a return to a world she could trust. For the moment, this nameplate served.

With her fingers still gripping the door handle, she spoke loudly enough to feel embarrassed, "If I will look at this brass plate long enough, I will hear his voice and then I will be okay. It will speak to me. Patience is all that is required."

Like a child whose reading brings praise from adults, she sounded each syllable of the physician's name over and over again.

"Dr. Kenneth Coughman, M.D.!" she yelled as once more she tugged. Again the door resisted.

She screamed, "By God, I'm opening this door! I'm not leaving here. If I have to break this sucker down, I'm going through this door!"

Following another desperate tug, the door swung open with surprising ease.

Sighing, she asked out loud, "Is this some kind of a trick? Is someone or something messing with my serenity?"

Certain she now tottered on the brink of yet another humiliation, she could not decide whether to step into the waiting room like she had an appointment, or bolt. She lingered for a moment more in the doorway as she waited for a familiar wave of panic to wash over her.

As the open door released a breath of cool air, she concentrated on mustering the strength to stand in the half-open door and to wait upon clarity as the single option that might permit her to draw another life-sustaining breath. This brief respite felt positive, but still she knew from years of conditioning that anger could always be counted on to purchase a moment of much-needed, if still counterfeit, confidence.

"What does a closed door mean? Dr. Coughman would scold me and say, 'Sometimes a closed door is just a door.'"

The waiting room's fragrances fired within her a primal flicker of anticipation. Within moments, she recognized this familiar and merciless yearning was no substitute for the kind of hope that might birth any real plan.

A disturbingly frail girl sat behind the glass window absorbed in a dog-eared tome.

She might be pretty if she wore no makeup and hid the top half of her head beneath a peasant's babushka. But she is trying her best. Her chin doesn't at all fit her long face and her mouth is much too wide. Our daughter would have been about her age had she lived, but unlike this girl she would have been beautiful.

Rapping her knuckles hard against the glass, Jan attempted to smile at the girl, who now startled, glanced up to offer the bright eyes of one trained to placate. Jan recognized the girl's wet, gummy grin as evidence of some orthodontist's expert efforts.

"Where's Helen?" Jan managed in a gravelly voice before the girl could slide open the window with a squeak.

"She's… she's out today, ma'am. Dr. Coughman said she's ill. Or maybe it was her daughter. I'm not at all sure." The girl's protruding chin trembled like a spring.

Standing now rigid and as tall as possible, Jan barked, "Young lady, I must see Dr. Coughman as soon as possible!"

The girl shook her head.

"How can I make this perfectly clear and impress upon you the urgency? I'm one of the doctor's craziest patients. And right now I'm totally insane! Can you possibly understand that, sweetie?"

Before the girl could slide the window shut, Jan wedged her palm against the edge. "You need not be scared. I'm not dangerous, except perhaps to myself. But I'm in a world of hurt right now, little girl, and what I've experienced in the past twenty-four hours qualifies as the biggest emergency likely ever to stumble into this office."

Releasing the glass, Jan ran her hand across her forehead. "Believe it or not, I've resorted to praying and I can only be counted on to stoop to such a silly superstition when I'm totally terrified, which right now I just happen to be. When I'm only a bit scared, I cuss like a sailor on a three-day binge. But when terror strikes, which it does far more often than I care to admit, I resort to praying, and this is all pretty weird when you consider that I gave up believing in God about the time I reached puberty."

The girl spoke in a calm, low voice. "I'm real, real sorry, ma'am, but Dr. Coughman is with a patient. He will be through shortly, and I'll tell him you're here as soon as he rings me. You can sit over there."

Stomping her foot, Jan's breath formed an oval cloud on the glass window. Regretting that she had frightened this girl with a homely face and a personality dedicated to pleasing people, she considered making an amend but just as quickly decided against it.

Sighing, she said, "Thank you. You may not feel all that

calm at the moment, but you look the part, so I thank you for the favor."

Jan tried to catch a glimpse of her reflection in the glass. "I must look a fright. I'm really not the maniac I just claimed to be. But as Ken tells me far too often for my liking, fear is the most contagious disease on the planet."

Smiling down at the girl, Jan said, "You can't even begin to know how grateful I am that you did not run out of here screaming. Had I been in your sneakers, I would have either done that or called the police. When Ken gets done, please tell him that Jan Macdonald-Love absolutely must see him. And mark this request urgent, young lady. Do you understand?"

The girl nodded before stretching her wide mouth toward a cheerleader smile, but as this affectation faded, her countenance again reflected a solemn self-protection. She said in a monotone, "I will certainly tell him, ma'am. I'm so sorry I jumped, but I didn't hear you come in. You can wait here. When the doctor calls, I promise to tell him you're here. He has lunch scheduled for the next hour, but maybe he can put that off for a bit. I certainly can't speak for him." The girl slid the glass window shut with a snap and returned to her feigned attention to the book.

Jan collapsed into a deep sofa and squeezed her eyes tightly shut, sighed.

Oh what I'd give for a drink right now. Scotch on the rocks! So what if I get a little drunk? But then what if I drive home and get another D.W.I. Oh my God, one more of those and the law jerks the old driver's license.

But if I were to get drunk, wouldn't that be great fun? A lit-

tle buzz sure would feel good right now. And if Ken doesn't get done with his patient soon and give me his full attention, I just might drive straight to the club and end up in jail and let that most respected and famous do-gooder ass-kisser I made the mistake of marrying bail me out, much to his humiliation, which I have to admit would be so much fun to witness.

Oh my God, I don't think I have been more scared than I am right this minute. Why can't I stop shaking? I'm not willing to feel this way much longer. Coughman had best hurry.

Rising to her feet, Jan raised her voice. "Young lady, by chance do you have a cigarette I could bum?"

Staring into the book, the girl did not respond.

Forget it, kid. I don't need a cigarette. Go right ahead and pretend you didn't hear. I'll just sit here and either die or go all out psychotic. After all, that window is as effective as the Great Wall of China. You're safe from the likes of crazy me, but if you don't slide that glass open again in the next sixty seconds, I swear I'll scream and rip off every piece of clothing I have on and I'll run outside completely naked so that Coughman will have to commit me.

The phone buzzed again, startling the girl. She fumbled with the receiver before placing it to her ear. She paused, frowned, then nodded several times. Jan tried to read her lips as the girl glanced up at her.

Another pause. Sliding open the window, the girl announced, "The doctor said he'd be right with you, ma'am."

Jan stared straight ahead and chose not to acknowledge the message.

"Ma'am, are you okay?"

Delighted that the girl was concerned, and hopefully now on edge, Jan decided against manipulating her further. She nodded and the girl slid the glass closed.

Jan muttered, "You're a spoiled brat. I could have easily toyed with you and scared the holy bejeebers out of you, but then what's the point? There is no good reason except that I despise all spoiled little perky air-headed co-eds. You, little lady, remind me way too much of me. So it's easier to despise you than it is to face the truth about myself. But if you're not very careful, in twenty-five years or so you will end up every bit as frightened and addicted and miserable as I happen to be at the moment, sitting here trembling and scared out of my mind. So no, I will not mess with you. Life will do to you far worse than I could ever do."

The slightly stooped physician stepped into the reception room and smiled at Jan with tired eyes. His bifocals appeared ready to slide like skis off his long thin nose, but as if they could defy gravity, they remained put two inches below eyes that beamed reassurance.

She attempted to stand but dizziness returned her to the sofa. She did her best to force a most disingenuous smile. She knew Coughman could read all the signals.

"Good afternoon, Jan," he offered in a tone so soft and pleasant she thought it might be suited to hypnosis. He extended his hand.

She again thought of standing and yet her legs would make no bargain.

"Come into my office, Jan, where we might visit. How wonderful to see you. What a surprise."

The girl lifted herself from the office chair to glimpse Jan shuffling into the physician's cozy office. Jan gave her what she hoped was a wicked smile.

Before closing the door, the doctor pointed toward the same comfortable sofa she had occupied for one hour each week during the past year. She scooted one foot in front of the other until she reached the sofa and she turned slowly to face him before falling into it. The doctor smiled as he reclined in a chair opposite her.

Dropping her eyes, Jan fixed her gaze on the carpet.

He can grin at me, and I don't resent it. But I resent just about everyone and everything else. What is wrong with me? Why am I so scared? Why can't I stop shaking?

"What brings you to see me today?"

His question felt suddenly overwhelming. Jan leaned forward while remaining on the sofa and stared at the floor.

"You're in a safe place, Jan. You know that."

Raising her head, she managed a nod as a long cord of phlegm dangled like a nylon rope out of one nostril. Leaning toward her, the doctor handed her a tissue.

"Thank you," she whispered, wiping her nose.

"What's this about, Jan?"

"Insanity!"

"Jan, how many times have I told you that you're not insane?"

"You must be wrong, Ken. I really hate to disagree with you, because you are the one man on the entire planet I think I trust. And about all I know right now is that I must trust someone."

"What makes you believe you're insane?"

"Yesterday I was alone on the banks of the Rio Grande in the Big Bend and from out of nowhere a man appeared and called me by my full name. Only my long-deceased mother ever called me by my full name. Tell me, how did he know that?"

"Go on."

"He told me he was the messenger, or some other weird gobbly-gook, and that I was to go with him somewhere. That's all. I drove away at a hundred miles per hour until I reached a bar in Lajitas. I went there because I was too frightened to be alone in my motel room."

Jan examined the wadded tissue in her hand. "Don't worry, I didn't drink anything but a Sprite. The bartender said I could stay and use the phone. I tried to call Chuck at home, but of course, he refused to answer. So I called the church and left three messages. Needless to say, he never called back."

She sniffled as she shook her head. "And then this weird bartender drops to his knees and begins to jabber some non-sense about seeing a little Mexican man standing out in the desert and this ghost told him I'm supposed to go back and find Royal."

"Who is Royal?"

"He's the man who knew my full name."

"And the bartender dropped to his knees before telling you this?"

"Just like that. One minute he's standing gazing out the window, and the next he's on his knees, grinning liked he'd just won the Power Ball."

"Why do you suppose he told you that?"

"I hoped you could tell me. At first light, I drove straight out of Study Butte and didn't stop until I reached the Mid-land airport, where I caught the first available flight to Dallas.

I rented a car drove straight here and scared your little girl out there half to death. But Ken, never in my life have I been so frightened as I am right now."

"I can see that, my dear."

"What were those men up to?"

"I can't say."

"They scared me, so badly I didn't know what else to do but to run home."

"I know."

"Can you do something?"

"I am going to increase your dosage on the Zoloft."

"That's it?"

"For now. You have an appointment with me next week. My suggestion to you is that you go home. Get some rest and between now and by the time I see you next, attend at least one AA meeting. Two would be better."

"That's all?"

"That's enough," he said, standing and smiling at her.

"I'd hoped for more."

"You'll get through this latest panic attack. Remember as I've often told you, they never last long."

"But those men?"

"They were just messing with you. Likely they schemed this up for God only knows whatever reason."

"But the man knew my full name."

"This is the information age. He read your name in a hotel log and went to the Internet and guessed correctly. There is probably no more mystery to this than that."

"But this man was on the Rio Grande near Boquillas Canyon and my hotel was in Study Butte and that's more than

70 miles away."

"So he followed you. There is a rational explanation to all of this. These men were in cahoots and they were set out to frighten you. Now, go home and rest, and the next time you take your medicine, take two instead of one. That will help significantly. I'll see you next week."

"I have no good choice but to trust you, but I think you're mistaken. There is more to this than you make it sound."

"Perhaps, but I doubt it."

CHAPTER FIVE

Sitting in the mansion's only downstairs den, Jan studied the fleeting shadows parading across drawn drapes. She recognized the familiar phenomenon of her husband's high beam headlights sweeping the mansion with light and muttered, "God, I so hate this mansion. What kind of church would buy its preacher a mansion? A sick one. Wouldn't it be wonderful if I could set this house on fire, escape my own misery, and rid myself of Chuck, all with a single match? Coughman tells me a fifth of anything hard would kill me quickly."

She stood and pulled the drapes back in time to see her husband cut the lights on his latest shiny new Mercedes, an annual gift from an adoring congregation. She dropped once more into a leather sofa to continue her muttering,

"Okay, so I go buy a fifth of Jack Daniels, down it fast, light a match to the huge arrangement of dried flowers in our kitchen, and then pass out and die peacefully before the flames engulf me and poor old Chuck sound asleep in his big lonely king-sized bed upstairs. It just might be my solution and my only real option. I can make a painless exit while killing the man I despise, and simultaneously devastate forever his sick church with the loss of this iconic old house. I could be killing three birds with one stone. Talk about headlines!"

She grinned. "And once the authorities figure out this was

arson, this fire will become one of the great legends of Dallas and in time will assume the same status as the assassination of JFK. I swear, if I ever discover that Chuck sent those men to the river to scare me, I'll torch this old house and kill the man and, of course, myself."

As Chuck fumbled with the keys in the back door lock, he rattled the door. She groaned in disgust.

God, the man is such a complete klutz. What a loser! He can't even open his own backdoor without waking the dead.

The howl of a neighbor's beagle signaled the beginning of their war. Each would hurl hurtful salvos until one of them made a dramatic exit, which, no doubt, would be followed by hours of isolation.

"Jan, I'm home," he yelled. "Tell me, how was your trip?"

"I'm in the downstairs den," she answered in a flat tone.

"Hi," he said stepping into the den wearing what in most circumstances proved a disarming grin. He extended his hand toward her shoulder, but she stepped away from his attempt at demonstrating what she knew to be a disingenuous demonstration of affection.

"I called here three times," she said.

"Let's don't fight. I've had a rough day, as usual. But we're both home now and this day is done, so let's enjoy the evening and keep it peaceful."

"Fine by me, I'm a bit tired myself. But, I do need to ask you a most important question, and I do need for you to be one hundred percent honest.

"Jan, have you ever known me to lie?"

Buster, your entire life is a lie!

She rose from the sofa and walked quickly into the adjacent downstairs kitchen where she retrieved a bottle of diet ginger ale from the refrigerator.

"I'll have whatever you're having," he called.

She lifted a second bottle from the refrigerator's door rack. As she returned to the den, she tossed the unopened bottle to him with a forced smile.

"How do I open this thing?"

She felt tempted to answer with sarcasm, but reined in the impulse in the hope she might actually discover the truth behind the men who frightened her. "Chuck, it's a twist-off cap."

"Oh, of course, oh how stupid of me. You know, Jan, in some ways I'm gifted beyond measure, but in other ways, I'm a real dunce."

Buster, trust me, in most ways you're a dunce or worse, a real bore not to mention the biggest hypocrite in the world.

"What is it you want to ask me?"

"Oh yes," she said before clearing her throat. Sitting now very erect across from him and doing her best to appear relaxed, she said, "Do you know anything about three men scaring me down on the Rio Grande?"

"Three men doing what?" A quizzical expression contorted his latest facelift.

"Three men scaring me down on the river at the very place where I used to go as a girl. One was a very tall man with hippie-length hair, and this dude crept up behind me and called me by my entire name."

"What did he look like?"

"His skin was dark and swarthy, like he'd spent his life outside. His eyes were pale blue and penetrating. He was very tall, maybe even six-foot-six. His hair was tied back in a ponytail, salt and pepper in color. He was dressed in khaki work pants and a wrinkled work shirt of the same color."

"What did you do after he spoke to you?"

"What do you think? I ran like hell and jumped in the Porsche and drove probably a hundred miles an hour until I reached Lajitas. I was much too scared to go to my motel room so I found a bar open and went in anticipation of being surrounded by normal people who would totally ignore me, which I hoped would return my mind to sanity."

"Oh my God, Jan, please tell me you didn't drink."

"Only a Diet Sprite, I swear, but that is not the point, Chuck.

"So what is?"

"Three men terrified me on the river, and I must know the truth as to whether you had anything to do with this."

"Jan, I have absolutely no idea what you're talking about. I would never intentionally frighten you or anyone else. You know that." Chuck took a sip of his ginger ale. "You said there were three men. Who were the other two?"

"One was the bartender in Lajitas, and the third was a little Mexican man who seemed to more float than walk. This tiny fellow was dressed in glowing white linen, and he sort of floated into the bar. The bartender crumpled to his knees as if he had been shot, and then approached me and told me I must return to the river to find a man he called Royal. I assume Royal is the name of the tall man who scared me on the river."

"What did you do then?"

"I ran to the Porsche and drove to my motel room in

Study Butte where I double locked the doors. I jumped in bed and hid under the covers until the phone rang."

"Who called?"

"Em."

"How did she know where to find you?"

"She made a lucky guess. But I'm glad she did, because I was tempted beyond belief to walk down to the motel lobby and buy me a fifth of Jack. And if I'd done that, I would not be alive today."

"I'm glad, very glad, she called you. "

"Me, too." Jan paused. "So, Chuck, I must know the truth. My sanity, and maybe even my life, depends upon it. When did you hire these men to frighten me?"

"Frankly, I find your question insulting, demeaning, and way out of bounds. And you know me. I don't return them when they're out of bounds."

Jumping to her feet, Jan hurled the crystal glass half full of ginger ale against the marble façade of the room's fireplace. "So what in the hell is going on? Who were those men?"

"I have no idea. But I think I can help you, if you will only let me."

"How?"

"I'm flying to Austin next Monday to lecture all morning at the seminary, and then I'm scheduled to play golf at Austin Country Club with old Homer Ruff, who just so happens to be the head of the Texas Rangers. I know him well. The man is good at what he does, and I'm guessing we can have these clowns behind bars by this time next week."

Jan sat in a chair across from him with her knees touching his. Chuck dug in his coat pocket to find a handkerchief, which he handed to her. She accepted the handkerchief with a cautious smile and managed a tepid, "Thank you."

As she attempted to return his handkerchief, he grabbed her wrist and jerked her toward him until she landed in his lap. She screamed as she struggled to free herself. "Let me go!"

"Jan, hush! The neighbors will call the police."

"Good! I hope they do. Then I can charge you with domestic violence. I wonder what your congregation and your buddy, the President, would think about that. I swear to the God I refuse to believe in that if you don't let me go in the next thirty seconds, I'm screaming until the cops come."

Still smiling, he released his grip to see her rise to her feet and tremble before him.

"What was that about?" she asked with fresh tears streaming down both cheeks.

"I meant it to be about love and comforting my distraught little wife."

"You call that comforting me? I feel sorry for you because you really don't have a clue how to love or how to comfort anyone but yourself. Are you so sick as to believe I want you to manhandle me?"

"I merely drew you to my lap so that I might cover you with kisses."

"The very thought of you kissing me makes me ill. I don't want you to kiss me. Ever! Do you get that, big-shot preacher man?

"Unfortunately, I do."

"All in the world I want from you is the truth about what happened to me on the river yesterday."

"Didn't you hear my offer to involve the Texas Rangers?"

"I heard you, but I don't believe you. Your offer is nothing more than a slick ploy to trick me so that you can alert those men to flee to Mexico where you and I both know the Rangers can't investigate."

Chuck rose and attempted a smile as he extended his hand to her. "Baby, let's go upstairs and make peace."

"Upstairs! You have to be the densest man on the planet. I wouldn't go upstairs with you if you put a gun to my head. Do you understand? Tell me, what did I just say?"

"You said you wouldn't go upstairs with me even if I put a gun to your head."

Grinning, she said, "Now we're getting somewhere."

Jan walked around the back of her chair, until it stood between her and her husband. "Okay, don't tell me anything. Tomorrow morning, I'm out of here at first light and off to the airport where I'm flying back to Midland where I left the Porsche. Then I'm driving straight to the river where I will do my own investigation."

She shook her finger at him. "When I find that tall scary man, I'm going to offer him $25,000 of our joint savings to return with me to Dallas. Once in Dallas, I'm going straight to the Dallas News with this character in tow, and he'll spill the beans to their religion editor so that he will write an expose regarding just how cruel and sick you really are. Then I'm hiring the meanest lawyer I can find and suing you for divorce. Then I'm taking more than half of our estate."

Jan dusted her hands together in triumph. "My plan is to leave you penniless and totally exposed for the con man you really are."

"Whatever." Chuck turned toward the stairwell. "I'm going upstairs to change clothes and stretch out for a while before I eat. What's for supper?"

"You're on your own tonight, Mister Big Shot. There are leftovers in the fridge. You won't starve."

"What are you going to do for dinner?" he called from the stairwell.

"I'm much too upset to eat tonight, so I'll probably just hang out here and seethe in my anger and maybe down another diet ginger ale or two."

Jan listened for him to close the bedroom door before she turned to enter the downstairs kitchen. An enormous bunch of dried flowers attracted her attention.

Oh, those would work. I'll shove them in the pantry where they will ignite the discarded grocery bag, and in no time this place will be on fire. But before I light them, I must remember to bring a pillow in here for my head. I definitely want to be comfortable when I die. So I'll down the fifth of Jack in here and then light these flowers. I'll stagger to the pantry and toss the flaming flowers onto the stack of grocery sacks and then I'll collapse on the floor with my head on the pillow.

She raised the bottle of ginger ale to toast herself and her scheme. *This will work, but there is just one problem. I don't think I'm ready to die. The better plan is to find that tall man down on the river and bribe him to help me ruin Chuck. Maybe I can even convince him to become my lover. After all, I'm still quite a looker, and he was sort of cute in an outdoorsy kind of way.*

Jan giggled. *I think taking on a lover at this chapter in my life would be great fun.*

The telephone's brutal ring interrupted her fantasy. She

sighed as her mood slipped precariously close to her familiar dance with despondency. Lifting the receiver to her mouth, she spoke in a monotone bereft of any hint of emotion. "Hello"

"Thank God, you're home. I've been worried sick about you. When did you get back?"

Jan rolled her eyes. The last person she wanted to talk to now was Em. "I flew in this morning, rented a car, and drove straight to Coughman's office where I scared the crap out of some little girl he had working there."

"What did he say?"

"To my relief, he didn't say I was imagining things or that I had experienced a psychotic break. And I can't tell you how relieved I was to realize he believed me."

"What did he do?"

"He increased my dosage of happy pills and told me to attend an AA meeting before I see him again next week."

"Taking those pills is not recovery."

"Em, please don't preach. I swear, if I never hear another sermon, it will be too soon, way too soon."

"Sorry, baby, but you know me. When it comes to recovery, I'm a purist."

"Coughman is convinced I need these pills, at least for now. And, of course he is a firm believer in AA."

"I know, sweetie. Forgive me."

"Okay, you're forgiven."

"What are you going to do now?"

Jan shared with Em the highlights of her plan, all the way from retrieving her Porsche in Midland to divorcing Chuck, but she included only a few details about going to the river and returning with the man named Royal. "The long drive home will give me some time to think."

"I want to fly back to Midland with you. You need protection, if you go to the river, which I seriously think you shouldn't. Promise me you won't go there."

My God, woman, get a life. "Em, that won't work. I appreciate your support, but I need to do this alone. I know you mean well, but honestly, you'd just be in the way. You have to understand this."

"Well then, I'll turn around and fly right back to Dallas, as long as you swear you won't go to the river and find that dangerous man. You can spend all the time you need to be alone on the way home. How about it?"

"But I'm not sure I can get tickets at this late hour."

"My Harvey sits on the board of Southwest Airlines, so we have tickets. Trust me. I'll meet you on your front steps tomorrow morning at 7:00 am. Don't oversleep."

"I'll be ready, and thank you for being such a good AA sponsor and an even better friend. Goodnight, Em."

"Goodnight, baby."

My God, I really don't want to take Em with me, but I can make this thing work. I'll dump her at the airport and then drive non-stop to the river.

CHAPTER SIX

Only minutes after takeoff, Jan peered out the jet's portal
Somewhere down there a stranger knows my full name.
What's more, he just may know something very important and
I must find out what it is. I am absolutely convinced he is real.
I definitely saw him and heard him speak. While I may be crazy in
some ways, I did not hallucinate. So I must find him and I will if it
kills me. I swear it on my daughter's grave.

As Jan studied dry West Texas 30,000 feet below, she
mulled over the events of the previous day. She had spoken
not so much as a word to her sponsor since they buckled
their seatbelts. Nevertheless, throughout the one-hour flight,
Emily Sands attempted one rapid-fire cheery question after
another, but nothing softened Jan's resistance.

Upon landing in Midland, Emily tried again. "Now let's
go find that gorgeous red Porsche I covet. I'd convince Harvey to buy me one, but I don't want to bother learning how
to drive a manual transmission. Tell me, do they come with
an automatic?"

I've never been so scared, but I can't let that get in the way. I'm
returning to the river.

Once out of the terminal, Jan pointed toward acres of
automobiles glistening in the bright October morning. As she
strode toward the Porsche, she ignored the racket of Emily's
new Prada heels clattering on the asphalt. Aiming a key at

the Porsche's door lock, Jan concentrated on not allowing her hand to tremble.

"Jan, I've changed my mind," said Emily. "I can't let you even think about returning to the river alone. Let me pay the parking fee and buy your first tank of gas, and then we'll head back to Dallas together."

"I told you last night I was going to the river to find a man the Lajitas bartender called Royal. You cannot go with me. I thought I made that clear, and you agreed not to interfere."

"Now that we're here, I have reconsidered. I absolutely cannot allow you to go back to that dangerous river any more than I would abandon you to a rough South Dallas neighborhood on a Saturday night. There is nothing good about that old river. Nothing down there but murderers, rapists, drug runners, and filthy poor people who carry every disease imaginable. No, I won't hear of it. You're returning to Dallas with me this very minute."

"You can catch the next flight to Dallas and be home in an hour." Jan settled into in the car's front seat and partially rolled down the window before deciding against unlocking the passenger door. Through the narrow opening in the window she said, "To hell with the danger, I'm returning to the river and I'm doing whatever it takes to find that man."

Emily pounded her fists against the Porsche's red hood and screamed, "Jan, listen to reason. To go down there is suicide. I know you hate your life, but you cannot do this thing. I love you too much to allow it."

As she moved toward the driver's side of the car, Emily tried to squeeze her fingers through narrow space in the slightly rolled-down window. "Don't you see, if you go there and get killed, Chuck wins? If you get murdered by some monster down there, Chuck will portray you as a martyr and he will, no doubt, remarry some naïve little trophy wife who will consistently support his sick, self-serving agenda, and he will get everything he's ever wanted, and you, my friend, will be forever dead."

Emily flattened her hands against the glass. "Is that what you want? To die in the unholy cause of helping Chuck Love fulfill his every selfish dream?"

Jan only smiled. "I'm returning to the river."

One more time Emily screamed, "For God's sake, be reasonable!"

Jan winked. "But remember, I don't believe in God, and now is not the time for reason. Reason can give rise to fear, and right now I can't afford to be afraid. I must be courageous or I'll never find that man who may know something very important I need to know."

To signal her impatience, Jan revved the Porsche's engine until it roared. "When you get back to Dallas, please be so kind as to call Chuck. He won't be in, of course, because he's off to Washington again to play sycophant to that idiot the American people elected President. Assuming he's left the voice mail on, please leave the message that I've returned to the river. He won't care, but I suspect I do owe him that much information."

Jan buckled her seatbelt. "There is still that much decency left in me, I suppose."

Once more the engine roared. Emily rapped her knuckles on the glass and screamed, "Unlock the passenger door. I'm going with you."

"From here on," Jan yelled, "I must do everything alone." She then slipped the transmission into reverse with a loud, metallic click.

"Damn it, get out of that car this very minute, or I'm going back into the terminal and calling the Highway Patrol. This red Porsche will not be at all difficult to spot. I'll tell them you're suicidal and they must take you to the closest hospital, and place you in restraints and hold you there until I can come and take you home."

Jan allowed the Porsche to speak for her with one last loud roar. Grinning through the open window, Jan said, "Stand back, Em, I'd hate to run over your expensive new Neiman-Marcus pedicure. I think it might smart a bit."

"If you drive off, I swear I'm calling Chuck, even if he is at the White House, and I'm telling him you've decided to commit suicide."

The Porsche's new tires squealed against the asphalt as they sprayed tiny pieces of gravel at Emily. Jan glanced into the rearview mirror. A thick cloud of exhaust fumes and dust momentarily obscured her well-dressed AA sponsor, then cleared in time for Jan to see Emily hurl her Gucci bag to the asphalt and stomp both Prada-covered feet.

As the Porsche rumbled through the airport exit, Jan rolled down both windows and breathed in the dry morning air. "I'm off to river," she screamed, "and into the biggest adventure yet. I just know it! I don't know how I know it, but I do, just as surely as I know the sun came up this morning. This will be the defining journey of my life. All I have to do is find a man named Royal and do whatever he tells me to do."

With the sleeve of her denim shirt, she wiped the tears

from her eyes, and then pressed the accelerator.

This is all pretty crazy, but for the first time in years, I'm not afraid. No, I'm only excited. God, I feel alive again for the first time since I married the oaf. Damn, this is a hell of a feeling. I only hope it lasts.

CHAPTER SEVEN

s the Porsche's super-charged engine rumbled its impatience behind the single stop sign in Marathon, Texas, Jan studied the features of the historic Sage Hotel for any clue pointing to something more promising than the absurd conclusions that had long infested in her mind like barn swallows.

Oh, I don't really know what this thing is all about, but right now I need to find out if this man Royal is real or merely another frightening creation of my poor old alcohol-saturated brain.

Lifting her foot from the brake pedal as her car rolled into the small hotel's front drive, Jan steered the Porsche like it was an obedient horse being hitched to a familiar rail. She exited the convertible posing as a woman driven by the kind of purpose that in her University Park world is often expressed by an air of determined self-assurance.

Confidence, much less self-assurance, had never been hers to claim.

Lingering in the lobby's doorway, she fumbled with her purse in search of either a cigarette or her cell, whichever surfaced first.

A balding man with both elbows resting on the surface of the front desk lifted his gaze only long enough to offer what she read to be an effortful smile. "How can I help you, ma'am?"

She attempted a smile of her own. "Sir, I am hoping you might provide me with some much-needed information."

The man's rather dour countenance quickly turned into a grin, revealing two gold front teeth and stretching his face in the direction of warmth, if not genuine kindness. "Well, you've come to the right place, because everywhere out here between the river and Alpine, this front desk is considered the foremost visitor information center for the entire Big Bend. What is it you'd like to know?"

"Do you know a man named Royal?

"Not personally, but our local priest sure as hell does. In fact, this old priest, whose name is Father Brady O'Shea, is real tight with Royal. He even brings him to our dining room for a cup of coffee ever so often, but that old skinflint never buys the man a full meal."

"How do I find your priest here in Marathon?"

"You want to meet him?" He lifted the telephone receiver from its cradle. "I'll have to call him on the desk phone. But it ain't no problem because I have his number right here somewhere."

Fumbling with a flock of discarded wads of pastel paper scattered about the imposing desk, the man grabbed one small wad and grasped it in his fist like it was a long-lost coin right out of a New Testament parable. "Eureka! I found it his number. Now before I call him, let me warn you about old Brady. He's about as old as these mountains and he's crazier than a rabid skunk. If you find him home, he'll likely be out in the shed next to the house hanging upside down."

"Why?"

"Because he's convinced himself he can ward off the Alzheimer's Disease that way."

"Is he a real priest?"

"Real enough, I reckon. He's about all that this dying old town and its sad old church can support. Now whatever you do, don't go into his shed."

"Why?"

"Because he'll talk you all the way into next month. I swear, people can drown in that old man's words. I'll call him for you."

The desk clerk spun the rotary dial with the care one might give to whittling hickory with an unusually sharp blade. "Hello, Brady there is a lady here at my desk wanting to come see you. Okay if I send her your way?"

Hanging up, he smiled. "He says come on, but he also told me to tell you that he only hears confessions on Thursday, and this ain't Thursday."

"How do I find the church?"

The man gave her directions to the old adobe church, which he claimed would be located beneath a tall wooden cross that could be seen from any point in town.

As the Porsche rested its big engine, it seemed to sigh as it cooled. In what was once a yard, Jan paused to read a faded pasteboard sign rocking in a breeze scarcely stiff enough to rustle a clump of tall, withered weeds. The hard caliches appeared as though it had not tasted rain since Noah. A rusty nail secured a scrawled proclamation to one post supporting the porch's sagging roof.

The sign read: *Father O'Shea is in the shed.*

She scanned the porch and then the scant shade a starving cottonwood managed to cast upon the parched ground beneath her. As the breeze suddenly kicked up dust into a distinct plume, a boisterous sneeze coming from the shed ended the hot afternoon's compact with silence. She turned to face a crude, unpainted building and thought the thing leaned so precariously, even one more sneeze might topple it. The building's old door hinges squawked in the breeze like a fiddle abused by a bad bow. The sound reminded her of the agony she endured each time some boy in her high school algebra class had dragged his fingernails across a blackboard.

This is too much. I'm not at all up to this. Emily is so right—I am insane. But I'm also out of here. I'm driving back to Dallas to-night, and I will do whatever it takes to forget any of this nonsense ever happened. I'll divorce Chuck and ruin the bastard, but then, he deserves it. I'll take half of his money and make out the best I can. I don't know exactly how I'll make it, but I somehow will. I always have been a survivor.

As she turned toward the Porsche, a voice every bit as raspy as the old rusty hinges interrupted this latest attempt to convince herself to abandon this adventure once and for all. "Now who's tramping about out there?"

Turning about, she said as forcefully as her tight throat would permit words to slide, "Uh, uh… my name is Jan, and I'm from Dallas, and I was hoping to visit with Father O'Shea."

God, get me out of here! I can't go into that awful shed! Even from this distance the thing stinks like a cow barn.

"Well, Missy, do come in out of the sun. You must be the young lady Ollie called me about not two minutes ago. You have a lovely voice, so please be so kind as to step into the shed, child, and let these tired old Irish eyes be filled up with the spectacle of your beauty. I suspect you're every bit as fetching as a young country lass straight off the farm."

Stepping into the shed, she said in a soft voice, "My name is Janet Macdonald-Love, and I'm from Dallas."

"Good to meet you, young lady. My name is Father O'Shea, but most folks out here call me Brady. Please dispense with any formality and do the same. And do come all the way in, because the glare is too much and my cataracts are far too advanced for me to see you unless you are fully in the shade. You need not be afraid, because I'm as harmless as an old armadillo."

Her legs felt ready to fold beneath her like a frail table bearing too much weight. *Do I run out of here screaming or do I stay? This is too much!*

She scanned the interior of the old shed in what dim light the sun could squeeze through holes in the slightly pitched roof.

God, I'm insane to be in this suffocating dump. This old shed could collapse at any second and no one would ever find my body. I don't want to die in this old shed. How inglorious. How utterly absurd this all is, and how convenient for Chuck if I die here.

Thin streams of light poured through a thousand wall cracks, causing row upon row of sealed glass jars to glisten.

"Father O'Shea… uh, I mean, Brady."

"I'm up here above you, child."

She raised her eyes. More a skeleton than a man hung upside down with both legs wrapped at the back of his knees around a wooden beam. Denim overalls as faded as the old man himself covered the bottom half of his frame. He wore no shirt and both bony shoulders resembled the claw end of a framing hammer. His caved-in peach-colored chest was home to a sprinkling of hair bleached to the color of fireplace soot. With his pointed bald spot aimed at the floor, sweat rolled off his pate with the slow drip of water escaping through a cracked pipe. Circling his inverted gleaming dome clung a rim of hair as orange as the ocotillo blossoms in spring.

"Well, Missy, I can see from up here that you admire my collection. But that is not at all surprising, because folks drive hundreds of miles to see my collection of the lower life forms of The Big Bend."

"Brady, I came to ask you about a man named Royal. The desk clerk at the Sage said you and Royal are friends."

"Of course we are. I practically raised that pup when there was a bishop alive with the good sense to entrust the both of us with the responsibilities of a real church where we could do some good for the Lord Jesus Christ and his kingdom right here on earth."

"Tell me about him, please."

"What exactly do you want to know?"

"To begin with, is he dangerous?"

"Only to himself, and that's because he is a crazy, unrepentant radical. "

The upside-down old man lifted his right hand to his head to wipe a large drop of perspiration threatening one eye. "The boy is a Franciscan, and all Franciscans have to be a little crazy to take the solemn vows they do. The vow of poverty is a mighty heavy cross to bear in this old world where greed drives everything in the halls of power, whether those halls are in Washington or Rome."

With her eyes now focused to the darkness, Jan studied

the shelves laden with glass jars, each one containing a spider or some kind of insect.

Ever since I married Chuck Love, I've been as imprisoned as the poor bugs this crazy man keeps in these jars.

"But I'll tell you this, Missy. Young Royal must be the craziest of the lot because the boy is a mystic. He lives for prayer rather than the other way around, if you catch my meaning. The Apostle Paul admonished us to pray without ceasing, and Royal lives his life just like that irascible old Pharisee admonished two millennia ago. He prays without ceasing, and because he does, he hears things and sees things most of us know absolutely nothing about. Missy, this man lives closer to God than he does even to his own ego. And in this old fallen world, that's one mighty rare quality."

"Is he a priest?"

"He was a priest in this diocese until he got cross-wise with our bishop all the way over in San Antonio. But when it comes to bishops, it's not hard to offend those fellows. They can be a bit thin-skinned and sometimes even a little prissy."

As Jan scanned the shed in search of a place to sit, she said, "How did Royal offend the bishop?"

The upside-down old man chuckled as he spit a wad of something wet on the dirt floor. "He wrote a twelve-week series of brutally honest newspaper columns that appeared in every daily in this state. He challenged the church to sell off all of its non-sacred real estate in Texas and give one hundred percent of the money to the poor on both sides of the border. After the third column appeared, the bishop called Royal to inform him that he was no longer a seminary professor, but instead he was now a priest to the tiny church in Redford.

But in only a few short weeks, the bishop dismissed him from there as well."

"What did he do after he was dismissed?"

"That's the beautiful part of all of this. He walked and hitchhiked his way downriver to a village on the other side of the Rio Grande in Mexico, a tiny and desperate place called Boquillas. He adopted those good people and they him. And now, he's their priest, but the humorous part about this is that no bishop in Mexico even knows he's down there doing all the good for those people."

Without notice, the old man released his firm leg grip on the overhead beam and dropped to the dirt floor, landing squarely on his back with a disturbing thud.

"Oh my God," Jan shrieked. She stepped toward him as he lay face-up in the dirt and grinned at her. Grime filled the creases in his wet face. "Brady, are you okay?"

"I'm fine, Missy, just fine. I fall like this every day because I've not yet learned a better way to get down. My young doc over in Alpine claims I'm going to break my neck some day, but what does he know? The fact is, I'd much rather die of a broken neck than Alzheimer's. So I ignore his warnings and let the government pay him through my Medicare. I have about as much use for the government as I do that young pup's advice."

With the old man still on his back and smiling at her, Jan knelt over him like an adoring supplicant. "Are you sure you're okay?"

"I need a couple of minutes to find both of my legs before I attempt to stand."

Jan extended her hand to the old man. "Father, let me

help you to your feet."

"Very well." Slowly the old man rose to his feet and tottered before her while holding fast to a grin that appeared permanently etched on his face.

"So Royal is a priest in Boquillas."

"Yes he is, but like I said, no Bishop in Mexico or anywhere else has appointed him." Chuckling, the old priest dusted off his overalls. "You might say he is the only self-appointed parish priest in the entire world. I don't know of another one, do you?"

"No, but I'm not Catholic."

"What are you, child?"

"I'm what you might call a reluctant Presbyterian."

"Why are you reluctant? The Presbyterians I know are good people. I like Presbyterians because they have a long tradition of thinking rigorously about their faith."

"I'm reluctant because I'm married to a Presbyterian minister who holds two distinctions. One, he is currently the most famous television evangelist in the world, and, two, he is this world's biggest ass. I think I hate him more than I ever believed possible to hate anyone."

"Bless you, child. So what is this famous man's name?"

"The bastard's name is the Rev. Dr. Chuck Love."

"I've never heard of him, but then that's not at all surprising because I don't own a television."

"Thank you, Brady, for saying you've never heard of him. You can't know how refreshing that is to hear."

"Well, then I'm very glad I've never have heard of him. Tell me, child, how might I be of service to you?"

"I need to find Royal."

"Don't we all? What I mean is that we all need to find what Royal has found. And if this world knew what he knows, all wars would cease, enemies would become friends, hatred would be nothing more than a most unpleasant memory for humankind to recall only for the purpose of studying its former power, and every form of evil would be vanquished by the greater powers of love. It would be literally 'On Earth as it is in Heaven'. Oh, forgive me, child, sometimes I get carried away and I wax almost poetically when I should be silent. It's one of my worst traits."

Smiling, Jan said, "You're forgiven. Please tell me how can I find Royal."

"That's easy, child. Drive to the Boquillas Canyon parking lot on the Texas side of the river. Park, and go to the riverbank, and then find yourself a salt cedar to sit under. In time, Royal will find you. And when you see him, tell him old Brady said to come see me. Tell him we're long overdue for a visit. And remember, go with God."

"Yeah, whatever," Jan mumbled over her shoulder as she ambled toward the waiting Porsche.

"I know this. Without Royal, those folks would have no priest."

Without Royal, I'll have no answers.

CHAPTER EIGHT

Chuck sighed. *This car is idling roughly. I don't like this. Something must be wrong with the engine.*

He depressed a button on the door and the window rolled down. *Gee, it's colder than I thought. Oh God, don't let this car conk out of me. I don't think I'm up for another humiliation.*

Stepping from the door of the gatehouse, a uniformed guard clutching an ivory-colored clipboard swaggered toward him with a distinct air of authority as he displayed the requisite smile of courtesy. Chuck turned the corners of his mouth slightly upward to reciprocate, although he didn't feel at all up to smiling.

Why didn't I plan ahead? This is Jan's fault. I swear that woman had me so rattled before I left Dallas. I should have reserved a Cadillac or Lincoln Town Car instead of this embarrassing Buick. I hope this is no bad omen. Oh stop it, man! You have an earned Ph.D. from Princeton. Remember, you're above superstition. Cognitive correctness, boy, cognitive correctness! That, and trust in God.

As the guard leaned into the window to welcome him, Chuck held on to a smile he knew could influence. "Good morning, sir. I'm here to see Mr. Barrett, Mr. Buck Barrett. I'm Dr. Love, the senior pastor of University Park Presbyterian Church in Dallas. The President has invited me to offer the inaugural prayer, assuming he wins, which, of course, no one doubts he will."

"Thank you, sir. Permit me to check the manifest."

God, help me. I pray for your strength to fill me up. I pray for your wisdom to consume me and to make me its instrument. I need to be far more than I am capable of being on my own. God, never in my life have I ever wanted anything so badly. Never! Guide my thoughts. Please, give me the right words. Amen.

The engine sputtered.

Why in God's name did I rent this piece of junk, but I can't think of that now. I can't let her ruin this. Please, God, take from me every thought of Jan. This is way too important to me, to this nation, to the kingdom, to allow that selfish, spoiled drunk I married to ruin this.

Glimpsing his reflection shimmering in the rearview mirror, he attempted to rein in doubts by remembering what he'd been told for the whole of his life: he possessed the qualities required for leadership.

As he admired his handsome face in the rearview mirror, he reminded himself, *I am one of the elite, the crème de la crème. I'm a born leader. Do not my friends at Dallas Country Club tell me frequently that I am a natural? Do I not know personally almost every bigwig CEO and corporate president in Dallas. And to a person, do they not count it a privilege to know me?*

Do I not travel in the most exclusive circles? And, am I not the hub around which most rotate. Did not D-Magazine recently name me the most respected man in Dallas? Did not Time Magazine feature me on its cover this year?

I am some body, a real player in Dallas, and I also just happen to be the biggest name in American Christianity.

I will be confident. I am a real winner and these people up here are fortunate to have me. It is they who will do the begging, if any begging is to be done.

He cleared his throat as the guard returned to say, "Please drive straight ahead and park in a visitor slot, Dr. Love. Mr. Barrett is waiting for you, sir. And welcome to the White House."

The guard smelled of the same aftershave Chuck's father had splashed on his face each morning. With the tips of his white-gloved fingers, the guard brushed the shiny brim of his military cap and prolonged his smile to signal the transaction between them was now finished.

Chuck returned the friendly gesture. *Remember, Spinoza, Chucky boy. 'None are more taken in by flattery than the proud who wish to be the first and are not.' Why do I listen to Spinoza? The man was an atheist. My God! I place no trust in man. I trust only in God!*

Tapping the accelerator, his confidence returned as the Buick's engine responded. He glanced into the mirror once more to admire his perfect smile.

Perhaps the Buick is a good choice after all. It does demonstrate a certain inclination toward frugality, which is always a virtue.

He parked the car and turned off the ignition switch before he rested his head against the steering wheel. With both eyes squeezed shut, he prayed aloud, "Lord, God. Please, let this opportunity be your will. I've worked for the whole of my life for this moment and I pray to God that this dream will come true. In Jesus' name, Amen."

Done with his prayer, he stepped into the bracing chill of the new morning with briefcase in tow. Immediately he spied a young woman dressed in a pleated khaki skirt and navy blazer. As she waved at him he whispered, "Don't let me blow this. O God, don't let me blow this."

When she smiled at him, he noticed that her hair so perfectly framed her face even the brisk winds appeared reluctant to muss it.

What a pretty girl. If our daughter had lived, she would have been about this girl's age. Stop it, Chuck. Don't remember. Don't go there. Ever! You promised yourself not to return not today, not ever!

Chuck winked at her and immediately regretted the gesture, lest she think him flirtatious.

Cognitive correctness consists of only positive and accurate thoughts: I will land this job. I will become an invaluable asset to this president and to this great republic. God created me for this position and from the very beginning of time I have been destined to take on this enormous responsibility. I am definitely God's peacemaker, equal to the task. In fact, I am likely the only man on the planet who is right for this position. God has blessed me more than most men and this administration will be blessed to have me. This is my destiny.

Walking toward the young woman, he said cheerily, "Good morning."

The confidence is back. I do feel good, in fact, very good. I can do this. I'm at the top of my game. Nothing like perfect timing.

And as he drew closer he said, "Top of the morning, young lady. How are you?"

The girl reminded him of Jan, when she was young and so beautiful every thought of her made his spirits soar. *Don't go there, Chuck. Jan is poison. Memories bring you down, and right now is not the time to be down.*

"Good morning, Dr. Love. Welcome to the White House."

"Thank you," he said dropping his eyes to read the woman's name on the brass lapel tag. "Brandi. What a delightful name. It fits you to a T. It's perky, yet warm. Just like you appear to be, if you don't mind hearing such an observation from a geezer."

"Oh no, sir. It's a privilege, Dr. Love, coming from you. Thank you. Please, let's go inside. It's nippy out here."

As he held open the door of the East Wing of the mansion, he said, "Do you work for Mr. Barrett."

"I'm afraid I do. I mean, oh, please excuse me, I should not have said that. What I meant to say is that I do. Yes, Dr. Love, I do."

Smiling, Chuck paused to run his fingers through his hair, which he was certain the wind had mussed. "Think nothing of it, Brandi. I'm acquainted with Mr. Barrett and I suspect he's not the most pleasant man in the world."

"Nevertheless, that was most unprofessional of me. I do hope you will forgive me."

"Your secret is safe, Brandi. Perfectly safe."

She sighed, smiled, and said, "Please follow me, Dr. Love, and I will escort you to his office."

"Brandi, thank you, but I know the way. This is not my first visit with that wily old goat."

Smiling knowingly she said, "Thank you, Dr. Love, for understanding. You're a kind man. I can see why it is so many people admire you, but I was wrong…"

Leaning toward her, Chuck placed his hand gently upon her shoulder. "Brandi, not another word now, do you hear?

I know he's a boor. In fact, everyone from here to his hometown of Lufkin, Texas, knows he's the backside of a horse, but he's also very good at what he does. And the President trusts him. So congratulations on being so insightful! I know the way to his office. You can get on with whatever else you need to do. Thank you for the welcome. And God bless you."

Chuck turned a corner in time to see Buck Barrett stepping from his office and into the wide hall with a cordless phone trapped between one elephantine ear and a shoulder wide enough to haul two-by-fours by the half dozen. The man's torso was shaped like a 50-gallon oil drum while his legs appeared to be constructed of elongated pipe cleaners. His wide shiny pate was bald and to his admirers and critics alike resembled a miniature replica of the Capitol's dome.

In his more than half century in Washington he had earned a reputation for efficiency born of brutality. He was known in both political parties to be fiercely loyal to his friends and he could also be counted on to do whatever was required to humiliate, or even destroy enemies. His reputation for expediency was legendary

As he barked into the phone wedged between his ear and shoulder, Chuck noted sweat pouring off the man's head in small streams.

Buck said, "Good-bye," before dropping the phone into a wide pocket in his navy trousers. "What a pain in the neck that senator is! What a useless, petty, and self-serving little martinet! You know what? I despise all Democrats! It's not politically-correct to think this way, much less say it out loud preacher, but there are times—and this just happens to be one of them—when I am convinced we'd be a lot better off if we'd limit the vote to white men who own land. Enact that law, and the Democratic Party dries up quicker than shallow water in a Texas July."

Chuck grabbed a doorknob of a closed door and held on so as not to be blown down the long hallway by the older man's hot breath.

"But now excuse me, preacher. I rant too much and far too often. It's just one of my many vices but we won't go into that, at least not out here in the hall. Welcome, son. Welcome to the White House and to the exciting world of the executive branch of this great government of ours."

He slapped Chuck on the back before grabbing his one free hand. "Come in, son, into my office so we can catch up. How's everything down your way?"

Both men sat, Chuck in a high back leather chair facing Buck, who propped his enormous tasseled loafers on the desk.

Ramming an unlit cigar in his cavernous mouth, the large man blurted out, "Preacher I do believe I just asked you a question."

"Well, it's been warm in Texas, Mr. Barrett—"

He coughed, then said, "Now I told you the last time you were up here to call me Buck. My friends call me by my first name, and I suspect you and I soon are destined by our shared devotion to this President to become friends, in fact, very good friends. And my many enemies, well, they call me names I dare not repeat in front of a preacher. And the fact is, I deserve everyone of them and I'm more than a little proud of that fact."

He grinned, revealing a top row of teeth stained a dull

gray by decades of voracity. "So, it's been a bit warm down in Texas, you say."

Chuck nodded.

"You know, I'm from Lufkin myself. I do miss the sweet smell of rain in the pines. Well, enough reminiscing. We thank you for your willingness to say the prayer at the inauguration."

"My honor, Buck."

"But preacher, I didn't ask you to take time out of your busy schedule to come all the way up here to discuss some prayer. Did I now?"

"No, I suppose not."

Good God, what does the President see in him? I can't imagine being his friend. For that matter, I can't even imagine working with him. He is so into intimidation. This is the only way he knows how to relate, but I won't be intimidated, by him or by anyone else.

"No, son, you and I have something much more important to discuss here. But then, don't get me wrong. Prayer is of course mighty important, but what I mean is that we have plans for you. And they're what I would call some mighty interesting plans, seeing how you're known for being, shall I say, just a tiny bit on the ambitious side."

"Yes sir, I mean, Buck, the President has spoken with me about this."

"Well good, then. We can cut to the chase."

"I don't understand."

"Don't play stupid, preacher. You know very well what I mean."

"Sorry, but I'm afraid I don't—"

"Okay, then let me spell it out for you. This President

wants you as an advisor, which is by far the most absurd idea I've heard in my half century inside the Beltway. But he wants an advisor who is a preacher and at the moment he happens to want you. Now hear me out, preacher. You and I both love this President, but let me tell you something about him you don't know. The man is his own worst enemy. But then, that's true for most of us, is it not?"

Chuck nodded. *I don't like where this is going. Not at all! How do I respond to this boor and at the same time keep alive the dream?*

"Most of the time we can keep him from making decisions that would be his undoing, but in the case of your appointment, we failed. The President made this decision before we could talk him out of it. So now, I've been given the assignment of training you and, in the President's words, prepping you to come on board in late January. And to tell you the truth, I do believe I'd rather have the Democrats win than to have you up here messing everything up."

Jumping to his feet, Chuck barked, "Sir, I assure you that I have no intention of—"

"Sit down, boy, and shut your famous trap. You're ready to go on the defensive and yet you have absolutely no idea what I'm talking about. You're known for speaking, but for now, son, you'd be most wise to shut up and listen to the voice of experience. Can you do that?"

Chuck grimaced and felt suddenly nauseous. *I hate this game. I refuse to play this man's insane game. God, why does this have to be so hard?*

"Let me tell you the way it is. This position you're being offered doesn't mean diddlysquat. It's one hundred percent image. You will sit with the Cabinet, but you will not utter so much as a syllable without it first being scripted and vetted. You will say precisely what it is we would have you say—not one word more or less. And if you should happen to stray from your script in a moment of Holy Ghost inspiration, you will be out of here quicker than a tomcat with his tail set ablaze. Do I make myself clear?"

Chuck stared at the man, but Buck refused to blink.

"Nod yes or I'll call up the President this minute and tell him you have no interest in this position. He'll say, 'That's too bad' and he'll appoint another preacher by lunch time."

God, I hate this. But what choice do I have?

Chuck nodded

"That's better. Now you can go back to Dallas and hold on to your pulpit tighter than a dairy farmer's grip. If you feel so inclined, you can brag all you wish that you know the President on a first-name basis, and such. But if we ever read you quoted in print media or hear your famous voice on CNN or Fox or anywhere else speaking beyond the most narrow limits of the script we've provided, it will be very bad for you very soon."

"That sounds like a threat."

Buck laughed so loud and pounded his fists on the desk, the sound rattled the leaded-glass windows in his ornate office, "Well, it should son, because that is precisely what it is. You're quite astute. Even more so than I gave you credit for."

With jaw set and teeth clinched, Chuck stared at the man. *God, what do I do with this boor? He's in the way of everything I've ever wanted, but unfortunately he's also the way to every thing I've ever dreamed of. So I will say nothing. I will say absolutely noth-*

ing. There is far too much at stake here.

"Now let me tell you what you must do. Son, you need to bring your pretty little wife in line."

"And just what does bringing my wife in line entail?"

Jerking his bandy legs from the desk, Buck jumped to his feet and bellowed, "You know exactly what that entails! The woman's a liberal and we can't have a bleeding heart within 100 miles of this bottom-line no-nonsense, law and order administration! She's also a drunk! And we know she runs off all over the country on wild trips and that kind of nonsense won't even come close to fitting with the image the President wishes to project. Do I make myself clear?"

Chuck stood.

Buck motioned for him to sit. "Excuse me, Dr. Love. I get a bit riled sometimes. Let's both sit down for a bit and let you think this thing over, because if you walk out of here right now, it's all over for you. Do I make myself clear?"

I hate everything you represent, mister. Everything! I don't know if I can do this. This is all so wrong and so against everything I believe.

"Yes sir, perfectly clear."

"Good," Buck said sitting again, this time keeping his feet on the floor. "Now preacher, you're the Bible expert here, not me."

"And your point, sir?"

"Get on back to Dallas and do as the Good Book says, and bring your pretty little wife around. She is to answer to you, if I remember my Scripture correctly. You are to be the head of the house, so act like it. Take charge!"

"She is in recovery."

"We know that. In fact, we know everything about her and also about you."

"Exactly what is it you want me to do?"

"Turn her into a born-again evangelical and right-thinking Christian. In other words, bring her around to our way of seeing things. Fail, and you're not setting foot into this White House again."

"Sir, I mean, Buck, you don't understand my wife."

Throwing both hands in the air in exasperation, Buck hollered, "You're dead wrong about that. I do understand your wife, and the indisputable fact is that the woman's got her head screwed on backwards. That's all that's wrong with the girl. Get it turned around, man! Bring her around to our point of view or you're out of luck with this White House."

Buck dropped his arms again to his side and grinned. "Now fly home and do what needs to be done. Frankly, none of us up here care how it is you do it. Just do it! You've got plenty of time still. But if you fail, this President will pretend he's never heard of you. You've got my solemn word on that."

Chuck turned away from Buck Barrett and exited his office without speaking. In the hallway he happened again upon young Brandi who, sensing his tension, hurried her pace so she might accompany him to the door.

Opening the door for him, she placed her free hand upon his wrist. Surprised, he turned to face her as she said, "Dr. Love, he is evil. If it gets me fired for saying this to you, so be it. But the man is totally evil."

Chuck gently pulled his arm away and stepped through the door and into the cold morning air.

You are so right young lady. I certainly didn't expect this. Now what do I do? God, what do I do? I will have to reason with Jan. Either that, or bribe her. Bribes are all she understands. So I'll bribe her, one more time. That's the only way. God, I hate this. This is all so unfair. I've worked all my life for this and now my crazy wife stands in the way of my dream.

CHAPTER NINE

The sun slipped behind a towering wall of dramatic clouds as Jan's Porsche rolled upon the gravel lot of the Sage Hotel. Distant thunder shook the mountains and sent cool breezes to blow grit and an assortment of dried desert vegetation rolling down the sidewalks and the main street of the tiny town. For protection against the dust, she wrapped a silk scarf about her face as she made her way to the hotel's entrance.

Ollie Matson recognized her immediately even with her pretty face partially hidden behind the silk. "Well, I see you made it back."

"Oh my God, you were so right, that old man is crazy."

"You found him in the shed?"

"Just as you said, he was hanging upside down."

"Did he tell you about Royal?"

"Yes, he said he was not dangerous."

"That's what I told you, ma'am. He's a very good and most trustworthy man."

"But I've got to be certain. I can't afford to be wrong on this. My very life is at stake."

"Well, lady, I'd bet a whole lot, and probably even my life, Royal is one hundred percent safe. Why don't you sit out on our porch for a bit and let me buy you a beer? The sun is down and the storm may hold off some. You can enjoy one of our rockers and sort this thing out."

"I can't drink beer or anything else with alcohol because my shrink back in Dallas tells me one more little drink will do me in. But I definitely do need to feel better. Is there any place in this town to score some weed? I can still smoke weed without it killing me, although my sanctimonious AA sponsor would be horrified if she knew how often I toked. What she doesn't know certainly can't hurt her, right?"

Ollie grinned. "My personal stash is depleted, but we have a regular supplier right here in good old Marathon."

"Where?"

"Cross the railroad tracks until you come to a row of small businesses on the other side. Drive behind those buildings until you reach the alley. In that alley behind the bakery, you'll see an old Mexican sitting on a fifty-gallon drum smoking a cigarette. He'll be wearing a bandana around his head. Just drive right up to Juan like you were ordering a burger at a drive-through."

He paused to answer the desk phone and then smiled at her to signal he was back. "Roll down your window and tell him how much you want. He'll name his price. Pay him, and he'll toss you a baggie or two full."

"Does he sell on the metric system? I mean, should I order in grams or what?"

"No, keep it simple. Just order a baggie. That should do us for tonight." Ollie popped the cash register's drawer open and withdrew a twenty-dollar bill and handed it to Jan. "Last week the going rate for a baggie was $30."

"What about the police?"

Chuckling, Ollie said, "The only police we have is our

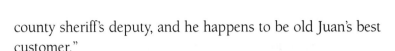

county sheriff's deputy, and he happens to be old Juan's best customer."

Jan turned to exit the hotel and felt immediately emboldened by the cool breezes whispering the kind of encouragement she had learned to trust. Lightning in long serpentine tongues of fire licked the bare distant peaks.

I love thunderstorms. I love talking to thunder. That's about as close to God as I care to come. If there is a God, he or she must certainly move about in a thunderstorm.

Jan fired the ignition of the Porsche and rolled the car out of the parking lot and onto the desolate highway. As she stared into the darkness, the fiery sky tempted her to continue driving west. A sudden and deafening clap of thunder, however, persuaded her to turn back to Marathon.

I have that man's twenty dollars, and I may be a broken woman, but I'm definitely not a thief, so I'm going back to score some weed and get as high as thirty bucks of Mexican grass can take me.

She brought the Porsche to a full stop in the middle of the empty highway to make the requisite U-turn. With her back tires squealing, she sped back into the direction of the town's dim lights while lightning filled her rearview mirror with both drama and fiery hints of promise. Once back in Marathon, she followed the desk clerk's directions precisely. Soon she found a man perched on an oil drum drawing upon a cigarette.

She pulled the Porsche close to the man, who ignored her. "Good evening," she said. "Oh excuse me, *buenas tardes*."

The shadowed figure on the fifty-gallon drum said nothing as his cigarette flared with each long draw.

"Looks like rain."

Only the thunder responded to her attempt at pleasantries.

"Oh hell, how much for a baggie?"

"Thirty dollars."

Jan reached into her purse and retrieved Ollie's twenty and her ten and handed it to the man as she sat tall in the bucket seat to scan the scene in every direction. The man tossed a baggie filled with what in the dim glow of a distant street lamp appeared to be marijuana. The small plastic bag landed in her lap. Clutching it to her breast, she attempted to embrace it.

Oh, sweet grass, I love you. God I, really do love you, and it's been way too long. I'm going back to that hotel and I'm going to get high enough to figure out what I must do.

Thank God for Mexico and for cheap grass. I'm going to be fine, and I'm going to find the answer tonight. I may go to the river and I may not. This grass will heighten my consciousness as it calms me, and then the thunder will tell me exactly what to do.

Once on the old hotel's concrete front porch, she found Ollie waiting for her in a rocking chair, one of the half dozen now rocking in the new breezes of the coming storm. Even in the darkness, she could tell the man was wearing a smile as he held high a fistful of white cigarette papers.

"It's been so long since I smoked any pot, I'd almost forgotten where I hid these papers. Once you've rolled yourself a joint, roll me one, but don't light it. I'm on the desk for another half hour."

Jan took the fragile papers in her hand and located a

rocker that would afford her the best view of the night sky. With her shaky right hand, she poured a small bit of weed into one of the papers, but the breezes serving as the storm's first heralds spoiled her effort.

"Damnation," she screamed, missing the relief she was certain she would find in that initial drag on a joint.

Through the window Ollie motioned for her to come inside. In the deserted lobby, she managed to roll four joints, one for herself and three for the desk clerk. Lighting her joint, she took a protracted drag and held it for as long as normal breathing allowed.

As a veil of thin smoke escaped her nose and mouth, she handed the three freshly rolled joints to Ollie. "This is some really good stuff. God, I have missed doing this. I'll meet you on the porch, mister," Jan said with a wink. "It's almost party time."

Ollie returned the wink "I'll be there soon, real soon."

The joint surprised Jan by remaining lit. Settling into the rocker providing her with the best view of the sky, Jan drew over and over again on the joint. *I'm beginning to feel the buzz, so I suppose it's time for me to talk to God.*

In a whisper, "Okay God, if you want me to return to the river, light up the skies."

No sooner had she finished her command than a long bolt of lightning spit a ball of fire directly over her head where it hung suspended before dying in an audible crackle. A cold wind now blew against her face threatening to extinguish her joint.

"Okay, Old Man, if you exist, make it thunder twice."

A single, deafening clap of thunder ensued.

This is ridiculous. There is no God. And there is no good reason for me to return to the river, except for the curiosity burning a hole in my heart. Sometimes I hate this curiosity. But I also love it, because it drives me and defines me. I'm not at all like the stupid women in my husband's sick church. Sunday after Sunday, they sit before that oaf and believe in their heart of hearts that the fool is speaking for God from his tall, antique pulpit. Ah, but I know better...

She savored a last long drag on the joint.

Yes, I know better, Chuck Love does not speak for God, simply because there is no God to speak for, only money, power, and even more prestige than the bastard already enjoys. Greed is all that Chuck Love can possibly speak for, because that is all he knows. Greed and ambition, those are his gods. And at the moment, my god is whatever grass I have remaining in this bag.

As the first drops of cold rain began to pummel her, Ollie rapped his fist on the windowpane. He motioned frantically for her to return to the lobby. She dropped what remained of the joint to the porch and ground its wet remains beneath her heel. No sooner had she entered the warm lobby than hailstones shattered the front windowpanes before rolling across a colorful Navaho rug to melt against a far wall.

Stepping from behind the counter, Ollie spoke through a smile seemingly fixed permanently upon his face. "It appears we're going to have to move this party inside."

"Can we smoke pot in here?" Jan said.

"No, we can't, but then, we're not allowed to smoke pot anywhere in Texas, are we?"

Sighing, she said, "I guess not. But won't you get fired?"

"Who is going to fire me? The owners live in Dallas, and I'm the manager, and desk clerk, and everything else."

"But what if some guests comes into the lobby and finds you smoking pot?"

"I'll just offer them a hit. It's no big deal. I smoke pot in here with guests from time to time. And of course, I've smoked it with our town deputy more times than I can remember."

"Good," said Jan as she rolled herself another joint."

"What's got you all jazzed up about our friend Royal?"

"I bumped into him on the river and he knew my full name and said he had some kind of message for me."

"So?" Ollie blew several rings of smoke toward the low ceiling.

"He scared me. Only my now-deceased mother ever called me by my full name. And I don't want some man I've never met to know my name and then to tell me he has some kind of message for me. To me, that's all real scary, in fact, too scary for my liking."

"But your curiosity is about to get the best of you, right?"

"Right! But, you know what?" said Jan. "Maybe it's the pot talking, but I'm tired, damn tired, of being afraid."

"Me, too," said Ollie stretched out on the lobby's cowhide sofa, and drawing hard on a joint before sending a string of smoke rings toward the ceiling.

"What are you afraid of, although it's none of my business," said Jan.

"I don't mind telling you. Ever since I came out the first semester of my senior year at West Texas Baptist College, I've been afraid of being hurt again. Consequently, I made a deal with God, or perhaps the Devil, I've never been certain which. And the deal was this: I'd forever give up one hundred percent of my dreams and the curiosity that drives them in favor of living my life between the two poles of panic and boredom. That's what I've done for the past twenty years, and as a consequence, I've pretty much wasted my life standing day in and day out behind that desk over there, making money for other people. And to tell you the truth, ma'am, I'm tired of my life behind that miserable desk, but even more I'm tired of allowing fear to drive my life."

"I can certainly understand that," said Jan as she managed to exhale a cloud of smoke without choking.

"When fear is the fabric of your life, it becomes your very essence. And that, my dear, is the short definition of a tragic life." Ollie paused again to float another fragile smoke ring above his head. "A life driven by fear is not worth living."

"Were you a shrink in another life?"

Ollie laughed until the joint tumbled to the floor. He picked it up and drew deeply from it. "Hey, I've got an idea," he said between puffs. "Let's make a solemn pact right here and right now to act courageously for once in our lives."

"What exactly does that entail?"

"It's simple. We make the pact, and then you let me buy you breakfast in our dining room. With only an hour to daylight, our kitchen will be open any minute now."

"Sounds great. Pot always makes me hungry."

"Immediately after breakfast, you return to the river to find Royal, and I go upstairs to the converted broom closet I've called home for the past twenty years, and I write my resignation letter to the owners."

"You know, you're one very wise man."

"In truth, I'm nothing more than a coward and a lowly hotel clerk. But thank you." Ollie's smile released the joint between his lips. It tumbled to the floor again where he ground it to death. "After I mail it, I drive straight to Sweetwater where I confront everyone who rejected me four decades ago, including my mother, who is still alive, and also my three sisters, one of whom is married to a fundamentalist preacher. I hang around Sweetwater long enough to find a job, and then I stay there for the rest of my life so I can force the people of my hometown to deal with their own bigotry. What do you say? Is it a deal? Are you willing to make this solemn pact to be courageous?"

"It's real scary to think of going to find Royal all alone. Would you go with me?"

"Can't do it, ma'am, because my part of the pact is to go home and risk being rejected all over again. This pact is based on courage, and that means we must do what we are to do all alone. Will you agree to it?"

"I suppose so, but I'm not certainly looking forward to encountering that awful man again."

"Well then, if you will, step over here to the sofa and shake my hand. We have to shake on it to make the pact official."

Jan rose from the chair. Her legs felt wobbly and ready to fold beneath her, but somehow she managed to remain upright long enough to clasp the hand of the man reclining on the sofa.

She stared into his face as a steady stream of smoke leaked out of both his nose and his mouth. "You sound like you have learned to accept yourself. I envy you."

"I learned from a living legend who has devoted his life to prayer. Somewhere or somehow he discovered that the truth is invariably love and that love is all that can possibly conquer fear. This man lives so simply and so compassionately that one would swear meeting him is tantamount to encountering Jesus himself face-to-face."

"Wow! I've never heard of such a man. I've got to meet him. Tell me, what's his name?

"Oh, you've already met this living saint. His name is Father Royal Cranfield, the very man who frightened you."

"Oh my God," said Jan. "That settles it. I'm taking off at first light and driving straight to the river."

Well, I guess this means I've made my decision. I'm definitely returning to the river, even if it kills me, which it just might.

CHAPTER TEN

A raven's caw sent an echo deep into the shadowed canyon where it ricocheted back and forth between Texas and Mexico as though it could not decide where to settle for the day. The bird's cry summoned Jan's eyes to the sheer sunlit limestone walls jutting a thousand feet above the river.

Scanning the cliffs hurriedly for any glimpse of feathered plaintiveness or other signs of life, she shifted the Porsche's transmission into neutral. After her tap on the brake pedal, the convertible slowed to a halt, crunching the parking lot gravel beneath its tires.

The hidden bird cried again, this time from a greater distance. Beneath the first clouds of the new morning, the river turned dark and sullen, even sad, she imagined, as she recognized it was all too easy for her to become. She twisted her body in the convertible's front seat to face the sun rising to paint the mountains in myriad pastels

He's not here. I'm going home. This is ridiculous. Oh, why did I come back? Whatever did I hope to find?

Ken Coughman is right. Those two men, Royal and the bartender, were merely playing a cruel trick. The people in Marathon may think this priest is some kind of saint, but I suspect he is at best a very sick practical joker, and I want nothing to do with him or with any other man. I'm heading back to Big D and divorce the Big C and take as much money as the law allows from that famous preacher.

Before she could shift the transmission into reverse, an emaciated, solemn-eyed man with skin the color of cinnamon stepped from behind a mesquite tree and into full view in the gravel lot. The new light the rising sun cast across the desert made the beads of sweat dotting his brow glisten like dewdrops on a ripe summer melon. He wore no shirt and even from a distance she could see he was so thin that his ribs pushed hard against his skin.

What she suspected to be an unwarranted, if not altogether bogus, smile revealed no more than the minimum teeth required for the man to bite. In one hand he gripped a tattered straw hat while he attempted to stuff his other hand in a pocket so frayed it scarcely existed.

God, doesn't anyone in this pitiful country ever wear a shirt? I'm out of here. No, I'm not. Not just yet. Maybe this peasant knows Royal.

"Hey, do you speak English?" she called.

"Sí, señora."

You could have fooled me. I would swear that sounds a whole lot like Spanish.

"Do you know a tall man named Royal?"

"I'm over here, Janet."

Remaining in the Porsche's front seat, she turned to see the tall man smiling.

Just like Chuck. Look at that big toothy grin. The fool thinks he's going to sweep me off my feet. But guess what, mister, you may have those poor suckers in Marathon fooled, but not me. No man is ever tricking me again. I've got your number, Sweet Pea, and you don't even know it. But you are no different than every other man on this planet. God, I so hate men, every last untrustworthy one of them.

"Morning, Janet. I'm pleased you came back. Didn't expect you to see you quite so soon, though. In fact, I wasn't sure you'd come back at all. I really put a scare into you. I regret that, but I couldn't see any way around it. I was given the assignment to tell you what I did and being upfront is my way."

She drew hard on a cigarette. "You terrified me, so badly that I flew straight home after encountering a bartender who went psychotic just as the sun came up. But then I suspect you know all about that. Is there anyone down here who is not insane?"

"Likely not."

"I visited with Father Brady—"

"Well now, talk about the glorious manifestation of full-blown insanity! Brady's more than just a bit addled these days. Too many years in the desert sun and far too many spirits coursing through his pickled liver—now that's a sure-fire recipe for insanity. Father Brady is certifiably crazy, but I do love that old goat. I confess I do."

Royal shook his head in amusement. "Let me guess. That sweet old padre told you I could be trusted."

"Did you also read that in your crystal ball?"

Royal folded his arms and took a step backwards. "No, not exactly. But why else does one seek references? And knowing Father Brady, I'm sure he told you about the newspaper exposés I wrote some time ago and how it is I have exiled myself to beautiful Boquillas."

"How did you know my name? No one but my mother,

who has been dead for years, ever called me by my full name. And by the way, my psychiatrist says you are in cahoots with the bartender in Lajitas."

Smiling, Royal said, "To tell you the truth, I have no idea what it is I'm being accused of."

"You and that bartender are conspirators."

"Well if we are, why did you come back?"

"Because I also think you may know something."

"The truth here is that I do, in fact, know something. But if this bartender and I are co-conspirators, wouldn't that negate any good motives on my part?"

"It could be that you are a good and honest man as Brady claims. He did say I could trust you and so did the clerk at the Sage."

"Oh, you mean Ollie. But what if Ollie, Brady, and this bartender in Lajitas and I are all conspiring against you. Have you considered that?"

"Of course I did. I've yet to meet a man I could totally trust. I'm not even certain I trust my psychiatrist, and I trusted the hotel clerk only because I was a little high on pot. And as strange as this sounds, I've learned to trust my pot-smoking partners more than other more respectable people."

"Your psychiatrist claims I'm in cahoots with a bartender and you obviously believe him, which can mean only one thing."

"And what is that?"

"You trust your psychiatrist. By the way, it's a sound idea, seeing you're likely paying this man a good bit of money."

I hate this man. I'll swear, all men are alike, all know-it-alls. All arrogant! All condescending.

"Are you always this arrogant?"

"Most times, I'm even more so. Good-bye, Ms. Macdonald-Love, and again, safe journey."

"But wait, what if I did come to trust you? What then? Would you tell me what this is all about?"

"From the way you describe your mistrust of men, I'd say for you to trust me would require some kind of a God-ordained miracle, you know, some kind of real epiphany. And nowadays those are few and far between."

"But what if I did? Would you tell me what it is I am to know?"

"Janet, my assignment—"

"What assignment?"

"My assignment is to take you to a holy place high above the village of Boquillas. Folks here call this place The Thin Place and this is where Juan Diego would have a word with you on behalf of our Blessed Mother. That's the sum of what I know about you—that, and, of course, your name."

"Who is Juan Diego?"

"He's Our Blessed Mother's messenger."

"Why doesn't he come to me himself? Why did he send you?"

"I have no idea."

"Where is this Thin Place?"

"If you'll be so bold as to step out of the car and trust me sufficiently to follow me down to the river, I'll be glad to show you."

"But what is it?"

"The Thin Place is a holy place high in the Sierra del Carmen. For centuries, people have gone there to pray, and, in doing so, they have worn thin the membrane separating the world of the Spirit from the material world. And now it seems you have been invited there also. I am to be your guide. It just may be one of the holiest places on earth."

This is absolutely nuts. I'm not going up in those mountains with this strange bird. I don't care what some upside down priest in Marathon says. This is all way too weird.

"If you want to see it, follow me. If not, head on back home and please do be safe."

Yanking the key from the ignition, her hand so trembled she feared she would drop it. As she stepped out of the Porsche, her body felt stiff and her legs frozen. Nevertheless, she forced herself to trail behind the tall man as best she could before he disappeared from view in the dense river cane.

"Would you please slow down?" she said.

He ignored her.

What if this is a trick? What if he is taking me down there to assault me?

Concentrating on not stumbling, she trained her eyes on the ground. She ran head first into the small of his back as he stopped abruptly at the river's edge.

"You did that on purpose just to make me look foolish."

"Excuse me, Janet. I didn't mean to have you crash into me. For one so on edge, you might want to pay a bit more attention to where you are going."

I despise you! You are just like Chuck---an arrogant, patronizing know-it-all boor.

"There it is—"

"There what is?"

"The Thin Place!"

"I don't see anything but a bunch of mountains."

"See that tall spire up there? That's Pico del Carmen and that's what we call The Thin Place. That's where Juan Diego has summoned you to climb."

"Who's crazier, me, you or this Juan fellow you're so fond of? I'm not climbing up there—not now, not in a million years, not ever! Do you hear me, mister?"

"Suit yourself. No one is making you do anything. You are only invited. You can accept the invitation or reject it. The choice lies with you."

The tall man turned to face her and, wearing a broad smile, he said, "Good-bye. This new day is well upon us, and the Border Patrol has not yet arrived to check this crossing for drug runners and other bad guys. It's time I imposed upon my brother, sweet Pablo, to row across to carry me home. I have work to do today."

Waving to the boatman on the Mexican side, he said, "Do take care, Janet. It was so good to meet you and I'm sorry our visit has been cut short by my need to get to my work. The next time I pray, I'll convey your regrets to Juan. No doubt, he will be disappointed, but he is a very understanding and forgiving fellow. Adios."

As she watched him signal the boatman with one last wave, melancholy seized her as though it meant once more to possess her soul. The same shirtless cinnamon-colored man she had seen scramble into the Johnboat earlier now rowed from the Mexican side against the currents as the sun rose to play in the river. Questions tormented her as she watched the man bump the boat's bow gently against the Texas bank. The tall priest stepped in and they shoved off the river's edge.

I'm heading straight home if I have to drive all night and half of tomorrow, and I plan to pretend none of this ever happened. If I should ever think of this again, I will erase the memories with alcohol and, no doubt, that will be the death of me.

Either way, I will not remember this madness. No, this never happened. None of it! This man Royal doesn't exist. And neither does Brady and neither does that crazy bartender in Lajitas.

None of this is real. I'm out of here and I will never come back. Never!

CHAPTER ELEVEN

Buck Barrett turned the headlamps to bright as the Cadillac Escalade eased into an alley before it rolled to a stop. A short man shaped like an avocado stood no more than six inches from the front bumper. He stared at the driver before raising one hand to shield his eyes.

Delighted he had temporarily blinded the man, Buck grinned behind an unlit cigar stub as he cut the headlamps. Dazed, the man stepped awkwardly toward the passenger side while attempting to avoid a puddle.

He pulled open the door and slipped into the front seat where he settled. As he stared into the windshield, he said, "Okay, Barrett, what is this about? And tell me why it is we have to skulk around like spies in a dime novel when my office at the CIA is likely the most secure one thousand square feet in all of Virginia."

"One can never be too cautious, Ramps. With what I'm about to tell you, I can take no chances. This information is far too sensitive for any place other than here."

"How do you know this car is secure?"

"I had your boys at the CIA check it out thoroughly."

"Seeing how I'm the Deputy Director of the CIA, there is a certain irony to this, don't you think?"

"Perhaps, so let's just say I feel far more comfortable sharing state secrets on my turf and my turf happens to be the front seat of this car. My office may not be secure. I don't trust everyone at the White House. Truth is, I'd be a fool to."

"What is it you want me to know?"

"Ramps, right now only a handful of people know what I'm about to tell you: the President, the Secretary of State, the Secretary of Defense, the Joint Chiefs of Staff, and the heads of state of two sovereign nations, and their top military people. You will be one of the very few to learn the most sensitive information to come out of the White House since the Manhattan Project. And I trust you because of your record of service and your devotion to this President."

"What is it that is so important to take me away from my family and my warm cozy den on this miserable Sunday night and place me in a dreary alley not three blocks from your warm, and I might add, luxurious office?"

"The President needs you to bend the law."

"Barrett, that's ridiculous. I'm not breaking the law for—"

"Not even to save this President?"

"Is the President in danger?"

"The President may be in the worst kind of danger."

"Barrett, I didn't get this job by breaking laws."

"You are one of the most trusted men in this government. That's why you're perfect for doing what must be done to save the President."

"How exactly is the President in danger?"

"I'm getting to that, but all of what I am about to tell you is top secret. Can I trust you with this?"

"Quit playing games and tell me what endangers our President."

"A woman."

"What woman?"

"The wife of a Dallas preacher."

"The wife of a Dallas preacher is a threat to our President? Get serious."

Barrett let his silence speak for him.

"How?"

"The President is bringing Chuck Love, Dallas preacher and world class sycophant, to his cabinet immediately following the election."

"Everyone in this town knows that secret. Is this why you believe Love's wife is a risk to the President? What kind Oval Office paranoia is this? The man's wife is probably nothing more than a homemaker and brownie baker for Jesus back in Dallas. I'm out of here."

"There is more—"

"Well, this had better be good."

"In March of next year, we will attack North Korea."

"In more than three decades of service to this country, that's the craziest thing I have ever heard. You have a well-deserved reputation for being cruel, but no one has ever called you delusional. Man, you've been watching too many spy movies. Have you thought of retiring?"

"Shut up, Ramps and listen. This is the truth. Beijing and Moscow have both been apprised and are secretly in on the attack. Of course, publicly they will condemn it, but secretly we have been assured we have their full support. We will hit Pyongyang with a new type of low-yield and very smart nuclear bomb on March 1st and take out their entire regime with one blast. The radioactivity in this new gadget is close to negligible. In fact, it is so low; it will all but dissipate within forty-eight hours. We estimate the casualties will be no more than ten thousand, give or take a thousand. Now, that's one very humane bomb."

Barrett rolled down the driver's side window to spit and then said, "The South Koreans have been secretly preparing to invade for two years now, and their army will cross the 38th Parallel on March 3rd, once the radioactivity has dissipated sufficiently. We estimate that in less than two days, what little remains of a leaderless North Korean Army will surrender immediately to the South's superior forces, and the North and South will finally be reunited. The entire world, especially our enemies in Teheran and in every other world capital where totalitarianism and anti-Americanism reign, will be placed on immediate notice that this new century belongs entirely to us. Ramps, the 21st Century is to be the American Century."

Ramps shook his head. "Insane, absolutely insane!"

"Our greatest legacy to our grandchildren will be a world that is safe for a robust American economy. We have a very small window of opportunity here. A few days less than one month after Chuck Love arrives in Washington, he will go before the American people and declare that our liberation of North Korea is God's will for the United States."

"Insane, insane, Barrett," said Ramps in a louder tone.

"He will tell the American public he's been praying about this, and this pre-emptive attack is exactly what God would have us do. And the craziest part of this whole scheme is that the citizens of this nation are so gullible and willing to believe in this preacher that they will buy every word he utters on our behalf."

Ramps pulled hard on a lock that refused to cooperate. "Barrett, open this door and let me escape this madness before I, too, go insane."

"We estimate no more than five thousand South Korean casualties. Since no American lives will be lost and because 'America's Preacher,' Dr. Charles Love, has assured the American people that God has ordained this swift little war, we'll be in and out of North Korea in less than a week. Believe me, the world will be better off for it. And if I believed there was a God, I would say 'Thank God.'"

"That is the most irresponsible idea I've ever heard coming from—"

"I'm disappointed to hear you say that, Ramps. I took you for a team player."

"The issue here is World War III—"

"But, you're so short-sighted for a CIA man."

"So, if this is the truth, how come I don't know about it?"

"For reasons of national security, the President intentionally left you guys out of the loop."

"You and I both know that makes absolutely no sense. That's never been his way. But assuming this is true, why are you now bringing me into the loop?"

"Because we need your help."

"What in God's name could you possibly need from the CIA at this point? Here you are, telling me you are ready to launch World War III and I don't know about it and now you claim to need our help? Are you completely out of your mind?"

"You see Ramps, we need this preacher's wife to commit suicide."

"You're not just delusional, you're also a sociopath!"

"We have the Reverend Dr. Charles Love exactly where we want him. He's the most respected man in America. Everything he says, people believe to be true simply because this man of God says it. But guess what?"

"Oh, I can hardly wait."

"Our famous preacher is also the father of an illegitimate child, who is a twenty-something year old retarded woman living in a government-subsidized housing project in a small county-seat town in a southern state. I will not disclose her identity or whereabouts, at least not at the moment. Turns out, our boy was ethically challenged some several decades back when as a youth minister he just happened to capitulate to temptation with a sad result of a most embarrassing teen-age pregnancy."

Once more Ramps attempted to unlock the car door. Turning to face the large man filling the driver's seat he said, "This is nothing but sick, salacious gossip, and I will not be subjected to it. Unlock this door, Barrett, and let me the hell out of here."

Barrett said, "Chucky boy's well-connected parents paid for the abortion, but there wasn't one. After the child's birth, Chucky's Mama and Daddy were kind enough to pay this unwed mother $100,000 to go away. She took the money and did just that for a year. But she came back and when she did, Mama and Daddy Love agreed to pay her $5,000 a month until the child turned eighteen, which occurred more than ten years ago. She took the monthly payments and promised to stay quiet until our people found her and she spilled, shall we say, one hundred percent of the beans for a small fee."

"Does Love know you are in possession of this incriminating information?"

"Not yet and neither does his Bolshevik wife. But if she were ever to find out about this top-secret plan, she would blow the whistle and we'd all be up to our ears in alligators before the ink in the morning headlines had time to dry."

"So tell her the truth about her husband's past and she divorces the preacher and takes him to the cleaners. The President finds another preacher and your problem is solved."

"I wish it were that simple. You see, the President wants Chuck Love. The good reverend is coming up here convinced we don't know about his decades-old indiscretion. He actually believes the President wants him because of his fame and sterling reputation as a man of impeccable character."

Ramps reached again for the lock, this time resting his thumb upon the thing as Barrett rolled down the window on the driver's side to spit out the remainder of his cigar stub.

"He's a household name and the most respected man in America, but even more, the President wants him because we can own this hypocrite's soul. We can make him do whatever we want. And for the immediate future, we want him to convince the American people that God would have us liberate North Korea."

"And what if he doesn't choose to cooperate?"

"It's simple. *The Washington Post* will receive an anonymous tip that will expose him for the phony he is."

"Barrett, don't you know anything about the statute of limitation?"

"Ramps, when it comes to baby rape, there are no statutes of limitations."

"I've got to hand it to you. You have more than lived up to your reputation. You are every bit as evil as people say."

"Coming from a CIA man, I take that as a compliment."

"Why don't you just pay her off?"

"She's a Bolshevik, you know the type, a real bleeding-heart. Not the kind we can buy off."

"Half the voters in the country consider themselves liberal and we don't kill them for it, at least not yet."

"Ramps, once push does come to painful shove in Dr. Love's personal circumstances, he just might break down and tell his nutty wife everything about the attack we're planning and his pivotal part in it. We can't afford for anyone to know this until we hit North Korea. She's a crazy lush and as unpredictable as Texas weather in spring. But for this to work, we need her completely silent, which means out of the picture. She is a variable we simply can't afford."

"Does the President want her gone, or is this all your idea?"

"The President doesn't know her like I do. He's been led to believe she's one hundred percent for him. Her famous husband bribes her with lavish gifts and she agrees to fly up here every so often and makes nice-nice with the President and First Lady. But I tell you, the woman's a loose cannon, and if she were to catch wind of our plan, every news organization in the world would have this story on the airways so fast that the North would invade the South and World War III would turn from a remote possibility into a certainty. We can't risk that because we know Beijing would be required to support their crimson comrades, even though they don't want to. Of course, Moscow and every other world capital would condemn us outright. The world markets would collapse overnight and I wouldn't be surprised if Congress didn't begin proceedings to impeach this President the very next day."

Barrett cleared his throat. "You can see the stakes have never been higher for any president since Nixon."

"This has to be *the* most irresponsible idea I've ever heard. Chuck Love is a decent man. What little I know about the guy is good. My recommendation is to abandon this fairy tale and leave the North Koreans to their misery. Sooner or later, that regime will implode. Those poor people are suffering under the cruelest form of tyranny, just as they have for the past half-century, and there is little we can do for them until the whole system collapses, which trust me, it will. But to attack them is madness. It's sheer madness, Barrett!"

Ramps shifted in his seat. "I plan to forget we shared this bizarre moment of fantasy. And my recommendation to you—and I offer this in the strongest possible terms—is that you put this insane scheme out our your mind, leave Chuck Love and his wife alone, and do your very best to serve this President in his second term with the good sense and level-headed restraint."

Barrett started to speak, but Ramps held up his palm. "I'm also going to assume that out of some perverse motive, which I confess is presently lost on me, you made this whole bizarre scenario up. Because, if I thought for a moment there was any real truth to what you say, I'd be in the Oval Office the first thing tomorrow morning doing whatever it took to convince the President of the unequivocal foolhardiness and outright danger of this hare-brained scheme."

Ramps pulled on the now unlocked door handle. "What you tell me is so bizarre it cannot possibly be true. I don't know your game, Barrett, but I now know that you're not only the meanest man in this administration, you also just have to be by far the most insane."

Pushing open the Town Car's door, Ramps said, "And please let me thank you in advance for never contacting me again. Good-night, Mr. Barrett."

"We're not done, Ramps. We're far from done, friend."

Ramps slammed the car door with a thud that reverberated through the damp night.

CHAPTER TWELVE

Seated in his favorite recliner, Chuck shifted his weight from one side to the other, but no arrangement of torso, legs and arms soothed him or brought comfort. He longed for strength and courage but could never quite muster enough of either when faced with the prospect of doing battle with his wife.

God, I'm wrapped tighter than a bolt of new wire. I hate this. Even more, I hate her. I hate the life we share and everything about it—the pretense, the stress, the constant drain of money, but most of all the lies. It has got to get better and soon. I can't go on like this for much longer without cracking wide open. God give me strength.

"I can do all things in him who strengthens me," Chuck said to himself.

God, I so wish I could believe those words are true. I once did, but no more. This sick relationship has eroded my faith. I doubt I'll ever get it back. Too much heartache. Too much disappointment. Too much everything!

The sound of the Porsche coasting into the driveway sent a chill through him, and his brow beaded in perspiration, and his hands trembled. As the back door bolt clicked with the turn of her key, his head felt like it had been pumped full of helium.

Jan cleared her throat for effect before launching into

what he knew from experience would be some phony affectionate expression he would end up despising. "Well, as you can see, I didn't get smashed on the highway."

"You're a day late," he said. "Are you also a dollar short, as usual?"

God, now why did I have to say that? I might have avoided a fight, but not now. I swear I am so impulsive sometimes.

"Reverend, it just so happens that I did give some thought to the idea of calling you," Jan said in a flat, caustic tone. "But then, since my calls have never seem to be all that important to you, I said to myself, 'I'll just let sweet Emily do the calling for me. After all, my important husband is off doing the Lord's work and far too busy to take his embarrassing wife's phone calls.'"

"Where have you been?"

"I flew to Midland with Emily," Jan said as she searched a kitchen cabinet for a clean goblet.

"Emily left word here and at the office. I know that much.

Filling the goblet to within an inch of the brim with tap water, she said, "I think it so very sweet of Emily to call you, don't you? The woman is incredibly thoughtful. But then I suppose she lives with the illusion that you are capable of caring for someone other than yourself. Poor naïve Emily, I must disabuse her of such nonsense the next time we speak."

Jan took a sip from the glass and followed the last swallow with what he read to be a triumphant smile.

In a show of exasperation, Chuck spread his arms wide. "Does it take two days to drive back from Midland?"

"You know, Chuck, I'm tired, very tired. Besides, you bore me. Sad to say, but you always have. The rest of the world seems to wait with bated breath to hear what you have to say, but not me. No, your wife finds you terribly boring."

"Answer me, Jan! Where have you been?"

Falling into the sofa with her arms outstretched, she continued with the demonstration of feigned glee. "If you must know, I was with another man. I met him just outside the Mexican village of Boquillas."

"Where's Boquillas?"

Tossing her head backwards, she roared, "Oh my sweet, dear darling Chuck, my long-suffering and most respected and revered cover-boy husband. You, my dear, are so very, very predictable. Here I tell you that I've been with a man from Boquillas, and you ask me about Boquillas. How typical, but how pedestrian."

"Jan, I gave up years ago caring about your obsession with sin. If you want to sleep with another man, I don't care any more. Years ago I realized marrying you was the biggest mistake of my life. Let's face facts. You are a worthless, disgusting drunk and a self-loathing, no-good little tramp who hasn't got the self-esteem God gave a skid-row whore."

Rising from the sofa, she said, "Good night, preacher boy. I'm off to bed. Being with that other man plus the long drive has worn me out. Sweet dreams."

"Jan, wait. Please." Chuck rose to block her exit. "There is something important we need to discuss."

Do this with surgical precision and with tact or everything is lost. Don't let your hatred ruin everything you've dreamed about or worked for. Don't do that. She's not worth it.

"Say it, Chuck."

"Please sit down. I need you to hear this, all of it. This

concerns you."

"Okay, I'm seated, so spit it out. You're known as America's greatest orator. Surely you can make it quick so I can get to bed."

"It's time you and I faced this charade we call a marriage."

"Oh, is that all you have to tell me? You must have thought long and hard before coming up with this keen bit of riveting insight. Why, I'm proud of you for being so astute. You and I can actually agree on something after all. Who'd a thunk it?"

"We should dissolve marriage, but not immediately"

Jan rose to scratch her head. "Not immediately? Why waste time? Let's split everything fifty-fifty, shake hands, and walk away, remaining the very good friends we are now. How about it?"

If I wasn't a Christian, I think I'd choke the woman. How could I imagine I ever loved her?

"No, I have a different idea. In fact, I have a proposition."

"For once you're not boring me."

"I visited with Frank Stevens last week. You've met Frank, I believe."

"He's a lawyer and the golfer who won the club tournament a year or so ago."

"That's right."

"We must keep all this confidential."

"Of course, who would want the world to know we are both so miserable."

"Frank drew up a contract that states I will pay you one lump sum of one million dollars, if, that is, you will remain married to me for the next four years and choose to be civil. Simple civility is all that will be required."

Chuckling, Jan said, "Now, preacher, tell me where is it that you plan to put your baby-soft little mitts on one million sweet dollars?"

"My position with the administration plus my speaking engagements will pay me one-half million dollars per annum. That, along with what I will continue to be paid by the royalties from my books and recorded sermons will be more than enough, even after taxes. And I will also be paid the $300,000 by the church because I have no plans to resign even while I serve the President. In fact, he wants me to remain in this pulpit. It fosters the image we're after."

She spun about full circle to glower at him. "So, you're attempting to buy me off, is that it, Chuck?"

"What I am proposing is that we turn the last four years of this mutually disappointing relationship into a business partnership that benefits both of us. In four years, you will walk away from me a rich woman. In fact, you will be set for life," he paused as his voice choked, "and I will give you my solemn promise in writing never to interfere in your life or to have any contact with you at all."

Chuck's tears flowed, rolling down his cheeks where he caught them in a handkerchief.

"All I've got to say is congratulations. You've finally made it, Chuck. You've hit the really big time. Whoever says nice guys finish last doesn't know my husband, the famous Dr. Chuck Love, a real live Princeton Ph.D. Why, you just have to be the nicest man in all fifty states." Jan headed toward the stairs. "No deal, mister. Now, I'm off to catch some much-needed sleep."

"Janet, listen to reason. You simply can't afford to turn

this down. You'll never get another offer like this. Never in a million years."

"Being bought and paid for is not my idea of a good time. No deal, Preacher. Good night. I'm headed back to The Big Bend first thing tomorrow."

Chuck collapsed in his chair where he buried his face in his arms and wept.

CHAPTER THIRTEEN

The Escalade idled behind a high, tin-roofed, unrestricted hangar at Langley that had not been used by the Air Force since Saigon fell. In the shadows from the shoulders up, a tall angular figure lit a match, for a moment illumining a clean-shaven jaw line.

Barrett read the signal and blinked the car's headlamps once, and the tall figure appeared more to float than actually stroll toward him. After opening the big sedan's front door, the man stooped to ease inside.

"Good evening, Mr. Daemon." Barrett held up his hand and pointed over the man's shoulder. "Before you get into the car, my friend hidden there behind you in the shadows must frisk you. I hope will excuse the inconvenience, but a man in my position cannot be too careful."

As a bulky figure emerged from the darkness, the tall man more grunted than actually spoke his consent. The bulky man patted him down with surprising speed and then once more disappeared into the shadows.

Daemon opened the car's front door for a second time to slide into the front seat. "Mr. Barrett." He nodded. "Tell me what is it we might discuss that might prove of mutual interest."

"Very good! I like a man who gets to the point. Let's put it this way. I have it on very good authority that your first-born son is under investigation concerning a bit of unpleasantness down in Miami."

"And if he is?"

"How would you like for that murder investigation to go away instantly?"

"I would think most kindly of anyone who could pull off such a miracle. Tell me, how much does this sleight of hand cost?"

"Mr. Daemon, how very crass! Oh, I'm so disappointed! Frankly, I expected much more from you. My sources tell me that you're most perceptive. No, Mr. Daemon, you've got me all wrong. I'm a patriot, quite pleased to leave extortion and the like to you fellows in the mob. Of course, I hope you know I intend absolutely no disrespect to you personally, sir."

"Mr. Barrett, I might take issue with you regarding that remark if you were not the President's muscle. It's prudent to overlook insults, because a man in your position can get away with quite a bit, that is, for as long as he is in your position. Otherwise, all bets would definitely be off."

"My sources are right after all. You are perceptive and quite astute. I do enjoy doing business with savvy people."

"How it is you propose to make disappear this current unpleasantness regarding my son?"

"It is all quite simple, Mr. Daemon. In the backseat, there is a briefcase containing $50,000 in small unmarked bills."

"And how do you wish I invest this money, sir?"

"Mr. Daemon, I would like it very much if you would keep it. In said briefcase, you also will find a complete set of counterfeit FBI credentials—badge and all—and yesterday's *Dallas Morning News*. On page one of the Metropolitan section, you will find a most interesting feature story regarding Dallas' most famous citizen, a Dr. Charles Blythe Love, best-selling author and senior pastor of University Park Presbyterian Church."

Barrett rolled down the big car's front window to allow the night's drizzle to wash against his left cheek. "Now, Mr. Daemon, if the American people were to read sometime before the general election in the *Dallas Morning News* that this man's wife had committed suicide—and what a great tragedy that would be to all concerned—there would be another brief case appearing at this same spot at this very hour, the day after that story was published. No doubt the story would make the front page in every daily in America and in most of the European papers."

Barrett stared through the front windshield as if he expected the bulky man to emerge once more. "This second briefcase will contain one-half million dollars in unmarked small bills, and it will all be yours. And quite coincidentally, and I might add, even miraculously, overnight the Justice Department will decide that your beloved son had absolutely nothing to do with murdering an ATF officer in Florida. All charges will be immediately dropped and your son will be a free man."

Barrett searched his inside coat pocket for a cigar. Finding none, he pushed the button that rolled up the Escalade's front window. "But if we should read in the same paper that her death was accidental, the briefcase will contain $250,000 and all charges will disappear and your son will be a free man."

"Sir, you may consider this woman a statistic."

"Very good, Mr. Daemon, but I do have one final word. If

anything should go awry, please understand that I have never met you and the investigation of your son will speed up and the Justice Department will see to it that your first-born is convicted and he will be incarcerated until he is put to death by lethal injection sometime within the next five years. Do I make myself perfectly clear, Mr. Daemon?"

"Spectacularly so, Mr. Barrett."

Daemon reached into the back seat and retrieved the briefcase and then pushed open the car door to disappear into the night.

Chapter Fourteen

The potholes in the primitive gravel lot adjacent to the Rio Grande filled with shadows like ink poured into a thousand tiny desk wells all at the same time. With her foot resting on the brake pedal, Jan stretched her arms above her head in the convertible with the top down and whispered, "God, my back is killing me. I've driven 12 hours only to stop twice."

So help me, I don't remember when I last ate. If I climb out of this car, I'm afraid I'll collapse. I'm just that dizzy. Why did I race to get here? What do I do now?

Does my back hurt more than my head? It's a contest and either way I lose. If I eat, I'll feel better. But where do I find food out here? This is not exactly Dallas, but I couldn't stay in the same city with the man who offered to pay me to be his wife. I had to run away, so here I am again.

The river ignored her complaints as it rattled past. A lone cardinal perched on bare mesquite branch sang over and over again a five-note serenade she decided was devoted to sympathy for every life defined by heartache.

Thank you, little redbird. It's reassuring to know someone in this old world is still capable of making music.

The bird jerked its crimson tufted head from side to side as if to inform her that she and this tiny creature shared the trait of hyper-vigilance and sadly the angst that drives it.

"My kingdom for a cold beer, little red bird. Everything I own for just one iced cold beer! Right here! Right now! O God, how I could do with a drink. Why in God's name did I ever give the stuff up? Well now, let me count the reasons: for starters it makes me totally crazy and—"

"Evening ma'am," spoke a man's voice into the Porsche.

She snapped her head to the left side. A young mustachioed man dressed in drab olive trousers and matching starched shirt exuded the brash, even condescending, air she'd experienced in men who wore badges. His smile revealed a pleasing contrast to the coal black mustache that turned his Hispanic features even more handsome. The young man's skin was so dark, she wondered if he might be part African-American. His shoulders were wide to the extreme and the muscles in his upper arms threatened to pop the stretched seams in his starched shirt.

Jan stepped out of the car and decided immediately his smile was hazardous to the hearts of all naive females. It carried an audacity that viewed itself exempt from repercussions. Such men considered taking liberties their birthright. She was not at all surprised to see him impose—without permission—one high-top boot upon the convertible's narrow rear bumper. He stretched his smile into a grin she suspected was not only his trademark but likely the most dangerous weapon in a well-stocked arsenal.

Trembling before the man, Jan said, "My God, you scared the fool out of me. Who are you?"

"Pardon me, ma'am. Allow me to introduce myself properly. My name is Aaron Flores. I'm with the Border Patrol, and at your service."

Border Patrol! I wonder if he can be trusted.

"Do you by chance know a man named Royal? He's tall—"

"Everyone on this stretch of the border knows Father Royal, ma'am. In fact, most people in these parts regard him as a man who will someday become a saint."

"So he's harmless?"

"That would be but one way to describe the good padre. He's also wise, learned, kind, sometimes mysterious and more."

"Do you know where I can find him?"

"Since he's not here, I suspect he's on the other side of the river lost in prayer. That's his habit each night following his meager evening meal. I've shared many a tortilla and frijoles with him the times he's slept on this side of the river. It's always the same with Father. Royal. He eats barely enough to stay alive and then prays for hours before turning in for the night. An hour before first light, he's up even before the roosters, praying again."

"I must get over there and talk with him before he sleeps. Does the boatman operate his ferry at night?"

The officer grinned beneath the neatly trimmed mustache. "Ma'am, it's illegal to cross the river here. Has been since 9/11."

"But I was here just a day or so ago and a man rowed over here not ten yards from where you and I are standing and invited me to cross over, for a fee of one dollar."

Flores said, "That skinny little man just happens to be my uncle. That cagey old hombre knows full well he's violating gringo law by inviting tourists to ride across, but Pablo doesn't care because the laws on this side of the river don't mean a thing to him. I've warned him I don't know how many times, of course, that if I should catch him, I'd have to haul him in and he would be charged with illegal entry into the United States."

"You would turn in your own uncle?"

"No, but I don't want Pablo to know that. So I threaten him every now and then, but none of it does any good."

"What if he came over here to take me across, would you arrest him?"

"No, but I'd arrest you."

"That's not fair!"

"Not much has ever been fair on this border. From the beginning, the line we've drawn separating these two nations has been a tragedy marked always by one constant, injustice."

She approached the young agent. "How can you be Hispanic and work for the Border Patrol? That makes no sense."

"Makes perfect sense, ma'am. Like you, I am an American citizen, and this is a well-paying job for a poor kid from a backwater barrio in Presidio with no more to recommend me than a high school letter in football. I earned a junior college diploma on a free ride that lasted until I blew a knee in the final game of my sophomore year, and then I said good-bye to any chance to play Division I ball. As soon as I got off the crutches, I signed on with the patrol. The pay is good, the benefits great and the retirement sweet."

"But the laws you enforce strangle the lifeblood out of Boquillas. I've been coming here since I was a kid and for all of those years the poor people of Boquillas have depended entirely upon what few meager tourist dollars they make. You're destroying their economy by cutting them off from the only income they have. These people are not terrorists! They are nothing more than a village of desperately poor people doing whatever it takes to survive."

She turned toward him until they stood face-to-face. "Have you no conscience?"

"I'm paid to enforce federal law, ma'am. In fact, your tax dollars pay my salary."

"But there are good laws and there are immoral laws. To cut off the flow of the few dollars that reach those desperate peasants is a bad law. In fact, it's immoral and it's just plain wrong. Make no mistake, I've never been a big champion of the poor, but any law that keeps those people from making a living just has to be wrong."

"Ma'am, I couldn't agree more." Officer Flores shook his head. "But it is not my job to question the law, only to enforce it."

He grinned. "And that's what I do, with the exception of Father Royal. He is free to cross at will. Most patrol agents down here know that and look the other way. One of our supervisors in Alpine even claims the man is invisible. If we regard him as invisible, how can we possibly arrest what we can't see?"

"But those are your relatives over there. You said so yourself."

"That is true."

"That's the most ridiculous law our government has come up with yet! Sir, this law you are so determined to enforce is cruel and any man with even so much as half a conscience would disobey it. We enact laws to keep desperately poor Mexicans out of our country. It's wrong, it's all very wrong and what you're doing here enforcing this law is a big part of that wrong."

"Ma'am, you sound a whole lot like a hellfire and brimstone preacher."

"Like a what?"

"Like some radio preacher."

"Hardly. I want nothing at all to do with religion, and, believe me, I've never read the Bible. I don't even like poor people. They make me nervous and I suppose that's because I'm afraid someday I'll end up just like them. Still, fair is fair. And the law you enforce, except when it comes to Royal, is so very unfair as to make me want to wretch."

"From the looks of the fine car you're driving, I'd have to say you're not exactly destitute. But then, you may have stolen that sweet ride, but you don't much look like the carjacking type. In the barrios down on the river, folks would likely call you some pretty rough names in Spanish that in English would translate into being just a bit of a hypocrite, if you catch my drift."

"Oh listen, I confess to being a hypocrite and a big one at that. I'm wealthy and I'm totally unapologetic about it. There can be no question that I'm extraordinarily rich, at least by the standards of the people subsisting on the other side of this border you're so determined to protect. But none of it is my money. Every penny of it belongs to my famous husband. He made it, all of it. But he won't let anyone get away with calling him a self-made man. No, he loves to remind everyone ad nauseum that he is not a self-made man, but rather God-ordained phenomenon."

Jan paced back and forth in front of the officer. "Every

time I hear him say that, I want to kill either him or myself or both of us at the same time. The man is such a phony. Now if you want to see a real hypocrite, he's it. Me? I just dabble in hypocrisy. I'm a real bush leaguer compared to this man. Believe me, he's the world's all-time grand champion."

Chuckling, the man said, "I take it you're not terribly fond of your husband."

"I hate him. But to be perfectly honest, I hate myself as well."

"What does he do?"

"Now, that's a very good question. Let me think."

She peered at him as if to examine his face. "The truth? He impresses the rich and powerful. I suppose that's what he does best. He also plays a bit of golf at a very exclusive club, which by the way disallows membership to Hispanics, Blacks, Jews, and other so-called undesirables. And he glad-hands anyone who is anybody in Dallas. When he's not doing that, he invests the rest of his energy loathing me and doing his dead-level best to make my life miserable. Making me miserable just may be what he does best. But then, he also has a way with the rich and powerful."

"What's his name? I might have heard of him."

"Oh, I suspect you've heard of him all right. But his name is not at all important. All that is important right now is that I get over to Boquillas and find Royal. Perhaps I can do that tomorrow or some day when you're not here with those binoculars you seem so attached to."

Jan leaned against her car. "I do believe I'm as tired as I've ever been, Señor Flores."

"Please call me Aaron."

"Okay, Aaron. Because you won't let me cross that stinking river down there, I will be forced to drive all the way back to Marathon, which as you know quite well, just happens to be one very long 100 miles from here. Seeing as how I didn't bring any camping equipment—"

"Laws are laws, Mrs. Love."

"God, does everyone down here know who I am? What the—"

"Father Royal told me you might come tonight. I'm leaving here in just a bit." Flores winked at her. "When I do, the headlamps on my vehicle will signal my uncle. If I blink them, he will come for you then."

"You were putting me on all along, weren't you?"

He nodded.

"You know who my husband is, too, don't you?"

"I like hearing him preach on TV. For a preacher, the man is thought-provoking and what he says actually makes a lot of sense. I don't always follow all of the big words he uses, but I get most of what he has to say. I do like his idea of correct thinking."

Flores pushed back his cap to scratch his head. "What's he call that thing? 'Cognitive correctness.' Yeah, I like that stuff a lot because it comes in handy in this work."

He stood up straighter and shifted his shoulders back. "It just so happens my supervisor in Alpine is also a really big fan of your husband. He claims he's by far the smartest preacher he's ever heard, and hardly a day goes by that he doesn't quote from your husband's book, *On Getting Everything You Ever Wanted*! I've read that book myself. It's quite good and I do my best to practice the seven spiritual principles I learned in it."

"Why did you put me on for so long?"

"Because you are much like your husband in that you are thought-provoking. Besides, you were teaching me about the mother country. Why interrupt such a superb lecture?"

"My God, if you're not just like all men—insensitive, rude, manipulative—"

"I was indeed rude. Please forgive me."

"Tell you what, I'll consider doing just that if you will blink the lights on that Jeep and signal your uncle to row across this river and take me to Boquillas."

"Sure, I do owe you that one little professional courtesy. After my sweet old uncle rows across in the darkness and takes you directly to Father Royal, I will be at least ten miles down the highway and I will know absolutely nothing at all about this latest breach of old Uncle Sam's law."

"Well then, I'll forgive you and I also ask you to forgive me for being so, well, preachy. I hate that about myself. I really do."

"No apology necessary, Mrs. Love. None whatsoever. Please give my uncle my warmest regards. The man speaks English, and will understand if you offer a hello from his favorite nephew. But be certain to tell him this particular greeting is from Aaron, because at last count the man had about sixteen or so favorite nephews."

"You can count on it."

"Good night, Mrs. Love." He edged toward his vehicle. "There's another long stretch of border to check over by Castalon. More illegal drugs come across that stretch than any other two miles on the whole of the Rio Grande from

Brownsville all the way to El Paso. Safe journey, ma'am."

"Good night, Aaron. I appreciate your help and again I apologize for being preachy. It's a family trait, I fear."

God, I'm scared, but I'm determined to cross the river to Mexico. But what choice to do I have? I can't stay here all night. God, I hope there is something to eat over there that won't kill me.

I'm climbing up into those wild mountains with a man I don't even know. I must be totally out of my mind, but I'm going. I wish I believed in prayer, because if I did I would definitely pray right now. But honestly I don't. I don't even come close to understanding my motives in this thing. Nevertheless, I'm going! Right now, all I know is that I am to climb those mountains even if it kills me and guess what, girl? It just might.

But then, I'd rather be dead than Chuck's bought-and-paid-for whore. Perhaps dying in this remote village in Mexico is the scenario my overly active unconscious has chosen for me to meet a dramatic end. I suspect I'm more prepared to die than my conscious mind knows.

CHAPTER FIFTEEN

Shadows loitered on the river's muddy banks as they waited to meld with the approaching night. A hush settled upon the vast desert only to be disturbed by a breeze rustling the creosote. As if cued by tranquility, the moon climbed to transform the river into a churning flow of fresh buttermilk.

As she watched the Jeep's taillights disappear into the darkness, Jan draped a sweater about her shoulders. She shivered as she pondered questions for which she would discover no answers.

Somewhere, across the rushing water, a coyote's howl sparked a gregarious antiphony from a pack not far from the vigil she now kept on the gravel. A sudden eruption of flapping of wings signaled an escape concealed by the deepening veil of darkness, followed by a desperate thrashing coming from the river's edge.

This is crazy! I'm out of here. Why in the—

"Janet," a man's voice called.

Startled, she screamed, "What?" She stumbled, then broke her fall on the convertible's warm hood. Resting her hand upon the car door's latch, she screamed into the darkness again.

The night refused to answer. Not even coyotes howled.

That's it! I'm gone. This is by far the craziest idea I've had yet. I'm so scared I don't think I'll ever sleep again. But where do I go? Alpine? That's exactly what I'll do, rent a room in some dump under a false name and get so drunk on cheap tequila I'll be dead by morning. It's the only way. I'm not up to this pain any-more. I'd rather be dead than slink back home to my insufferable husband exhausted, confused and even worst defeated. I'd rather die a thousand deaths than have that arrogant prig be right even once.

Returning to the car's front seat, she turned the ignition key until the engine's growl pierced the stillness. As the car's headlamps flashed, she accelerated and then slammed her foot against the brake pedal. The Porsche slid no more than a few feet on the loose gravel.

Before her stood Royal, grinning so wide that his teeth glistened in the brightness of the car's high beams.

"What the—"

"Good evening, Janet," he yelled above the engine's silky purr. "I came to take you across in Pablo's boat,"

Jan leaned to her left to project her voice beyond the windshield. "I've changed my mind. I thought I desperately wanted to go across, but now I don't. No, I'm off to Alpine to drink myself into an early grave. And don't try to stop me. I've had enough of you and your crazy ideas, thank you very much."

Stuffing both hands in the pockets of his tattered khaki trousers, he stepped closer. "Then why do you keep coming back down here?"

Refusing to answer what she considered a question rife with tricks, she said, "I thought tonight you'd be in Boquillas praying. I hear you waste a good bit of every day on your knees."

Still smiling as he rocked back and forth on his heels, he said, "I spied Aaron's signal. Poor Pablo is hurting tonight. At the moment he is at home nursing a pulled muscle and unfortunately will miss tonight's fiesta. So I volunteered to row across and to bring you back to Boquillas to celebrate."

"Celebrate what?"

"Chico, who happens to be one of Pablo's many grand-sons, hauled a monster of a catfish out of the river today. That fish must have weighed every bit of sixty pounds, per-haps even more. But who really knows? We have no scales in Boquillas, but as we speak, all the women in the village labor under Mamacita's militant supervision as they fillet and fry the great fish one paper-thin sliver at a time. Those precious saints are preparing a banquet fit for royalty. The pun is defi-nitely intended and I use it as often as I can get away with it."

Royal stepped to the passenger side of the Porsche and leaned close enough for her to feel his breath against her face. "Tonight there will be dancing in the plaza to the music of the finest Tejano band from here to Ciudad Chihuahua, and washtubs stuffed to the brim with iced cold cerveza. Believe it or not, our ice is hauled in twice a week all the way from Musquiz. That's more than two hundred miles on a dirt road riddled with potholes the size of washtubs."

Jan folded her arms and turned her head away. "But I don't want to go to Boquillas and have no interest in celebrat-ing anything. I just want to die. Besides, I can't drink beer or any other alcoholic beverage anymore, unless later tonight I decide to kill myself with a bottle of very bad tequila."

"Oh, but Janet, our village fiesta would be much more pleasant than suicide. You will enjoy the merriment and the catfish is delectable. Honestly, it's the best on the border, and the way Mamacita breads and seasons a fillet of Rio Bravo *gato pescado* is the most delicious fare anywhere. No chef in the world can do it any better."

"God, I am so hungry. I haven't eaten all day. Actually, I must be too tired even to remember."

"Good then, it's settled." Royal stepped around the Porsche and gently pulled open the door. "If you brought a bag, grab it, and I will row you back across the river before all the catfish is devoured."

Jan sighed before dropping both feet to the gravel. "I am hungry," she said as she stood up. "I really don't have to kill myself tonight, do I?"

As he followed her to the car's trunk, he said, "When Señor Pablo and Señora Graciella heard that Aaron had flashed the lights, they invited you to sleep in the one-room adobe house where I stay. I will sleep under the stars and also under one of Graciella's heavy quilts. On most nights this past summer I slept outside, but now they are turning brisk."

She again sighed and announced in a weak voice, "Okay, I will cross the river with you. Besides, I'm much too tired to drive all the way back to Alpine."

Turning off the car's engine, she watched as streams of moonlight frolicked on the water. She could ill afford to allow this or any interest in beauty to distract her from the determination to protect her soul from the onslaught of the despair now so determined to take her life.

He whispered, "Where the light shines, darkness possesses no power."

"Listen, if this is a sermon I'm changing my mind. I do

not possess either the words or the energy to convey to you just how much I despise being preached to. Believe me, if I never hear another sermon, it will be much too soon."

"No sermon tonight, Janet. I offer only a humble invitation to discover holiness in the river, in the moon, in the night, in the deepest silence possible, and also at 'The Thin Place'."

"You know what? You are one strange and very likely not-to-be-trusted individual."

"Half of what you say is true. I am indeed very strange. I appreciate your recognizing this gift. But then, I have no interest in being conformed to this world, which is a place where there is so little use for love. The Lord's brother taught, 'Friendship with the world is enmity with God.' This is universally true and so is the fact that I can be trusted."

Royal turned toward the river, then stopped in mid-stride. "But as I promised, there will be no more sermons tonight. We must attend to your physical needs and then we can discuss the spiritual disciplines required for receiving from God the greatest of gifts, which, by the way, will likely make you also very much a stranger in your own world. And this is only an observation and in no way is intended as a sermon."

"I can't remember if I ate anything in Dallas before I took off. That was too many hours and way too many miles ago. Right now I don't believe I possess the strength to do myself in tonight."

"Wonderful news!"

"Oh, what the hell? Let's go across. Maybe I can catch some sleep in that bed you're not so fond of. Tomorrow I'll ask you to row me back to this side, since your friend Aaron tells me that the Border Patrol claims you're invisible. I'll drive back to Dallas and check myself into a hospital and do my best to drain some more jack out of my husband's insurance. I enjoy doing that, because every time the man loses money, he becomes apoplectic. And believe me, I take delight in seeing him turn crimson and shake like a dog left too long in the rain. The man is so predictable, he's boring."

Jan lifted a small overnight bag from the Porsche's trunk. "Do you suppose there is still anything to eat over there?"

"Oh, please follow me and there will be plenty of food." Royal stepped toward her and reached out his hand. "Be so kind as to allow me to carry your bag to Pablo's boat, so that we might ride the moonbeams."

Once upon a time the idea of riding on a river of moonshine would have held enormous appeal for this old depressed drunk. But no more! No, I am powerless over alcohol, and tonight I would ask God to restore me to sanity if, that is, I happened to believe in God.

But I don't. So I won't go there! Not tonight! Likely not ever! Oh well, Mexico, here I come.

CHAPTER SIXTEEN

Perched on the crown of a crumbling limestone wall, one rock piled on top of the other, Jan gazed at two walrus-sized guitarists with what interest her fatigue permitted. From a distance, their quick hands appeared perfectly synchronized as they whipped tight strings stretched above the wide oval holes in their two big guitars.

God, I hate it that those men are staring at me. I don't want to be subjected to the gawking of peasants. Those old men have probably never even seen a rich and attractive American woman like me before.

She averted her eyes from the musicians as the decision for suicide lingered like a violent storm waiting to erupt.

Oh God, I can't do this here. I simply cannot fall apart. Now is not the time.

Panic circled her like a pack of jackals, and she was sufficiently familiar with this tactic to recognize it would not be long before the forces of terror launched another attack. Because suicide had long been a forgone conclusion except for when and how, she decided she could not allow the sight of these obese musicians to fuel any more memories of her mother forcing her to attend Dallas debutant balls.

Noting her attention, both musicians smiled, each displaying open and vacant mouths.

That's it. I'm going back. Where is that silly priest? I'll convince him to row me back across tonight.

But God, I'm so very tired. Can I drive back to Marathon or Alpine at this hour? I don't think so. I'm stuck here.

Why did I come here? Why did I set myself up? When it comes to setting myself up, I'm the grand master.

Sighing, the new breath she inhaled so surprised her with the rare gift of invigoration she dared to glance at a line of girls, each of whom wore a festive and brightly colored hand-sewn skirt. Though fatigue and a lifetime devoted to sadness weighed down her eyelids, she wondered how long she might keep them open. Considering a new tactic for keeping herself awake only resulted in bewilderment. *Why can't I break free from my past?*

As the peasant girls danced, Jan silently begged her cruel memories to fade, allowing her to savor the spectacle of this celebration and to see it as beautiful, even romantic. But failure wrapped around her like a thick cloud, as she realized no amount of merry-making could hold at bay the devastating powers of self-loathing.

The world will judge me harshly. She sighed, once more resigned to the darkness waiting to engulf her.

When the fear lifted, as if by magic, she wondered if she was being set up for yet another emotional ambush. She inhaled before releasing a series of measured breaths, while in front of her the dancers' feet flew to the music's frantic tempo.

Two of the older girls attracted the attention of gang of boys wearing half-buttoned shirts and boots polished enough to reflect the lit torches circling the plaza. Each young man gripped a longneck bottle of Lone Star Beer, as one by one they punctuated their swigs with loud obscene belches, which appeared to be the single requisite for inclusion in their fraternity.

As they tossed their heads back to gulp, Jan imagined them to be a flock of herons grazing in salty Gulf marshes, and their audacity coaxed her to smile.

At the periphery of the celebration, several younger boys dashed back and forth between dim moon shadows, whooping and yelling at the end of every dance as they lit and then tossed firecrackers with squeals of fiendish delight. Following each pop, village curs contributed to the cacophony and their chorus spawned a long-distance serenade provided by a concealed pack of coyotes.

How can these people possibly celebrate anything? God, they are so desperately poor. They have absolutely nothing.

What do they have to celebrate anyway? They must be fools. Don't they know they are the poorest of the poor?

I pity them, I really do. They are a stupid people. There is nothing I can learn from them. Stupidity never taught anyone anything except perhaps how to be even more stupid.

Why did I ever come down here? If they are fools, I am the bigger fool.

A tempting new fragrance suddenly turned her toward the admission of hunger. God, what is that wonderful smell? Whatever it is, it is making my mouth water. I don't know when I've been so weak and famished.

The priest ambled toward her carrying a platter piled high with a smoky fare.

I don't care if what that man is carrying on that plate kills me, I'm eating it. After all, not a half hour ago I was willing to use cheap tequila, but now it appears I will likely die from food poisoning.

Either way is fine with me. Who cares? Death is still death, however one gets there. Tomorrow's headlines will read: Botulism Kills Pastor's Wife on the Border.

A boy no older than ten trailed behind a man clutching a blue plastic tumbler She received it with a nod and eyed it with suspicion. "Is this water safe?"

"It's from our spring," Royal said. "The public water supplies in Mexico are another matter, but our spring is one hundred percent safe."

"I'm thirsty." She sipped. "Mm, this is very good."

"Drink your fill, Janet, and young Paco will gladly go and fetch you some more. Isn't that right, Paco?"

The boy nodded, his mane bouncing with each movement of his small head.

After taking a bite she said, "Wow! This is the best catfish I've ever tasted. This is really, really good stuff. Thank you, Royal, and thank you, Paco."

I'm going to get fatter than an old cow, just as my mother always warned.

Bowing, Royal said, "I will pass on your compliments to the chef, who just happens to be Mamacita. She will be most pleased."

Turning in the direction of the river, she said, "But Royal, isn't this river polluted?"

"Unfortunately it is, but for now the fish is safe to eat, the utensils are clean, and the water pure. There is no call for anxiety."

"Why is the river polluted?"

"Greed, I suppose," he said with a sigh. He motioned for her to join him on the limestone wall.

Holding fast to her plate and full tumbler, she sat next to him. "What does greed have to do with it?"

"Greed is always love's executioner. It has been from the beginning and if we don't learn to transcend it, someday we will end up killing the entire planet and ourselves with it."

"I often think of killing myself."

"I'm most aware of that sad fact, and I am very sorry to hear of your pain."

As she chewed a large bite of the fried fish, she said, "Why? You don't even know me."

Royal slid from his place on the wall until he stood in front of her. "That's true, I don't. But Juan Diego does and I trust his judgment."

"I don't know about all of this magic you seem so fond of."

He stepped toward her. "Janet, you're tired. When you're done eating, you must rest and then when you are strong again and, of course, assuming your willingness, we will climb the mountain where you will meet Juan Diego face-to-face."

"Thank you, Royal, for being kind. You are patient and I don't know anyone who is really patient. I am dog-tired. But I do feel better. This food is really very good. Give me time for another two more bites, or maybe three, and I'll follow you to the guesthouse you mentioned."

"It's more of a guest-hut, but it suffices. Take your time with the dinner. Down here, hurry is the devil. Taking life slow is just one of the countless blessings these people enjoy. Perhaps you will stay long enough to discover them."

A delicious meal, a decent night's sleep, and I'm out of here.

CHAPTER SEVENTEEN

A rooster contemptuous of the morning's tranquility intruded upon the silence The bird's frantic crowing stirred her as the sun stretched hospitable beams through the window to warm Jan's face.

She blinked and lifted both hands to find her eyes. Rubbing vigorously, she forced open lids that felt like they'd long been cemented shut. Her vision was blurred yet still she scanned the bare adobe walls in the hope of discovering any credible clue that might whisper a word of reassurance. Once she felt up to entertaining lucidity, she wondered why she was lying in a mesquite wood bed lashed together by rawhide straps and draped in homemade quilts.

God, where am I? And why am I staring into a red sky through a window that has no glass. How long have I been here?

Hearing again the rooster's raucous reveille, she hoped it was not a signal for any coming threat. She was not enough awake to do battle with anything and yet dark forces that were still ill defined stalked her, just as they had done the night before, presenting her now with the choice of suicide or breakfast.

She held her breath and yearned for even the slightest symbol of hope to appear.

The crackle of a fire permeated the brisk morning with a fragrance wafting through the open window, carrying with it vague invitations. She had trained herself not to rely upon her conclusions as any reliable guide and as she considered various options she remained determined not to be manipulated.

If happiness ever occurred in any life, she was certain it was something akin to winning the lottery, a blessing intended always for others. But one of her several disciplines in self defense was to remind herself often that every dream she'd ever dared pursue had ended in heartache, if not in all-out disaster.

Perhaps there is some sane answer to why I am lying in this bed. But for the life of me I cannot begin to imagine what it might be.

The fragrance of frying meat blended with the scent of coffee to evoke a yearning that at least for the moment trumped suicide.

"Good morning." The voice came from outside her window.

"Who's out there?" she said.

After placing one heavy booted foot and then the second through the window, Royal stood at the foot of her bed, grinning. "I've prepared two very plump breakfast tacos for you. These delicacies consist of freshly-laid eggs—picked out of a warm hen's nest not one half hour ago and scrambled to perfection—fat sweet chunks of chorizo, goat cheese, slices of juicy red onion, and just a pinch of serrano. May I also present to you a piping cup of black coffee? I can also provide you with sugar and cream substitute.

"I've never been served breakfast in bed."

"Well then, it's high time for you to enjoy this gift. How

do you take your coffee?"

"Black."

"Good, that's the way it is, black and strong enough to be mistaken for a cup of Texas crude."

"How long did I sleep?"

Royal braced his back against the adobe wall and slid down it until he rested upon the dirt floor. "Right at eight hours give or take a few minutes. Obviously you were a bit done in." With his eyes level with hers, he smiled.

Oh, let the poor man smile. After all, he fixed you breakfast. Chuck has never done that. I'm too hungry to fight.

Besides, if I eat, perhaps I can put off the terror for a bit and that's not at all a bad idea. I'm always most vulnerable to its persuasions when I'm tired or hungry or both.

Mm, this is a delicious breakfast. The people down here may be desperately poor, but they know how to eat. I wonder how many calories are in just one of these tacos.

As Jan chewed the first bite, she said, "Royal, may I ask a question?"

"Of course."

"Why are you kind to me?"

"Easier than being rude."

"When men are kind to me it means always the same thing."

"Oh?"

"They want something."

He smiled.

"Why are you smiling?"

"Would you prefer I frown?"

"I would prefer you tell the truth. Tell me why you are

kind to me. I can't help but be suspicious.

"Janet, you asked for the truth and this is it. Juan Diego has summoned me to take you to the top of the mountain, that is, if you agree to go. The decision lies entirely with you. If you are willing, I will take you. If not, then, of course, I will not. The issue between us is that basic."

Royal rose from the dirt floor to tower over her place in the bed. He turned to gaze through the window as the new morning lit the distant mountains like torches.

"Now about kindness. I strive to be kind to all people, although I always make this attempt imperfectly. The Apostle Paul said that 'love is first patient,' but he made kindness his second descriptor of the great mystery that is love. One cannot follow Jesus without being kind. I think of kindness as my foremost religious expression."

"You will excuse me if I don't trust you."

"Who could blame you for being skeptical? This must be all terribly strange, even scary. You've come down here to the Rio Grande on a vacation, I suspect, only to discover that someone whose been presumed dead for five hundred years is very much alive and calling for you to come to him atop a tall, imposing mountain. Even to the most open mind this is an unbelievable invitation."

Royal tossed the remains of his coffee out the window and then returned to his place on the dirt floor. "I know I am trustworthy. No doubt, my kindness feels like a ruse. So, if you don't want to believe me about Juan Diego and The Thin Place, I cannot blame you. In fact, I told Juan Diego I didn't think you would believe me."

"What did he say?"

"He didn't say anything, he only smiled."

He is making this whole thing up. Does he really expect me to believe that a five-hundred-year-old man actually talked to him? But what is his game? Why does he want to take me up that mountain?

"Royal, sometimes my curiosity makes me terribly impulsive."

He grinned.

"Did you hear what I said?"

Royal nodded.

"I came down here to The Big Bend on impulse but perhaps even more because I knew it would worry my husband. There are probably other motives I have not yet identified."

"Okay."

"You may be a good man and I could be misjudging you completely, but I can't believe you actually talked to a five-hundred-year-old man who would have a word or two with me up on that mountain. Well, Royal, what do you say to that?" she said with the edge of annoyance now amplifying her tone.

"Like I said, who could blame you for being skeptical? This tale is much too bizarre to believe—except for one important fact."

"And what is that?"

"A man who has been dead for more than five centuries did speak to me and did request that I bring you to The Thin Place."

Tears now flooded her eyes as she trembled. "I've made a huge mistake coming here."

"You certainly appeared to enjoy the celebration last

night. Plus you tasted Mamacita's delectable fried catfish, and you obviously slept well throughout the night in a comfortable, not to mention free, bed."

Royal rose from his place on the dirt floor and stood facing her with his hands on his hips. "How could any of this be a mistake?"

"But I must go. I can't stay here. I don't believe this story, but the strange thing about all of this is I suspect you are telling me what you believe to be the truth. Perhaps you can believe it true and be quite sincere, and still be wrong."

"I'm not wrong Janet, but it is perfectly okay that you don't believe me. I have absolutely no doubt it is also okay with Juan Diego."

Jan wiped the tears from her eyes with the corner of her pillowcase. "Royal, you leave me with three choices."

His smile broadened

"One, you are a liar. Two, you are a living saint, or three you are a lunatic. I'm placing my money on choice number three."

He held his smile as he raised his hands above his head in a stretch.

"Doesn't that anger you?"

"What can I do to help you get back across the river?" he said with his hands still above his head.

"Avoiding my question?"

"I'll go to the river's edge and wait for Aaron's signal. When I see it, I'll come back and escort you to the boat and row you across myself. Likely Pablo is still a bit sore."

"Royal, why don't you fight with me?"

"I have no reason to fight."

"But don't you want to be right? Don't you possess the courage of your own convictions? Why don't you stand up like a man and fight with me?"

Jan raised her fist and shook it at him. "Come on, argue with me. Do your best to convince me. I dare you!"

He placed one leg through the window. "I don't wish to fight."

"Why? Are your afraid of me?"

"I'd prefer to help you go home, if that is your wish. I have absolutely no interest in fighting."

"Every man I know needs to be right"

"I'd rather be kind."

Oh brother, now I've heard every imaginable line.

"What about that fellow, Aaron? Will he arrest me?"

"As long as I row, he will consider you also invisible."

"Royal, why aren't you angry? I as much as called you crazy. Don't you want to take up for yourself?"

"I didn't hear it that way."

"How did you hear it?" She withdrew her feet from the warm bed and dropped them to the cold dirt floor.

"I heard only your skepticism and what intelligent person would not be skeptical? No, I'm not angry. In fact, I'm not even disappointed."

"What will you do now, once I've gone back to Dallas?"

Straddling the window, he said, "I'll pray. Later this morning I will celebrate mass and the rest of the time, I'll simply be."

Turning to face her, he spoke with an unexpected urgency. "Once young Aaron signals, the window of opportunity opens, but no more than for a few minutes. When the signal comes, we'd be wise to move quickly."

Good, because if I eat any more of this taco, I'll be the size of a sow hog.

Jan shuffled across the cold dirt floor to gaze at the Texas side of the river through the hut's front window. Before her, on the Mexican side, Royal dragged a Johnboat into the knee-deep water. He then turned about and tied the small craft to the trunk of a mesquite.

Oh, as my oaf of a husband says all too often, 'Discretion is the better part of valor.' I'd best get on back to Texas and forget all about this Thin Place nonsense.

CHAPTER EIGHTEEN

Emily and Harvey Sands shivered as they waited for the mansion's doorbell to roll through the first stanza of *Onward Christian Soldiers.*

"Nauseating," she whispered as the cold night turned her opinion to vapor.

"Predictable," he murmured. "But let's be nice."

A breeze rattled broad oak leaves waiting for autumn to turn them crimson before releasing them to November's caprice.

"He is such a jerk, Harvey! I can't blame Jan for wanting to leave the man. He's so incredibly selfish that I find it difficult to understand how he is able to convince so many people of his heart-felt sincerity. Can't they see him for the phony he is?"

"It's not our place to judge, Em."

"I know that, but with him I can't help myself."

She wrinkled her nose. "Everything about him is so self-serving, and yet he boasts of being a big-time Christian and an example to the whole country. I despise hypocrisy and to tell you the truth, I sometimes hate the man. Now Harv, that's a confession of a very dangerous sin because I know we risk our eternal salvation when we allow ourselves to slip into hatred. While I don't find it comfortable, I do confess to hating the suffering he inflicts upon poor Jan. I also resent him for what he gets away with."

The front door opened allowing a rush of warm air to be lost in the cold.

"Do come in, dear friends, come in out of the chill," said Chuck with a smile. "You are so thoughtful to dash over on such short notice."

Emily offered a knowing glance to her husband before together they trailed like mourners behind their host down a long hallway and past several closed doors. One open door revealed a walnut paneled room housing a pool table covered in burnt orange felt. She thought it odd a minister, even this famous and wealthy preacher, would own a pool table.

No sooner had the thought arrived than she chided herself for entertaining it.

Chuck pointed to a banana-yellow love seat in the smallest of the mansion's dens. "Please sit down and make yourself comfortable. Can I get you anything? Coffee? Hot tea? Cocoa? I believe I even have decaffeinated."

"No, thank you," said Emily.

Harvey wagged his head. "What is this about?"

"About Jan. What else? Emily, I would never put you on the spot…"

Of course you would, you big jerk. What kind of fool do you take me for?

Emily smiled as the muscles in the small of her back tightened. "Are you going to ask me if she's drinking again?"

"Yes, that's the most pressing question at the moment, I suppose."

"The answer is an unqualified no. She is not drinking, but I confess to being terribly worried about her. In fact,

I've never been so worried about any one of my friends as I am about Jan at this very moment. She's very close to the breaking point."

"I know she's depressed, Em."

"Obviously."

"May I be perfectly candid with the two of you?"

Harvey nodded while Emily said, "Oh, why not?"

"I'm on the threshold of a being appointed to a most important position."

"Are they going to make you a bishop?" said Harvey with a feigned ebullience his wife thought treasonous.

"Presbyterians don't have bishops. No, this is not an ecclesiastical appointment. Let's just call it a secular appointment of significance."

"What exactly do you want from us?" said Emily.

"It's more what I need from you. And at the moment I need your help."

"How can we help you?" said Harvey.

"Before I can assume the responsibilities of this position, I must be certain Jan is, well, let's just say, squared away."

He held out both palms toward them. "Surely I don't need to explain myself. I need her to be normal or at least as normal as she can be, given her years of irresponsibility. I cannot emphasize this enough. You see, I can't just take off and fly around the globe, which this new challenge will require me to do often, until I know for certain that she is safe here in Dallas and under her physician's watchful eye. The nature of this new position is so image-sensitive that I simply can't afford to have her running off here and there on one hare-brained scheme after another."

How do we figure into this... opportunity?" said Emily.

"I need you to help me with some kind of intervention."

"With what?"

"Jan's behavior is bizarre, erratic, impulsive and often volatile. If I say the least little thing the wrong way, she immediately misinterprets my meaning and blows up, making me always the bad guy."

"She's in a world of hurt, Chuck."

The preacher nodded. "That's precisely why we must do an intervention and do it as soon as possible. Getting her into a good psychiatric hospital right now to be evaluated and then placed on an effective regimen of medication and treatment will return her to some semblance of normalcy. Or at the very least calm her down to the point where she can function without acting like a madwoman."

Chuck rested his chin against his hand. "She fights—and by that I mean, tears into me—at the drop of a hat. She is so unpredictable I never know which Jan will be coming through the front door, the lovely girl I married or the preachy, bleeding-heart, and insane ideologue she has deteriorated into. It's no picnic living with a mentally ill spouse. My marriage has turned into a living nightmare."

"Being an ideologue does not qualify her as mentally ill," said Emily.

Chuck searched the inside pockets of his sport coat for a pack of cigarettes he carried but seldom smoked. Finding none, he settled again in his chair and sighed.

"Of course, she's depressed," Emily said, "but tossing her in a hospital is an over-reaction, like hitting a tack with a sledgehammer. That, I cannot and will not support, at least not until I have more information"

"What if I can provide it? Will you help me then?"

"I'd have to see compelling evidence first." Emily dug in her purse until she successfully located a cigarette, which with shaky hands she wedged between her lips. "Okay if I smoke?"

Chuck nodded. "Jan's off in the Big Bend again, but then you know that since you flew to Midland with her."

"She's convinced she met a tall stranger who knew something important about her."

"What more evidence do we need, Emily? Can't you see she's hallucinating?"

"But how do we know she didn't actually see this man? And until we know more, I'm not for putting her in a hospital." Emily shook her head. "I love her way too much for that."

"Listen to reason. There's no man down there on the Rio Grande who knows Jan. This latest delusion is nothing more than a symptom of her illness."

"What if she actually did meet him and he told her something important about her life, or even about you? What if he actually exists and you lock her up in the hospital? What then? That could kill her Chuck. And if it doesn't kill her body, it would surely destroy her spirit. No, I can't be any part of a decision to hospitalize her until I know for sure that she is delusional."

"But what if her psychiatrist recommends hospitalization?"

"I'd have to be persuaded by a competent doctor who knows what the hell he's doing."

"Once she comes home, I plan to have her evaluated by Dr. Harry Singleton. He's one of the finest in this town."

Emily rose from her chair to glower at Chuck as she lit the cigarette. "To be perfectly honest, I don't care who it is or how reputable he is. I have no interest in participating in your little scheme."

"You drive a hard bargain, Emily."

And you're the rear end of a mule!

She smiled in satisfaction before retuning to the chair where she drew hard on the cigarette.

"Chuck, there is something I need to share with you," said Harvey. "I was about to contact you when you surprised us this evening with your call."

"What is it, Harv?"

"A fellow dropped by the office late this afternoon, not thirty minutes before I was headed out the door. He claims he was with the FBI, and he even had the badge to back it up."

"What did he want?"

"He wanted to know about Jan. That's what bothered me. He said he was doing a background check on you for security clearance, but what troubled me about this fellow is that he kept pumping me with questions about Jan."

"What kind of questions?"

"Well, for instance, he wanted to know if she played tennis at the club regularly and what other organizations she belonged to and her typical daily schedule, and such as that. I don't know anything about Jan's daily routine. That's why it bothered me."

"Don't worry about it, Harv. This new opportunity involves the federal government and a requisite security clearance."

"Well then, that solves the mystery, doesn't it? I was afraid Uncle Sam was harassing you guys and nothing would rile me more. You know what I think of big government, Chuck. I don't trust it, never have. Em says I'm even a bit paranoid. Maybe I am and maybe I'm not—"

"You are, Harv, trust me, you are," said his wife.

"Thanks for your concern," Chuck said. "I'm undergoing a routine background check, that's all. We can't be too careful when it comes to national security. We dropped our guard and look what happened on 9/11."

"But this guy was strange, even sort of slimy, if you ask me. I've been around long enough to learn to trust my guts, and my visceral reaction to this fellow was not at all good. Something wasn't right about this agent, but I can't put my finger on it."

"Harv, I'm sure he's legitimate enough. There are things to worry about, but me being checked out by the FBI is not one of them."

"He looked haggard, even dissipated. Throughout the whole of our interview, which lasted every bit of a half hour, the man never removed his shades. Doesn't that strike you as odd?"

"In Dallas, summer's glare lingers."

"The skin on his face resembled hail damage."

Standing to shift his weight from one foot to the other, Chuck spoke with a tone reserved for benedictions. "Harv and Em, thank you for coming over. You've been most helpful."

As Harvey stood, Chuck slapped him on the back of his

shoulder and steered him toward the hallway. Emily followed.

Beneath the marble entryway's massive cut-glass chandelier, Chuck said, "Bless you. And thank you for coming over tonight on such short notice. I will be in touch. And most especially, I thank you, Emily, for being such a caring friend to my wife in her time of need."

Oh brother, you didn't hear a thing I said.

"Now you are absolutely certain there is no reason to worry about that FBI fellow?" said Harvey.

"None whatsoever, Harv. Rest well now."

The door closed behind them.

As they stepped onto the front walk, Emily said, "He's so manipulative it's disgusting."

Lost in thought, her husband mumbled, "I'm not so sure Chuck is right about this. There may be more to that fellow's investigation than a routine background check."

A screech owl abandoned to the city cried out to a night preparing to usher in the season's first freeze.

CHAPTER NINETEEN

Following a one-hour drive from the river to Marathon, Jan stomped her foot and sighed as she spotted frail old Brady alone on a cowhide sofa in the Sage's lobby. She gave thought to scolding the old man, but no sooner had the urge appeared than she resisted the temptation. She attempted to sort out suspicions from theories, and yet, she knew that too much introspection could lead those head games that typically devolved into a crippling depression.

Why am I so angry with that old man? Does it matter? I'll ask Dr. Coughman.

The priest pressed the *Midland Times* so close to his mangled wire spectacles, she guessed his vision to be more impaired than she imagined. Obviously lost in a front-page story, he appeared only slightly less eccentric than when she had visited with him as he hung upside down.

His pale blue eyes swung back and forth like the pendulum on a grandfather clock. With a start, the old priest glanced up to stammer, "Why, why good morning, Missy."

Jan stood tall and erect. "Why aren't you in church this Sunday?"

"Why, if it's not the young lady I met the other day in the collection shed. What a delightful surprise."

As he released the paper's front section, it alit with a sound upon a red-and-black Navajo throw rug. He peered over the thick bifocals and attempted a grin that revealed a crop of teeth she thought much too straight to be real.

A sigh dropped her into a high back leather chair, where she told herself if she rubbed her eyes hard enough, tears would arrive to make her feel somehow better. "Forgive me, Father. I was rude. There is no way you deserved that."

"Now there, child, I hear confessions only on Thursdays. My custom is to read the paper here before Mass. The paper and three mugs of coffee cut perfectly by two full tablespoons of real cream are my only two Sunday morning sins, but without question others will follow later in the day. I praise God for each and every one of them and believe me, I plan to savor them to the fullest, thank you very much."

The old man attempted to stand to tuck the front of his clerical shirt into his frayed khakis. The effort threw him off balance. He dropped into the sofa. "No apology is required, my dear. Tell me, did you find our friend, Royal?"

Jan nodded.

"Well, good for you. How is that brilliant trouble-maker?"

Jan rose from the high back chair and turned to face the vacant clerk's desk behind which Ollie Matson had stood for more than two decades.

I wonder if Ollie ever made it back to Sweetwater to face his demons. I hope to hell he did.

Turning to the priest she said, "Royal is well enough, I suppose. The truth is that I didn't stay around long enough to find out much. I was only in Boquillas overnight and I left at first light this morning. Royal was good enough to break the law by rowing me across the river."

"Well then, Missy, it's a real coincidence that you're here.

Not ten minutes ago a tall beanpole of a character dressed better than a fellow stepping off the cover of GQ was here firing one question after another about your whereabouts and such. Likely, you passed him going out on your way in."

"Who was he?"

"He claimed he was with the FBI and he even had the badge. But of course, my eyesight is so pitiful these days I couldn't read a thing on that man's silver badge. As far as I know, he could have been old J. Edgar Hoover himself. Did you know I once actually met J. Edgar Hoover one time years ago when I was in Washington?"

"What would the FBI possibly want with me?"

Chuck! He's having me tailed, that sorry bastard. Now, how the hell do I get back to Royal without this private dick catching me? No doubt, he means to abduct me and carry me back to Dallas.

"I have no idea who he is, child. I told him about you stopping by the shed the other day, but I left it at that, except I told him you were off to search for Royal down around the mouth of Boquillas Canyon."

"Did he ask anything else?"

"No, Missy, that was the sum of the interrogation. He thanked me and kinda smiled in a way that made me wonder if he was up to no good. Then he was out of here before I could assure him that he was welcome for my latest service to Old Uncle Sam."

Father Brady chuckled under his breath. "And what do you know? I glance up and see you standing here before me with this man off looking for you somewhere else. Now, that's quite a coincidence, isn't it?"

"Chuck must have called the police. Oh God, I'm so sick of his conniving."

"How's that, Missy?"

"Nothing, Father. I must get back to Boquillas at once and find out who this man is and what he's up to."

Jan stood and hitting her one fist into her open hand, she headed toward the door. She paused to turn her head toward the old man. "My husband is a sorry bastard and a manipulative son of a bitch."

"I don't believe I understand."

"Believe me, neither do I, Father," she said as she strode toward the front door.

She abandoned the lobby for the concrete porch in time to hear tires spinning as they spewed gravel. Stepping to a sidewalk fractured by the encroachment of cottonwood roots, she glimpsed a dark sedan, a Lincoln Town Car, streaking south past a forest green and silver highway sign that read: *Big Bend National Park.*

A sulfur-colored dust cloud hung in the morning, suspended between her refusal to be duped by hope and the prospect of being assaulted once more by terror. As she watched the cloud dissipate to reveal a distant range of lavender mountains, the desert drew a long and miserably hot breath.

What the hell do I do now? How do I escape this private detective's net? And how do I get back to Mexico without being arrested by the Border Patrol?

And what do I do if I should make it back to Royal? Do I climb that big mountain with a madman who claims to talk to a five-hundred-year-old man? Or do I drive straight to Alpine and kill

myself with a cheap bottle of cactus juice?
What do I do? God, help me, what do I do?

CHAPTER TWENTY

Laughter lingered above the river like a gauzy fog. Slowing the Porsche to a halt, Jan searched the gravel lot for any sign of the priest. The place was jammed with late-model vans, pickups, SUVs, and motorcycles abandoned by visitors heeding the call to explore the desert on foot or risk crossing the river illegally.

With the engine purring she gazed at the distant spire and whispered, "So that's The Thin Place."

She returned her attention to the lot, but spotted no vehicle bearing any marks of authority. Relaxing a bit, she turned to glance again toward the river. Two boatmen rowed their primitive crafts hard against the currents in their determined effort to return tourists to Texas.

God, it's like 9/11 never happened. It can't be more than one o'clock and the place is teeming. Where is the Border Patrol?

Jan tapped the accelerator. The car rocked up and down as its tires rolled over deep potholes. She smiled to find a space wide enough to accommodate the convertible, and once she eased the car between two SUV's, she switched off the ignition and yanked on the parking brake.

A brown-skinned man appeared out of nowhere to stand before the car's front bumper wearing a smile she knew far better than to trust. "I watch the car, señora," he said in a proud yet soft voice.

Jan did her best not to appear startled. "Thank you."

She dug into her wallet until her fingers happened upon two one-dollar bills, which she placed in the man's hand. He snatched the money, grinned for what seemed much too long for sincerity, and then bowed as low as his ample middle would permit.

Stepping from the convertible, Jan studied a line of tourists as one by one they exited the two Johnboats and huffed up the river's steep embankment. Their breathy banter and distant peals of laughter suggested the kind of fun that she had seldom allowed herself. Mumbles followed by howls floated across the dry morning like a song carried by the wind.

How can they possibly be so happy?

The first to make it up the embankment's mud steps was a lean, statuesque woman whose obvious devotion to exercise had stretched her body toward limber. The muscles in her lean, tan legs rippled as she sauntered toward the lot.

As the woman paused to wipe perspiration from her brow with a red handkerchief that matched her shorts, Jan noted that, while her hair had turned the color of fresh snow, life had apparently spared her face the indignity of wrinkles. Jan wondered if this wisp of a woman might be somehow immune to disappointment.

"Afternoon," sad the woman in a cheery tone that spared Jan the temptation to immerse herself in melancholia.

Jan forced a smile she knew to be dishonest. "Did you by chance happen to run into an Anglo fellow over there? This fellow is a priest named Royal. He's tall and ties his hair in a ponytail, if you can believe it. That style died 40 years ago, but he doesn't—"

"Sakes, child. You've met Royal? Why, lucky you," she said, still panting from her climb. "I not only know the man, I'm head over heels in love with him."

"You love him?"

"He's a huge part of reason I'm in the Big Bend. The man's had the greatest influence on my life, and all of it for good, I assure you. He's the most spiritual human being I know. He is authentic and such an effective mediator of the Spirit that to be in his presence is to be blessed. Unlike most of us, the man is willing to live his truth, which is that this life is really only about one thing, expressing love in much the way God offers it. But then that is not surprising because he's a Franciscan."

"Do you live in Boquillas?"

"I live in Redford where I'm one-third of the faculty of the Redford Elementary School."

"Isn't that where Royal once served a church?"

"He served the church there until a year ago and I was a member of his parish. I still belong, although we're currently without a priest. Before that, I taught sociology at Trinity University in San Antonio, where I came to know Royal. He was a professor at the seminary in San Antonio, and we became very good friends and Starbuck coffee-drinking and book-sharing buddies and fellow rabid yellow-dog Democrats, and you name it."

She chuckled as she shook her head. "If it was fun and also a bit on the wild side and uproariously irreverent, we probably did it."

"I didn't know he was a professor."

The woman nodded with vigor. "Once upon a time he was arguably the most-respected scholar in his field in the entire Catholic Church."

"What was his field?"

"Christian mysticism. The man's a mystic, a dedicated contemplative, and a scholar, and that, my dear, is a most rare concoction in this old cynical and oft vicious dog-eat-dog world. But as far as I'm concerned, Royal is the Almighty's finest exemplar of simple humility. One doesn't happen upon such genuine selflessness much any more, not in the priest-hood nor anywhere else, unfortunately."

The woman paused to raise her arms and stretch. "The man is definitely one of a kind, if not a holdover from another age. Prayer has all but eroded his ego as he has disciplined himself to dwindle down daily into his own nothingness, which he claims is the goal of all good spirituality."

Without warning, the older woman extended her hand. "Excuse my rudeness. I'm Amy Windigo."

Jan leaned toward the woman's warmth in the way a sun-flower in summer bends toward the morning's first light. "My name is Jan. I'm from Dallas."

"Now let me impart to you a bit of information you might find most helpful. If you're considering traveling across the river with old Pablo down there, you will definitely be pinched. I can one-hundred-percent guarantee it. That man's outrageous, not to mention legendary, rudeness is something you can count on, my dear. Getting pinched both on your way into and out of his ridiculous little boat is a slam-dunk. You see, that wily old pirate loves to pinch pretty women on the bottom and he grins every time, even if he's threatened within an inch of his life, scolded and/or cursed, the old lech-erous fool."

She folded her arms and squinted into the distance. "But he doesn't do it to me because he knows I know his secret. Old Pablo can't swim."

The woman unfolded her arms and shook her finger toward the river. "If that skinny little hombre ever falls out of his boat, he will sink quicker than a millstone. So I tell him every time I get in or out of his boat that if he pinches me, I'll shove him into the river. I was a varsity swimmer at UT a hundred years ago. Before you get into his boat, just tell him you know how to swim. He will act as dumb as a brickbat, but believe me, the old reprobate knows more than enough English to catch your meaning. Do that, my dear, and spare yourself some major humiliation."

"Is Royal in Boquillas now?"

"He is. The last time I saw him, he was headed for the river with a gaggle of ecstatic and jabbering boys and girls, off to noodle a catfish."

"To do what?"

"Noodle! It means to wade into the river in nothing but your skivvies until you're about shoulder deep and search with your hands beneath rocks until you come upon a big old slumbering catfish. Then grab the poor unsuspecting creature by the gills and jerk him out of his hiding place and toss him on the bank. Royal claims he's the grand champion, and to hear the villagers tell it, no one on the border does it better."

She turned to face Jan. "How is it that you know my sweet Royal?"

"I don't really know him. In fact, it's more the other way around. He knows far more about me than I know about him. I met him here only a couple of days ago. I must say our introduction was more than a little bizarre. He is so mysterious."

"But what do you expect from a mystic?"

"He was your priest?"

"Come, sweetheart." She crooked her finger at Jan. "Follow me to that rock over there and let's sit for a bit if we're to discuss Father Royal Cranfield. This man is so complex no brief stand-up conversation can possibly do him justice. Besides, I'm winded from that steep climb out of the river, and I hate to admit it, but I'm not nearly as spry as I once was."

Jan followed the older woman to a flat boulder half submerged in the river.

"Now, where shall I begin?" said Amy. "For starters, he's brilliant and a first-rate theologian and the most self-aware man I know. Royal hears God speaking to him almost every day."

"What, for example, has he heard?"

Dropping to nestle her knees upon the rock, Amy said, "Recently he's heard God calling him to convince the church hierarchy in Texas to do something significant and substantive for the poor who languish in grinding poverty on both sides of the border."

"But isn't it arrogant to believe you can hear directly from God?" Jan said.

"I've heard that all of my life, but I never believed it."

"Well, I'm married to a preacher and there is not a bigger phony in the world, and yet with every fiber of his being, he is convinced God speaks to him every day."

Amy rose again to shield her eyes from the sun before scanning the river. "Let me share with you what Royal considers the litmus test. If what one hears tells him or her to ascend the ladder toward more recognition and greater financial gain or the garnering of power, the message is coming from the ego. However, if the voice calls one to greater humility and the kind of service where no financial gain is attached, the voice is likely God's. Royal likes to say, 'Sacrilege is the ego's fruit; while sacrifice is the sign of true obedience.' He claims this to be the difference between self-aggrandizement and sainthood."

"But isn't his coming down here to be with these peasants a waste of his talent and education?"

"Royal finds a strange, inexplicable joy in sharing their plight. He owns precious little and yet, unlike most men, he also wants for even less. Without question, he's the most content man I know. He's discovered the secret of happiness and his life radiates joy like I've never before witnessed in another human being. How many of us can truthfully claim joy?"

"Not me," said Jan.

"On my better days, I dare to tell myself I might be a little happy," Amy said in a wistful tone. "But there is no way I am always centered, at least not in the way I witness the serenity that has become his beautiful spirit."

"Have you ever climbed up in those mountains to where he calls The Thin Place?"

"Once. By your question, my hunch is our friend invited you to make the climb."

"He says a five-hundred-year-old man is up in those mountains and wants to tell me something important."

"Well then, my dear, you should go because if Royal tells

you that there is a five-hundred year old man high up there in the Sierra del Carmen who wishes a word with you, then it is true."

Jan jumped to her feet to face the big mountain and raised both hands high as though she found it impossible not to sing aloud or scream, whichever came first. With her fists clinched, she yelled, "Wow!" so loudly her chest ached.

"Yes, wow!" yelled Amy.

Turning toward Jan, she said, "It's all true, all of it, girl. And the climb, although at times a bit taxing, is not at all dangerous."

"So I can trust him?"

"Like you can trust God, my dear."

"But I don't trust God because I don't believe in God. Besides, Royal scared me. He just walked up and announced my name and—"

Royal

Amy chuckled as she rose from the rock. "He's a mystic, Jan. He hears voices coming from a realm the rest of us know very little, if anything, about. That's who he is. And if he said you should climb to the Thin Place, by all means, do so."

She dusted off the seat of her shorts. "Well, it appears the parking lot has just about emptied out, so hopefully no one has blocked me in. Unfortunately, that happens often in this small lot. Sometimes I have to wait for hours to get out."

Jan said, "I take it he's not a charlatan."

"Sakes, no. The man's a mystic and perhaps even a prophet, but I'll leave that role and the attendant danger for him and God to sort out. But trust me, he's the real deal. I've known the man for close to twenty years now and he is by far the most trust worthy human being I've ever encountered. In fact, there is no one I trust more."

The crunch of gravel silenced them as they turned to see a dark, dust-covered sedan rolling into the half-empty lot.

"Isn't that the car I saw leaving Marathon?" Jan whispered.

The sedan's door opened with a squeak amplified by the desert's emptiness. A thin man extricated himself from the front seat and stood expressionless as he scanned the gravel lot with several quick bird-like jerks of his head.

His demeanor struck Jan as odd, even suspicious, but neither woman commented. Dressed in a charcoal business suit so absurdly enigmatic to this wilderness, he made a parody of the world from which he had come. Even from a distance, it was evident that beads of perspiration glistened on his narrow forehead, separating combed-back hair from the top rim of silver shades.

In his right hand, he gripped a leather case while with his other he snapped his second finger against his thumb with enough force as to mimic a tremor. The corners of his mouth were turned down to suggest the habit of disdain and his eyes remained hidden.

Jan sensed they burned with intensity. His stare challenged her determination to remain unfazed and she gave thought to running.

The man is staring a hole straight through me. Do I know him? What could he want? No doubt Chuck sent him. I wonder if he's a private investigator. But why would he tell Brady he's with the FBI? Isn't that illegal? And what would the FBI possibly want with me?

"Afternoon, ladies, it appears I'm lost," he said across lips Jan wasn't at all certain had moved."

"Where you headed?" said Amy.

The man appeared disinterested in the question.

Taking a step toward the man, Amy said, "Sir, I asked where you are headed?

"Panther Junction," he said in a cool tone of voice.

"Well, you missed it. It's about forty miles back up—" Amy shrieked, "Oh my God, watch out!"

The roar of what sounded to be a low-flying jet shattered the stillness. Jan spun about with her eyes turned skyward. A gray football-shaped cloud streaked like a missile, just inches above the mesquites.

Before she could gasp, the seething cloud wrapped itself about the man's head. He dropped to his knees and wailed as he slumped, then tumbled face-first to the hot gravel. Groaning and gasping, he rolled to his side with a final dying howl above the roar.

"Run!" Amy yelled. She sprinted toward the river where she stumbled and fell. Righting herself, Amy scrambled on all fours toward the mud embankment's edge where she rolled to her back. After sliding feet-first down the long slope, she splashed into the water.

Jan watched her disappear under the surface. She turned about to study the fallen man, and then darted toward the embankment where she followed Amy into the river.

As Jan struggled to raise her head into the air, someone gripped her left elbow, squeezing all feeling out of her arm. Thinking she was tangled in a fishing line, she pulled as hard as she could but to no avail. She gave thought to screaming but realized she could not open her mouth without taking in even more muddy water.

Choked and desperate for air, she kicked the river's rocky

floor and managed to push her head just high enough to suck in a single breath. Opening her bleary eyes, she discovered Amy on the river's muddy bank, leaning toward her, all the while clasping her arm with both hands to keep her from the currents.

"What happened?" gasped Jan, blinking and sputtering.

"Bees. African killer bees! No doubt, they've killed that man. The last I heard, they were still in Central Mexico, never this far north. Are you okay?"

"I'm alive but, God, I've never been so scared," she muttered, coughing.

"Jan, stay in the water—"

"But I'm freezing!"

"Better cold than dead, sweetheart!" Amy shifted her weight and leaned back against the embankment. "Hold on to a root as though your life depended on it. If the bees come after me, let go and drift or swim as far away as you can. Keep your head below the water as much as possible."

She glanced toward the parking lot. "I must go to that man. If the bees are gone, perhaps I'll drive him to the hospital in Alpine, assuming he's still alive. If not, I'll take his body to park headquarters and turn it over to the Rangers. But I have to do something—"

"Don't leave me. I'm terrified!"

"You'll be safe here, Jan. If I don't come back for you in five minutes, get out of that water and drag yourself into the sun. But if you should hear me scream, swim like the devil. Understand?"

After releasing Amy's hand, Jan gripped an exposed acacia root and nodded. She watched as Amy crawled on all fours up the mud embankment, slipping and sliding backward with every step. Within less than a minute, the cold water convinced Jan to disobey the older woman's admonition. She pulled herself out of the river where she lay upon a slab of limestone, drawing one heaving breath after another.

God, now I know how those catfish feel that Royal jerks out of this river. I can't stop shivering. I must be hypothermic. I have a change of clothes in the car, but there is no way I'm climbing up to that parking lot. Not with those bees up there. I've never seen—

Amy called, "Jan, he's gone. And there is no sign of the bees either. It's safe to come on up. I have no idea how he survived. A dead man can't drive a car."

Amy held high the man's brief case as if it were booty. "He dropped his case, but there is nothing inside except one very expensive camera. No ID or anything. We need to signal Pablo and get him to carry us back to Boquillas. We must tell Royal about the man and these bees."

She waved her arm in a semi-circle. "Come on, girl."

Jan attempted to push her stiff body off the rock slab but there was not enough strength in her arms. She thought of screaming, running, or doing whatever might be required by survival, but she could not stand.

God, I can't stop shivering. I don't think I've ever been so cold in my entire life. I'm frozen stiff.

What am I doing here? This is crazy. No, I am crazy. I'm going to die in this desert. At least I will be finished once and for all with this pain.

Go ahead, God, and take me. Oh never mind, I forgot. I don't believe in you. Please forget I prayed. I plan to forget it immediately.

CHAPTER TWENTY-ONE

"Ah now, son, do come in and welcome, sir, to the White House," said the President.

Chuck imagined his head attached to a swivel as he swung it from left to right while attempting to absorb even the minutest details of this spacious dining room. "Thank you, Mr. President."

Taking his hand, the President said, "Now son, I don't believe I've ever asked you which you prefer, Chuck or Dr. Love?"

Chuck stood tall and erect like he was a soldier reporting for duty. He dropped his eyes to study a miniature ivory elephant adorning a knee-high mahogany table between himself and the President. "Please, sir, call me Chuck, if you will be so kind."

"Good, then, Chuck it is. Tell me, how was your flight up?"

Chuck nodded and forced a smile, stretched as broadly as he could. "Fine, Mr. President, just fine."

"And how are things down in Texas?" The President pointed him to a chair at a long table. Three men of various ages occupied the other chairs. In unison, they smiled at him.

Following the President's lead, Chuck seated himself. He held his expression as he nodded to each of the distinguished gentlemen, all of whom rested their curious eyes upon him.

He drew a breath. "Super, Mr. President. Sir, we Texans are perhaps even sinfully proud to have a fellow Texan up here in the White House doing such a splendid job for our great country. I don't know anyone in Texas who is not busting his buttons, overjoyed that our former Governor is now President."

Chuck scanned the room to note the faces of each man. All of them appeared to approve of his comments.

"Ah now, thank you Chuck, that's most generous of you, but you and I both know that close to half the good citizens of Texas, and for that matter clearly half of the rest of Americans, pray to God every night before they turn in that I will lose the upcoming election. Let's not talk of that most unpleasant, but thankfully still remote, possibility. That's not why we've invited you up here this morning. No sir, we have something else of at least equal importance to discuss."

The President turned to acknowledge the presence of a large man who filled the doorway like dark storm cloud waiting to erupt in violence. Rising a few inches from his chair, the President pointed to the man. "Ah now, I believe you are acquainted with Mr. Barrett, my able Chief of Staff."

"Good morning, Buck, uh, I mean, Mr. Barrett."

"Buck will be fine," muttered Barrett with a contemptuous scowl.

"And allow me to introduce you to the other gentlemen I've invited to this meeting." Returning to his chair, the President pointed to a thin balding man. "This is Secretary Abrams, who, as you know, is Secretary of State."

"Mr. Secretary, an honor, sir."

The man nodded.

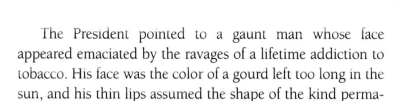

The President pointed to a gaunt man whose face appeared emaciated by the ravages of a lifetime addiction to tobacco. His face was the color of a gourd left too long in the sun, and his thin lips assumed the shape of the kind permanent pucker that signaled their function as a cigarette's home.

"And this is Secretary Cabell, Secretary of Defense."

"An honor, Mr. Secretary."

"Likewise, Dr. Love." As the man spoke his fingers ran nervously all over his forehead like long-legged spiders.

Pausing to allow Secretary Cabell to say something more, the President took a sip of ice water from the glass previously prepared for him. "And finally, this is Mr. Searcy, our most able Homeland Security Secretary."

They exchanged the same courtesies.

"Please be seated, gentlemen," said the President as he turned to face Chuck. "I believe in cutting right to the chase. After the election, which no one, including, I might add, the Democrats, doubts we will win, we will ask you to join this administration in a new cabinet-level position. I believe Mr. Barrett has apprised you on the particulars."

"Yes, he did, sir," said Chuck before nodding at Barrett.

"Good. Ah now, son, today you don't have a security clearance, so I will be necessarily somewhat guarded, and therefore, speak in generalities. Nevertheless, what I am about to tell you must be kept in the strictest confidence. Do I make myself clear?" The President stroked his chin like it sported a beard.

"Of course, Mr. President."

Stroking his non-existent beard even more fervently, the President said, "Ah now, son, early next spring we will preemptively attack a little mud patch of a nation, and within forty-eight hours, we will liberate millions of people who have suffered for more than sixty years under a ruthless Stalinist regime."

Perspiration beaded upon Chuck's forehead, and he patted his inside coat pockets in the hope of locating a handkerchief he could not recall packing. Finding nothing, he raked his sleeve across his forehead as he often did on the golf course after 18 holes.

God, I hope I don't appear too nervous. I certainly can't afford to appear weak in front of these men. Why didn't I pack that handkerchief? It's Jan's fault. She had me so frustrated I couldn't think straight.

"Ah now, our question for you, son is this: can you support this action?"

"Of course I can, sir. And I will. I want nothing more than to rid the planet of the evils of totalitarianism. What can I possibly do?"

"I'm getting to that, but first let me say I'm glad to hear that. Please understand, this situation is a bit more complicated than a mere bombing attack with conventional weaponry. You see, we plan to strike their capital with an extremely low-yield nuclear device that will immediately decapitate their government."

The President waved his hand as if shooing a fly. "The radiation will be so minimal as to take out absolutely no more than 10,000 of their citizens. Once the radiation has dissipated, which our experts at the Pentagon assure me will require no more than twenty-four hours, we have arranged for a friendly and neighboring democratic nation to have its well-equipped army invade. We have it on excellent authority that, by the end of the week, this war will be over, and this nation will be forever liberated. Once we set up a new democratically-elected government, our friendly nation will withdraw its troops and, within a period of no more than three days or so, we will have forever eliminated from the earth yet another dangerous, and I might add, nuclear-armed despot."

The President's broad grin struck Chuck as contrived and perhaps even menacing.

"Ten thousand dead is a quite a sum, Mr. President."

"Ah son, no question about that, But if you will, weigh the number 10,000 against the literally millions of people we will free. And add to that number the uncontestable fact that we are making the world much, much safer for our children and for our grandchildren."

"That certainly makes sense, sir. But I confess, Mr. President, 10,000 dead is hard for me, as a man of God, to countenance."

"Ah now, son, it's a smart and extraordinarily clean bomb."

Chuck pushed his chair back from the table an inch or two. "Sir, with all due respect, that's still a lot of fatalities—"

"Mr. President, if I might add something here, sir," said Secretary Cabell."

"Certainly, Mr. Secretary. Please proceed."

"Dr. Love, the vast majority of the people we will take out are die-hard Marxists whose families have been big players in this corrupt and tyrannical regime from the beginning." Secretary Cabell's words exited his mouth like a swarm of angry hornets attacking a would-be predator. "With all due respect to your religious sensibilities as one who proclaims the message of the Prince of Peace, please believe me, this world would be much better off if these people were eliminated. They are the enemy of everything we in this great Christian republic hold dear, and for fifty years they have posed a major threat to the world's security. They absolutely must be taken out. The sad fact is they give us no choice other than to exterminate them."

Chuck squirmed as his knees bumped against the underside of the table.

Secretary Cabell rose from his chair to nod at the President, who returned his signal. Cabell focused his eyes on Chuck. "Sir, because of your influence in my life, I am a born-again, evangelical Christian. I was baptized only two years ago and my wife and I wouldn't think of missing worship on Sunday. Even more, we're probably your biggest fans. The little woman and I never miss your Thursday evening broadcast out of Dallas. And although I've never had the privilege of meeting you personally, I've considered you my pastor for a long time."

Chuck didn't dare blink as he waited for the Secretary to continue.

"Let me share with you something more about this regime. These are bad people and the simple, yet incontrovertible, fact is that they don't deserve to live. They have murdered and tortured their own citizens for six decades."

Leaning toward Chuck, Secretary Cabell's grin slipped into a scowl far more at home on his face. "The suffering their people have experienced is identical to what the children of Israel endured in languishing in bondage for four centuries.

This President is to be their latter-day Moses and you are to be our nation's great prophet."

He leaned back again and laced his fingers over his chest, as if to congratulate himself. "Like the God of Exodus, we have heard the cry of our fellow human beings and we mean to liberate these brothers and sisters, not just in the cause of national security, but even more for God's sake. Our cause is not only just; it is also holy. Consequently, we are absolutely convinced of the rightness of this. Believe me, Dr. Love, this decision has been preceded and informed by a great deal of earnest prayer on the part of this President and every member of this cabinet."

Turning to face the President, Chuck said, "So, Mr. President, exactly what is it that you want me to do?"

"Sometime after the election, you will to go on national television right here in the Oval Office and share with the American people what we plan to characterize as a pastoral conversation. And in this chat, you will quote Scripture frequently in making the point that the Almighty would have this administration eliminate all vestiges of this ruthless tyranny from the face of the planet. We will leave the details of your Bible quotes to you, but our people will write your script and you will follow it verbatim. And in this speech we will compare the few people we must kill to Pharaoh's army that the Lord drowned in the Red Sea so that his chosen people might forever be free."

The President lit a cigar and drew hard on it until it flared. He glanced at the fiery tip before he continued. "Our experts at the Defense Department assure us we can accomplish this surgical strike with the strong likelihood of absolutely no loss of American life. Once we unleash this very low-yield nuclear weapon, every other totalitarian regime will fall into line immediately by holding legitimate elections within six months, or they too will be hit."

I can't afford to allow the thought of killing a mere ten thousand people to become an obstacle to my lifelong dream of bringing the entire world to Christ. These people are probably better off dead, so I can't let some old-fashioned moral construct stand in the way of what God has called me to do.

I have to go along with this. There is no other way.

"Ah now, son," said the President, "because you proclaim to a national television audience that our crusade is ordained by God and that the United States is, indeed, the New Jerusalem and the Bible's bright and shining city on a hill, the American people will believe you. The voting majority will have no problem with us doing what is required of us to rid this planet, once and for all, of every despot who now abuses his power and causes so much suffering."

He poked the air with his forefinger. "And you, sir, will go down in history as every bit as important to the Christian movement as Martin Luther, Albert Schweitzer, and Mother Teresa and saints of their caliber. In fact, after our successful little war of liberation, you'll be even more admired than the Pope. Your place in history will be guaranteed. I wouldn't be surprised if in the end you didn't rank up there with the likes of Martin Luther King, Jr., and who knows? There will probably even be a statue erected in your honor right here in D.C. long after you're in heaven. Your grandkids can bring their kids to see it and feel the kind of genuine pride that transcends words."

Chuck bowed his head as if in prayer. His entire body trembled with anticipation and excitement.

"Ah now, Chuck, I must be brutally candid with you here. If you can bring yourself to do this, you're definitely our man. No religious leader is more trusted by the American people than are you, sir."

The President leaned back in his chair as he gazed at the ceiling. "But if you cannot go along with us on this, well, let's just say we have other capable candidates waiting in the wings. Of course, none of them is as well known or respected as you, but we have no doubt that the men we have in mind can definitely do the job. But you, sir, are without question this administration's first choice."

Chuck sighed and again wiped the sweat beading on his brow with his sleeve.

"Ah, now son, I wish we could offer you the luxury of a great deal of time to think this over, but the fact is the election is only days away, and currently I've got more domestic problems to untangle than mulch a cow has ticks. All of this is to say we need an answer, Chuck, today, like this minute."

The President tilted his head toward Chuck and stared into his face. "What's it to be? Can you do this for God and for your country, or not?"

Chuck raised his eyes to study the face of every man present. All of them now stared at him.

Don't appear too eager. Make it appear you are reluctant. Reticence here is good for your image. It demonstrates character. Make them wait and they'll admire you even more.

Still shaking but attempting to sound confident, he said, "Yes, I suppose I can do it, sir. Yes sir, I will do it. I can't bring myself to think long about the idea of so many dead, but I trust you, and I agree with your argument that some must die so the majority might know the sweet taste of freedom. We didn't ask these people to be tyrants, did we, Mr. President?"

"Not by a long shot."

"And we've warned them, have we not?"

"Ah son, for the past 60 years, we've told them repeatedly through the U.N. Security Council that the United States will not tolerate their kind of tyranny nor their continued viola-tion of human rights. Sixty years is long enough, Chuck. In fact, it's much too long. This new century belongs wholly to America, and we view it is our sacred duty to God and to the American people to say finally to the tyrants of this world, 'Enough is enough.' We are convinced one slightly radioac-tive, and, again I might add, unusually smart bomb will make this point very nicely."

Jumping to his feet, Chuck Love said, "You have yourself a new cabinet officer, Mr. President. I accept."

"Ah son, that is absolutely wonderful news. I knew we could count on you."

Every man at the table applauded, and still smiling, Chuck took a bow. He then circled the table, as he shook hands one-by-one with each secretary and finally with the President.

"I knew we could count on you," said the President through a thick cloud of cigar smoke.

You've done it, Chucky Boy. You've finally made it to the big time.

Thank you, God. Thank you, and now please make me an instrument of your peace.

Amen.

CHAPTER TWENTY-TWO

Curled in the fetal position on the cold gritty floor of Pablo's metal boat, Jan shivered as she asked herself if her cramped legs would ever move again. Even before the question could be fully formed, she recognized any plan to extricate herself from the boat would prove a tough sell to her stiff muscles.

Pablo gave a final forceful tug on the oars, pushing the boat's battered bow into the soft mud on the Mexican side where it rested. Satisfied, he nodded.

Please, God, let me stand with a steadiness that makes it possible to get out of this stinking little boat without falling on my face and making a complete fool of myself. Oh God, you know I don't believe in you, nevertheless, I beg you. Please.

The river rattled past and she thought its cadence cruel as she resented its effortless flow. She was much too cold and far too numb to think of anything but the urgent issue of exiting the boat. High above an etching of benign clouds, a lone red tail hawk squawked in a manner she imagined derisive.

Have your fun, stupid bird! I'm down here shriveled up like a miserable little mudpuppy and you soar. Go ahead and taunt me! I've been taunted all of my life by someone, so why should you treat me any differently?

Like slaves inured to cruelty, her legs finally fell to one side. Although she expected the pain to be excruciating, she breathed deeply, as if she could inhale courage from the autumn breezes. Either she could try to climb out of the boat or wait until the hypothermia turned deadly. She shivered at the choices.

Jan gripped the little boat's gunnels with fingers as numb as her legs and pulled herself upright. Pain shot through her lower back, but subsided enough to convince her she had made the right decision. She would not return to the boat's inhospitable floor and instead hoped for a safe landing on the slick mud.

A quick movement on the bank distracted her from her preoccupation with agony, and she glanced over her shoulder to spy a chubby dark-skinned boy darting into a sun-lit clearing from behind a stand of agaves. This shirtless waif paused only long enough to present a giggle she read as yet another taunt. He announced above the water's roar in perfect English, "Señora, the father is waiting with the burros. He is ready."

Are this kid and the hawk in cahoots? No conspiracies now, old girl. Remember what the good doctor said, "No conspiracies."

Okay, so this kid never met the taunting hawk and vice-versa. I can accept that, but God, I hurt. I don't believe ever in my life have I been so sore and cold and stiff. Oh God, please take me home to Dallas, and to a hot shower and a warm bed! That's what I crave. That's all I care about.

Stepping out of the boat with no particular show of effort or strain, Amy said to the boy, "Why, thank you, José."

She then turned to Pablo, who had not said a word as he rowed them across the river. "Thank you, Pablo, for bringing us to Royal and for not pinching us. That was so thoughtful on your part."

Facing Jan, she said, "Well, my dear, it appears Royal is ready to take you up the big mountain."

A dog hiding its mood behind a mud-caked mask trailed the boy all the while raising his ragged burr-infested tail. The skinny animal slinked toward them growling threats, each of which was marked by an incongruent wag of the tail.

"Ocho, now you be sweet!" said Amy.

She turned once again to Jan. "We call him Ocho because he was born on August 8th. Of course like ninety-nine percent of the males on this planet, he's one hundred percent bluff, but if you rub his belly, he'll count you as a friend for life. Now tell me, isn't that just like a man?"

"I suppose," said Jan still shivering in the boat.

I'm freezing, still. I can't get warm and I can't stop shaking.

She looked up at the sound of a snort. Royal gripped two frayed halter ropes, each of which was attached to a burro bearing loaded packsaddles draped in water stained green canvas.

"Welcome home, señora," he called.

From the boat Jan yelled, "Royal, I'm so wet and cold and miserable. I don't think I've—"

"I said, welcome home." As he stood erect near the bow of the boat, Royal grinned. "Down here folks ordinarily respond with a heartfelt gracias when offered such a greeting."

"Well, thank you then, I suppose."

Still smiling, the priest said, "Are you ready?"

She thought Royal's smile every bit as bogus as the idea of a five-hundred year old man wishing to speak to her on the summit of the big mountain high above. Gripping the boat with white knuckles, she said, "Ready for what?"

"To climb the mountain, of course."

"Are you out of your mind?" Jan released the gunnels to throw her head skyward. "Royal, I'm still soaking wet, and so cold I'm close to being hypothermic. I just saw a man attacked by killer bees, and if I don't get some dry clothes on soon I'll catch my death of cold. And you expect me to climb a mountain? My God, I can't even climb out of this miserable little boat!"

She gripped the gunnels again. "Oh I'm sorry, Pablo, I didn't mean to demean your boat. Forgive me."

Pablo remained silent.

"The sun will dry you out in no time. There's no humidity in this desert."

Releasing the boat's gunnels long enough to throw her hands in the air, she said, "But I must pack. And I'm not even sure I can walk. My legs feel paralyzed. I don't know if I can move them."

The priest turned to rub the neck of one of the burros and then faced her again. "Pack what?"

"You can't possibly expect me to do any climbing without a change of clothes. And I'm going to die if I don't get out of these wet things."

Royal shrugged. "So stay there in the boat, and Pablo will gladly row you back across the river and you can grab your bag. Then our good friend here will do you the service of rowing you back again. I'll strap your bag to the back of sweet little Josephina here and she'll gladly tote it up the mountain." He turned to face the smaller of the two burros. "Right, Josephina?"

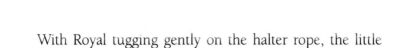

With Royal tugging gently on the halter rope, the little burro nodded.

Gripping the gunnels once again, she said, "But, I'm sore all over, and my legs are killing me."

Royal led the two burros to within a foot or so of her face, then paused. "No better way to treat the soreness than to stretch it out by walking. We're getting a late start but we still have time to climb a good bit before dark."

She sat suddenly erect in the boat. "Royal, will you ask Pablo to row me back across the river, but would you also be so kind as to tell him not to pinch me? And another thing, do you see the Border Patrol? I also have no interest in going to jail."

Royal slackened the halter rope, and the little burro brushed his silky muzzle against Jan's cheek. Jan pushed the animal away.

"Oh, I suspect our friend here will likely not pinch you if, that is, you tell him you know how to swim," Royal said, "and at least for the moment I see no patrol car on the far side. Most agents can be counted on not to hide the fact they are present, because the majority of them are related to these people. Those fellows don't have much stomach for arresting family and friends. It appears safe enough to cross."

Still in the boat, she turned to scan the river only to think better of crossing back into Texas. Again she turned to face Royal. "But what about the bees? Amy and I saw a man being attacked—"

"They are no longer a problem and neither is the man."

"But how can you know that?"

Royal grinned in a way that annoyed her.

"Juan Diego told me."

"But…" she said as she pounded her fists against the cold gunnels.

He's not listening. I hoped he might be different, but he is like all men, a know-it-all.

"Trust me, Jan. They are no longer a problem and the man is gone."

"You can believe what he says, honey," said Amy.

Jan shoulders sagged as if they had melted. "But what if they come back?"

"They will not," said Royal, as he stood tall and erect above her place in the boat.

His grin had slipped into a slight, and perhaps, even re-assuring, smile. She thought this expression something she might trust.

Jan sat up straight and turned to Pablo. "Listen to me, Pablo, if you even attempt to pinch me, I promise I will slap you out of this boat and not care one bit if you drown."

Pablo stared straight ahead.

"I don't think he understands," she yelled at Royal and Amy.

Royal's old confident grin returned. "He understands all right. He just doesn't want you to know he understands. Our good friend Pablo will not pinch you once you tell him that you know how to swim. You do know how to swim, do you not?"

"Of course I can swim!"

Turning away from the boat, Royal led the burros back to the trail where he paused and gazed toward the big mountain's distant summit and then faced her. "Good. Apprise him of that fact again for emphasis, and I promise he will exempt you from humiliation. Deep down, he is a most gracious soul. But the truth is that he will not pinch you only because the poor hombre can't swim."

As she turned to the stoic boatman, Jan said, "I can swim like a fish, so now will you take me back for my overnight bag?"

"Hurry, my dear. Time's a-wasting," yelled the priest as Pablo opened his eyes and slipped over the side of the boat to dislodge his craft from soft mud.

Jan glared at the boatman with a sternness she hoped he would read as her refusal to be subjected to any gesture even implying lechery. Amy took one step toward the priest who dropped the halter ropes to embrace her. Even over the water's rush, Jan heard the woman say, "I love you, Royal."

Royal said, "I love you, too, dear Amy. Now go have yourself a very lovely week and I do hope you will return next weekend. As usual, we still have much to discuss."

As the woman released the tall man from her arms, he smiled at her with an intensity that struck Jan as something far more than mere friendship. She wondered if the priest drew strength from this woman, or if it was the other way around, or if their relationship might be secretly sexual. No sooner had the latter question arrived than she dismissed it, but not before rebuking herself for even considering anything salacious.

Amy turned to the river. Jan stared at her and wondered if her forced smile covered a mix of emotions. Amy strode toward the boat Pablo held steady by the bow while its stern rocked in the currents. As she approached, she sang a taunt celebrating the fact she could swim. First she sang it in English, and then she sang it in Spanish, all the while smiling.

Still on the cold floor of the boat, Jan stared at Pablo until he nodded at her.

Oh hell, it appears I'm climbing this stupid mountain. But why am I doing this? I've come this far and I can't walk away now. If I do, my curiosity will make me crazier than I am right now. As good old Dr. Coughman reminds me all too often: the mind detests unfinished business.

Therefore, I must trust this man. I really don't want to, but what choice do I have? So, I'm climbing the mountain even if it kills me, which it well might.

CHAPTER TWENTY-THREE

"**M**y God, every view up here is breath-taking," said Jan. "I can't believe I haven't hiked this trail before. In all the years I came down here as a child, and even prior to my marriage to Chuck, I never once even thought to venture into the Sierra del Carmen. I had no idea what I was missing."

"Perhaps beauty is not so much in the eye of the beholder," said Royal, "as it is in the soul of the beholden."

Pausing to breathe deeply, Jan said, "What did you just say?"

"Gratitude is the soul's rejoicing."

"You know what?" Jan panted. "You make absolutely no sense."

"I've been told that. But you see, the world values reason and making sense while I value other gifts."

"What do you value?"

"Beauty, truth…"

"How far to the top of this mountain?"

"Not far."

"Well, thank you for that precise bit of helpful information. I feel so much better now. Let's keep going while I still have strength."

"God strengthens."

"No sermons, Royal. Remember you promised."

"Excuse me, madam," he said with an exaggerated bow. "I forgot."

Bending to place her hands on her knees, she said between labored breaths, "How did you know I was coming back?"

"Mamacita did. She packed everything for our journey and impressed upon me the utmost importance of making ready. She stood in her tiny kitchen, stared out the open window at the Sierra del Carmen for the longest time as she mumbled over and over again in Spanish as if she was in a trance, 'The señora will return today. The señora will return today.' And when Mamacita speaks, I definitely listen."

Jan shrugged.

"She is a *curandera*, you must realize. She knows things science has not yet discovered. What I find most fascinating about her is that she's never spoken into a telephone in her life; nevertheless, she makes long-distance calls every day. To her, prayer is breath. She speaks far more to God than to people."

"Has she ever been to The Thin Place?"

"When she was young, she practically lived there. Today the climb is too much for her. But it was on this mountain that she received the vision that blessed her with the gift of healing. She has been a healer ever since. She prays for her patients, always in Spanish, touches them upon the head, and then utters words nobody but God understands. To the surprise of some skeptics, but of course not to Mamacita, those for whom she prays far more often than not are fully restored."

Breathing hard, they rounded a switchback in the steep

trail. The burros snorted and Royal stopped.

"We'll let them rest for a bit. It's better they rest standing up than have them sit in the trail. I know of a campsite not far from here. Centuries ago the Mescalero Apaches and the Comanches frequented this saddle. When the sun is fully out, you can still see the scars left by their fire pits. It's a very good campsite and is nestled snugly behind a rocky false summit that will protect us. The winds can get fierce up here once the sun slips behind the Chisos Mountains."

"That's hard to imagine. It's so calm right now and so warm I don't even need a jacket."

"But once the sun drops behind these mountains, you'll need it."

He turned to face the burros. "Come, ladies, we have less than a mile before we make camp and there you can graze to your hearts' content."

Josephina snorted as Jovita sat.

"Oh my," said Jan. "What do we do now?"

"Well, it looks like I was wrong," Royal said. "We don't camp up there after all. Jovita has chosen our campsite."

Jan knelt in the trail before Jovita, and peering into the animal's limpid eyes, she whispered, "Well, sweetheart, it appears you are free to make up your own mind. Do you realize how very fortunate you are? I've never been able to do that. You can act on exactly what you want while I cannot. You're a simple beast of burden and I'm a wealthy, college-educated, and most cultured alcoholic with a country club membership, an unbelievably miserable marriage, and a depression that would kill me if given the opportunity. Now I ask: which of us is more fortunate? You? Yes, I'd say you are."

Leaning toward Jan while holding fast to Josephina's halter rope, Royal said, "When did you begin conversing with burros?"

She lifted her eyes to meet his. "Oh, I'm not conversing, I'm confessing. But thank you for interrupting, because if I ever really get serious about confessing my sins, I don't believe I could stop."

Royal grinned and shook his head. "So Jovita has become your priest?"

"She'll do. At least she listens and that's more than I can say for my husband."

Stroking the burro's long ears, he said, "I've long been enamored of sweet little Jovita. But to be perfectly honest, I have to say she is not the first priest I've met who also happens to be an ass."

The priest turned to lead Josephina a few yards farther up the rocky trail. After a slight tug on the halter rope, the burro followed the priest until they both disappeared behind a huge boulder.

"Don't leave me here all alone!" Jan yelled.

As Jovita deigned to rise slowly in the trail, Jan hugged the little burro's neck and managed to steal a free ride that returned her to a standing position. In the hope of riding Jovita to wherever she might find the priest waiting for her, she attempted in vain to lift her leg high enough to mount the burro. The animal snorted, kicked, and bucked until the packsaddle slid to its side.

Still grasping the halter rope but spinning like a top, Jan screamed, "Royal, help me! Help me! This stupid donkey is attacking me. She means to kill me."

Jovita discovered enough slack in the rope to swing her long neck back toward Jan where she sunk her teeth into the fleshy part of the woman's arm immediately above the elbow.

"Yeeow!" Jan screamed as loudly as she could.

As Jovita released her grip, the woman dropped to her knees in the trail. She rubbed her wounded arm and sobbed. The burro turned away and once again sat on her haunches from where she stared into the fast-approaching dusk.

Jan crawled to the boulder's base where she rested her back against its rough surface. Drawing her knees toward her and wrapping her arms about them, she sobbed. When she sensed Royal's presence, she wiped her eyes to find him hovering above her like a juniper tree blocking the setting sun. She did her best to read meaning in his smile, which she chose to accept as both genuine and strangely comforting.

Kneeling before her, he placed his hand beneath her quivering chin and lifted her teary eyes to meet his. He then sat cross-legged in the middle of the trail with his hand still holding her chin. "Janet, are you okay?"

Chuckling behind her still-heaving shoulders, she said, "You know, for a man who is supposed to be wise, you can really ask a stupid question."

She glared at him with faked irritation. "Your stupid donkey over there just bit the fire out of my arm before hurling me to the ground like I was a rodeo cowboy. Of course, I'm not okay. I'm exhausted, close to starving, and so sore I may never walk again. And, by the way, once we get off this mountain, I plan to sue you for everything you own."

"Jovita can be a mite naughty at times, but she is not a donkey."

His smile now annoyed her and she looked aside. Attempting to stand on legs that refused to support her slight weight, she said, "What the hell is she?"

"A burro."

Alone on sore knees in the middle of the trail, Jan said, "What's the difference?"

"Nothing really, except in Mexico she is called a burro."

"Well, whatever she is, she is a killer and a menace to society."

He offered her a hand and she surprised herself by taking it. As he pulled her to her feet, he held her steady. "After a good night's sleep and a couple of delicious meals, you'll feel much differently about her."

Rubbing her sore arm, Jan said, "Sleep? Where are we going to sleep?"

Royal kept his grip on her shoulders. "We'll sleep right here, and this big rock will protect us from the gales that visit this mountain most every night of the year."

Jan stamped her foot. "But I don't want to sleep here. I want that ancient campsite you spoke of earlier."

"Jovita won't budge. Once a burro sits, she's done for the day."

"But can't we whip her or something to make her go?"

"We can't do that for two reasons: one, we don't have a whip, and two, even if we did, to whip her would be to abuse her. I cannot even imagine abusing her or any other animal."

Jan joined Royal in stroking the seated burro's long ears. "Can't we push her up the mountain?"

The priest's laughter angered her, and she whipped her head around to show her contempt.

In a tone she considered patronizing, he said, "Jan, little Jovita weighs six hundred pounds, I weigh two hundred, and you weigh probably a hundred. That's three hundred pushing six hundred up the mountain. Does that sound feasible to you?"

Jan glowered at him. "Royal, what is to prevent me from absolutely hating you?"

"The Holy Spirit, I would hope."

Pounding her knees with her fists, Jan cried, "Listen, there is no Holy Spirit, there is no God, there is only you and me and this six-hundred pound ass sitting here on the side of this desolate mountain squarely in the middle of nowhere. And if that stupid burro is a fool, I'm a bigger one."

As she attempted to stand, her legs betrayed her. She broke her fall by sliding down the side of the boulder, bracing herself against the burro's rough hide until she landed in the trail.

Once seated in the rocky trail, she said, "Okay, Mr. Know-Everything Priest, that's it. I've had it. Tomorrow you're taking me down this mountain, and I'm jumping in my Porsche and driving straight to Dallas, and when I get there, I'm reporting you to everyone from the President to the Pope."

As she attempted to stand again, she turned her face to the boulder and sobbed.

This is the dumbest thing I've ever done. I just must be the most gullible woman on Earth to believe for even one second that a man who's been dead for five hundred years wants to speak to me. It serves me right being up here with this madman and his killer burros.

But what is his game? Does he mean to humiliate me even

more? Or does he mean to extort a fortune from Chuck?

I have no idea, but tomorrow I do know this: I'm going back to Boquillas, crossing the river, and then I'm heading back to Dallas.

As a strong gust of wind stung her face with grit, in the corner of one eye she caught a flash of something white. When she spun about to investigate, it darted among the brush and rocky terrain to disappear.

She yelled to Royal, "Come over here. I think I see something."

The wind seemed to steal her words as it carried them away from the mountain and deep into Mexico. With her eyes squeezed shut, she attempted again to summon the priest.

Even before she could form the words in her mouth, his resonant voice stunned her. "The winds are early tonight, so I've brought you a quilt to cover you and to protect you. I have our camp set up on the other side of this boulder, and I've begun preparing a delicious stew."

"Stew requires a fire. How did you make one in this wind?"

"The boulder protects the fire. I brought some dried prickly pear soaked in kerosene. One match lit it, and then I simply tossed on a few twigs I also packed, and bingo. Mamacita was good enough to place a dried and discarded wooden shingle in my pack, and that will provide enough fuel to cook all the stew we can eat."

Taking the quilt from the priest and snuggling under it, Jan said, "I saw something back that way." She pointed toward the trail they had moments before climbed.

With his hand serving as a visor, he turned about to face the wind. "Well, I don't see anything now. What do you think it was?"

"I don't really know, but it could have been a man," she said as she rearranged the quilt to expose only her face. "Yes, I think it was a man."

"Was he a Gringo or a Mexican?"

"I couldn't see him exactly, because the wind was too fierce and the dust too thick, but he was dressed all in white and even his serape was white."

Royal turned toward her and offered his hand. The long silence between them compelled her take his hand.

He gently pulled her to her feet. "Now, if you will allow me, I will lead you to a bedroll as fine as any bed in a five-star hotel, and I will prepare for you a dinner fit for a queen."

"The thought of sleep is competing in my mind with the idea of a meal. I honestly don't know which one holds the most appeal at the moment. But believe me, I'm up for either one."

The wind blew hard enough to push them back down the trail a step or two. To keep her from falling, he placed his arm about her shoulders as he led her up the trail one step at a time. "Move a bit to your right because Jovita is sitting in the trail squarely in front of us."

From deep within the quilt, Jan said, "That ass, I think I absolutely must hate her." She sat down and buried herself within the folds of the quilt.

After what seemed an hour later, the priest lifted the edge of the quilt. Jan opened her eyes. Royal had spread twin bed-rolls upon the rocky ground on either side of a small fire that crackled with all manner of hospitable invitations. A wire grill rested upon the circle of rocks forming the fire pit.

At one end of each bedroll, the priest had placed an empty packsaddle, meant to serve as a pillow. A fragile column of smoke rose from the flames and remained intact until it climbed above the boulder's protection. The wind howled all about them, but seemed wholly unwilling to invade this pristine site.

Dropping the quilt to the ground, Jan ambled to the first of the twin bedrolls. She sank to her knees, then lay on her side and rested her head against the empty saddle frame covered in green canvas.

The priest paused long enough to pick up the quilt, which he then spread upon her. "You will need this in a few minutes. Once the wind dies down, the temperature will drop to near-freezing."

"Thank you," she said, as the wind howled. "Thank you."

Crouching before the small fire, he turned toward her. "You're welcome."

Sleep came within moments, and with it arrived a recurring dream of childhood where her mother chased her with a belt, screaming threats. This nightmare awakened her, and through bleary eyes she saw the priest kneeling above her and holding a large tin cup of hot stew. His smile spoke of a world she knew little about.

Attempting to return his smile, she took the cup wrapped in his kerchief. "Royal, tell me about love."

"What do you want to know about it?"

As she sipped the stew, she said, "Tell me what it is. Define it for me. I once thought I knew, but in truth, I didn't. I'm dead serious; I really want to know what it is. You asked me one time why I came down here, and I guess the real reason is that I was desperate to know what it means to love, and to experience love."

She set the cup to one side. "Somehow, I thought I might find the answer down here. I suppose that was terribly foolish of me; nevertheless, that is what I thought."

The priest settled upon the ground next to where she lay. "I don't think love can be defined."

Holding fast to the quilt, she sat upright. "Why not? Anything can be defined, can't it?"

"No," he said between sips of his own cup of stew. "There are some things that simply defy definition, and love is one of those things."

"Why?"

He stood and towered above her as he swallowed the last drop of stew. "Because love is a mystery, and mysteries, by their very nature, refuse to be defined. I will tell you, though, that all love comes from God and comes to us. We are to be love's mediators. In other words, we don't create it, but it is our job to express it."

"So if I don't believe in God, then no love comes to me. Is that what you're saying?"

He shook his head. "You are as much loved by God as I am or as any person on this planet is."

Royal stepped toward the dying embers the fire. "That's enough for tonight. I'm turning in. I'm way past tired."

Without having to wait long, sleep came to Jan again. This time her dreams contained a brief but pleasant memory of a trip to the Texas State Fair with a high school halfback she had long ago convinced herself she would love forever. As her mother's threats returned to eclipse all possible pleasantness contained in her latter dream, she awakened with a start to discover the beaming face of a little man above where she lay.

His smile disarmed her and she relaxed under the quilt. "Who are you?"

The little man with snow-white hair did not speak, but only held his smile.

"Are you the angel of death? Am I dead? Is this heaven? Oh my, this place is so beautiful."

Jan sat straight up and pushed the quilt off her shoulders. "No, I don't think I want to die, after all. I want to live and to remain here for the whole of eternity. May I do that? Please tell me I can. Oh, I beg you, please tell me I never have to leave this beauty. Please."

The man dressed all in white said nothing.

Jan attempted to caress the cheek of the little man, but her fingers failed to touch anything. She blinked her eyes, hoping to sharpen her eyesight as the vision of the little man faded from view.

"Royal!" she yelled as loudly as she could.

CHAPTER TWENTY-FOUR

Following the ring of a borrowed White House telephone, Chuck lifted the receiver. "Harry, thank you for returning my call."

"I'm afraid I only have a moment. Apparently my next patient is late, and I can talk until she gets here. What's this about?"

"I'm still in up here in D.C. I'm catching a flight back to Dallas tonight, but I called because I really do need your help."

"No doubt this is about Jan."

"She's begun hallucinating. She thinks she's seen a man down in the Big Bend. Of course, I doubt he exists, but if he does, he's one in a long line of weirdoes who claims to possess some kind of mystical powers that end up always costing me money. She's back down there as we speak, and God only knows what kind of trouble she's gotten herself into."

With the receiver pressed to his ear, Chuck turned about to wrap the long cord about his torso like a lariat. "Not an hour ago, the President of the United States offered me a position on his cabinet with the enormous responsibility of making peace in the world. At the risk of sounding grandiose, the future of our nation may actually depend on having Jan back in Dallas, sober, straight, clean, and most of all sane."

"You're painting with a mighty broad brush there, friend."

"Can you understand how terribly urgent this is?"

"You're being offered a most important assignment and her instability is standing in the way."

Chuck plopped his tired frame on the White House hallway desk from which he had borrowed the phone. "So, what *do* I do?"

"What exactly are you asking, Chuck?"

"Do I go down to the Rio Grande and find her? I'd have to haul her back to Dallas, toss her in a hospital against her will, and then make a scene that will, no doubt, hit the papers."

Chuck mussed his hair with his free hand and then searched for his comb in his inside coat pocket. "If the media gets a hold of this, this deal disappears. I don't think I've ever been so frustrated in my life. Here I am being offered the opportunity to see to it that peace in our time actually becomes a reality. The President's plan can work and, what's more, it absolutely must. But for me to do what I am convinced God would have me do, my sick wife has to get well real fast."

"Given Jan's history, I would not be surprised if she's resumed her drinking and has experienced an alcohol-induced psychosis."

"Doesn't she need to be hospitalized?"

"Jan's diagnosis is one hundred percent Dr. Coughman's call."

Chuck jumped to his feet. "Harry, I'm desperate. This is the chance of a lifetime and Jan's illness is the immovable boulder in my path."

"Call Dr. Coughman. That's the only way to do this thing. I can't help you with this. All I can do is guess regarding her condition and remember a guess is not even close to a diagnosis. I should not have even guessed. I had absolutely no right to do that."

"The *only* solution is to hospitalize her, Harry," Chuck yelled into the receiver. "I want my wife back! Evil has her in its grip and I want her back. I absolutely must have her support. I'm deserving of that. This is not too much for any man to expect of his wife. Everything depends on this. *Everything!* Somehow I'm must find her and put her in a hospital. Enough is enough!"

"Chuck, call Coughman!"

I can't do that. The man detests me, and he will be of no help, whatsoever. What do I do? God help me, what do I do?

God help me. Please God, I have no idea what to do.

"Thanks, Harry, I'm sorry I bothered you." Chuck dropped the receiver into its cradle as he fought against the flood of tears he feared might send him spiraling into another attack of panic if he dared release them.

I can't have another one of those episodes here. God, help me be strong. Please help me be strong.

God I'm begging you… please!!!

He paused only long enough to smile at the woman who had allowed him to use her desk phone. "Thank you, ma'am. You have been most kind."

"I hope everything is okay, Dr. Love. I mean, with you and with your wife."

You idiot! That woman heard every word. If she tells Buck Barrett, this opportunity dies and with it everything I've ever worked for.

Oh well, I can't worry about that now. No, my challenge now is to return home and somehow find Jan and then convince some shrink to put her away for years.

CHAPTER TWENTY-FIVE

Throughout the whole of that night, the wind punished the ridge as it conspired with the desert to shroud the dawn in a saffron veil. The storm wailed in discordant arpeggios, and as dawn arrived to pierce the darkness, curiosity tricked Jan into opening her eyes.

She inched away from the fire's dying embers. The grit stung, forcing them shut, but not before a trickle of tears escaped to mix with the dust. Twin meandering paths on her face descended toward her delicate chin.

"Wow!" she cried, catching a mouthful of desert.

She rubbed her eyes with a shirtsleeve and yet failed to soothe the irritation. Jovita decided to stand and the priest nudged her flank gently with his knee. The little burro ambled down the path as the wind flailed the sotol stalks, turning them into buggy-whips.

Returning to the safety of the boulder, she watched the wind buffet him as Royal tended the burros. *God, I so wish I knew his secret?*

"Will the burros be okay today in this wind?" she yelled.

"They are blessed with lashes that block out the sand, and fortunately their ears can rotate counter to the blow. Their Creator engineered them quite well for storms." From a small burlap bag he withdrew a fistful of twigs and deposited them into the fire pit with the care one might give a fine piece of heirloom china.

"What are those sticks for?"

"Kindling."

"Surely that is not enough wood?"

"It will have to be."

"Why don't you go gather some more wood? Something bigger?"

He shrugged, "This will do."

Kneeling, he retrieved a clipping of dry kerosene-soaked ocotillo from the bag, sniffed it, winced, and signaled his concentration with a turn of his mouth. For a few seconds he managed to repel the wind with one broad hand as he used the other to light the tip-end of the cactus before dropping the flame into the kindling. One by one he placed larger sticks upon the twigs, and in minutes a tiny column of rising smoke became a robust flame stretching toward the burnt orange sky.

With an eye on the incipient fire, Royal pulled a scarred and battered iron skillet from the pack, the handle of which was secured to a piece of broomstick by a tightly wrapped rusty wire. He withdrew a small can, pried off its lid with a pocketknife, and then poured its oily contents into the hot skillet.

From a linen bundle he removed two corn tortillas and dropped each into the skillet now swirling in a fragrant smoke. Once the tortillas were seared golden brown, he lifted each from the skillet and laid them side-by-side to cool on the kerchief.

With a wooden implement carved in the shape of a miniature shovel, he dug into what had once been a mustard jar.

He spread a scoopful of frijoles upon each flattened tortilla. He then rolled each thin tortilla into a tight rope before returning them again to the skillet to heat. After they sizzled for a second time, he removed them gingerly with his fingertips and laid them upon the kerchief. With a satisfied smile signaling an ebullience she decided to trust, he turned to her and said, "This, my dear, will be a breakfast you will not soon forget."

"I don't know if you're right, because if this food kills me, I suspect I'll forget it real soon. But I no longer want to die," Jan said with a smile. "I suppose now is a good time to trust you."

He rose.

"Where are you going?"

"I left six small bags of grain on the ground where I unloaded the packs last night. I must feed the ladies by hand this morning, because the wind is much too fierce to spread the grain on the ground. Enjoy your meal. I only wish we had some of Mamacita's goat cheese to go with it."

"Aren't you going to eat?"

"You come first, then the burros."

"Yum," she said taking a bite from the tortilla. "This is delicious."

As he stepped into the wind, Royal paused to wave at something behind the curtain of dust.

Still wrapped in the quilt, Jan inched like a caterpillar closer to the determined little fire. She watched the tall priest drop to his knees.

Look at that man praying in a dust storm. How can he be so disciplined and faithful? I've never known any one who was that sincere and honest. Whatever the outcome of this journey, I'm glad I made it because for once in my life I've met someone who actually walks the talk.

Windblown and caked in dust, Royal stepped toward the fire.

Emboldened by the new energy coming from her meager meal, Jan said, "Royal, tell me about Juan Diego."

"Ah, Juan Diego, the sweet saint of Mexico. Did you not just see him? He is accompanying us on this climb, you know."

Buoyed by his cheeriness, Jan could feel old resentments falling away one by one like autumn leaves. "He came to me in a dream last night, but it might not have been a dream at all. He may have actually come to me."

Jan extricated her arms from the quilt's tight grip long enough to stretch. "But this morning I didn't see a thing except the backsides of two burros, which I must say was not a particularly lovely piece of scenery. Not a Kodak moment, if you catch my drift."

Royal's smile silenced her as she waited for what might come next.

He chuckled "Their backsides are probably not their most photogenic angle, but you must admit that their eyes are beautiful and their long ears iconic."

Stepping close to what remained of the smolder and its thin column of smoke, Royal knelt next to her. He paused before sitting cross-legged directly across from her, raised his arms in an exaggerated stretch, and yawned. "Ah, sweet Juan Diego. He is hidden from your view at the moment by the thick dust, but he is only yards away, just behind my left shoulder."

Jan liberated herself from the quilt and crawled closer to the fire's embers where she leaned as far forward as she could. Holding her hand above her eyes, she scanned the mountainside for Juan Diego, but could see nothing but the curtain of dust swirling up the trail like a thick orange storm cloud.

She coughed, "I don't see a thing. Are you sure he is there?"

"Yes, he's there. I can't see him either, but trust me, he's there not ten yards away."

"You wouldn't lie to me would you?"

"No, ma'am, I would not." He yawned again.

"Why can I not see him?"

"Likely, he doesn't wish to be seen, at least not just now. When he wants to be seen again, he will make himself visible, and we will see him and then perhaps we will know why it is he has summoned you to the Thin Place."

Jan rose, stepped away from the fire to feel her way into the orange cloud. "I don't see him," she yelled. "In fact, I can't see anything. The wind is too strong and the dust too thick. I can't keep my eyes open."

She returned to the fire and sat directly across from the priest while he poked at the embers with a small stick. "Do you think he came to me last night?"

Royal tossed the stick into the embers and sighed. "Oh, I don't really know, but I suspect he did."

"So, you don't think I was dreaming."

Royal rolled to his side, propped himself up on his elbow. "Did you feel really good after he left?"

Jan's smile stretched into places in her face wholly

unaccustomed to expressing happiness. "Oh my, I don't think I've ever felt so good in my life." A laugh slipped from her mouth before she could stifle it.

Did I just laugh? My God, I haven't done that in forever. What is happening to me?

"Then he was more than a dream." Royal leaned toward the fire and blew gently upon the struggling flame. "That's the effect every encounter with holiness has upon us mortals. We experience real wholeness, which among other things, means all anxiety evaporates."

"Is it a kind of euphoria?"

"Far more than that. Euphoria is always temporary, while this experience is more substantive and much longer lasting," he said catching his breath.

"Does it remain with us forever?"

The priest now spread the full length of his body upon the ground and tucked his large hands beneath his head to form a pillow. Following the little stream of smoke with his eyes, he said, "In a way it does, because it is the first taste of true spiritual transformation."

"What exactly is spiritual transformation?"

Rolling again to his side, he said, "Spiritual transformation means that God blesses us with a whole new head and with a whole new way of seeing the world and an entirely new way of being a human being in this old fallen world."

"Give me an example of what that looks like."

"Well, to begin with a transformed person predicates even the smallest decisions upon what it means to express love, while the rest of us usually base our decisions on self-interest or self-protection."

Sitting suddenly upright, he smiled. "Transformed people live to express love, while the rest of us live only to defend our egos and to satisfy our several appetites."

Jan jumped to her feet. "Oh, I want to be transformed. Tell me, what must I do to make that happen?"

"Not so fast. Remember, living as one who is dedicated to love is not easy. In fact, it is downright dangerous."

Exhilaration faded from her face. "Why is it dangerous?"

He placed his hands upon her shoulders, drew her close, gazed into her eyes. "Because love is not much valued in this world. Remember, this world kills its prophets, and two thousand years ago it crucified our Lord, Jesus. So be very careful what you pray or wish for."

Jan shrugged. "Let's sit by the fire again so you can tell me about Juan Diego."

Royal sat so close to the smoldering embers his boots rested in the fire pit. Leaning toward her from the waist up, he said, "Juan Diego was born and raised in what today is Central Mexico. He was one of the very first of the indigenous people of his world to be baptized when the Franciscans followed the Spanish explorers to this new land."

Jan sat upon her knees and stretched toward him to hear every word. "When was this?"

"In the sixteenth century," he said before turning his head away to spit beyond the boulder's protection.

Jan rose to her feet. "May I come sit by you? I don't want to miss a word of this."

"Certainly," he said with a fresh smile.

She crawled on all fours around the small fire pit, rolled to a sitting position next to him, and then pressed her cheek against his shoulder.

He surprised her by wrapping his arm about her and drawing her close to his side. "Comfortable?" he said.

"Very much so." She wondered why she was neither angry nor scared. "I'm very comfortable. Please continue telling me about Juan Diego."

Royal held her close as he spoke. "Juan Diego was so devout he would walk fourteen miles every day one way from his humble home to the Franciscan mission where he received instruction. It was on one of those walks that he encountered a vision of the Virgin Mary, who instructed him to tell the bishop that she wanted a chapel to be built on the very hill where she appeared to him."

Jan's slight frame trembled against his.

Royal paused. "Are you okay?"

She lifted her head. "I'm okay. I'm just crying."

"Why?"

She laid her head on his shoulder. "I have absolutely no idea. I just am. Now, please tell me the rest."

"Juan Diego did as the Virgin commanded. He returned to his village and managed somehow to see the bishop, who, of course, didn't believe he'd actually seen the Virgin Mary. Nevertheless, the bishop was surprisingly kind to Juan Diego, in that he didn't dismiss him out right. He told the little peasant to bring him a sign. Needless to say, Juan Diego was disappointed, and he even considered himself a failure. Consequently, the next day he took an alternative route to in his fourteen mile walk to the mission."

Jan's sniffles turned to heaving sobs as her body trembled against his. He held to her even tighter.

"The Virgin appeared to him again. Poor Juan Diego dropped to his knees and confessed his failed attempt. The Virgin only smiled at him and summoned him to the top of the hill, where he discovered roses blooming in the dead of winter in a rocky place where only scrub and cactus ordinarily grew. Juan Diego removed his mantle from his shoulders and gathered the flowers in it. He then returned to the Virgin at the base of the hill where he spread his mantle upon the ground. To his astonishment, the roses had been transformed into a perfect likeness of the Virgin imprinted upon his mantle. He immediately carried this likeness of the Virgin to the bishop, and the bishop was so convinced of the veracity of Juan Diego's story, that he set about immediately to build a chapel in her honor on the hill where she had appeared. Juan Diego built a hut adjacent to the chapel, where he lived for the rest of his life. And for all the years remaining to him, he devoted his life to serving the Virgin Mary."

Jan pulled away slightly to gaze upon his face as best she could with her eyes flooded with tears. "Is that true?"

"Every word."

She thought his smile reassuring.

"Now Jan, we'd best pack up these burros and get on our way. We have many miles to climb today. The wind is dying, and once the sun is high in the sky, it will turn into a gentle breeze."

"Will the storm be transformed?"

"Oh, something like that, I suppose," he said, still smiling.

CHAPTER TWENTY-SIX

With a trembling hand, Chuck answered his cell phone on the third ring. Following a long drag on his cigarette, he said, "Thank you for returning my call, Dr. Coughman. I cannot tell you how much I appreciate this courtesy. Unfortunately, I'm still at Reagan here in D.C., waiting to catch a plane in about an hour's time."

He rose from the airport chair to pace in a tight circle with the phone pressed to his ear and the cigarette wedged between his lips.

"You are welcome, Dr. Love," Dr. Kenneth Coughman said. "What is this about?"

Chuck ceased his pacing and sighed. "Okay, let me get right to the point. You need to hospitalize Jan. The moment I return, I plan to go find her, wherever she is, and bring her back to Dallas. You will commit her and do whatever it takes to see she gets well immediately. And it is of the utmost importance we do this in complete secrecy. No one, and by that I mean absolutely no one, can know about this."

He paused long enough to exhale the cigarette smoke. "I need her to be well. I cannot emphasize this enough. But I can tell you that her wellness or her recovery—or whatever it is we call her becoming an appreciative, polite, and cooperative human being—is so important as to be tied to issues that are bigger than you can possibly imagine. I can't explain it to you with any greater clarity, lest I violate a solemn oath, but I will tell you that at this moment there is no issue in your practice that can possibly take precedence over Jan's mental health. None, sir!"

Pacing and dragging on the cigarette, Chuck said between breaths, "Absolutely none. Trust me on this. And there can be no publicity."

"Dr. Love, I've been your wife's psychiatrist for a bit more than a year now, and I can assure you never once have I thought she required hospitalization. She didn't need it when she first came to me and she has made marked improvement since then, sir, with all due respect."

With his free hand Chuck clinched his fist and shook it. "Doctor, you are mistaken," he yelled. "She definitely needs to be hospitalized. I know her better than you. At this very moment she is down in the Big Bend somewhere doing God only knows what, and for all I envision, she's out of her mind drunk once again. She is delusional. My very good friend, Harry Singleton, with whom I believe you are acquainted, says she is likely so depressed she has become psychotic."

"I know Dr. Singleton well, and he is a fine psychiatrist. However, permit me to reiterate, Dr. Love, your wife is not now, nor has she ever been, in need of hospitalization."

Dropping his frame into the hard plastic airport chair, Chuck blew a steady stream of smoke out of his nostrils. "Well, then, you give me no choice but to dismiss you immediately. My wife will be seeing another psychiatrist when I return her to Dallas, sir. I'll be notifying you where it is I need her records sent."

Coughman cleared his throat. "Your wife's treatment is

entirely her decision, sir. But if she requests her records, I will be glad to send them to whomever she selects to be her psychiatrist."

"Listen, Coughman, I'm not going to blow the biggest opportunity in my life simply because my wife is a lush you haven't helped one bit. Do you hear me?"

Dr. Coughman said, "Good day, sir."

Jumping to his feet, Chuck hollered into the cell phone, "Coughman, don't hang up on me. I'm not done!"

The phone line went dead.

Chuck cursed, threw the phone down, and looked up just in time to see other passengers staring at him. As heat rose from his collar, several people in line near the check-in counter backed away. Chuck sank into his chair and put his face in his hands.

CHAPTER TWENTY-SEVEN

At every switchback Royal tugged on the harness ropes, halting the sure-footed animals. With every pause Jan mumbled words of encouragement to herself between breaths, as she measured a resolve she was not at all certain could be sustained. For the first two miles, she had forced an affable banter she suspected he could read as a cover for the myriad self- doubts that swarmed in her mind like angry yellow jackets.

As each new step taxed her shallow breathing, an ache climbed its way up her thighs before turning into a wrenching back spasm. She debated whether to choose feigned courage or the more sensible option of begging for an entire day of rest.

Oh my God, how I do love the ease of the country club existence. And what is so wrong with that? I was out of my mind in thinking I could do this. I can't do this. I can't! I'm way too old and out of shape!

She paused to permit her misery to be succored by the spectacle of ancient mountains connected to deep, shadowed valleys. The sight would have taken her breath had not the climb already robbed her of it.

God, what am I doing up here? But the view is incredible, unlike anything I've ever seen. I wish I were in shape. Let's face it. I'm not! I can't believe I'm so out of shape.

As she peered into the purple Sierra Madre more than one hundred miles away, she considered dropping to her sore knees like a supplicant to beg this machine of a man for mercy. The next instant, she thought better of the idea of humiliating herself.

At noon they finally stopped and Jan perched herself on a big rock adjacent to the trail. In minutes, the pain in her back eased enough for her stand and turn fully about in her search for Juan Diego. Seeing no sign of the man, she returned to the rest on the rock.

The burros remained still as they munched the grain the priest fed them by hand. Once they were nourished, Royal approached her place on the rock. For the next several minutes they shared in silence a meal of stale corn tortillas filled with cold frijoles right out of the jar followed by gulps of tepid water from their two canteens.

Feeling stronger but still far less than sanguine about making it to the summit, she wondered what to say. Instead of mounting any argument, she decided for a sort of Delphic silence between them.

I love the beauty of this place, but I'm really not sure I can make this climb. But I absolutely have to do it. There is no real choice in this. The days of my disobedience are behind me. Even so, I don't know if I can do this.

Once the sun reached its apex, the first hour of afternoon turned the thin air so hot she was forced to give up first all chatter and then even lucidity as one torturous step at a time they climbed. At three o'clock, she surprised herself by dropping suddenly to her knees before expending what breath she had remaining to cry, "God, why don't those dumb burros sit down? I've had it! I can't go another step, Royal. I swear I can't. I'm sorry, but I have had it. I was not made for this. I'm a spoiled city girl and a burden to you. I'm so sorry to disappoint you, and even more, Juan Diego, but I don't think I can climb another foot up this mountain."

The priest said nothing as Jovita snorted before chewing a portion of grain she had stowed in her mouth.

"Royal, please tell me you heard me. These burros are traitors."

Moving close enough to cast a shadow upon where she lay, he pointed. "*Buenas tardes*, big fellow." He dropped to his knees before crawling on all fours up the trail no more than three yards.

She began to cry. "This is no time for your prayers! I want to go back. No, please let me restate that: I need to go back. This heat is making me sick to my stomach. I can go no further. I was completely out of my mind to think I could climb this mountain. I'm very sorry, but I can't do it."

He's not hearing me. God, what is he doing? Oh, I can't believe this: he's crawling like dog.

"What are you doing, Royal? Don't scare me. Please, I'm not up to this." On legs that felt as though they had been reduced to bungee cords, she struggled to stand and was grateful to discover she could.

Thank God for small favors.

Emboldened, she said, "What are you doing down there? Please take me down this mountain. I need to get down. I'm feeling sick, real, real sick—"

"But look, we have a visitor."

"What?"

"We have been joined on our journey by a friend." He pointed to the trail.

Following the line of his finger, she spied a diamondback the girth of which she judged to be that of a fire hose.

My God! What a monster! That settles it. We're going back,

"Please take me down this mountain. I'm not only sick, I'm now also terrified. You can't know how much I hate snakes."

Ignoring her, he said, "*Buenas tardes*, big fellow. And how are you this fine day? I wonder how big you are? I suspect you are every bit of six feet. You've been on this mountain for some time. What a delightful place to spend your life. You are truly magnificent. Look at the exquisite pattern in his markings, Janet."

God, he's actually talking to that awful thing. This man is completely out of his gourd. What if the thing jumps up and bites him and he dies and I'm left to die alone on this mountain?

"Royal, please!"

Darting its forked black tongue into the hot afternoon, the big snake slithered undisturbed toward a limestone boulder where it disappeared into a crevice. The priest rose and turned to smile.

"Did you hear me?" she yelled.

"Time's a-wasting, Janet."

"Do you realize you're insufferable? Surely, I'm not the first to share this keen bit of most unpleasant insight with you."

"Time to get on up this mountain, sweet lady."

"I am not sweet, and I cannot possibly climb another step."

He turned to lead both burros upward one slow, breathy step after the other.

What choice do I have? None! The man is going up this mountain and I don't dare try to go down by myself, not with a monster snake waiting to sink its poisonous fangs in me.

Why in God's name did I climb this mountain? And where is Juan Diego when I most need him?

For the next two hours, a will drawn from the instinct for survival and nothing else she could imagine pushed her one halting step after another up the steep, rocky trail. She no longer possessed the strength to plead her case, and yet she knew if she refused to climb, he would only outwait her with a contrived patience she recognized to be his clever gambit. And yet, if she turned back, she would travel alone, vulnerable to dangers she was too tired even to dread. She had fallen into his trap and she hated herself for it.

So this is it! This is where I die. I wonder if he will have his way with me first? Is this his plan? Oh, he's not going to do that. This man is not at all a criminal. He's not evil. He is just a little crazy. Perhaps, I will die from exhaustion, or maybe that monster of a snake will do me in, but more likely my heart will fail.

"Only five hundred more yards, Janet. That is all! Then we will camp for the night in a lovely spot, and there I will prepare you a meal fit for a queen."

"I can't go one step farther. Not one more. Those burros have betrayed me. And what's worse, you have tricked me."

"They've been magnificent, and I have not tricked you."

"No, they are traitors and you have to be the cruelest man on this planet. I want to die right here and right now. I don't care if a five-star hotel is only five hundred yards up this trail,

I can't take another step. Not another one. Why won't you listen to me?"

"You are a courageous woman."

"Quit manipulating me! You know good and well I now have no choice but to remain here with you."

"I'll go ahead while you rest. Once you feel stronger, simply follow the trail and I will have our camp set up and a sumptuous dinner waiting for you." Kneeling to touch her brow with the tips of his fingers, he smiled. "I can do all things in him who strengthens me."

"Don't touch me! And don't you dare preach! How many times do I have to tell you that?"

He stood again to step backward. "Take your time. I'll be up ahead a bit waiting for you. Tomorrow will be much, much easier. In fact, it will be less than a mile from tonight's campsite to the Thin Place. You will make it with no difficulty. A good meal, a night's rest and God's grace will strengthen you."

"I don't want to be strengthened. I only want to die."

"Oh, but you will feel much stronger."

"I hate it when you say that, so quit it! See if I ever place my trust in any jackasses again. They are traitors and you, Mr. Big Shot Professor, are a sadistic priest. You should be forever banished from the church, and I am a complete idiot for ever having trusted you."

"They are burros and I am indeed a sinner, but I am not sadistic. There is a great chasm separating my ordinary sins from sadism, a great chasm, indeed."

The discordant clang of a cowbell returned her gaze to the trail. Two big copper-colored men lumbered toward her with sweat streaming off their heads. As they trudged the steep grade, they huffed like steam engines. Each was dressed in sweat-stained khaki shirts and tattered trousers covered in crudely sown olive-colored patches. Following these two came three more, and then as many as seven, and all of them traipsed ahead with their sweat-soaked khaki hats in hand and bare heads bowed in the thin hot air.

Oh my God, who are they? What are they doing out here in the middle of this wilderness? Are they dangerous? They are dressed like soldiers, but are they?

The first man's huge glistening belly had bullied its way through the buttons on his rag of a shirt, except the bottom one which held, at least for the moment. His navel winked like a big empty eye socket with each ponderous step, and the menacing smirk he displayed beneath a scraggly gray mustache signaled danger. Dust and what from a distance appeared to be layers of caked-on soot masked their faces.

God, are they ghouls or are they men?

"Uh, Royal we have company and they sure don't look like Boy Scouts."

Turning to face the men, he smiled. *"Buenas tardes."*

"Ah, buenas tardes, amigo," bellowed the fat man breathlessly. When he stooped to place both hands upon his knees, his huge belly hung low enough to eclipse the tops of his boots.

"Come share tortillas and frijoles with us, amigos."

She counted as many as ten lathered mules trailing behind these filthy men. The last of the group was a frail boy. He gripped a rope linking the train of big mules that snorted and stomped, and clanged their steel shoes, ringing them against the rocks. The mules whipped shaggy tails to and fro, and made a hissing sound as they snorted the rarified air through expanded nostrils.

The fat man grinned in recognition of the obvious—the sight of his caravan terrified her. He let loose with thunderous bullfrog belch, then lifted his head to grin widely enough to reveal a crooked line of broken teeth.

"Why the mules?" she said.

"Not now." Royal's tone contained caution.

Each animal was piled high with as many as a dozen canvas bags and atop each pile a pair of rifles were secured with taut ropes.

"What are they hauling?"

"You don't want to know."

"Why the guns?"

"Deliver us from evil," he said.

She stepped toward Royal and wrapped her arms tightly about his waist.

My God! Oh my sweet Jesus! Help me! I don't believe in you, but please help me anyway! Oh God! I can't face this.

Sauntering toward the priest with no change in his grin, the obese man said, "We will take the beautiful woman off your hands. She will serve well as our booty, and because of your generosity, we will let you live. What a deal? No?"

"What?" she screamed. "Royal, don't let me go! Please, don't let them have me."

"Easy, Janet. Easy," he said as he wrapped both arms about her. She buried her face in his shoulder.

The fat man glowered.

Speaking loud enough for the fat man to hear, Royal

prayed, "Father, deliver us from evil."

"Quit praying and do something!" she screamed.

"Have the woman disrobe and show us her full loveliness. Oh, I can tell she is delectable; just perfect for our pleasure."

"Hombres," said Royal in the bold tone of authority the circumstances now mocked. "No one may touch this woman. She is holy. She belongs only to God—"

"But you are mistaken, she is ours."

"No, you are the one who is mistaken," said Royal."

The fat man lunged at Royal and grabbed him about the neck before unsheathing and pressing a Bowie knife against the soft tissue beneath Royal's chin. "Release her, or I will cut your throat," he snarled.

Royal raised his hands shoulder high and said with amazing calmness, "Deliver us from evil."

"Don't let them hurt me!" Jan screamed as she released her grip on his waist to dance about in a panic.

Mouthing the prayer over and over, he watched as the men now swayed in an ill-omened motion not unlike the subtle, and oh so slight, bob of a rattlesnake's head seconds before it strikes.

"We will take her with us," the fat man bellowed, bringing reflexive grins to the faces of his comrades. "And if you make trouble, you will bleed to death on this mountain and the coyotes will drag your pitiful remains so far from this trail that no one will ever find them. And once they are finished with you, the buzzards will pick your bones before the sun bleaches them snow white."

"Deliver us from evil."

One by one, the men grunted and whistled through the

gaps in their teeth.

"Royal, please! Don't leave me to these pigs."

A sinewy man, his arms and torso a canvas for grotesque tattoos, grabbed her about the shoulders and flung her to the trail.

Covering her eyes with her hands, she curled herself into a ball. "Don't! Don't hurt me! Please don't hurt me. I beg you—"

"We will permit you to watch our sport," said the fat man. He pressed the blade so hard against Royal's chin a steady stream of blood rolled down his neck. It streamed around a band of sweat and grime until it soaked into his collar. "We are hungry lobos."

The wiry man ripped Jan's shirt from her torso. She shrieked.

"Deliver us from evil!" Royal yelled.

"Royal, do something. They mean to kill me."

The tattooed man stepped out of his threadbare khakis to stand naked above her. He raised his clasped hands in a parody of triumph, eliciting roars from his gang of filthy comrades.

His chin bleeding against the blade, Royal called again, "Deliver us from evil!"

Before the fat man could retaliate, the sinewy man screamed and slapped his arms to his sides as though his stiff body had, much like Lot's wife, been suddenly transformed into a solid pillar of salt. The fat man released the knife, and it dropped through his thick fingers to clatter against the rocks.

"No! No!" bellowed the fat man before his circle of comrades collapsed in unison. The big mules snorted and kicked and bucked. As he fell to his knees to bury his face in his arms and whimper, the frail boy who had clung to the rope released his grip.

After he knelt to cover her with his shirt, Royal wrapped his arms about Jan. She hugged her knees as she trembled.

Garbled mumbles turned her eyes again to the khaki men and the whimpering youth, all of whom now withdrew from them on all fours. After raising themselves one-by-one on uncertain legs, they scrambled down the mountain like a flock of spooked roosters, leaving behind echoes that lingered long after they disappeared. The mule train still bound together by the rope galloped down the mountain's north slope in the opposite direction as their steel shoes kicked up a thick curtain of dust.

"What's happening, Royal?"

"Be still. Be very, very still. We're in the presence of holiness."

"Those men are not holy. They are vile and the worst kind of men. Evil. Oh my God, they are the very worst."

"They are gone. And we have a visitor. He is with us again."

"I'm much too frightened to open my eyes."

"But there is nothing to fear. Look for yourself," said Royal, smiling at the dark-skinned man who stood before them dressed in glowing white linen.

"Take me home. Please, I beg you. Take me home!"

"Open your eyes and see for yourself Juan's beautiful face."

With her hands over her eyes, Jan screamed, "I've had it, Royal! Take me home! No more evil men! No more big snakes! No more of your tricks! Either you take me home, or I'm heading down this mountain alone. I can't take any more. I'm losing what little is left of my rum-soaked mind."

"He's gone."

Jan pried open her eyes.

The priest removed his bloodstained shirt that had covered her nakedness. He then rose to walk toward one of the canvas bags that had tumbled from the mules in their mad dash down the mountain. After using the fat man's knife to cut open the canvas bag, he dipped one finger into its white powder, returned it to his lips, and tasted. "If I had to guess, I'd place my bet on this being cocaine. Whatever it is, it is not good."

"Take me home! Please!"

Returning to where she trembled, he knelt before her to lift her head to rest it on his knee. "You're safe now."

With her chest still heaving she said, "What happened?"

"We were delivered."

"Delivered? How?"

"We will make camp here for the night."

"But I don't want to make camp. I want to go home. I'm much too scared to sleep. Those men meant to murder us."

"They did, indeed."

"Will they come back?"

Royal shook his head.

"But how can you be so sure?"

"I just am. They will never come back. Their mules are likely still running down one side of this mountain while they are scrambling down the other."

"Why?"

"Because those men are more frightened right now than ever they imagined might be possible."

"But what scared them? Why did they run? How come they didn't kill us?"

"I'm going to the burros to fetch you two quilts, one for a cover and the other to be rolled into a pillow. You can rest while I prepare dinner."

Won't you answer me? Oh, forget it, I'm too scared to beg.

As she lay trembling on the rocky ground the first cool breeze since dawn washed against her face.

"We are hungry lobos," the wind sang.

God, I've never been so scared in my entire life. Never! This is sheer madness. I am out of my mind. Why am I making such a fuss? I deserve to die.

Chapter Twenty-Eight

Chuck pressed the phone's receiver to his ear and paced about his spacious office. "Buck, I'm returning your call. I landed here in Dallas not an hour ago and just now reached my office. What's this about?"

"Pleased to hear from you, preacher. And you know perfectly well what this is about. It's about…"

As he collapsed into his chair, Chuck winced.

"…your pretty little Bolshevik wife."

"Buck, I'm doing all I can—"

"You're not doing a damn thing, now isn't that the real story here, preacher? Our people tell me the little lady is down in the Big Bend at the moment, and, seeing how you are in Dallas, I'd say you're not doing a whole lot to bring her in line. Now don't try to fool me, boy, because when it comes to your wife, I know more about that little bitch than anyone else on the planet, including you."

Chuck jumped to his feet, thought better of protesting, and sighed. "What is it you want me to do?"

"You know very well what I want you to do," Buck yelled. "Good God Almighty, preacher, how many times do I have to spell it out for you? Go down to that God-forsaken desert, find the woman, escort her home, and then do whatever it takes to bring her into line. And to do that, you must get her into a good Dallas hospital. Now, be so kind as to tell me exactly what part of this necessity you are having some difficulty grasping."

"It's not that easy."

"It's every bit as easy as a bunch of flies finding a fat horse's ass in the dead of night. Just drop whatever it is you're doing at the moment and catch the next plane down there, wherever the nearest airport happens to be—Midland or Odessa—and alert the highway patrol or the Texas Rangers. I hear you're tighter than a shiny new screw with the governor, so I suspect you can arrange all the help you need. If you like, I'll get the Border Patrol and even the Department of Interior people involved. We know how to keep unpleasantness out of the papers. But do whatever it takes, boy. Find her and get her admitted pronto to a good head hospital in Dallas. And do that real soon, or your dream will dry up quicker than cow piss on soft sand. Do I make myself clear, preacher?"

Dropping back into his office chair, Chuck said, "Perfectly, Buck. Perfectly."

CHAPTER TWENTY-NINE

The wind ripped their campfire, snapping the flames like signal banners caught in a gale before sending sparks soaring high to disappear amid the stars. Wrapped snugly in a quilt, Jan whimpered with her head bowed as Royal studied the pot of hot water. Once the surface bubbled to a slow boil, he emptied a handful of dried vegetables into the steam and then pared a long green onion, dropping each thin slice into the stew as he cut.

The noise of the spew returned her thoughts to the snake and to the men. She raised her head. "Royal, I once so wanted to die."

"Those men came precariously close to granting you that wish."

"What really happened?"

"They saw Juan Diego and that little saint scared them so badly they're still running."

"Will they come back?"

"Never into these mountains again. At this very moment, they're still scrambling down the west slope of the big Sierra, begging for their lives with every breath."

"Oh, I can't believe that."

"I understand."

After ladling a cup of stew into a tin cup, he handed it to her. "Here, have a taste of this delicious stew."

She didn't take it. "I can't eat. All I want is to go home."

"Obviously God wants you to live and to climb to the Thin Place."

She attempted to stand. "How do you know?"

Kneeling beside the fire, he placed the cup full of stew on a rock and poked the flame with a stick. "We were delivered."

"But what if whoever or whatever scared those men only meant to save you? You're the good one, not me. I'm a drunk and a selfish, miserable, materialistic spoiled brat."

He turned to smile at her. "Oh, let's not burden this gift with questions."

Royal leaned toward her with the cup and, dipping a spoon into its hot broth, he held the spoon high. After a moment to let it cool, he gently placed it to her taut lips.

She hesitated before opening her mouth. "What are you doing?"

"I'm doing my best to feed you."

"But I don't want to eat. I just want to get off this big ugly mountain as fast as humanly possible. I'm terrified of those awful men, and I'm afraid they will return tonight to kill me in my sleep, if, that is, I can sleep."

Urging the spoonful of stew toward her lips, he said, "I suspect God very much wants you to live through this night, because the Virgin herself has summoned you to the Thin Place, and we can easily make it there in the morning."

As she parted her lips, he rolled a second cooled spoonful of stew onto her tongue.

"Mm, this is really good." After she received a third and then a fourth sip, she closed her eyes and sighed, releasing tears that somehow escaped between sealed lids. "Royal, tell me about angels."

"Why?"

"That must be what those men saw, an avenging angel. And if I'm right about that, then I've been wrong about most everything all of my life."

"About God, we've probably all been wrong about many things."

"But why do we have to be wrong instead of right?"

"Because God insists upon being a mystery. So we do the best we can. We make our guesses, we love as best we know how, and we call it faith. But a big part of what we are so convinced we are so right about is likely very wrong. Perhaps God arranges it to be this way to keep us humble."

"What do we know about God?"

He leaned toward her. "Mercy and also mystery, of course."

She could read emphasis in his grin and frowned in reply. "That's all?"

Pulling his shoulders back, he said, "That's enough, don't you think?"

She turned her frown to a smile. "But whatever scared those men was not so very merciful."

Royal stood above her to stare into the fire.

She lifted her eyes to meet his. "Mercy is not scary, is it?"

Stretching his long arms toward the sky in a yawn, he said, "But only a loving heart can fear no judgment."

"Those men were terrified. Never in my life have I seen men so scared."

"They had reason to be afraid."

"But why would they be afraid if God is mercy."

"If you don't know God is mercy, you might believe God

to be about most anything, including vengeance."

"Do you believe God loves those awful men?"

Royal nodded.

"That makes absolutely no sense."

"You're right, it doesn't."

"I don't know if I believe in God or not. Right now I'm much too cold and much too scared to know what I believe or don't believe."

"Listen." Royal held up a forefinger. "A whippoorwill calling to its mate."

"What's so unusual about that?"

"Whippoorwills don't live at this altitude."

"You're a strange man, Royal, a very strange man indeed. Not an hour ago, seven of the most evil men on the planet attempted to kill us, and now you hear a bird that is not supposed to be up on this mountain with us."

"I am, indeed, strange. Sometimes I even go so far as to ask myself why. But I always come away from that question with the same answer."

"And what do you say?"

He laughed. "I usually say, 'I don't really know.'"

Jan pulled the quilt over her shoulders. "I'm confused and so scared."

"Please eat some more stew and then you can rest."

"I didn't realize I was so hungry, and never in my entire life have I been this tired."

He fed her until the cup was empty. Jan then laid her head upon his lap and soon grew drowsy as she listened once more to the whippoorwill.

What is a whippoorwill doing up here? More mystery! More

beautiful, exquisite mystery. God, I thank you for it. I so love it all.

"Amen," Royal said in response to the bird's song.

Jan closed her eyes and fell into a deep sleep.

CHAPTER THIRTY

The morning awakened Royal as it warmed him little by little into consciousness. Enough aware to focus his eyes, his initial thought was to scold himself for sleeping late. Yawning, he rolled lazily to one side to discover the woman gone.

My God, O my God, where is she? Was I wrong? Did they come back and take her?

Fumbling with the rumpled quilt, he discovered the stem of a cut rose bearing a single sharp thorn that pricked his finger as he picked it up.

She came in the night with Juan to lead Janet to the holy place. Oh my God, I slept through it and Janet is with her this moment.

Then again, had I not slept, she likely would not have come. After all, this journey has absolutely nothing to do with me. There is little else to do but wait and, of course, pray.

But the little burros are hungry and I must feed them.

He listened. Only a lonely wind swept up the big mountain, raising clouds of dust that turned the day's first light into a soft russet tone. He wondered if it might be too cold for her high above him at Pico del Carmen.

I hope Janet took a quilt, but then, Our Blessed Mother's warmth is always sufficient. She needs no quilt. In our Mother's presence, she needs absolutely nothing.

Royal laid the rose upon the ground, studied it once

more, and sighed. "Thank you."

He pulled from the pack what little kindling remained. Balancing one twig carefully upon the other, he formed a miniature structure that resembled a tiny-pitched roof hay barn filled with small pieces of kerosene-soaked cactus. As he lit the cactus with a match, he said, "Thank you."

A breeze fueled the incipient flame. The curious burros drew close to bump their muzzles against him.

Grateful for their company, he smiled at them. "In a minute, ladies. I will feed you in just a minute. First I must pray."

He dropped to his knees and folded his hands and prayed as the wind tore at the flames, whipped his long locks, and stung his face with grit.

CHAPTER THIRTY-ONE

The first clouds of the new morning to collect about the peak were, Royal suspected, little more than benign harbingers of a peace that would extend into the still distant evening. The desert's heat could quickly convince them to erupt into that violence indigenous to the high country where flashes of fire are punctuated by a deafening roar.

Royal stood up and stared toward the horizon. The threat of another storm invited more prayer. He dropped to his knees again as the two burros looked on.

Protect her, Juan. Keep her safe, O Blessed Mother. I beseech you in Jesus' holy name.

Mumbling an "Amen," he opened his eyes. The clouds had thickened and his thoughts slipped once more in the direction of worry.

God, I hope she is safe.

One cold drop of rain and then a second splashed against his furrowed brow, reducing prayer to distraction. No sooner had the rain been unleashed than all threats of fury dissipated and left a long benevolent rainbow joining the Sierra to Texas.

For the second time the sun blessed the morning with warmth as the winds tore asunder all remaining danger.

Thank God! O, thank you, Mary, Mother of God.

For hours he lay prostrate on a rock and mixed prayers with dreams as the burros pretended to graze. As he sensed the air turning cool, he opened his eyes and rolled to his back to discover a flock of gray clouds once more toying with the peak. A scattering of pebbles rolling down the trail toward where he lay distracted him from his attempt to read the clouds' intentions.

Sitting up abruptly, he said, "How are you?"

Jan dropped to her knees before where what little remained of the timid fire more sputtered than crackled. "Royal," she said in a throaty voice.

He stood. "Good afternoon, Janet."

"How long was I up there?" From a kneeling position she stretched out to lay face forward on the ground.

He crept to her side. "Are you okay?"

"Yes." She squeezed her eyes shut.

"Can I get you anything?"

"No." She rolled to her back and covered her eyes with her hands.

"Would you like to sleep?"

Jan smiled. "That would be wonderful."

"I will prepare your bedroll and you can sleep for as long as necessary. I will be here when you awaken."

Rolling to her side to face him, she said, "I've been so wrong. So terribly, terribly wrong." She opened tear-filled eyes to study his face.

"Now is not the time. Now is only the time for sleep. We'll have plenty of time later to talk. Oh, by the way, Juan left you the gift of a rose."

"I know."

"Sleep and when you awaken we will talk."

Again she rested her head upon her arm and closed her

eyes. Sleep came to her in moments bearing a dream. In it she knelt as she trembled before the visage of the Holy Woman, the Mother, her Mother, and at the same time, everybody's Mother, who only hours before had spoken to her the holy words she was now certain would remain forever written upon her heart.

As she slept, Royal sat upon a rock and gazed upon her face in child-like wonder as she uttered, "I will Mother, I promise I will do my best."

His wonder turned to joy as she said, "Amen."

Once more her breathing assumed the rhythm of sleep.

CHAPTER THIRTY-TWO

She slept and he tended the fire while he kept a vigil over her throughout the whole of the night. An hour before dawn, the mountains on the Texas side of the twisting river far below attracted a storm the way hatred is drawn by rumors to a lynching. Wild serpentine tongues of fire snapped at the bare rocky summits as thunder crashed, sending rumbles to shake the Sierra.

He knelt beside where she lay to study the single rose stem resting in her open hand. Once the first streams of light lit the big mountain, he said, "Janet, you must wake up. Another storm is not far off and this one appears dead-set on driving us down. We must go now."

He gathered what little food remained along with their scattered gear and stuffed everything into the packsaddle bags along with his rolled quilt. Turning to the burros he said, "Ladies, it is now your responsibility to carry this holy woman to safety. I'm counting on you not to sit down. And once we're off this mountain, there will be a bag of fresh grain, cold spring water, and two apples each awaiting you."

The burros twitched their long ears and sniffed the cold as he crept back to where she lay. "Janet, you must wake up."

As he attempted to lift her, she opened her eyes and smiled. "Was I only dreaming, Royal? Tell me, was it all a dream?"

"We must get off of this mountain. We cannot wait. You must—"

A deafening clap of thunder split the air and seemed to shake the ground as well.

"Where are we?"

"We're not one hundred yards from the Thin Place, and we must go down now."

Again, thunder rocked the mountain.

"Royal, I've been so wrong—"

"Not now."

"I don't want to leave. I'm not ready to go. There is so much more to learn, I must go back up there today."

"A storm is taking dead aim at us and if we remain up here, we'll be killed."

"But God will protect us."

"We are always to trust God, but never to tempt God, especially when we're up this high and vulnerable to the Sierra's bellicose inclinations." He slid his hands beneath her waist and shoulders and lifted her.

"What are you doing?"

"I'm carrying you to Jovita. She will take you down."

The storm hurled cold rain against them while he settled her in the packsaddle. "Let's go, Jovita. Let's get this sweet woman to safety."

"I can't do this!" Jan said from the rude saddle.

Royal attempted a smile. "Hold tight, we're going down."

Jan wrapped the rope about her hand. "Juan Diego will protect us. He delivered us from evil; he will keep us safe."

"Hold on real tight as though your life depended upon it, which it just might." He tugged on the frayed harness ropes and the burros followed him one slippery step at a time. She released her grip, slid out of the saddle, and landed face-first in a puddle.

Towering above where she lay, he leaned toward her. "Please stand up and climb back on."

As the rain whipped them without mercy, she sat upright and hollered, "I must pray, Royal. Then we can go down."

"Be reasonable! Now is definitely not the time for prayer!"

With her hands folded, she yelled into the raging storm, "Oh, God, forgive me."

The storm answered with yet another ear-splitting clap of thunder.

CHAPTER THIRTY-THREE

Buck Barrett spoke into the phone even before it could ring in Dallas. "Okay, preacher, I know you're there. This is Buck Barrett at the White House. For once show me you have some balls and pick up the damn phone"

The pastor's recorded eloquent voice answered with a polite request for the caller to leave a message.

Buck chomped on the end of an unlit cigar and scowled as he waited for the machine's beep. "Since you're refusing to pick up, let me tell you how it is, Chuck. This administration must hear you've satisfied your end of our bargain in exactly two weeks, or upon my recommendation, the President will name another spiritual advisor. We've got a very good, chapter- and verse-spouting, big-haired evangelical in the wings whose wife is a tea-totaling, card-carrying Republican. She, like all right-thinking Americans, regards liberals as Goddamn Bolsheviks."

His voice turned ice cold with threatening undertones. "I do hope I make myself clear. Feel free to call me with questions, although I cannot imagine why a man as smart as you claim to be would have any. I'm looking forward to hearing some splendid news from you in forty-eight hours or less regarding your precise plans to bring your wife around. Otherwise you'll read of the president's disappointment on the morning front page. Your signed declination letter is sitting right here on my desk at this moment, and all I have to do is hand it to the President."

Barrett held the receiver in front of his mouth like a microphone and spoke through clenched teeth. "Don't force my hand."

At home in Dallas, Chuck stared at the upstairs den's vaulted ceilings. "God, I hate that man."

CHAPTER THIRTY-FOUR

Young Oonie Garza peered through the old church's crumbling shutters at the big sedan rolling across the parched yard. He waited to see what sort of person would climb out.

Every citizen of Marathon—from the school district superintendent to the seasonal ranch hands—agreed Oonie was the most talented basketball player ever to don the Matadors' black and gold and arguably the finest athlete ever to come out of the Trans-Pecos.

Because his average remained consistently above ninety percent, the *Alpine Avalanche* covered his every move on the court and had crowned him a full-fledged phenomenon by the end of his freshman year, when he led all scorers in his district by more than twenty points per game. And his junior season, papers as far away as El Paso and Ft. Worth dispatched an army of sports writers to cover his feats, and in every small town west of the Pecos his was a household name, and he was regarded as a force to be reckoned with.

There was even consideration given to naming one of Marathon's dusty, unpaved streets after him, once he graduated. Opponents and fans alike initially had nicknamed him "Magic," but this troublesome moniker failed to gain traction in the predominantly Catholic town where superstition was frowned upon by the faithful.

Although his astounding athleticism was the talk of West Texas, Oonie was also known widely for another and far less glorious reason, which in polite conversation was termed "the problem." If the boy became overly stressed, whether by the challenges of multiplying fractions or assenting to the demands of his teacher to attempt nominal declensions in English, he would let out a sudden and unexpected blood-curdling squeal followed with the firing of a sizeable wad of saliva or mucous. When Oonie spat at some target, his aim proved as accurate as a deer hunter peering through a well-sighted scope.

The word in the streets was that when Oonie expectorated, he never missed, and to no one's surprise, there existed equal amounts of curiosity and concern regarding this bizarre behavior coming from an otherwise normal boy. The only real argument was whether he had been blessed by the angels or cursed by the Devil.

Ever since he began bringing glory to Marathon by making baskets at an unprecedented pace, the general consensus in town swung to the side of the angels. Some even believed the oft-told tale that Oonie had happened upon an angel in the desert who had blessed him with the gift of uncanny accuracy.

By the time he reached high school, someone in authority had attempted to convince Oonie's guardian, his Aunt Lita, to have the boy examined by a head doctor in El Paso. She, however, refused because Doagie Broadside, and a number of visiting college scouts had convinced her to subscribe to the angel theory. After all, believing her nephew had been blessed was less troubling than subjecting him to the methods of a science she knew nothing about and refused to trust. Furthermore, the idea not only satisfied her, but had also proved to be a source of enormous pride.

In the cafés and coffee bars as far away as Ft. Stockton and Van Horn, ranchers and townsfolk alike often swore over cheeseburgers and frosty mugs of cold beer that NBA scouts had been sighted prowling the dusty streets of tiny Marathon and hanging out in the school's unventilated and musty old field house. Some professional team, perhaps even the Spurs, were certain to sign the boy no more than sixty seconds after he graduated from Marathon High School.

But when it came to Oonie's physical well being, Aunt Lita called one hundred percent of the shots. Even with this control, she relied upon the advice of Esperanza Zuniga, who was the most respected *curandera* in all the Glass Mountains.

And following Esperanza's wise counsel, Aunt Lita struck an agreement with Oonie's teachers, Father O'Shea, and Coach Broadside for the boy to leave school and venture to the church's sanctuary to pray until the urge to spit subsided. This arrangement worked to the surprise of few and to the delight of Doagie Broadside.

Through the broken shutters covering the tall church windows, Oonie now studied the tall gaunt man who untangled his long legs from the car's front seat. The boy gave consideration to spitting, but just as quickly he decided against the urge, since he'd promised both God and Father O'Shea that he would never desecrate the church sanctuary with spittle. For Oonie, the house of God was definitely off limits.

Aunt Lita, and in far less measure Coach Broadside,

had taught him to respect the sacred, and therefore, he resorted to prayer each time the compulsion to spit came over him.

Oonie held his breath as the tall man staggered one halting step at a time toward the church's red door. Oonie backed away from the window. Pressing his shoulders against the wall, he wondered if this man had been shot. He'd once witnessed a hunter die of buckshot wounds on the frozen muddy bed of a pickup before the horrified shooter could make it to the emergency room in Alpine.

As far as Oonie was concerned, this scary staggering stranger looked every bit as wounded as the man he'd seen drawing his last breath. His dying whimper caused Oonie to spit so frantically that no more saliva would well up in his mouth for a full twenty-four hours.

As the doorknob turned with a long squeaking sound, Oonie slipped behind the door and held his breath. He squeezed his eyes shut, concentrating on his promise to God never to spit in this or in any church.

"Anyone in here?" said the stranger.

The warped floorboards creaked beneath the man's weight. Oonie opened his eyes wide enough to watch him through the crack in the half-open door. The intruder pulled a blue-steel revolver from a shoulder holster concealed beneath a charcoal colored suit coat.

The man's quick yank on the door revealed the tall skinny boy glued to the wall like a movie poster caricaturing shock. The kid grimaced as he stretched both hands high above his head and stared with wide eyes straight into the stranger's opaque silver shades. Oonie rolled a juicy wad of spit back and forth in his mouth.

"Who the hell are you?" said the stranger.

"Oonie. Oonie Garza, sir."

Cautiously returning his weapon to the holster, the man said, "Is there a priest that goes with this dump?"

"Yes sir, there is, but he's not here."

"Who are you, the handyman?"

"I'm a high school student. I just come here to pray when I feel the need."

"Will the priest be in any time soon?"

"I can't say, sir. His schedule is unpredictable."

Bracing his weight on the rear pew, the stranger said between hacking coughs, "Kid, is there a drugstore in this town?"

"The closest store is in Alpine. Forty miles, sir."

"Which direction?"

"West."

"Did a woman from Dallas happen by here in the last day or so?"

"No one comes to this church but the people who worship on Sunday. We seldom have visitors, sir."

The man slumped into the pew where he struggled to sit. He rolled to his back and lay flat and still with his face pointed toward the thick spider webs draping the rafters like bunting. "Kid, I'm hurting. Is there a doctor anywhere close by?"

"Only in Alpine, but we do have Esperanza and she is as good as a doctor. She's our *curandera*."

"She's a what?"

"A *curandera*. She heals by faith."

"I got hit by a swarm of bees down on the border a couple days back, and I can barely see. I'm so swollen and hot I think I must be dying."

The man pulled out his money clip and peeled off some bills. "Listen, kid, I'll give you $50 if you'll drive to the drugstore in Alpine or wherever it is and ask the pharmacist to sell you something for bee stings. If he needs a prescription, I'll give you another hundred to slip him. I never yet met a pharmacist who wouldn't take a bribe. But if you run off with my money, I'll track you down, kid, and kill you and then your mother. Comprende?"

"I can't leave town during school, mister, but I can drive you to Esperanza's house. She has all sorts of medicines and she will cure you. She is the best, sir. My Aunt Lita says she is even better than a city doctor and I believe her. I've seen Esperanza heal people of all kinds of diseases, even rattlesnake bites."

"Okay, take me to this witch doctor."

"Her powerful poultices will make you well. She is of God, sir. Even Father O'Shea says she is sanctified."

"Take me, kid, before I die in this stinking church."

"If you can stand, sir," Oonie said, "I will hold you up and walk you to the car."

As the man attempted to stand, his sunshades slipped off his nose and dropped to the floor. Oonie gasped. This man's eyes were more swollen than even those of a prizefighter he'd once witnessed lose a bout in the border village of Santa Elena on the Mexican side.

One slow step at a time, Oonie half dragged the man to the car. Firing the engine, he turned to the stranger who lay with his head against the door and wheezed. "You will be okay, sir. Esperanza will see to it."

Chapter Thirty-Five

A coal oil lamp flickered in a window as the burros clopped past the small adobe house and into the sleepy village. They stopped at the rusty wire fence separating Boquillas from the vast wilderness of the Sierra del Carmen.

Royal could scarcely place one heavy foot in front of the other. Yet with every pause, the burros nudged him on with their muzzles. Josephina and Jovita snorted in anticipation of their happy rendezvous with fresh hay, grain, apples and an endless supply of cold spring water.

Slipping in and out of consciousness, Jan rocked in the packsaddle with each step the burro took. For the past hour, she had awakened time and again, but only long enough to inquire as to their whereabouts.

The priest did his best to answer, although exhaustion interfered with any accurate assessment. What few words he did manage proved useless because, even before he could hazard a guess, sleep would overtake her. And yet, as if by a miracle, she clung to the slack in the diamond hitch that bound the packsaddle to the animal.

At the village horse corral, Royal came to a sudden stop. Both burros plowed into his back and knocked him face-first into a puddle. He rolled over and forced a grin as his eyes rested upon the woman now tottering in the saddle.

"We're home, Janet," he said with his head half submerged

in muddy water.

With eyes closed, she slid out of the saddle and braced herself against Jovita's flank. Attempting a smile that would not come, she dropped to her knees and landed next to the priest, whose mud-caked face wore a mindless grin.

"Are you okay?" he said.

Rolling to her back she raised her head a few inches. "Royal, I must go home."

"But we are home."

"My home is in Dallas with my husband. I must go there as soon as possible to tell him what Our Blessed Mother would have him know. I cannot waste time. What I've been given to say is important, much too important for me to lie here in the mud."

Rolling over, she staggered halfway to her feet. With her auburn hair matted against her head and her face caked in clay, she balanced on rubbery legs before tumbling forward. As she lay still in the mud she said, "I must return, but I can't. I'm exhausted. I've never in my life been so used up. Never!"

Jan's voice turned to a whisper. "O, Mother of God, give me courage. Please, Mother of God, give me the strength required. I'm too tired to go back. Much, much too tired, too weak, too hungry, too everything."

CHAPTER THIRTY-SIX

Peering through a tear in her screen door, Esperanza Zuniga, the town's *curandera*, pressed her grandmother's rosary beads against her thin, moist lips. She gave thought to whispering a prayer with a solemnity reserved for impending danger.

Her mother had long ago bequeathed the words she uttered to ward off dark spirits, and they had always proven reliable. For more than five decades, Esperanza had healed those who came to her, casting out dark spirits while protecting her own soul, and yet she could recall offering this prayer less than half a dozen times in all those years.

Now sensing danger, she bowed her head behind the torn screen door and prayed:

"Protect us; we are frail.

Do for us what we cannot do for ourselves.

Keep us in the light and safe from the coming evil.

We ask this in the name of our Savior, Jesus. Amen."

She sighed as she watched Oonie exit a big car she did not recognize. "I pray for our most blessed one, Lord. Protect this precious child. He cannot know he brings evil into this house. Forgive him, for he knows not what he does, and strengthen my heart to do now what must be done. Amen."

Esperanza searched for clues as the tall agile boy pulled

open the passenger door. He stooped to drape over his shoulder a lanky semi-conscious man.

"Deliver us from evil," she prayed through the beads.

Spotting her silhouette in the screen, Oonie yelled from the yard, "Esperanza, I'm bringing you a sick man. Bees stung him and he is very hot. His eyes are swollen shut."

She opened the screen wide as the boy more dragged than walked the man into the front room and to a tattered sofa where he carefully rested the stranger's limp body. Esperanza knelt beside him to examine his swollen eyes. Oonie lifted the man's long thin legs and propped them upon the sofa's arm.

"Remove his shoes," she said. "This man is sick, Oonie. Both his body and his soul are poisoned."

Placing her fingers to the man's brow, she said, "His fever is high, at least 104."

Oonie stood. "I must get back to school. I was at the church praying when this stranger drove up. He came into the church, Esperanza, but I don't know why. He said he was sick and asked me to drive to Alpine to buy medicine. When I told him I could not, he collapsed in a pew, so I did the only thing I could. I brought him here."

"You did well, Oonie."

"But why did he come to the church?"

"Darkness is sometimes attracted to the light."

Oonie frowned.

"It's well that you don't understand. You are young and still innocent, greatly blessed by the angels. There is no darkness in you and your heart remains pure. Now get on back to school and learn your lessons well. Tell no one of this man. I will heal him of his wounds, but I must leave his soul to God. I have no power to deliver him from evil. Only God can do that and I pray he will."

"Is he dangerous?"

"Evil is always dangerous. But you need not worry, Oonie. I will be safe, and you and all of us will be safe. But tell no one of this man. Do you understand?"

"I think so, Esperanza. But why can't I tell the principal? He would call the sheriff in Alpine and have this man arrested."

"This man is much too dangerous for us to speak a word of him to anyone. You must trust me and tell no one. Do you promise?"

"Okay, I promise. But are you sure you're going to be safe with this man in your house?"

She smiled. "I am certain of it, child. Now return to school."

The screen door slammed behind him as the boy's agile feet hit the front porch. He leaped into the yard. "Be careful, Esperanza," he yelled as he dashed off.

Esperanza returned to the man lying on the sofa. With deft fingers, she searched beneath the man's jacket until she discovered the revolver stuffed snugly in its leather holster. She removed the weapon and carried it across the worn linoleum floor where she deposited it in the highest drawer of an ancient pie safe.

His moan drew her close. Standing only inches from his swollen face, she said, "Sir, you can rest now. I will heal you of your wounds and I will pray to God for you. Only God can heal your soul."

The stranger lifted his head no more than half an inch. "Where am I?"

Ignoring the question, she prayed in silence as she hovered like a cloud above where he lay.

Deliver us from evil. O most holy One, please deliver us from evil. Deliver us...

CHAPTER THIRTY-SEVEN

As streaks of new sunlight streamed through a dingy window, the stranger opened his eyes, blinked, and attempted to lift his swollen head from the pillow. Dizziness distracted him, but only for a moment, from the pounding ache inside his head. He lay sprawled on a sofa with both legs dangling off one arm.

"God, where am I?" he said across dry lips. He squeezed his eyes so tightly shut he feared he might slip once more into unconsciousness.

An old woman knelt before him. "Sir, you are in God's house."

He tried to focus, but with each attempt the room spun in wild patterns. He snapped his eyelids shut and blinked them open again. This time he spied a watermark on the ceiling in the shape of an anvil. Fixing his gaze on it, he said, "Who the hell are you, old woman? And where am I?"

"My name is Esperanza and you are in God's house."

"How did I get here?"

"Had a kind soul not brought you here yesterday, you would have died. You are sick, sir. I remained with you through the whole of the night. It is morning and the fever has broken. You will be well soon, but until you're strong, you must rest."

"What are you, some kind of doctor?"

"I heal by faith, sir."

"I only have faith in my snub-nose thirty-eight." Fumbling with his empty holster still strapped to his shoulder, he jerked his head up but again the dizziness returned him to the pillow. "Where is the gun, bitch?"

"Put away, sir. No guns are allowed in this house."

Searching his forehead with his fingers, he discovered what felt like an oversized spongy teabag. Gripping it, tepid streams of water dripped upon his face. "What is this?"

"A poultice, sir. It has absorbed your fever."

He flung it to the wall and forced a scream, "God, what the hell have you done to me? I don't believe in witchdoctors."

"It is nothing more than pure mineral water from the springs at Balmorhea and a blend of desert herbs. It's harmless to your eyes and yet it works miracles with fever. Your fever has broken, sir."

"How is that possible?"

"I read fever with my fingers. I was up with you throughout the night. For thirty minutes of every hour, I rubbed a raw egg gently against your forehead, and then returned the poultice for the remaining thirty minutes. The egg and the poultice absorbed your fever."

"Woman, help me stand. I need to get on my feet and I want my damn gun back. No argument. I'd prefer not to kill you. Understand?"

"You are not well enough to travel today, sir. I will return the gun when you are strong enough to go."

He coughed with such violence his half-raised head fell back hard against the pillow. "Listen, old woman, whatever your name is, I don't want to have to hurt you. Give me the gun and I'll be on my way."

Again he tried to stand, but his legs buckled and he tumbled face-first against the linoleum with a jarring thud. "Now give me the damn gun, bitch," he mumbled.

Esperanza pressed the prayer beads to her lips. "The gun is put safely away until you are able to leave. You are in God's holy place, and you and I will both be safe for as long as you are here. I will pray for your soul. I will pray for you to give up the evil you intend."

From the floor he said, "Go get the gun, old woman. Give me the damn gun."

"Do your best to sit up, sir, and I will help you back to lie down on the sofa."

He no longer had the strength to resist and he allowed her to take him by one arm and hand and raise him from the floor. Clinging to her, he tottered to the sofa and collapsed.

CHAPTER THIRTY-EIGHT

The intrusive buzz of the office intercom startled Chuck. He picked up the receiver while concentrating on not permitting any hint of annoyance to leech into his tone to tarnish the unparalleled successful image he knew he must maintain.

In his most recent bestseller, he'd characterized every expression less than patient as an indicting, not to mention embarrassing, sign of spiritual immaturity. His theory required a discipline he was frequently less than certain he felt up to, and yet he maintained that no negative feelings should ever be expressed unless first tempered by at the least a half hour of prayer.

This was a rigor he knew he must keep, no matter the intensity of any personal challenges. He sometimes wondered if Satan—whose existence he refused to acknowledge—might be real and had in secret arranged, even before creation, for Jan to be in his life to defeat him.

"Yes, Margaret, what is it?" he said as cheerfully as he could manage.

"Oh my God, Dr. Love, this is all so exciting I can hardly breathe. The President's secretary, Helen Jensen-Wade, is on the other line and wants to speak to you. Never in a million years did I think I'd take a call from the White House."

"Thank you, I'll take it." He punched a button on his

phone. "Hello, this is Dr. Love."

"This is Helen Jensen-Wade, the President's appointment secretary. The President has requested you return to Washington as soon as possible to speak with you in person here at the White House. What shall I tell him, sir?"

"Uh… Ms., Ms.? Excuse me, but what did you say your name is?"

She repeated her name.

"Do you know what this is about?"

"No, sir, I do not."

God, I wonder what old Buck is up to now. Oh how, I hate this.

No, that's not right. It's Jan I hate. Why does it have to be this way? A man should be able to count on his wife's full support.

"Well, Ms. Jensen-Wade, I will have to secure tickets."

"We've taken the liberty of doing that for you, sir. You are scheduled to depart DFW tomorrow at 6:00 a.m. on American Airlines flight 299 and you will arrive at Reagan at 9:45 eastern. The President will have a limousine waiting to take you directly to the White House. You can rest for a couple of hours here before meeting with the President for what I understand will be a private lunch."

"Uh, Ms. Jensen-Wade, will other members of the president's staff be present?"

"I'm only authorized to arrange the appointment. Thank you, sir. I will tell the President to expect you tomorrow. Have a good flight."

They hung up.

God, I hate Buck Barrett. I'll bet every penny I have he's behind this command performance and that means I'm being set up to be humiliated even before I touch down in D.C. I loathe that man. I truly do.

That little girl I met at the White House is right. Buck Barrett is evil. Why does it have to be this way? Why in God's name does it have to be so hard?

I despise Jan. God help me, I really do hate my wife.

CHAPTER THIRTY-NINE

The gaunt man's own snoring stirred him awake and into grogginess. He languished until an ancient memory attacked with a pain he had long striven to outrun.

He jerked his body and cried out like the terrified boy his father had once so savagely beaten. Blinking his eyes, he wondered how to defend against the dark memories of the horror that defined his childhood. Yet what concerned him even more was that, try as he might, he could not locate the familiar rancor that most days filled his heart and awaited his violent expression.

As his eyes cleared, he made out the silhouette of the old woman hovering above him like a cloud. But because rage now strangely eluded him, he did the best he could with a half-hearted growl. He was still much too weak and far too addled to feel embarrassed, and yet the fact troubled him.

He cleared his throat. "Who are you?

"My name is Esperanza, sir."

Something is wrong, very wrong! I can't think straight.

"Oh, you're the witchdoctor who took my gun. Old woman, I need it back."

She raised the weapon for him to see. "Here it is, sir, as I promised. You are now strong enough to travel."

As he sat up, the room spun, forcing his head back onto the pillow.

What is happening? That woman did something to me. My thinking is not right, not at all right. Where is the rage?

"Please be patient, sir. And if you will allow me to help you sit for a bit on the edge of this sofa, your balance will return. You are recovered. Your fever broke more than twenty-four hours ago, which means the poison has been drawn. Your strength will return because prayer has invoked the Spirit."

With his head drooping like a dead sunflower, he mumbled, "I don't believe in superstition."

"Please allow me to assist you so your confidence will return. If you try little by little to sit up, there will be no dizziness."

He did as she suggested and was relieved to discover the haze lifting. "How long have I been here?"

"Three days."

"When did I last eat?"

"I nourished your soul with prayer and your body with goat-cheese soup and herbal tea. You were conscious enough to swallow, thank God. And I carried your pans."

"My pans? What pans?"

"Your bed pans, sir."

"Why?"

She said nothing.

Carried my bedpans? She can't be in her right mind. This old woman doesn't know me. Why in God's name would she do that? She owes me absolutely nothing!

"God, I feel like I've returned from the dead. How long did you say I've been here?"

"You were here three days and you were close to death, sir. God delivered you."

Delivered me? What the hell are you talking about, old woman?

"How much money do you want?" he said as he rammed the revolver into its holster.

"I want nothing, sir." The woman returned the wallet to his inside coat pocket.

What's her angle?

Retrieving the wallet, he said, "Here, take this." He withdrew several bills. "You let me sleep off the effects of the bee attack. What I recall of it, I was in bad shape. I really don't remember much, but I believe you when you say you fed me, so I owe you."

He shook the money at her like a rag. "Here are five one hundreds. I consider that more than fair and should leave you with nothing to complain about and also with no incentive to tell anyone anything. Go buy yourself something. This room could use a color TV. While you're at it, buy yourself a dish and watch CNN like the rest of this unhappy world."

"I want nothing, sir."

"Take it, ma'am, and if you tell a living soul I was here, I'm coming back to do something, but for the life of me I don't know what I would do. But maybe I would do something, but I can't imagine what that something might be."

I can't hurt this woman. Killing is what I do. God, what is wrong with me?

She nodded.

He rose to stand and was surprised by his strength.

Why am I smiling?

"Where's the nearest place to grab some breakfast? I could do with some strong coffee."

"There is a café on our main street across from the hotel,

sir. And the hotel has a restaurant. If you care to travel to Alpine, you will find even more choices."

"God, I must look like the dead. I haven't shaved in days and my chin itches. I stink and my teeth feel like they're wearing angora." His stride across the linoleum reverberated throughout the tiny house like each step was a clap of thunder.

Pushing open the screen door with his shoulder, he spied a rooster strutting across the parched front yard. He pulled the revolver from the holster, gripped the gun's butt with both hands until his knuckles turned white, and aimed. And then surprised himself by pointing the gun up to fire into the sky.

Grinning, he placed the silver lenses again over his eyes. "Now, old woman, we're even. You were kind to me and, in exchange, I spared your rooster."

She watched as the panicked rooster scurried in a wide zigzag arc until it reached the dirt street. It ran in full circles, crowing the vivid details of its near brush with a bullet.

Before the screen door could slap shut, every dog in Marathon filled the hot morning with howls. The gaunt man scratched his head in bewilderment.

I could have easily killed that rooster. It was an easy shot. What the hell is wrong with me?

CHAPTER FORTY

"Welcome back to the White House, Chuck, my boy," said the President. "I appreciate you coming back up here on such unreasonably short notice. This trip is a tremendous imposition and I am, without question, taking advantage of your famous generosity."

Chuck scanned the intimate dining room and spied only one man, a short dark fellow he'd never met, following the President toward a table set for two replete with china bearing the presidential seal. This man was dressed in a white chef's frock, tall bubble hat, navy and white striped pants and spotless white shoes. Chuck smiled and nodded at the man before sighing as he considered the possibility he might escape Barrett's abuse on this trip.

"Chuck, please allow me introduce you to Oscar Trevino, White House chef. I discovered this fellow wasting his considerable talent in the only five-star hotel in Laredo and brought him with me as a part of our staff. The First Lady adores his interior Mexican dishes. The man is an artist, and I wanted him to meet you because he tells me he's one of your biggest fans."

"It's an honor, Mr. Trevino."

"Likewise, Dr. Love. I never miss your broadcast out of Dallas. No matter what, I make it home every Thursday night by 8:00 to catch your program, and I have read all of your

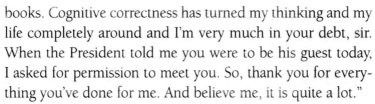

books. Cognitive correctness has turned my thinking and my life completely around and I'm very much in your debt, sir. When the President told me you were to be his guest today, I asked for permission to meet you. So, thank you for everything you've done for me. And believe me, it is quite a lot."

"Well, Mr. Trevino, I don't know what to say except that you humble me."

With a bow, the chef smiled as he quickly exited the room, leaving the door open.

The President beamed at Chuck and pointed to an empty chair. "Fine man, that Mexican. We're most fond of him here and that fellow can definitely work magic in the kitchen."

The President surprised Chuck by strolling toward a window facing south. Chuck waited for him to move toward the table.

"Today I've ordered my favorite snow crab salad, which is a far cry from his specialty, but at the moment the First Lady is in Tennessee campaigning with the Vice President and his wife. She doesn't much cotton to snow crab salad. Off the record, I think snow crabs and crude oil the only good things ever to come out of Alaska." He shook his head. "Forbiddingly cold country that state, beautiful, and thank God most of it still pristine, but much, much too cold for my arthritis."

He waved Chuck to a seat at the table.

"I'll join the First Lady for dinner tonight and campaign with her and the Vice President all weekend, but I had a bit of business to attend to here and I wanted some alone time with you for a heart-to-heart talk."

He stepped toward the table. "Please sit down, and would you be so kind as to say a prayer before we eat?"

Bowing his head, Chuck felt beads of perspiration on his forehead. He wondered how to wipe it discreetly. "Lord, we give thanks for this great President, your servant and our nation's leader, and we give thanks for this great republic, and we give thanks for this wonderful food and for the hands that prepared it. And may America be forever blessed. Amen."

"Good prayer, Chuck, brief, straight to the point and most righteous. Thank you, sir."

Raising his voice to speak through the open door, the President called, "Oscar, whenever you're ready with that salad, I'm more than ready."

He grinned at Chuck. "I'm as hungry as a big old she-bear coming out of her hibernation hole. The First Lady thinks that statement is crude, so I only use it when she's not within hearing distance. Me? I can't see anything wrong with it."

Oscar Trevino stepped into the room balancing two large china salad bowls on a silver tray, each also bearing the presidential seal. "Enjoy, Mr. President and Dr. Love."

The President turned toward the chef, giving Chuck an opportunity to wipe his brow with the linen napkin. "Thank you, Oscar. And if you would be so kind, please close that door on your way out."

The chef nodded and left the room.

"Chuck, tell me, how's the wife?"

"Fine, Mr. President. Oh, she's just… just fine, sir."

"Good, glad to hear it. Buck informed me just yesterday, I believe it was, she has been a bit under the weather as of late. Depression, I think. This First Lady was depressed for a full month after the birth of our first son. The docs know far more what to do about it now than they did fifty years ago.

Her doctor told her to buck up and get over it and that was pretty much it. In time, the cloud lifted, thank God."

Chuck hummed and raised his spoon high, as if offering a salute.

"Mm, this salad is tasty," said the President

"Oh, she's fine now, Mr. President. She's just fine. Thank you for inquiring. But she is quite well, sir, I assure you."

"I'll apprise Buck of her improved health before I take off for Tennessee this afternoon. Relieved to hear it. I've always been fond of Jan. She's a good one, Chuck, a real keeper."

That weasel. I swear I hate Barrett.

"Chuck, this room is secure. Would you believe that we have the FBI sweep the entire White House every day looking for electronic bugs?"

"No one at this level of government can be too careful, sir."

"It's all a real shame, but it's true. Sadly, this is the paranoid world we live in." He slapped his palms together and rubbed them against each other. "But enough about the gloom and doom realities of humanity's collective global hysteria. I invited you here to share with you two pieces of highly sensitive information, and then I have a question for you. Against the wishes of Barrett—who is quite capable, if not a mite paranoid himself—what I am to share with you is top secret. I know I can trust you with this."

Chuck nodded.

"Good, son. Good. Now, to begin with, even the Democrats' pollsters say—off the record of course—I am to win the election and more than likely by a landslide. That's the first point. We can't afford to say this publicly, of course, lest we be accused of political hubris, which for any politician from a justice-of-the-peace on up is the proverbial kiss of death."

He tossed his unfolded napkin on top of his plate. "The media makes certain the American people never forget Dewey's stunning upset defeat by Truman. And in a way, that's a good thing. Polls are just polls and the only vote that counts is the one on Election Day."

"I am certain you will win, Mr. President."

The President grinned and pushed his chair back from the table. "Now to the second and more important point: I will announce your appointment on January 31st. On Sunday evening, February 28th, you and I will appear in this office on a national television broadcast and, following what will be my surprise declaration of war against The Democratic Peoples Republic of Korea, you will read a prepared speech word-for-word on the teleprompter, composed by one of our most senior writers. And this speech will inform the American people of the heaven-sent revelation that God Almighty would have this administration liberate the long-suffering people of North Korea. March 1st is Independence Day in Korea, although it has not been celebrated in the North since the Communists took power after World War II."

His expression turned serious. "Nevertheless, on March 1st, 1919, Korea won its independence from the iron-grip of Japanese colonialism and this day is the South's biggest celebration and this will be our strike date. I will announce this attack with twenty-four hours' advance notice so that we might warn civilians to get out of Pyongyang while there is still time. Your job is to apprise the American people that this pre-emptive strike is not only blessed by heaven, but even more, mandated by God Almighty. Kim Jong Un can run, but he can't hide. Not from this bomb."

"Yes, Mr. President, from our previous discussion of this issue I deduced North Korea would be the target. I am proud to be a part of this courageous, and may I say, righteous decision, Mr. President."

Chuck detected a certain unctuous tone in his own voice, but chose to ignore it. "And I will gladly read whatever it is the assigned White House writer would have me say, sir. I believe very strongly that the liberation of our fellow human beings is invariably God's will, and if we liberate a people, we can be certain we are doing God's will."

"I'm so glad to hear you say that, Chuck. And I'm not at all surprised, but I am most comforted by your support of what has been the most trying decision of my political life. More comforted by your agreement than anyone else's, because I know you to be a man of God, with a direct line to heaven. But I do have a question that is a bit more personal in nature, and if you will be so kind to as to allow me to impose it upon you, sir, I'd be most obliged."

"Yes sir, Mr. President, go right ahead. To be of any service to you sir, is a great privilege." Feeling perspiration beading on his brow, Chuck wiped his forehead with his cloth napkin.

"Our people at the Pentagon have reevaluated their previous estimates, which are the ones we shared with you in our earlier meeting. You see, the bomb we plan to use to take out Kim Jong Un's government is a bit more lethal than first supposed. Instead of an estimated 10,000 dead North Koreans, the new number more closely approximates 50,000. Now, Chuck, I don't need to tell you that such a number is not only politically risky but also morally troublesome."

"Sir, that is a staggering number—"

"Yes, it is. So here's my question: what if we drop this bomb and, say, we kill 50,000 North Koreans? What happens to my soul?"

"I don't think I understand."

"Let me be frank. It's no secret that I have heart disease. I'm seventy years old, son, old enough to be your daddy. The docs tell me I'm fit enough for a man my age, in the sense the heart disease is under control. I'll very likely make four more years, but if I don't, I have complete confidence in the Vice President so the country will be fine. He's a very good man and he could take over today without this administration missing a beat."

The President stood and returned to the window. "But that's not the issue. No, the issue is my soul. What happens to my soul if I order the killing of God only knows how many thousands of human beings? Does my eternal soul go to heaven or do I spend an eternity burning in hell? That is my question Chuck."

"Sir, your soul is safe with God. You have been baptized and you believe Jesus is Lord, and even before you became our governor you were active in your church. And I've heard you say many times you're a born-again Christian. All-born again Christians are saved. God keeps promises, so you have nothing to worry about."

The President turned toward Chuck and seemed about to speak.

"If I may continue, sir?" said Chuck.

The President nodded.

"What in theology we term the "Just War Theory" originated with St. Augustine, who believed it was the obligation of a nation's leader to maintain peace. Augustine said, and I quote, 'A just war is wont to be described as one that avenges wrongs such as when a nation or state has to be punished...' Sir, predicated upon this foundation, your decision to liberate the North Koreans from a tyrannical and evil leader is most sound and I can assure you is also blessed by heaven."

"That's comforting to hear."

"Thomas Aquinas later developed three necessary criteria for a war to be viewed as just: authorized authority, just cause, and rightful intention. In his Letter to the Church at Rome, the Apostle Paul writes and again I quote, 'For he, (meaning the head of any state) is God's servant for your good.' Sir, you have divine authority, liberation is always a just cause, and your intentions are to make the world a safer place."

The President's beaming smile inspired Chuck to continue. "As I recall my American history, it was soon after his Second Inaugural Address that Abraham Lincoln began to view himself as God's instrument for saving the union and for liberating the slaves."

Emboldened to stand beside the Chief Executive, Chuck said, "Sir, war is an evil, but it is also at times necessary in this fallen world and I would say to you with all due respect that you have been appointed by God to be His instrument in this dark and dangerous age."

"Chuck, when we visited a few days back, I sensed your reticence regarding this venture. Have you changed your mind?"

"I have indeed. I've prayed about this thing and I now

agree one hundred percent with you and your advisors, un-swervingly on the side of liberating brothers and sisters from the yoke of tyranny. Like you, sir, I hate the thought of killing anyone, but I also know that when it comes to liberating a whole people, killing enemy combatants is necessary. Simply put, the end does in this situation indeed justify the means."

"So you believe that I'm on safe ground with God."

Chuck smiled. "I don't know of anyone who is more consistent with God's will than you, Mr. President. You are the exemplar of what it means to follow our Lord, Jesus, and you are by far the most faithful Christian to inhabit the White House since Abraham Lincoln. I'm most humbled to stand by you on this decision and I promise to stay by your side with every other issue that might challenge this administration."

As he spoke, Chuck bowed his head. "I cannot adequate-ly convey to you, sir, what a privilege it will be to serve you and this great nation of ours. We're on the side of the angels, Mr. President. I am absolutely convinced of it."

"My God, son, I'm so glad we had this chat. I can't tell you how I've worried over this matter. I want to do the right thing, but not at the expense of my own soul."

Chuck raised his eyes to look the other man squarely in the face. "God not only blesses you, Mr. President, God also blesses every plan for liberation. Thank God for political leaders with the moral courage to liberate the oppressed."

The President stepped toward Chuck, placed his hands upon the preacher's shoulders, and drew him close. "Chuck, my boy, I feel so much better, like a load's been removed from my old arthritic shoulders. I can't thank you enough, son."

"You're most welcome, Mr. President."

"Now how about some dessert, son? Oscar whips up the best strawberry cheesecake on the planet." He returned to the table and snatched his used napkin from the plate. "My internist, with no small amount of input from the First Lady, forbids me from partaking of this delectable treat, but the good doctor is not here either, so what do you say we share a taste of heaven?"

"Delighted, Mr. President. Thank you, sir."

"No, thank *you*, Chuck. Thank you. I cannot tell you how much better I feel."

The President pushed a button under the table, and within seconds Oscar opened the door. "Dr. Love and I would like a slice, no, make that a wedge, of that cheesecake you tempted me with earlier. And Oscar, I know I can trust you to prevaricate, if necessary, on my behalf if the First Lady should inquire of you regarding this harmless little indiscretion."

"Of course, Mr. President. I will consider it a state secret. My lips are sealed."

"Now, Chuck, do you see why I so value this fine patriot? And I know I can trust you never to tell a soul that he is in this country illegally."

Chuck's eyes widened as he watched Oscar retreat through the open door.

CHAPTER FORTY-ONE

"Royal, where are you?" Jan cried.

A breeze ushering a chill through the empty window blew against her face.

I am so sore. I don't think I'll ever get out of this bed.

"Royal," she cried again in a weaker voice.

Nearby dogs barked and, as their racket ceased, more breezes arrived to rock the mesquite branches above until they scratched like rambunctious cats against the hut's flat roof.

Where is he? Was it all a dream? No, of course not. I was there. I heard her speak to me. I met her servant Juan.

I must get back across the river and drive straight to Dallas. O God, give me strength.

"Good morning, Janet," Royal said grinning through the window.

How can he look that rested when I'm so sore and used up?

"What time is it?" Jan said.

"Since I don't own a watch, I can't tell you the precise hour, however, the sun hasn't even been up long enough to warm the morning. Winter's first real chill hijacked a stray breeze and bit so hard I was inspired only a few minutes ago to stop in mid-stride to sing the Doxology to this glorious new season. And not surprisingly, my solo invited every dog within a mile radius to join in. Together we awakened the entire village, but surely it's time for every soul in Boquillas to arise and celebrate the beauty of this new morning. I do love our gentle winters. Yesterday's storm is done with us and this new day promises to be gorgeous."

Royal stretched both arms high over his head and grinned. "Tell me, how do you feel?" he said as he finished yawning.

Ignoring his question, she said, "Royal, I must get back to Dallas at once."

"Whoa, slow down. You must first rest and then pray. You will return, but not today or anytime in the next few days, because the Spirit's work always takes time, in fact a good bit of time. Hurry can never be the Spirit's way."

Struggling to free herself from the quilts, she said, "But you don't understand. I absolutely must go."

Royal changed his grin into a knowing smile. "Oh, but I do understand all too well because, until I came here, I'd been in a hurry all of my life. What did I have to show for it but one self-orchestrated defeat after another? Please trust me on this. Hurry is never God's way."

Jan scowled and threw her head back against the rude pillow. "But you didn't hear the words Mary spoke and you didn't see what I saw. As faithful and as good as you are, you cannot possibly know what at this very minute is burning a hole in my soul. Royal, I respect you more than anyone I've ever met and I think I know what it means to love you, but *now* is not the time for caution. I absolutely must return to Dallas today. Please understand I intend no disrespect, it's just that I know the urgency of her message. I've been given an enormous responsibility, and that is what terrifies me. If I mess this thing up, people will suffer and possibly even die."

Resting in the empty window with his boots on the floor, Royal gave her a disarming smile, "What have you been instructed to do?"

"I don't know where to begin or even who to tell what it is I learned on the mountain, but I do know I must do something. Anything! Believe me, I'll pray on the drive to Dallas and by the time I get back, I'm sure I'll know. You must trust me, just as Mary entrusted her sacred words to me. But I don't have a specific plan, at least not at the moment. Please tell me you understand and give me your word you will support me."

He stood and maintained what she hoped might be a smile signaling flexibility. He braced his back against the adobe wall before sliding slowly to the floor, then faced her eye-to-eye while she remained in the bed, tangled in quilts and two sheets.

Lifting his gaze to the ceiling, he spoke so softly she could scarcely hear him. "Janet, impulsivity is dangerous and it is my biggest flaw. Look at me—I am in exile for the remainder of my life. Yes, I've discovered joy here on this side of the river among these people, but I cannot in good conscience recommend impulsivity."

"But I'm not being impulsive," she yelled, "I'm being faithful! I'm doing what I was told to do. You of all people should understand. After all, you took me up there. Even today I don't know why I consented to go, but I'm very thankful I did, because what I learned is so important that it must be shared as soon as I have permission. This is all very urgent, and I cannot waste a minute. I would have gone last night had I not been exhausted."

"Please listen, Janet."

She began to cry. "I won't beg you. On the mountain, I learned that a big part of loving myself means I would never again grovel. Please tell me you will pray for me and trust me. Surely you can understand."

"But your world will *not* understand the message you've been given. They will *not* get it, not at all and not in a hundred years. Given the opportunity, they will spoil it, which means among other unpleasantness, you could be hurt or even killed. This world rejects holiness because it threatens its tight grip on power. This is why Jesus was crucified and the prophets killed."

"You're scaring me even more."

"The words Our Blessed Mother spoke cannot be given to this world in the way she spoke them to you. You must comprehend this. She and her words are holy, and holiness can never be restricted, much less contaminated, by the flawed perceptions every language creates."

Royal stretched his hands toward her, palms up. "Believe it or not, you have already interpreted the words she spoke to you, because language is symbolic and imprecise. Words are fair game for interpretation, while holiness should never be subjected to our speculation. Meaning, nuance, connotation, and the like are always negotiated in the context of human transactions, while holiness can only be accepted as it is and for what it is, God's eternal truth. But this world finds it difficult, if not impossible, to grasp this. It's why most of us have created a god who far more reflects our image than we have given any serious consideration to what it means to become people who have been created in God's holy image and for

God's holy purposes."

Jan kicked at the quilt covering her legs. "But she spoke to me in plain English, using the very words we use! What you're saying only confuses me more. You're acting like the professor you once were, but I need you to be my sympathetic priest and my wise counselor instead. Most of all, I need you to listen."

Royal shook his head until his thick mane swished like the tail of a horse. Lifting his eyes to meet hers, he said, "Okay, let me say it to you this way. She is holy! We are not! It's that basic. She can use our language, because her heart is pure and because she knew you might, with help, grasp her meaning but not yet her full purpose. Her words are not derived from our consciousness but rather from the very mind of God."

Royal leaned toward her. "But for as long as we remain in our own consciousness, we risk making the mistake of believing we are in possession of heaven's message when, in truth, we're still confusing obedience with self-interest. Her language is not our language, and our language is not her language, even though the words are the same."

The worried scowl that had moments before erased his smile now returned, inviting her to hang on his every word. "Janet, what was given to you on the mountain can only be mediated through your being, and what this means is that somehow you must actually become her message. This is the only way anyone can convey holiness to the world, and of course, this requires months and sometimes even years of prayer. Her message can only be communicated through genuine meekness. Before you attempt to tell the world what she told you, you must first become meek."

Still wrapped in the sheets, she pounded her knees with both fists. "But how do I do that, Royal?"

"One only becomes truly meek when God makes her meek, and to become meek, you must first pray and pray and then pray some more, and you must listen like you didn't know it was possible to listen. And then, sweet friend, in time you will be made meek enough to convey Our Blessed Mother's message to this old fallen world."

Sobbing, she gripped her knees and buried her head in the tangle of quilts, "But if I accept what you say as truth, I could be too late."

"The Spirit intends you to become its humble expression and this is what Jesus meant when he proclaimed blessings for the meek. This was his way as well as the way of the saints. To become her message, you must take the time to pray and listen. Remember Jesus' beatitudes?"

"No, I've never really read the Bible."

"Well, Jesus once offered to a gathered throng of listeners nine blessings. And guess what the third blessing was.

Raising her eyebrows, she shrugged.

"It was blessings for the meek. And he went on to promise that the meek will inherit the Earth."

"What does that mean?"

"People who have been transformed into the image of God will one day be in control of this tired old world. And when that happens, there will finally be a lasting peace, and the kind of divine justice to will insure compassion will become the norm of all human interaction. And to put it simply: love will finally win because the Kingdom Jesus proclaimed and died for will finally become a reality right here on Earth."

"Therefore, I must ask God to make me meek. But what if it takes too long and I don't get the message to my husband in time?"

"In my experience, God is sometimes slow, but never late."

She folded her hands in mock reverence and bowed her head and said, "Okay, you win. I'll get out of this bed and creep as fast as my sore body will allow over to the chapel and begin my prayers at once."

"I don't win, God wins, and ultimately love wins," Royal said with smile returning to his tired face.

Janet returned the smile as she liberated herself from the tangle of bed covers.

CHAPTER FORTY-TWO

The pine doors of St. Joseph's Church hung so haphazardly on their hinges that the gap between them invited breezes with such force and frequency, no votive candle could long remain lit. Still, the villagers, and those few rare tourists who risked arrest crossing the Rio Grande, ventured into this oblong adobe chapel to kneel in prayer before a primitive, but still beautiful, icon of the Virgin carved from a rugged mesquite trunk. And before each petition, most of the faithful lit the small candles while trusting that even if the winds snuffed out the fragile flames, their petitions would survive.

Jan placed her hands on the rusty latch and was surprised by how easily the heavy doors swung open with a pleasant groan. The air inside was slightly musty, yet still cool.

The closer she drew to the altar, the more intense the acridity of spent candlewicks, and the sweeter the hint of a twig of sage smoldering in a tiny copper tray. This was only one of three buildings in the village that could boast of glass panes fitted snugly into window frames, and yet this luxury was a far cry from the standard for inspiration set by the exquisite cathedrals on both sides of the border where the sun's light was filtered through multi-hued stained glass.

The six narrow benches, three placed on each side of the sanctuary's dirt floor, served as pews for those few who attended mass on Sundays. Handmade, they were abused by the decades, oft patched, and repaired with clumsily struck nails. Each old bench was so infested with splinters she questioned how any worshipper could long sit without being tormented, if not impaled.

The altar was constructed of a single rude pine block better suited for a butcher shop than as a piece of liturgical furniture. Sunlight poured through transparent spaces in the otherwise garish green and red panes, sending elongated beams of brightness to illumine patches of dirt floor.

Perhaps as many as two dozen hand-carved icons of angels and an assortment of suffering saints adorned the adobe walls from ceiling to floor. At least fifty votive candles remained unlit, as the breezes wreaked havoc with what little smoke rose from two smoldering wicks.

She crept toward a space in the dirt separating the altar from the first two crude benches. Once there she dropped to her sore knees and whispered, "Here I am."

Silence answered, followed by a breeze that sent what scant smoke remained into the rafters, where it disappeared into a flock of cobwebs. She closed her eyes and then opened them to adjust her vision to the dim light. Regaining her focus, she turned her head in the hope of finding a sign or a symbol pointing toward clarity.

"I am here," she whispered a second time.

Adjacent to her knee lay a wadded scrap of paper ripped from a small spiral notebook and left in the dirt to rock back and forth in a subtle breeze on its tiny fulcrum. She retrieved the wad and held it close as she inspected it from every angle before unfolding it. Three words in English read: "Pray for Gregory."

This is my assignment? Is this why I climbed the mountain? Is this from you, O Mother of God? Is this what I do? Do I pray for Gregory?

Silence settled upon her. Soon yet another breeze rocked the two big doors back and forth until they groaned like two old men complaining. Gaining momentum, the breeze swept through the gap, swirling the dirt floor into a cloud.

She closed her eyes and whispered, "O God, My God, I speak this prayer on behalf of a man—or is he a boy?—whose name is Gregory. I have no idea who this Gregory is, but if this is what I have been commanded to do, I will do it. And if it is not, I will trust you to show me how to follow the message given to me. I do not understand; nevertheless, make me attentive because my thoughts do often wander. My soul is possessed by a disease that distorts my thinking, so please don't leave me here to languish. Show me what it is I've been asked to do, whatever that may be. And—"

The breeze whistled as it rattled the rows of tiny glass candleholders with such determination as to invite her eyes to investigate. Finding nothing out of the ordinary she turned to face the chopping block altar, closed her eyes, and whispered, "Well, okay then, I will pray for Gregory. Yes, I *will* pray for Gregory to be whole and well and to know you and to know he is yours. And I will pray—"

'The hatred in you has died, Janet," whispered a thought. Or was it a voice from beyond? She could not be certain but since she'd come down from the mountain she frequently heard a woman singing—a soprano—but she could not decide if she actually heard singing or if the song was all in her head.

I am praying for Gregory, and I have been blessed.

The whistle through the gap raised its pitch a quarter step.

So this is how it works? I pray for someone I don't know—a man or a boy named Gregory—and I am blessed. Am I doing the right thing? Oh, this has to be right. I will pray for Gregory until I know I am done praying for Gregory.

But how will I know? I will trust. That's all I can do. I will trust. But for now I offer more prayers for Gregory, although I have no idea as to what specifically to pray for.

A dog's bark followed the wind's modulation from high to a resonant baritone hum and back to shrill. She interrupted her prayer while doubts circled in her mind like birds of prey and threatened to erode her commitment.

Before returning to the prayer, she imagined who this Gregory might be. Was he a boy? Or was he some mother's sick baby? She didn't know anything about him except his name.

Since she had been mandated to pray for him, that is what she did, hour after hour for three long days.

CHAPTER FORTY-THREE

The sight of the lanky priest squatting like a vagrant on the faded red curb stirred a sudden unexpected outrage Jan managed to rein in. A thorough self-scolding left her shaken and teary.

As he braced his back against a gaudy pink wall of the Park Bar, one of the several failing former tourist spots in Boquillas, Royal appeared content in an off-handed manner that annoyed her, although she had no idea what to do with the thorny tangle of emotions welling within. He was shirtless, barefooted, and covered by nothing more than a pair of drab olive-colored shorts, ragged to the point of absurdity. A borrowed and tattered straw hat balanced atop his shaggy crown with a jauntiness she thought insensitive, altogether inappropriate, and she wondered what attitude this man intended to convey.

With his eyes closed, he took long sips from a plastic tumbler, with a lime wedge balanced on the rim. He seemed to enjoy his beverage.

As Coughman had taught her to do, she paused to question her feelings of disgust, if not rage, giving herself time to prevent any expression of them and thus kick up regrets for not constraining herself. She was not at all up to handling any tension between this man and the whirlwind of questions blowing in her mind.

Inhaling several hearty breaths, she pondered Royal's behavior and the motives underlying it. Since she had descended the mountain, a quiet curiosity had diminished, if not replaced, her former reflexive need to release her rage.

Are the voices of hatred really gone? Is the hag dead? God, I pray so.

And if she is, can I now be angry without obsessing about killing myself? Of course I can.

But why am I so angry? The man's done nothing to hurt me. Is it because he looks relaxed while I've been curled up in knots for the past three days praying? Do I feel tricked? Manipulated?

Yes! No! Oh, I don't really know. What I saw and heard on the mountain and everything I experienced was real, very real. But did I waste three days when I needed to return to Dallas? If so, it is his fault, and I will be angry, even livid, if that turns out to be true.

But for reasons I don't even begin to understand and certainly can't explain, I do trust this man and what happened on the mountain. After all, it was through him that I met Mary and heard her speak holy words

And yet three days ago, he told me I must become the message, and yet I still have no clue what that means. I confess it. I'm scared again.

But am I angry? Well, maybe. Does it matter? The only question that matters is what do I do now?

"Royal?"

Without opening his eyes, he responded with casualness she interpreted as indifference. "Good evening, Janet. Come join me."

"I've been in St. Joseph's for three days now on my knees, flat on my back, and lying prostrate and every other position imaginable, praying for someone whose name happens to be Gregory. A week ago, I had no idea what it meant to pray, except when I was so terrified I didn't know what else to do. Tell me, did I just waste three days on a total stranger?"

Following a long sip on his tea, he said, "No."

"How can you be so sure?"

Another sip of the tea. "Prayer is never a waste."

Groaning, she refrained from anger. "My knees are killing me and I'm not sure if I've permanently wrenched my back. And I confess that, on the third day, I frequently interrupted my prayers with curiosity regarding the whereabouts of the nearest chiropractor."

In a circular motion, she rubbed her lower back with the knuckles of both hands. "From the moment I arrived and knelt, I prayed only because I found a slip of paper wadded up next to where I knelt. One scribbled sentence requested prayers for Gregory. Of course, I did take breaks to venture outside to that foul outhouse, but frankly I've had it. To be honest, I'm not sure if it is the Spirit who is calling me back to Dallas or if it is the compelling lure of a sanitary flush-toilet, but I am more than ready to go home."

"What have you learned?"

Settling next to him on the curb, she pressed her aching back against the pink wall. "Well, I've learned I've done permanent damage to my tired, long-abused, and as a consequence, most unfit, forty-six-year-old body."

Jan swatted at a swarm of gnats. "Three times each day, women crept into the church to leave meals on the back-bench and then just as quietly they returned to pick up the dishes. Through everything, I never heard them. Sometimes

I did glimpse them moving to and fro in the shadows but I have *no* idea who they were or how they knew I was there. Other than that little bit of food, I've not tasted a real meal since you and I climbed the mountain."

She sat up and cast a sideways glance at him. "During a lifetime of insane thinking, I've starved my body, convinced I was obese. And as a result, I'm now very hungry, and I'm also stiff and sore and more confused than ever. That is the sum of what I've learned in the past three days."

With his eyes still closed he said, "Confusion is humbling."

"Oh, don't start with me, Royal. Please don't even think about it," she sighed. "I'm tired. I am close to fainting because I am so famished. In fact, I feel like I've just run a twenty-six-mile marathon. I am still exhausted from the climb and never before have I been this filthy."

Jan dusted off the knees of her pants. "Do you realize I've not bathed for a better part of a week? I suspect I'm humble enough or as meek and mild as I ever plan to be, thank you very much."

She shook her forefinger at him. "And I'll tell you this. I don't plan to become any more anything, including humble. I spent three days twisted like a pretzel praying for someone I don't know because you, my friend, convinced me that to leave when I wanted to go was to be impulsive. So, I've done what you suggested, and the first thing tomorrow morning I'm heading straight back to Dallas."

Jan rose from the curb to turn and stare directly into Royal's nonchalant countenance. "And if my three days of prayers were a waste of time, then so be it."

"How could any prayer be a waste?" Royal said.

"Hear me: I'm not up to another lesson."

"Pardon me."

"Tell me, do you know someone named Gregory?"

"I know several."

"Who, for example?"

"I know of St. Gregory, a major sixth-century luminary. An artist in Austin named Gregory, and a mechanic in Marfa, and a very good writer in Alpine who answers to that name—"

"Why do you suppose the prayer request for Gregory was written on a scrap of paper and left in the church?"

"Likely some tourist left it there. Gringos have done that for years, ever since the church was built sometime in the early 50's."

"A tourist! You mean I've wasted three days praying for a name written on a scrap of paper a tourist just happened to leave at that ridiculous altar? Is that all I've done?"

Jan clapped her palm to her forehead as she whirled around in the street. "Oh my God, what a fool I am. How could I be so stupid?" She stopped spinning to pace in front of him. "No, mister, I'm out of here. I'm heading straight to Dallas at first light, and I trust I can count on you to get me back across that river since the Border Patrol considers you invisible."

"Your husband was here."

"What?" Her frantic orbit came to an abrupt halt. "Chuck was here? When? Where?"

"Two days ago."

Stomping her foot, she said, "Royal! Why didn't you come tell me? Oh my God, where is he now?"

"I didn't want to disturb you."

"Disturb me? You wouldn't have disturbed me." She knelt in front of Royal. "Did he leave? Where is he? I must see him at once and tell him what it is I've experienced. I know now I am supposed to tell him everything because he has so many powerful connections, tons of them. He plays golf regularly with the Governor and, believe it or not, he is even tight with the President."

Royal squinted at her. "But what if you're not to return?"

"Enough is enough, for God's sake, enough is too much. It is time for me to do this my way." She stood up and looked down at him. "You know, it's time for some common sense, so please be kind enough not to manipulate me again. You know where he is and you're not telling me."

"Two days ago he appeared alone on the Texas side, and from what I've been told—third-hand in very broken English—he ran up against some unsympathetic border patrol agent. Apparently, Chuck tried every trick from bribery, which happens to be a felony, to invoking the President's name, but nothing worked with this hardcore public servant. The two boatmen who witnessed this unpleasantness from their hiding place in the rushes reported that Chuck threw a 'real gringo fit.' He even tried to slog across the Rio Grande with his trousers hiked up above his knees, but I am told he slipped and washed down stream a hundred or so yards. He finally managed to right himself only to trudge out of the river cussing."

Royal chuckled. "I'm very sorry I missed that."

"Oh my God. I hope he's not hurt."

"Nothing is injured except maybe his pride. Most of us

could do with a good defeat every now and then to bring us back to the reality that we're *not* the center of the universe."

"Poor man. I must go to him. Can you take me across right now?"

Royal shook his head.

"What do you mean, no? That young man named Aaron told me you're invisible to the Border Patrol, coming and going as you please. Now please don't be difficult, Royal. Unlike the rest of us, you can row across any time you wish."

"Very likely, your husband is already on his way to Presidio where he can legally cross the border. Once in Ojinaga, he can catch a bus to Musquiz, and from there he can pay any number of eager young men to drive him here. It's only two hundred miles from here to Musquiz, but then the road is terrible. And I can't lie to you: it's at least an eight-hour drive from Musquiz to the border because the road is so washed out."

"If you're right, he's still two, maybe three days away."

"But then again, he could have driven back to Alpine or Marathon for the night." Royal shrugged. "Who knows? But from the way I heard it, he was so eager to find you that I'll put my money, of which I have not so much as two coins to rub together, on him being in the Sierra de Madre this very moment, somewhere between here and Ojinaga."

"Royal, why didn't you go help him?" Jan sat down next to him. "You could have convinced that agent to let him cross."

"First of all, I didn't know he was there until long after the fact, and secondly, you overestimate my influence. While it is true that Aaron and some of his cohorts regard me as invisible, there are other agents—and plenty of them, too—who don't."

Royal looked her squarely in the face, his eyes bearing down on her. "But to tell you the truth, had I known it was your husband, I would have rowed across to Texas at no charge and inquired regarding the possibility of look-away. But it didn't work out that way, so here we are."

"What's a look-away?"

"It's when the law looks the other way while they know someone is committing a crime. Look-aways have been around for as long as we human beings have enforced laws."

Jan fidgeted, lacing and unlacing her fingers together in rapid succession. "Royal, I have no idea what to do. Do I take off for Dallas at first light or do I wait in the hopes that Chuck is coming?"

"I've a third possibility."

Jan's eyes widened as she waited.

"I could row you across at first light and we'll take our chances with the agents. And it might not be a bad idea to pray tonight for one of those look-away fellows, if you are inclined to make such a self-serving prayer. And then you can drive to Marathon, where there is only the Sage Hotel. From there, you can call the dozen or so motels in Alpine to see if Chuck has registered as a guest."

"And if I don't find him?"

"Well then, I recommend you high-tail it back here and wait for your husband, but even more importantly to wait upon Our Blessed Mother to make you her message."

"Oh, do you think she will?"

"We must hope so, seeing how your actual plans are a bit on the vague side at present. But if you run back to Dallas, you will no doubt be misunderstood. No, ma'am, now is not the time for you to get on back to Dallas—not now and not until you've actually become her words. And any kind of holy becoming takes time and patience."

Royal closed his eyes. "Most of all, it requires the great miracle that is grace."

"I'm tired, very, very tired." Jan inhaled, held it, and then took her time exhaling. "May I sleep again tonight in the bed? And tomorrow morning, will you row me back across? Between now and then, will you pray that Aaron or one of his buddies is on patrol tomorrow so you and I will be considered invisible?"

He opened his eyes and smiled. "Yes, three times."

Raising her eyebrows, Jan tilted her head toward him.

"Yes to all three requests."

Jan clasped her hands together, looked up at the flawless azure sky, and grinned.

CHAPTER FORTY-FOUR

The shoeless man in the charcoal pinstripe suit pants removed his coat and draped it across the back of the room's one chair. After tossing his unknotted tie on the floor, he lay stretched out on the garish turquoise motel bedspread, admiring the blue steel Colt, detective model, snub-nose .38 caliber revolver. He pointed it toward the ceiling as though aiming at a target overhead.

What superb craftsmanship!

From its two-inch barrel to its inlaid mother-of-pearl handle, he considered it a work of art. He admired the smooth-spin of its revolving six chambers and marveled at its amazing power in less than six inches of steel.

He snapped open the chamber and all six bullets tumbled out one-by-one like airborne infantry. They rested upon the bed cover for a moment before disappearing into the crevice between where he lay and the rock hard mattress. Once the gun was empty, he popped the chamber back into place, aimed again at the yellow plastic light fixture immediately above, and pulled the trigger repeatedly to hear it click.

Why was that old woman kind? There's no profit in kindness.

He examined the scars on his arms, some of them from cigarette burns. Thoughts of his childhood overtook him, and he wondered if he'd ever been kind to anyone. Maybe, before his old man took to beating him on a regular basis, each time he came home drunk, which was every night. He admitted he was not sad to see his father die.

Three more times he pulled the trigger, grinning wider every time it clicked. He rolled to his side and placed his sock feet on a stained throw rug. Standing, he scratched his head and gave consideration to stepping toward the shower. Deciding against it, he balanced upon the edge of the bed and did his best to rub the itch from his eyes.

The strange old woman appeared in his mind's eye. He puzzled over why she didn't call the law. Using their computers, they would have discovered his identity and pulled up any warrant issued against him, probably more than one.

He didn't know if she failed to act out of kindness or fear, but he decided to leave her alone. She had earned his respect.

He fell back into the bed and stared at the ceiling. He squirmed at the memory of his helplessness. While he was so weak, she could have overpowered him. Then he relaxed as he recalled how she had spent those three days tending to him.

Like I was her only son.

The man recognized her action as a different kind of strength, one he wasn't used to encountering. He preferred the gun, with its blue steel .38-caliber reality affording it the capacity to intimidate what it doesn't main or kill. Understanding the power of threat, violence is what he lived by. Kill or be killed: that's the code. He wanted actual power he could hold in his hand, not some fairytale God peddled by fools.

Still he didn't understand the character of her strength. God made sense to her, he figured, but how does she make sense of something that weird?

Maybe she is crazy.

He sat up and reached for the telephone, but decided against making a call when his fingers touched the receiver. He lifted the receiver no more than an inch before returning it to its cradle.

The thought of the bees attacking him made him shudder. He would have left any half-dead victim where he lay and not given his death another thought. Logic provided him no answer for why that tall skinny Mexican kid, who just happened to be hiding out in that church, saved his life. He could have summoned the authorities, too, at any time.

The man had one job left to do: arrange for some preacher's wife to commit suicide. How he would convince the bitch to kill herself wasn't yet clear, but he wasn't worried. First he had to find her.

Then, after he got his son off the hook with the Feds down in Florida, he would retire to some remote village in Mexico. No more hits. He could live out the remainder of his years under an assumed name.

Maybe I'll spend the rest of my life being kind, but I doubt it. After all, a man can't do what he doesn't understand.

Tomorrow he would head back to the border and figure something out. He was good at what he did.

Unless the damn bees came back.

He stood up, retrieved a bottle of cheap scotch from his suitcase, and poured himself a drink in a plastic cup provided by the motel. Setting it on the dresser, he scanned his face inch-by-inch in the dusty mirror. The swelling was almost all gone, and the redness had faded.

He caught the reflection of the telephone across the room

and decided that making a call required too much effort. Not used to confusion, his hesitation bothered him. He hated losing his focus. If he had it to do all over again, he decided, he would shoot that woman's fool rooster.

Peering closer at his face, he rubbed his eyes. The itch persisted, even when he pulled the lower lids down. He slammed down the scotch in two gulps.

He needed sleep before he returned to the border first thing tomorrow after breakfast. Then, after he found the preacher's wife and took care of business, he would quit. It surprised him that he yearned for the feeling of peace he'd discovered in that old woman's house.

God, I'd like to feel that again.

If he were honest with himself, he doubted he would ever enjoy killing again. The idea made him feel as if he'd gone insane. He crossed the room and, one last time, he reached for the phone and dialed the front desk.

A woman with a cheery voice answered. "Front desk, may I help you?"

"Room 215. Could I have a wake up call at 5:00 sharp tomorrow morning?"

"Certainly, sir. Will there be anything else?"

"That's all I need, thanks." *That, and a good night's sleep.*

They both hung up.

The man held the gun before his face and kissed it. "I love you. I really do. Tomorrow I'll be my old, deadly, determined, disciplined, and dangerous self again."

He placed the gun beneath his pillow and closed his eyes. He could feel a smile linger until sleep arrived to carry him away from his concerns and the questions that for hours had circled like buzzards over road kill.

CHAPTER FORTY-FIVE

The fog formed an elongated cat's tail that floated lazily above the muddy rapids. As Jan sat on the riverbank, she studied its subtle undulations. The early morning mist stole into her consciousness and shrouded her thinking until it was impossible for her to make a clear distinction between the subtleties of revelation and the maddening power of desire.

Yet the name for which she had prayed for three days loomed in her mind like a bright morning star that invites speculation simply by its reticence to fade. No birds sang, no dogs barked, and no sound intruded upon the incessant whisper in her head of the name Gregory above the water's din.

High above the long transient cloud, the sky remained clear, and in mere minutes the sun would rise to warm the desert and turn the heavens to cobalt and the mountains from deep purple to brown, rugged and forbidding. Life in the village would stir, children's laughter would again drift toward the river as if to add to its already boundless energy, and an old man would scold his goatherd. Women would chatter as chores bid them scurry, and a faint but clear soprano voice that had comforted her during her three days of prayer would once again sing only to her as it did every new morning.

Jan wondered if this voice was real or something she had

made up because she believed she needed to hear it? She next addressed a more serious matter: had she actually been assigned the task of praying for someone named Gregory or was she wasting precious time, when returning to Dallas had seemed so right and urgent three days ago?

She had been blessed, so she asked herself if she was now merely obsessing and thereby avoiding taking responsibility for what had been assigned, or was this newfound devotion to quietude and a clumsy effort at prayer a faithful response?

No matter how often she had revisited this question in the past three days, certainty still eluded her. Worse, she did not know how to know or even where to discover an answer, so she did what felt right. She remained still on the river's mud bank and watched as the fog continued to roll and curl in concert with the turbulence within her own soul.

As Royal approached, his boots crunched the dry mud immediately behind her. "Good morning, Janet. Aaron signaled while it was still dark and that means that no border patrol will show up for an hour or so. So, you'd best gather your things, and we'd be wise to be in the water in no less than half an hour."

"Royal, I'm not going back, not today, anyway."

Without waiting for an invitation, he sat beside her, pressed his shoulder gently against hers, and closed his eyes as if to savor the warmth of the day's first light blessing his face. "Might I ask what changed your mind?"

"I thought I could do this alone... well, not actually alone but with the help of Mary, and perhaps Juan Diego, but I'm stuck."

"How can I help?"

"Listen to what Mary told me and then support me in

whatever decision I make. I'm not at all sure I have her permission to share it, but neither do I wish to mess this thing up. You're a priest and, as you said, you've prayed to her for the whole of your life and I've only just met her. Before I climbed to The Thin Place, I thought every story about her was a silly superstition that exploited the gullible."

With a small stick, Jan drew a circle in the dirt lining the riverbank. "You can see my problem. I have no clear idea what to do."

Royal wrapped his long arms around his knees and drew them close. "I've prayed about this, and all I know is that I have no right to ask what our Blessed Mother told you, or even to be curious. What you've been told is to remain in your heart until you have permission to share it."

"Will I sin if I share it with you?"

Royal shrugged.

"Will I be forgiven if I commit this sin?"

He nodded.

"Then I'm willing to be a sinner because I desperately need guidance and your support. I'm far too new at this and way too ashamed to operate alone under the enormous weight of this many questions. It's not like I can return to Dallas and tell my psychiatrist I climbed a mountain in Northern Mexico with a maverick priest-turned-mystic and encountered a five-hundred year old man who led me to a brief face-to-face visit with the Virgin Mary."

Chuckling, he said, "I wonder what would happen if you did share the truth with your shrink."

"Just as you said. I would be judged delusional, psychotic, or whatever the correct diagnostic term is for being completely out of my gourd. Then I would be slapped in a hospital so fast and medicated so severely that the holy message I've been given would be forever lost. Remember, those are your words."

Royal smiled.

"And I can't tell my husband, not just yet, anyway. He's not prepared to hear this. His approach is so rational there is no place whatsoever for mystery. As far as he is concerned, everything can be explained, and that which cannot is relegated to a category marked 'never to be investigated.' His take on God is purely intellectual and, because it works so well for him, reason is the single path to the truth."

Jan shifted sideways to look Royal in the face. "You're my only real choice as a guide and confidante. Three days ago I thought this Gregory I've been praying for might show up out of nowhere and serve as my mentor, but no such luck. It appears you're it, if you are willing."

Royal stood and bowed before her. "I'm humbled."

"That's a good beginning place. You also taught me that. I've learned a great deal about what it means to be humble ever since I climbed the mountain and met Juan and Mary. Before that and the three days I spent in St. Joseph's, I never realized humility is that important. But believe me, I've learned first-hand that when one stands in the presence of holiness, humility is the only good response."

"What did our Blessed Mother say?"

"Juan came for me in the night and his smile was so bright it actually awakened me and then comforted me until I was not at all afraid. He laid a rose upon the quilts where I had been sleeping and then I followed him silently up the trail until he motioned for me to kneel. I followed his instructions and closed my eyes until, even with them still closed, I could see a light burning so brightly I was afraid to open them lest I be blinded."

Jan laced her fingers together, as if ready to pray. "In English and in the gentlest and most reassuring tone imaginable, a woman's voice first spoke only three words."

"And they were?"

"She said, 'Stop the war'!"

"That was it?"

Jan shook her head. "I waited with my eyes still closed and she said to me again, 'Stop the war.' And after she spoke these words for the third time and I opened my eyes, the Virgin Mary stood before me. This time she said, 'War is sin!' It was obvious she had been crying for the longest time. Tears filled her eyes and had stained her cheeks. It broke my heart."

"And then?"

"The light faded and I closed my eyes. When I opened them, Juan stood before me still smiling. The man glowed as though his entire being had become a torch. Then he too disappeared, and I lay prostrate on the rocky ground and prayed for hours because I thought that was the right response. Frankly I didn't know what else to do. Remember, I'm very new at this mystery business. And then I descended the trail and found you."

"What war is she talking about?"

"No idea. I wasn't aware some nation is preparing to go to war."

Royal sighed. "Nations war against each other all the time. Sadly, the violence never ends. But could our government be planning a war?"

"I only know this. I was blessed with a holy mandate to stop a war I know nothing about. And then I walked into St. Joseph's and knelt to pray, but even before I began, I discovered that wad of paper, opened it, and read the request of prayers for Gregory. Only because I didn't know what else I am to do, I prayed for Gregory for three whole days."

Jan's tone tuned anxious. "And I can't help but believe I'm wasting precious hours here, when Mary, the mother of Jesus, would have me somehow stop a war. Let's face it. The only man I know who has the influence to persuade anyone with power here in the United States is Chuck. Now you can understand why, four days ago, I was so intent upon getting back to Dallas as soon as possible."

Jan's hands fluttered like nervous birds. "Naively, I thought if I told him what Mary said, he could share her message with the President. And if there was a threat of war anywhere on the globe, he could stop it before it began. But the more I thought about it, the more I came to see Chuck would never believe me."

She shook her head. "No, he'd see to it I ended up in a psychiatric hospital so medicated I couldn't do anything. Tell me, Royal, how is a newly recovering drunk like me supposed to stop a war? I'm nothing more but an unrepentant sinner who is so narcissistic, I have enormous difficulty not being self-obsessed all of the time."

Grinning, he said, "I have no idea."

"Well then, neither do I. But I do know what I experienced on that mountain was every bit as real as this conversation." Jan shrugged. "I've asked and asked and asked, and all I hear in return is the wind blowing through that big gap in the chapel doors. And sometimes I even think I hear a woman singing."

"Janet, I have a suggestion."

"Good! What is it?"

"Continue to pray for Gregory."

"That's it?"

Royal nodded.

"But I thought you might know something. You're the expert here, not me."

"I know only that you're to become her message. But you're right. Your husband and his world will not take you seriously, so for the time being, pray for Gregory."

"But I'm tired of praying for someone I don't know." Jan pounded her fist into the soft dirt. "What's more, I don't even know how to pray for this man or boy, or whoever he is. I don't know the first thing about becoming her message. Remember, I'm the grand champion when it comes to avoidance. But I can't afford to mess this up. You said so yourself."

"You want my advice?"

"Why else would I jeopardize my eternal soul by revealing what she told me?"

"Pray for Gregory until you are extraordinarily clear what it means to become her message. In other words, pray for Gregory until you know what it is she would have you know."

"I'm not comfortable agreeing with this, but I suppose you're right. Honestly, I don't know what else to do, so the only faithful response is to keep up the prayers for good old Gregory. In the meantime, perhaps Chuck will somehow find his way here, and when he arrives, Mary or her Son or the Father Himself will instruct me as to what to say to him. At this point, I'm not even sure I would tell him anything."

She leaned sideways to nudge Royal's shoulder. "But I do feel better sharing this with you, so I suppose that's something."

He smiled and wrapped his arm about her and hugged her.

Jan returned his smile, with a hint of wistfulness. "Okay, I'm not going back to Dallas today. But before I return to St. Joseph's, would you break the law with me and be so noble as to row me back to the Texas side? I've not bathed in days and I smell like a dead skunk in summer."

"There's nothing I'd rather do. I'll drop you there and come back two hours later. That should be plenty of time to soak your tired, sore muscles."

"Oh, I can hardly wait. I am filthy and stiff. With a hot bath, I'll be ready to pray for as long as necessary. But who knows? I may be there the rest of my life, but praying for Gregory seems right until I am asked to do something else. Thank you, Royal, for listening and not thinking me insane."

"Dear lady, I don't think you're crazy at all. You are quite sane and now very much on the path to becoming holy."

"Don't scare me. I'm not ready to be holy, not even close, but I am willing to pray, so let's go to Texas."

With that, she and Royal rose and she walked toward Pablo's boat with an air of newfound confidence.

CHAPTER FORTY-SIX

Elbows braced on the breakfast counter of the Everybody Belongs Café in Alpine, the gaunt man behind the silver shades took a sip on his second mug of coffee for the morning. He rotated on a squeaky stool to study the scene unfolding in the street.

One media truck after another rumbled past and soon all were stalled to form a traffic jam so rare the town sheriff later boasted to a Midland television reporter that no one could recall the last one. Each vehicle proclaimed its identity through a colorful logo. CNN was first in line followed by ABC, NBC, Fox, and ESPN. Mixed in were vans brandishing the call letters from local TV stations as far away as Dallas/Ft. Worth and Houston.

Sensing that the woman who'd taken his order only a few minutes earlier had returned to the counter behind him, he said over his shoulder, "What's all the excitement?"

The waitress sighed in a showy demonstration of feigned disgust. "Well, you must not be from around these parts, because this is only the biggest thing to hit Alpine since the railroad tracks were laid more than a century ago."

As the snarled traffic honked its impatience, he said, "Tell me, ma'am, what is this big thing?"

"Mister, don't say you ain't never heard of Oonie Garza?"

He shook his head.

"My God, mister, where have you been?"

The gaunt man turned about on the stool until he was eye-to-eye with the waitress. "I'm only passing through."

"Oonie Garza *is* the best basketball player on the planet and that includes high school, college, and the pros. I ain't stretching the truth one-half inch. You ask anybody around here. Michael Jordan can't hold a candle to this kid. Neither can LeBron or Shaq."

"Who's he play for?"

"Marathon. Tonight Oonie and the mere mortals," she chuckled, "the other kids who make up his team, are playing the Balmorhea Bears and Balmorhea ain't got no kid over six feet, so it's certain to be a rout. The two school boards came together and decided to move the game to the Sul Ross field house to attract a bigger crowd and make more money. But even that place, which can hold half the folks in Alpine, won't be big enough. Everybody who's anybody, including the Governor himself, is coming in tonight. Maybe even the President will show up. He's a Texan, you know."

She gave a low whistle. "Just look at all them television trucks, mister. We ain't never seen nothing like it in this little town. This is for sure once-in-a-lifetime doings."

"How tall is this kid?"

"He's every bit of six-four, skinny as a rain-soaked scarecrow, but by the time he's twenty or so, he'll fill out just fine. He may go off to college for a year or two, but he'll be a pro in no time a'tall. And there ain't a college in the country that ain't after him like some big old nickering stud horse sniffing romance in the breeze. Some claim he's been offered cars and cash bonuses to sign, but I don't believe it. Oonie and his

Aunt Lita are God-fearing and law-abiding Catholics."

The light changed and the big trucks, cars, and vans rumbled past the vibrating café window.

The gaunt man rested his elbows on the counter. "How can I get a ticket to tonight's game?"

"They've all been sold, every game for the whole season. And even when we go to Austin for the State Finals, the UT field house will be sold out, too. Folks on television say the Longhorns want to sign him bad, but then everyone wants Oonie. The smart money is on Duke. And when it comes to his studies, Oonie does better than most. He's a right sharp kid and sweeter than a fresh-baked pound cake."

"Have you got a ticket?"

She eyed him with a mix of suspicion and sympathy. "Yeah, but I do believe I'd rather cut off my ring finger with my wedding band attached than give up my ticket to tonight's game."

The man leaned toward her wearing a scowl. "Everyone has a price."

Her sympathetic look faded. "There ain't a price high enough to convince me. I'm rock solid when it comes to holding on to my ticket."

"Not even a thousand dollars?"

Her eyebrows shot up as she gulped.

His face didn't move a muscle, not even a twitch. "I said a thousand dollars cash money right here right now on this genuine Formica counter top in exchange for one ticket to tonight's game."

"Are you serious?"

He nodded, never taking his eyes from her face.

"You'd give me a thousand dollars for a ticket to a high school basketball game?"

"Take it while you can, ma'am, because within ten minutes, one of the fine upstanding citizens of Alpine, Texas, will be obliged to relieve me of it in exchange for a ticket."

"Why, mister," she said as she grinned, "you've just bought yourself a basketball ticket, a reserved seat on row one right dab in the middle of the court."

Clenching his teeth beneath the sunshades, he said, "Congratulations." And with that, he pulled ten one hundred dollar bills from his wallet and handed them to her one at a time.

Checking both sides of all ten bills as if she could distinguish counterfeit money from real, she said, "Are these things good?"

"Good enough to spend, ma'am. If you don't believe me, take them to the bank. They'll verify them."

"No, I believe you. It's just I ain't never seen that much money in one little stack before."

"Now about that ticket—"

"Excuse me, mister. I plum forgot, I was so taken with these bills. I've got the ticket stuffed in my purse. Sit here a minute more, and I'll be back quicker than you can say, 'Oonie Garza'."

"Thank you, ma'am." He smiled at her without any genuine warmth. "It's a real pleasure doing business with you."

CHAPTER FORTY-SEVEN

At the door, the gaunt man presented the ticket to a girl dressed all in white. As she examined the thing before ripping it in two, he turned to observe the throng of which he was now a part, flowing like a fire ant swarm into what felt far more like some lascivious celebration of carnality than a high school athletic contest.

The thumping of the pervading bass defined the music as rap. Its ear-splitting beat pulsated throughout the building, shaking it. He wondered if the intense throbbing in his head might be a vestige of the stings.

Cupping his hands over his ears, he pushed his way into the gymnasium. An hour before tip-off, the arena was already more than three-quarters full. He glanced at the torn stub and read the numbers and proceeded at a crawling pace toward the first bench on the home side at center court.

A narrow sliver of glossy hardwood peeked out between the old priest he'd met days before at the Sage and an obese rancher dressed in faded denim. His shirt strained at the buttonholes and his straw western hat rested on an ample lap more than half invaded by his enormous belly. The denim fan smiled with the confidence of a man a checker jump away from self-congratulation and he followed that with a don't-mess-with-me nod as the gaunt man approached. The old priest paid the gaunt man no mind as he squinted straight ahead through Coke-bottle-thick cloudy lenses.

"Good evening, Padre," the gaunt man yelled above the pulsating beat.

Stunned that this stranger knew him, Father O'Shea glanced up to begin a quick search for any connecting memory. After several misfires, he smiled and bellowed above the cacophony, "Why you're that fellow with the FBI. Well, I'll be switched. Did you find our visitor from Dallas?"

"Almost," the man screamed as he attempted to squeeze into the narrow space. He turned to stare through the shades at the denim man. More gesture than substance, his scoot provided perhaps an additional inch of hospitality.

Fortunately, someone in authority thought to spare the crowd permanent ear damage by turning down the decibel level on the speakers. Conversation, although not easy, proved possible.

Settling as best he could between the priest and the rancher, the gaunt man turned to the priest and yelled, "Good to see you again, Padre. You a basketball fan?"

Brady tilted his head to speak into the man's ear, "An Oonie Garza fan."

No players from either team had yet taken the court, but two cheerleaders dressed in bright blue and gold led a tiny contingent of similarly outfitted fans in a hapless cheer for the opposing team, Balmorhea.

"Tell me about this kid, Father."

The old priest tossed his head back like a crowing rooster. "Why, he's only the best basketball player ever to play the game."

Struggling against a lifetime habit of appearing dour, the

gaunt man smiled. "Really?"

"He and his Aunt Lita are members of my parish. I chris-tened Oonie when he was only three months old."

"What became of his parents?"

"His papa came into this country illegally. One morning before Oonie was even two, the INS swooped into some of the bigger ranches in this area and hauled all the illegal hands to El Paso where they were deported. That was fifteen years ago, and he has never come back. For all I know, the poor hombre is dead and buried."

The priest's head rotated as he followed the motions of the cheerleaders. "Not six months later, the boy's mother was killed in a head-on collision with a drunk driver. Lita is his mother's older sister, never married, because, bless her heart, she's homelier than an old nanny goat. She took baby Oonie as her own and has raised him ever since in the admonition of the Lord. And there's not a soul in all of West Texas who won't tell you she's done a right good job with the boy."

"What makes the kid so special? Plenty of kids are good at this game."

"Well, that's the $64 million question. In fact, it's joined to the single most intriguing answer this old priest has ever shared with a living soul."

Father Brady shifted as best he could in the cramped seat and tried to look the man in the eye.

"Poor Oonie was suffering from some kind of baffling behavior disorder, but I was not nearly educated enough in the field to know what I was looking at. His Aunt Lita couldn't afford the cost of a mental health professional, even if we did have one."

Turning to face the priest the gaunt man said, "A disorder?"

"He couldn't connect with people, even though he desperately wanted to. Every time he experienced even the least bit of stress, he would jump to his feet like he'd just sat on a sharp mesquite thorn and scream like the furies before spitting a wad of saliva as big as an agate marble. No kid can function in a classroom if he's going to spit on people every time he gets a bit fractious. When Oonie was a first grader, Lita brought him to the confessional because she believed him possessed."

Wearing a quizzical expression, the gaunt man rested his eyes on the priest's old face. "And what did you do?"

"He was too young and much too sweet to have any sins—at least not the soul-jeopardizing kind—and he wasn't possessed. I've seen demon-possession up close, and believe me, it's not a pretty sight. So I did the only thing I could, took the boy straight to Esperanza, our *curandera*."

The man nodded. "I've met her."

"Then you know she is our local treasure. And I'm one hundred percent convinced—even as a former hospital chaplain in San Antonio with more than twenty years of experience—her way of curing folks, regardless of the severity of the ailment, is every bit as effective, if not more so, than anything the city doctors do in exchange for a bushel of money. Most folks in this town can't afford health insurance. It's an unimaginable gringo luxury. My God, what a racket the health care industry is! Oh don't get me started—"

The gaunt man patted the priest on the shoulder. "You were telling me about Esperanza."

"Esperanza is as close to a saint as any human being can possibly be and still be alive. Her uncommon and unusually deep faith is distinguished by a strong strain of mysticism, a holdover from her Mescalero Apache medicine man great-grandfather, and by a holy humility garnered from decades of daily prayer. One day she came to understand she had been blessed with the gift of mediating the Spirit with such clarity and with such astounding efficacy that she could actually heal the sick and change even the darkest heart to light. And not surprisingly, soon after this discovery she told me about this blessing. Because I trust the woman one hundred percent, I began referring ailing folks to her with every kind of complaint imaginable from gout to tumors and guess what?"

The gaunt man's slight smile returned to his face. "What?"

"To a person, they got well. And I don't mean they walked away just feeling better for the time being. No, these folks were actually cured. And what was even more incredible is that some of the meanest people imaginable turned their lives completely around. Or in the parlance, they repented."

"Did she cure the kid of spitting?"

"Not exactly. After five days of fasting and almost ceaseless prayer, she carried him out into to the desert at dusk in that old beat-up truck, provided him with a blanket and a bottle of water, and left him all alone. Poor Oonie couldn't have been more than six years old at the time, and a night alone in the desert will scare the devil out of even a full-grown man armed with a rifle."

The priest shook his head and chuckled. "And the boy's aunt let her do it, too, because she trusted Esperanza just that much. The courageous little fellow stayed there alone for the whole of that night because he didn't know how to find his way back. This desert is plenty big, but at night it gets even bigger. And since the dawn of time, the desert is where human beings have always gone to discover God. Anyway, an hour before sunup, she returned to find Oonie standing in the middle of the blanket, both hands raised to the sky, singing like he'd been born for the Metropolitan Opera. And the miracle is that he hadn't spit once all night."

"So she *did* cure him?"

"He still spits, but the night alone in the desert made him accurate. He seldom misses when he spits, shoots a basketball, tosses washers at our annual all-church picnic every August, or hurls a baseball. The boy's a right talented pitcher, but he's the best basketball player in the world. No one ever born comes close to doing what this boy does with a basketball."

"What happened to him out there in the desert?"

"No one knows for certain, but he told Esperanza an unusually small, dark-skinned man dressed all in white appeared to him that night and blessed him with the gift of unparalleled accuracy."

"Who was this man?"

"Juan Diego."

The gaunt man raised one eyebrow.

"He's a fellow who died about five hundred years ago, but before he died, he happened upon the Virgin Mary on a hilltop down in Mexico. That simple meeting forever changed the consciousness of this hemisphere. Countless rumors along with no small amount of evidence maintain and support the conjecture that this saint appears from time to time right here in the Big Bend. Off and on, folks in this desert—from desperadoes to the very salt-of-the-earth vaqueros and their señoras—have reported seeing him for more than a century now. And a few folks have even reported visiting with him, but always only briefly."

"A five-hundred-year-old spook appeared to this boy and blessed him with the gift of accuracy?"

The priest nodded as if trying to shake something off the top of his head. "Yes sir, that's exactly what I'm saying. Once you see him play tonight, you will be convinced that what this boy can do with a basketball is something way beyond natural, even supernatural. And whether or not folks understand what they're witnessing, his gift and the mystery surrounding it come directly from God. Even a blind man could see it. Skeptics will walk out of here, either unaware—or worse, unconvinced—his gift is a manifestation of God's grace."

The familiar scowl returned to the gaunt man's face as he pondered the old priest's story. "Sounds like you believe in a fairy tale because the boy became a superstar."

The old priest jumped to his feet and yelled as loud as his old lungs would allow, "Most people ridicule the story of Juan Diego's visitation, but not Oonie, not his Aunt Lita, and certainly not me. What happens on this court is about more than a basketball game. It's about the amazing power of God to transform the human soul."

The sound of taped trumpets blasted a shrill fanfare as both teams trotted onto the court. The crowd's cheer drowned out the scratchy blare of the recorded music. The Bears, sporting their gaudy, bright blue-and-yellow satin warm-up suits, trotted in a circle beneath their basket, practicing lay-ups as the Marathon players, dressed in equally garish black-and-gold satin uniforms, did the same at their end of the court.

"Once you see the kid play, you'll agree that what this young man has is amazing. Watching him will take your breath away. I'll wager there are at least one hundred college scouts here tonight and several pro scouts doing their best not to be spotted."

The gaunt man leaned toward the old priest. "Which one's Oonie Garza?"

The priest, now balanced on the bleacher before him, yelled over his shoulder, "He's not out yet."

"Why not?"

"Wait and you'll see."

As both teams broke rank to take practice shots under the watchful supervision of their respective assistant mentors, Coach Doagie Broadside stood at the scorer's table, looking like a celebrity, with as many as a hundred microphones shoved into his face. His big head generated a flood of sweat beneath the glare of the klieg lights, and the wide grin emblazoned on his always-ruddy face refused to wane. With a flair for the dramatic, he revealed to the army of reporters one detail at a time the latest regarding the life, talent, and no doubt, extraordinary future of arguably the greatest sports star ever to come out the Trans-Pecos and perhaps even the whole state. To even a casual observer, it was obvious Coach Broadside enjoyed the fleeting air of importance his young charge had blessed him with since the kid's freshman year.

When the overture from the motion picture *Rocky* boomed through loudspeakers suspended on long poles from the high ceiling, the crowd, even the Balmorhea fans, responded with thunderous applause. The gaunt man stood up and his gaze followed the crowd's attention to one end of the arena. Trotting out of the home team's locker room was the same tall kid who days earlier had draped the man over one skinny shoulder, dragged him to the car, and driven him to Esperanza's house.

The crowd chanted "Oonie! Oonie!"

The stranger mumbled, "I thought so. He just had to be the same boy who pulled me out of that sweatbox of a church and brought me to the woman who saved my life. Well, now, isn't that something?"

Tip-off occurred on schedule at straight up 8:00 p.m. and within two minutes of regulation play, Oonie had scored seven three-pointers with no points scored by Balmorhea. By halftime, he accounted for 58 points, 11 rebounds, 17 steals, and no fouls.

At the final whistle, the score signaled the predicted rout that was still deceptively tepid on the Marathon side of the ball. Nevertheless, the final score to be emblazoned as a headline in sports' sections all across Texas, and wherever else readers were fascinated with the phenomenon that was Oonie Garza, would read the next morning 76 to 18 in favor of Marathon. Satisfied, if a bit subdued, the crowd began their slow descent down the high bleachers.

The priest, who remained seated, turned to the stranger next to him. "Well?"

"You are right, Father. The boy is truly amazing. I've never seen anything like him. Never."

"What do you think about the blessing?"

"I think I might pay a visit to Esperanza."

"Why in God's name would you do that? I thought you were down here hunting that pretty little lady from Dallas?"

"I have no idea, Father, but it's very good to see you. Good night."

"Good night. Give Esperanza my best. And go with God, son. Go with God."

The gaunt man waited until the crowds had emptied from the arena. Stepping onto the court, he walked toward one end until he stood under the basket. He stared up at the net for several minutes without blinking.

Not until the janitors rolled their trashcans through the doors leading to the locker rooms did he stir. Without speaking to the worker who nodded at him, the man headed out the entrance toward the parking lot, already enveloped in West Texas darkness.

CHAPTER FORTY-EIGHT

Into the sanctuary's dim light, Chuck called, "Jan," in a soft and timid tone.

Jan had knelt at the rough altar, for how long, she did not know, as concentration on her prayers sapped her awareness of time and space. And yet, a familiar sound—rather a voice she recognized on some dim level—stirred her from the intensity of her discipline. Her mind was reluctant to awaken to her physical reality, and she fought the return and the myriad dreadful associations that distinct voice called forth.

While still on her knees in the dust, she turned in time to see the man's silhouette against the morning's brightness. "Chuck?" she whispered.

"Jan, I've been searching for you."

"Chuck," she said. "Oh my God, it is so wonderful to see you."

He eased toward where she knelt and placed his hand upon her shoulders like a brother might do. She did not flinch. Lifting her on wobbly legs until she stood, he drew her close but did not kiss her. "I've come to take you home."

"How did you get here?"

"I've been on the road, if you can call it that, for three days, bouncing around like a pinball on a miserably hot Mexican bus with no air-conditioning."

Jan suppressed a grin, as she edged backward until their bodies no longer touched.

"The illiterate farmer in the seat behind me held a rooster in his lap all the way from Ojinaga to Musquiz, which has to be the longest and most terrifying two-day trip on earth."

"Where did you stay the night?"

"Some pathetic little out-of-the-way mud hovel with no electricity and no bottled water and there I was served what I swear was botulism in a bowl."

"Didn't you eat anything at all?" Jan tried to sound concerned, as she wriggled free from his grasp.

"I swallowed no more than a spoonful of some kind of thin soup. But so far, thank God, and all of his angels in heaven above, I've not yet come down with 'Montezuma's Revenge.' No doubt, it's just a matter of time."

"What did you do when you reached Musquiz?"

"I chose not to attempt to sleep but instead paid a kid $100 down to drive me the next two hundred miles in what has to be the roughest pickup still running. The non-English speaking tattooed peon had no sooner switched on the ignition than I realized his truck had never known such luxuries as struts and shocks. Can you imagine a future member of the President's cabinet—"

"Sounds like you got a good dose of how much of the rest of the world actually lives." Jan tsked-tsked as she shook her head.

"Oh my God, you cannot believe what indignities I've endured." He dusted off the front of his jacket. "Here I am, every bit as determined as when I left Ojinaga three days ago, but also stressed to the limit of my ability to cope. I'm emotionally drained and precariously close to starving, and more physically whipped than I knew possible and yet, if anything, even more committed than ever to bring you home."

"I can't go back with you. Not now."

He gripped her on the shoulders. "That's the most irresponsible thing I've ever heard you say."

The preacher shook her until her jaw went slack. "Listen to me. I'm your husband and I say you're going back! I didn't risk life and limb coming all the way down to this miserable country full of unwashed peasantry to argue. So let's go grab what few belongings you brought over here and get out of this stinking place as fast as possible."

One at a time, she pried his hands from her shoulders until they stood eye-to-eye. "Chuck, sit down."

"I don't have either the time or the money to sit down. Do as I say, Jan. And do it *now!*"

Chuck jerked his thumb toward the door at the entrance. "The kid with the pickup is outside waiting to drive us back to Musquiz, and from there we will take a difficult, if not potentially lethal, bus ride to Ojinaga. And we can pray to a loving God that we'll get a more cautious driver this trip."

As he tried to link his arm through hers, she pulled away. "I left my new Benz parked in Presidio," he said, "and paid some local pirate fifty bucks to watch it. The minute I disappeared across the international bridge, I'm sure he called every member of his gang to chop it up. God, help us all!"

Tears flooded her eyes and coursed down her stained cheeks. "You must hear me, Chuck. This is important."

Chuck scowled at her. "As exhausted as I am at the moment, I will gladly help you gather your possessions, if you have anything over here. Three very long days ago, I spotted your car parked in the gravel lot on the Texas side and by God's grace—and nothing more—it appeared still safe."

When she didn't move, he said, "Jan, you're not listening. There's a kid out there with his motor racing and the greedy little bandit is charging me $10 an hour, and that's not counting the cost of gasoline. I'm also paying one hundred percent of his fuel costs." He grabbed her hand. "Where is your stuff?"

She shook her hand loose from his. With her shoulders quaking, she dropped to her knees and lifted her face to meet his eyes. "Chuck, you must listen. I cannot leave. Not now! Not yet! Not until it is time!"

"Time for what, Jan? Time for what?" He stepped toward her in a manner she considered menacing. "Look around you, woman, and please note that this place is a dried up, forgotten purgatory populated by a handful of illiterate peasants who've been down for so long they can only accept the tragic plight of poverty as their destiny. Nothing you or I can do will ever change that."

As he turned away from her, he spoke out of the side of his mouth. "Mexico is hopeless. Trust me, God never intended for you to end up in place like this."

Raking the dirt floor with her fingers, she lowered her gaze. "Chuck, please go outside and tell the boy in the truck to cut his engine and wait. No sense wasting gas."

"No, Jan, we're leaving together now!" He grabbed her elbow and squeezed. "You're coming with me, woman," he yelled, "*and* you're coming this very minute!"

She struggled to break free, but he tightened his grip. "Please don't make me get rough! You know I don't want to hurt you!" Chuck snapped his arm like a whip, jerking her up until they stood facing each other. "It's high time you minded me." He glared down at her. "No man of my stature should ever be subjected to your sick and self-indulgent disobedience."

He lowered his voice, but his tone turned bitter and frosty. "It's over, Jan, one hundred percent finished. From now on you will do as I say, and there will be no argument. I should have done this ten years ago and saved myself a decade of suffering."

As she jerked her arm to pull away, she spied Royal standing in the doorway between the two big open doors. "Royal!"

Whirling to face the intruder, Chuck snarled, "So you're the sociopath who abducted my wife, dragging her to this God-forsaken place and keeping her against her will!"

Unfazed, the tall priest smiled. "Are we okay in here?"

"None of this is any of your concern," said Chuck. "But I do want you to know that everyone from the FBI to the Texas Rangers has you on their radar and, as we speak, the State Department is negotiating with their counterparts in Mexico City to have you arrested and extradited back to the U.S. to stand trial for kidnapping, extortion, and terrorist threats."

Chuck wagged a finger at Royal. "You're a defrocked priest hiding from the authorities like the coward you are. Furthermore, you manipulated my wife to join you here, and, for God only knows how long, you have held her against her will in this nation of beggars. And, sir, need I inform you, in the eyes of the law, your actions are tantamount to abduction?"

"I'm okay, Royal." Jan waved him away with one free hand. "Chuck just arrived, but he won't be staying long.

He's going back within the hour. No need to worry. No need at all."

Turning again to face his wife, Chuck said, "Listen, Jan, I'm *not* going back without you! I'm the head of our household and the God to whom you were praying when I came in would have you know that. A woman's submission to her husband is God's will. So be the dutiful wife God created you to be and gather your belongings without making a fuss."

He glanced at Royal. "You'd be most wise not to interfere. I'd say you're in enough trouble as it is."

Royal maintained the strained grin that Jan recognized as dogged determination. "I'll wait for you outside, Jan. If you need me, call. By the way, I told your driver friend to cut his engine. No need to waste gasoline and pollute this otherwise pristine desert morning." He disappeared from the doorway as silently as he had arrived.

Chuck scowled at his wife, but she held up her hand, palm forward. "Chuck, please sit and let me tell you what has happened."

Jan took a deep breath. "It is all so beautiful and so wonderful and you don't need to be upset, not in the least. If you will but listen and do your best to understand, I believe we can both return to Dallas immediately and work together on something so important that you and I cannot even begin to imagine the full implications."

Sighing, he plopped down on the rude bench. "Okay, tell me what it is you believe you've learned this time. But make it quick. That kid is charging me by the hour."

"To begin with, Royal didn't kidnap me." She sat across from him in the cool of the darkened dirt-floor sanctuary with the desert breeze whistling through the doorway. "I came here of my own free will."

Chuck jumped to his feet. "He kidnapped you and he demands a ransom for your return. The CIA and the FBI consider him a terrorist. Those are corroborated facts, Jan."

"He did not abduct me and he wants absolutely nothing from you or, for that matter, from any other human being. You must hear me on this. The man is not a criminal. And the idea of him being a terrorist is ludicrous." She snickered. "If anything, he is a life-long pacifist."

Chuck wagged his head as if trying to dislodge a clod of dirt from his thick hair. "It's public record that his man threatened his own bishop. Why else would a man trick a married woman into running away with him into a foreign country and then keep her holed up in a building constructed of mud? Good God, look at this place Jan!" His gaze passed over the homemade benches and the bare dirt floor. "Don't you find this all a bit humiliating? I certainly do!"

Sniffing as if he smelled a foul odor, Chuck sat down, taking care not to touch the back of his legs against the bench. "Furthermore, he's manipulated, or far more likely brainwashed, you only to disgrace me. That guy is a sociopath and a seditious terrorist pretending to be a man of God. The sooner you face facts, the better."

"I came here because I chose to." Jan shook her head. "Royal didn't force me to do anything. Several days ago, he and I climbed the mountain behind this church and it was at the summit that I actually met the Virgin Mary. I heard her voice with my own ears and I beheld her heart-breaking countenance with my own eyes."

Jan's lips quivered. "Trust me, I'll never be the same because of it. *Never!* Seeing her was beyond belief, and her face... oh my God, Chuck, she was so very, very sad. Her tears broke my heart."

She put her hand on his arm. "She loves us, all of us, every human being on earth, rich and poor, and every ethnicity and every religion. And she is passionately concerned about the welfare of each man, woman, and child, and this is why she wants us to stop the violence at once. I can't bear thinking of her tears. My heart breaks every time I do. You can't imagine–"

Springing to his feet again, he said, "Good God, Jan, that's enough! Don't blaspheme! You didn't meet the Virgin Mary. You're a very sick and selfish drunk and more delusional than I imagined. Oh, my God in heaven, what evil has this defrocked devil perpetrated?"

Jan frowned and did her best to control the shakiness in her voice. "Sit down, Chuck, and hear me out. I'm not blaspheming and neither am I delusional. What I am telling you is the truth. I met an angel... well, at least I think he's an angel and this man who lived five hundred years ago led me by the hand to meet Mary. His name is Juan Diego, and I was on the summit of the mountain with him when Mary came to me to speak two messages with tears flowing down her cheeks."

"My poor, misguided, delusional Jan, you're so very, very sick." Chuck bowed his head, resting his forehead in his hand. His lips moved, but no sound came out.

Jan sat up straight. "With tears flooding her eyes and coursing in streams down her cheeks Mary said, 'Stop the war' and then she paused, and I said 'Yes?' and that's when she said, 'War is sin.'"

Chuck leapt to his feet. "Okay, I've heard enough, so go grab your stuff and let's get out of here. The sooner I can get you to a psychiatric hospital the better."

"She wants me to stop a war and came to me because of who you are. And she knew I would go to you because you're to be the President's spiritual advisor and that after the election you will have more influence with him than anyone else in the world."

"Enough of your nonsense, now let's go."

"Please sit back down, and listen to me. Please. I am begging you. She is convinced there is to be a war—"

"Get real!" Chuck screamed. "You didn't see or meet the Mother of Jesus, the Virgin Mary. You couldn't. The woman's been dead 2,000 years and she doesn't come back to visit with people. That is utter nonsense. I've never bought it and I don't plan to begin believing in magic any time soon."

"But she told me there is to be a war."

Chuck paced in front of her, gaining speed with every step. "This President is *not* going to declare war. Even if you did see the Virgin Mary, or St. Peter, or Peter Pan, or Big Foot, or whoever you talked to up there on that mountain, the fact remains that there is to be *no* war. *None!*" He stopped to shake his finger in her face. "Got that? There will be absolutely *no* war! Not so much as a single gun will be fired in anger. Not now, and not at any time in this President's administration, unless we are attacked first by a foreign power. So, you can relax."

Chuck sighed. "Now that I've listened to your latest

delusion, please be so kind as to get up from that bench, gather your stuff as I've requested, and climb into the socio-path's truck idling outside so we can return to Musquiz."

Noting his wife distracted gaze, Chuck turned to see the tall priest again in the open door smiling like a man holding a winning hand. "Now what do you want?"

"I don't want anything, Dr. Love. But I did return to inform you that your ride back to Musquiz doesn't seem much interested in waiting."

"Tell him to wait anyway. I've already paid that tattooed robber good money. He's as corrupt as everyone else down here, and if that kid is not real careful, I'll have the FBI on him, too."

"He's already gone."

"Gone? He can't be gone! I paid that peasant to stay put."

"If you stop browbeating your wife and sashay over to this door, you will see the dust cloud his little truck left hang-ing. Right now I'd say it's waiting to hook up with a rainbow."

"What? That bandit! That liar! That kid promised me he'd stay put. You did this!"

"All I did was listen to the boy's complaints. Apparently you offended the young man's sensibilities, since he charac-terized you as something akin to the back end of a fat burro. Anyway, he's now very much departed."

Beads of perspiration dotted the furrows in the preacher's brow and, blushing, he sighed. As he sank to the bench, his expression turned sullen.

"She said for me to stop the war, Chuck."

He closed his eyes and raised his hands shoulder high before declaring in a calm tone, "Jan, dear wife of mine and mother of our deceased child, on our infant daughter's grave, I swear to you there is to be *no* war. *None!* Not so much as one shot fired in anger. Do you hear me?"

"So why did she say I am to stop the war? And why did she say 'War is sin'?"

"How do I get out of here now that your friend—this disgraced priest turned enemy of everything that is right and decent about us as a nation—has just sent away our only means of transportation?"

Royal said in a cheerful tone, "Pablo will gladly row you across."

Chuck clenched and unclenched his fist several times before he spoke. "Father Cranfield. That is your name and former title, isn't it? I don't believe I addressed my question to you. If you will be magnanimous enough to remain out of this discussion between a husband and his wife, I would consider your disciplined self-exclusion a distinct and most gratefully-received blessing."

"He's right," Jan said. "Pablo is the only way out of here. And he will row you across and you can drive my car back to where you left yours. Somehow we'll figure a way for me to retrieve it when it's time for me to return."

"What about the Border Patrol?"

"I'd tell you about that if I am allowed to speak, Doctor," said Royal.

Chuck sneered at Royal. "Father, are you always this childish and this impudent?"

"Right now I'm on my best behavior."

Ignoring the insolence, he turned to his wife. "Will you go back with me if I believe you truly did see the Mother of

Jesus? And if I assure you yet again there is to be *no* war."

"But that makes no sense. If there is to be no war, why did she say what she said?"

"Believe me, my dear wife, I have no idea what you're talking about. Zero!"

"I cannot return until I know what she meant and even more what I am to do with what she told me." Jan's voice broke as she came close to sobbing. "I cannot disobey her. She is pure love and she gave me a message to safeguard until I can discover the meaning but even more how I am to convey her holy words. You go back with Pablo without me."

"Who is this Pablo?"

"He's our inveterate boatman," chimed in Royal, smiling in a way Jan sensed was intended to annoy her husband as much as possible.

"Excuse me, Father, but I believe I was addressing my wife and not you."

"He's the boatman and he will row you across," said Jan.

"But what about the Border Patrol."

"Am I free to speak, sir?" said the priest.

"Oh, why not? Go ahead!"

"They are not a problem this morning, Dr. Love."

"How can you be certain?"

"He knows these things, Chuck. You don't have to like him to trust him."

"I don't like him and neither do I trust him, but what choice do I have?"

Grinning, Royal said, "Well Doctor, you could stay here and climb up to The Thin Place and perhaps you too could meet Juan Diego. And who knows, maybe even Our

Blessed Mother. Then she could tell you first-hand what she wants from you. Seeing how you're in real tight with the powerbrokers in our nation's capital, you could be of some valuable service to the Holy Mother of our beloved Prince of Peace."

Ignoring the priest, he said to Jan, "Where do I find this Pablo?"

"I'll gladly introduce you to him," chimed Royal. "He rows gringos back across for $100 a ride."

"That's larceny!"

"Take it or leave it, Doctor, he's the only boatman we've got. It's either Pablo or you're stuck here with us. If you're lucky, Juan Diego just might show up and even convince you to climb the big mountain. And if that happens, I'll gladly guide you, just as I did your wife."

Facing his wife, Chuck said, "I'm coming back with the Rangers or the Federales or someone in authority. One way or another, you're coming home, woman, and then I'm putting you in a hospital and in Harry Singleton's care."

He dusted his hands together. "But today I will drive your car back to Dallas. I have no idea how you would get to my Benz, should you come to your senses and leave this madman, but you'll find it in long-term parking at the international bridge in Presidio, if it is still there. I will leave it there until I can make other arrangements."

He folded his arms and glared down at Jan. "When I made the decision to risk my life coming here, I had such high hopes this all might end differently. But I want you to hear from me two truths before I go: one, you did *not* meet the Virgin Mary. It *doesn't* work like that. It never has and it never

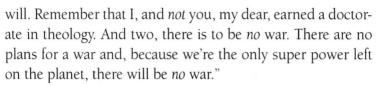

will. Remember that I, and *not* you, my dear, earned a doctorate in theology. And two, there is to be *no* war. There are no plans for a war and, because we're the only super power left on the planet, there will be *no* war."

Turning to face the priest he said, "And Father Cranfield, you and I are far from finished. I will do everything within my considerable power to see to it you are arrested and extradited to the United States and you are tried and convicted to the fullest extent of the law for abduction, extortion, and terrorist threats against my wife and me, and against the United States. As far as I am concerned, you're a one-man Al Qaeda sleeper cell. And sir, as I believe you are aware, I have friends in very high places and they will join me in taking great pleasure in seeing to it that you rot in a prison cell. Do I make myself clear?"

"Abundantly so, Dr. Love. Oh, one last thing. Tell Pablo you know how to swim."

"Why?"

"Just an inside joke, not something you'd appreciate. You're just a bit too uptight for our humor down here in what you called a pathetic country." Royal's expression turned serious. "Integrity requires that I not lie. In truth, it's not been a pleasure, but it has been quite interesting, even revelatory, and more than a little bit confirming to meet you, sir. I promise to take excellent care of Janet until she returns. In the meantime, *vaya con Dios*."

Chuck stood stiff, as though covered in heavy armor. "Jan, one last chance."

"I can't go back until I know what it is I've been given to do with what she told me."

"I should have known the power of delusion should *never* be underestimated. Have it your way for now. I'm gone, but I will continue to pray for you. And when you return, you're going straight into the finest psychiatric facility money can buy."

"Prayer is an amazing gift. It's such a privilege." Jan stood up and took one step toward him. "Thank you and be well. And I promise to return home as soon as I possibly can, but I have no need of a hospital or of a psychiatrist." She put her hand on his arm. "I want to love you, Chuck, I really do. And I will try to do that, as God gives me strength. Please tell me that you believe that."

He said nothing as he turned toward the river. Jan and Royal stood in the doorway and watched as Chuck negotiated the slippery riverbank. He waved his arms, arguing with Pablo, but at last appeared to give up and climbed into the unsteady boat.

Pablo grinned as he gripped the boat's stern with both hands. Once they shoved off, Chuck leaned over the side and vomited into the river while the bow bounced in the rapids.

CHAPTER FORTY-NINE

Esperanza cracked open the door to peer through the screen at the man ambling toward her. His cautious gait kicked up little puffs of dirt in her front yard, while it signaled a hint of reservation his bravado had earlier concealed.

Clutching her rosary beads to her lips, she squinted at him through the rusty screen. As he climbed the steps to her front porch, she latched the screen door. "Why have you returned?"

In the shadows, he stood a respectful distance from the entrance. "I hoped you might invite me in so we could visit for just a short while. Ma'am, I need your help. Actually, I need an explanation, but I don't think you are the one to provide it. But I think you're a part of it, if this makes any sense."

"I did all I could for you and there is nothing more I can do. The poison is gone, but I cannot heal your soul. Only God can do that."

The man shifted his weight from one leg to the other, and back again. "That's why I must talk to you."

"You threatened me, sir, and I will not invite you inside." Esperanza folded her arms across her chest. "Of course, you can push your way in, but if you do that, we will be where we were. You will threaten and I will pray for you as I did before. Fear between two souls is never God's will. God would have us be reconciled."

She shook her head. "But you do not know God. Your truth is a lie, and that makes you dangerous. I cannot invite you into my house."

"Will you take me to the desert and leave me at the exact spot you left Oonie?"

Her dark eyes narrowed into slits. "Why?"

"Ma'am, I honestly don't know." He took a step backward and looked down at his shoes for a moment. "But whatever happened here in your house did something to me. If I knew more, I would tell you everything," he said as he looked up, "but the truth is, now I am certain I must go to the desert to learn something and I have no idea what."

He shrugged. "And that's what is so strange, ma'am. I don't know why I'm asking you to help me. Something deep inside me has changed. And if I don't ask you to take me, I'll be making a mistake, even a big mistake. Other than that, I don't know what to tell you."

Esperanza unfolded her arms. "Will you hurt me?"

The man shook his head. "I swear I will not hurt you or anyone else ever again. Since you drew the poison out, I am very different. And frankly, this difference should terrify me, but it doesn't."

He ran his hands through his hair. "Confusion has never been a luxury I could afford. All I know is that I must go to the desert and I promise not to hurt you."

Esperanza put her hands on her wide hips. "And if I refuse?"

"I will go away and never bother you again. You have my word, ma'am."

She let her arms drop to her side. "I will take you tonight.

Be here at eight o'clock and do not bring your gun. Holiness comes only to the meek."

He stood on her porch after she closed the door, listening to his own breath. Several minutes passed, and then he turned around and walked out into the hot sunlight.

CHAPTER FIFTY

The minister rapped his knuckles softly against the half-opened door, after which he nervously cleared his throat.

Barrett stood facing the big office window with his back to the door. "Come in, preacher," he said without turning around.

Even from a distance and over Barrett's shoulder, Chuck could see a brisk November breeze scattering leaves across the faded White House lawn.

"Sit down, preacher," Barrett said, still staring out the window, "and make yourself at home."

Chuck hated the power struggles into which he was thrust every time his ambition compelled him to interact with this bully. He reminded himself to be cautious, even hyper-vigilant. If there was one predictable quality in this Washington powerbroker, it was the man's compulsion to remain in control, whether the contest was politics or a deceptively simple conversation.

As he fixed his gaze on the man's massive back, Chuck sat in the same high-back chair he had occupied in previous visits. An uneasy, close to unbearable silence ensued.

Whatever this man's game, Chuck would not be the first to speak. He would wait this ogre out, even if it required one tense hour after another. He dreaded what he suspected was to come next, the news he was no longer of use to this

President. He still maintained some hope, however, but only because he had been invited to return to Barrett's office.

Over his shoulder, the big man said, "Preacher, tomorrow the polls open here on the east coast at 7:00 a.m. And a mere twelve hours later, this President will be re-elected."

Fidgeting in the chair, Chuck said, "I'm sure that is true, sir."

"Every poll predicts it, but even more, my gut prophesies it. Nothing I trust more than my gut. It's one hundred percent right one hundred percent of the time. And about that I ain't bragging, I'm simply acknowledging a God-given gift."

Chuck thought it odd, even a bit perverse, to hear this man speak of God. He wondered if such a man ever prayed.

While gray clouds shrouded the city in the promise of a dismally cold day, Barrett cleared his throat. "That comes down to another four years, preacher."

"Yes, sir, and that is very good news for this country," said Chuck, and immediately regretted the observation.

Again Barrett cleared his throat and said, "How's the wife?"

Feigning confidence, Chuck said, "She's down in Mexico, sir."

"We know. She's down there with some disgraced lunatic priest and she's turned into a regular Jesus freak."

Chuck jumped to his feet. "Well, that's not—"

"Furthermore, you risked a good bit of political embarrassment, including becoming a huge liability to this administration, by striking out for Mexico and riding a bus and then in some kid's pickup all the way to a little border town not a stone's throw from Texas. You did your dead-level best to convince your wife to return but she refused. She can stay and commit adultery with a man who has taken a solemn vow to live a celibate life."

Chuck leaned toward Barrett. "Listen to me, I will not have you—"

Turning to face Chuck, he said, "Sit down, preacher. There is no reason to get riled. None whatsoever!"

Barrett held up his palm. "We're going to keep you, boy. The President of the United States loves you and he's most proud to welcome you to his second administration and he and all of us up here in the White House have no doubt you will be an inestimable asset to our rather ambitious agenda. The President is most impressed your wife is so dedicated to Jesus that she is willing to go to a third-world country and do such fine missionary work."

"She's not doing—"

"Of course she is. She's doing missionary work down there with those poor unsaved beggars. God knows they need all the sweet-Jesus missionary work they can get. And good for Jan, and good for you, that she's willing to sacrifice in the Lord's name."

Chuck gave up protesting, as he realized it would do no good. As he waited for Barrett to twist the next truth, his thoughts careened from one possibility to another.

Barrett strolled from the big office window to the large chair into which he collapsed. He lifted one leg at a time to the desk until he propped both big shoes on his desk each with a jolting thud.

Chomping on the wet stub of an unlit cigar, he grinned with his teeth still clinched. "Boy, now listen tight, because this is the way it all shakes out. You're to be the President's

Secretary for National Spirituality. Of course, the Senate and the House will have to confirm your appointment, but they will. You'll be easier than slick on chicken grease to get through. And your wife is a missionary and can't be at your side. But her cause is a most noble one, preacher. If she can do enough good work down there, perhaps she can help staunch the flow of illegal aliens crossing our border. Now wouldn't that be a dream story for *Newsweek* or *Time* to slap on their covers next spring? I swear, preacher, the whole of Latin America is hemorrhaging and no one has been able to stop it. Your wife could be the woman of the year. Who knows?"

Barrett turned his head to spit in a large brass vase adjacent to his desk. "But the second she crosses back into this country, she will be apprehended, secreted away, and placed in psychiatric facility operated by the CIA. This place is so secure not one member of Congress even knows it exists."

He narrowed his eyes into a scowl. "The place is so top-secret it doesn't even have a name. The CIA agents who even know about it call it 'The Hospital.' And if one of our fine members of Congress ever discovers its existence, it will be because you leaked it and your service will be no longer required. And then unfortunately for you, there is that little bit of former embarrassment you've managed to keep so well to yourself for all these many years."

Standing, Chuck said, "I have no idea what you're talking—"

"Sit down, preacher, and let me refresh your memory. It seems you have what down in the East Texas piney woods the homefolks call a 'love child' you've never even laid eyes on. How sad for everyone concerned."

Chuck collapsed in the chair.

Barrett managed a toothy grin with the cigar still in place. "Your parents helped you out of this scrape some thirty years back by paying the child's mother to keep quiet. Am I kicking up any memories?"

The big man paused, and Chuck read the man's grin as triumphant.

Through that devastating grin, Buck said, "And to make matters worse, this child, as I recollect, is just a bit on the backwards side. Isn't that right, preacher? Oh what an embarrassment this must be for a man of your considerable abilities."

Chuck bowed his head and could feel shame turning his face hot and, no doubt, crimson.

"Like I've told you before, we know *everything*. Now wouldn't it just be the worst kind of luck if *The Washington Post* were to get a hold of a story that you, sir, in a church youth group you were leading at the time, were more than just a little bit amorous with a young, under-aged virgin who tragically ended up with child? Including photos and birth certificates?"

Chuck's stomach churned.

"Preacher, the law books on that shelf over yonder say the same thing in all 50 states. Ain't no statute of limitation on aggravated sexual assault against a minor. Simply put, son, you raped a little girl who trusted you. And unless this girl's pregnancy was some kind of God-ordained miracle, then some fairly indicting DNA links you to this daughter, who is now a young adult living in poverty. What a pity a famous evangelist father dumped his retarded kid like she was a bag of garbage and has never even shown up to visit. That kind of behavior doesn't sound like the man the media calls 'the nation's pastor,' now does it?"

Defeated, Chuck leaned back in his chair. "What is it you want, Barrett?"

"Precisely what the President of the United States wants. I want you to be the Secretary of National Spirituality and for you to serve this President extraordinarily well. You will report directly to me and only to me and you will say *exactly* what I want you to say and not a word more or not a word less. When the time is right—and it won't be long—you will read word-for-word the speech I will prepare for you, announcing God has mandated this administration to liberate the world from every vestige of tyranny. This is to be *the* American Century, son, and we mean to democratize the world and depose every despot while we're still the only ones with the big guns. And a few weeks from now, you will convince the American people that God would have us bomb the North Korean commies back into the Stone Age. You beginning to catch my drift, boy?"

"And what if I should turn down this position?"

"It's a free country. But you don't know this town like I do. Up here in D.C., the craziest government leaks make their way into the Post and, as much as we try, sometimes we just can't stop them. It boils down to this: you can serve this President with distinction or likely serve more than just a few years behind bars back there in Tennessee. That's where this bit of misfortune occurred, ain't it? "

Chuck stood tall and threw his head back. "This is extortion!" he yelled.

"It's patriotism and we know you to be a super patriot and your beautiful wife is a most devoted woman of God dedicating her life to serve the less fortunate somewhere in the jungles of Central America."

Chuck protested, "But she is on the border in—"

"We know where she is. And we say she is in the jungles of Central America, working tirelessly every day to save the souls of those backward people, and her work is so important, so sensitive, and so sincere, that even the paparazzi will declare her off limits. The good taste of the American people will demand it. You see, we're ready to nominate you as the President's Secretary of National Spirituality and accept your wife as American's version of Mother Teresa. That's a win-win for a child rapist if I've ever heard of one."

Chuck turned away from the man and faced the office door.

Barrett raised his voice. "When she returns to the states, she will be kept safe for the duration of this President's second term in the CIA's secret facility, where she will be treated for her mental problems. As far as the media will ever know, she will remain the dedicated woman of God, laboring for Jesus in the jungles."

"This facility… is it like a prison?"

"It's a CIA-run hospital and it's one hundred percent secure. When you're finished up here, you will be reunited with her and by then she should be far more compliant. The docs that run this place are very, very good at what they do and their medicines are more than a little potent in helping folks change their minds. I'm presenting you with a once-in-a-lifetime opportunity to be of extraordinary use to this President and to this great nation."

Turning about to face the big man, Chuck said, "I'd say you're nothing more than a rank extortionist."

"You're just a bit on the fractious side, but who can blame you? You recently experienced that terrible misadventure down in Mexico. No, son, this is not at all how you describe it. It's a wonderful opportunity and, in the name of this President, I'm offering you the chance of a lifetime. You will be of enormous service to this administration, sir. No doubt about it."

"I really don't have any choice do I, Barrett?" said Chuck, stuffing his hands into his pants pockets.

"Oh what a sad and pessimistic view. And here I thought you were known for being positive all the time. My God, man, what a disappointment!"

"You have me just where you want me—trapped!"

Barrett smiled so wide his cigar stub dropped to the surface of his desk. "Not at all, preacher, not at all. Do exactly what we need for you to do and you get your wife back and you can hold fast to your sterling reputation. And then you're free to go on the lecture circuit and sell more books than you ever imagined possible. Who knows, you might even win the Nobel Prize. Now, if there is nothing else you have to say, I'm ready to end this conversation. Good day Dr. Love and welcome aboard. Welcome to your special place in history."

Chuck turned and moved toward the door to make as quick an exit as possible. He wanted to run but thought better of the impulse.

As he stepped into the hallway, he realized he might

faint, and the thought terrified him. Nevertheless, he managed to locate an ornate hallway chair, where he sat until his head cleared enough to imagine walking and his breathing returned to some semblance of normal.

CHAPTER FIFTY-ONE

Seated behind the old truck's steering wheel, Esperanza refused to turn toward the gaunt man. "Sir, the desert freezes at night this time of year so I brought two quilts, one for you to sit on and the other for you to use as a wrap. You will need the wrap, sir." Esperanza gripped the steering wheel with both gloved hands and stared straight ahead into the darkness.

The headlights on the old truck were dim enough to be illegal. Since his wallet contained counterfeit identification, the man would be an easy mark for any law-enforcement officer with access to a computer. Furthermore, he suspected the FBI didn't have a Daemon listed on its rolls and certainly not one with his first name David. But then there was the chance a sheriff deputy would know Esperanza and either not stop her, or if he did, would consider any passenger as not worth investigating.

The state troopers worried him. He wondered if he'd not made a mistake leaving his gun in his motel room. But no sooner had he thought of the gun than he realized he would never use it again. Although he didn't understand this jarring revelation, he did sense that whatever drove it was the very power now sending him into the desert to be alone on this cold night.

A huge jackrabbit shot across the road to disappear in

the darkness.

"How cold does it get out here at night?" he said.

"This is the last week of November and the freeze is still light, but next month the winter nights turn bitter. You will be warm enough in the quilt."

"What if I build a fire?"

"No one will come."

Turning to face the old woman and wearing the grin of expectancy, he said, "Who might come?"

"Perhaps no one. But if you pray perhaps someone."

"What if I don't pray?" said the man as he lit a cigarette.

"No one will come," said the old woman staring straight ahead and into the dim glow of the headlights.

"But I don't know how to pray. I've never prayed, not that I can recall. Perhaps as a child I did, I don't remember."

The old woman sneezed and cranked down the truck window. The cold night chilled the truck's cab. "Then you must be open. Openness is also prayer," she whispered.

"What exactly does it mean to be open?"

A massive mule deer jumped out of the blackness and into the road, his rack of antlers reflecting the truck's dim light.

The old woman said, "You say 'Help!' and you really mean it. That's all."

Turning to face the woman, the gaunt man said, "Will this someone be a supernatural being?"

"Perhaps."

"Who or what is most likely to come?"

"An angel."

"So I might actually see an angel if I just say 'Help!' and

I mean it."

"Angels are God's very best thoughts, and they come to every soul who is sincerely requesting help."

The man cranked the window down on the passenger side only long enough to toss his lit cigarette into the desert. With a wider grin, he said, "Have you actually seen angels?"

"Many times."

"How often?"

"Every day, because I see God's thoughts in everything. God is on your side, sir, but you have never known this and so now you must ask for help."

Fumbling with a pack of cigarettes in his shirt pocket, the gaunt man said, "I don't understand."

"When you ask for help, you are asking God to purify your heart and to restore your soul so you can be blessed with new eyes. And with these eyes, you will see you are greatly loved and are safe with God because God holds nothing against you. God loves you and God intends for you to become love's eternal message."

He chuckled. "Me, a message of love? Ma'am, you don't know me, but let me assure you that for the whole of my life I've been anything but love's message. Terror's message maybe, or death's angel, but nothing about me has ever been about love."

The old woman slowed the truck. "I do know who you are, sir."

With a new cigarette in his mouth, "Okay, tell me ma'am, who am I?"

"You are a man who as a child became frightened enough to believe you must choose evil, but now God has chosen you for good, perhaps for great good. In God's time, you will become what God from the beginning created you to be, love's very expression."

"Really!" the man said, as the unlit cigarette dropped into his lap and fell to the truck's floorboard.

"That is God's truth, sir."

"So I just wait to become something I've never been. Is that it?"

"We are here, sir. Step out of the truck and walk due west. When you can no longer see the road, you will be where I left Oonie. I will return at first light tomorrow."

The man shrugged, opened the truck's old door, and stepped down onto the rocky crude shoulder of the narrow road. He trembled alone in the cold as he watched the truck's taillights grow dimmer until the blackness swallowed them completely.

CHAPTER FIFTY-TWO

Fox News' morning anchor, Dan Slagle, opened his broadcast. "We're in Dallas, Texas, this morning in the most impressive office of a man known to most Americans regardless of their political party as this nation's pastor. Welcome to Fox News American Morning, Dr. Chuck Love."

Seated behind his big desk, Chuck squinted under the bright lights as he waited for his eyes to grow accustomed to the intense beams bearing down on him. "Thank you, Dan. And may I offer to you and to your fine crew a hearty welcome to Big D. We're so glad to have you visit us here in our fair city, even on such a bitterly cold day."

"Thank you, sir. Our sources tell us, Dr. Love—"

"If I can get away with calling you Dan, then it is only right you call me Chuck. Let's dispense with titles and formalities, shall we?"

"Sounds good, Chuck. Our sources tell us the White House has invited you to offer the inaugural prayer for the President's second term."

"Let me just say I consider this invitation to be *the* greatest honor of my life."

"But that's not all. The capital rumor-mill has been churning a good bit lately, which as you know is what it does best, and the latest rumor has it that you will be invited to serve on this President's cabinet in a newly created capacity.

Is this also true?"

Chuck leaned closer to the microphone. "The moment I say 'no comment,' most Americans will think it's nothing more than another way to say 'yes,' but in this instance it means just that. No comment."

"So you don't deny the rumors."

"Neither do I confirm them, Dan."

"Fair enough. So, Chuck, share with our viewers your opinion of this President."

"I admire the man tremendously—"

"Why?"

"He puts principle first, even before political self-interest, and also because he's a man of prayer. I will go on record as declaring him to be the most devout Christian in the White House since Lincoln. It's no secret he's a born-again Christian, which is the only kind of true Christian. If you think about what it means to have Christ within your heart—"

"But Chuck, the list of spiritual men who have occupied the White House includes the likes of Woodrow Wilson, FDR, and Carter. History regards those Presidents as men of faith, even devoted to God and arguably, with the exception of President Carter, these were all very effective Presidents, each in his own way, of course."

Chuck smiled and scooted his chair closer to the microphone. "History will prove me right on this. This President is a man of God and I am both honored and greatly humbled to know him as a close personal friend, as well as the finest President this nation has elected in the past century. You know from your own experience, Dan, what it's like to be in the presence of true greatness. One cannot help but be influenced tremendously and inspired by being in such close proximity to giants regardless of the professional field."

"Chuck, the President makes no secret that God has called him to this office."

"I admire him for making this perspective public. He truly believes, God has placed him in the Oval Office, and again he's not at all shy about stating this conviction often. And even when he was our governor back in Texas, I admired him for both his candor and his extraordinarily strong faith."

"My question is this: do you as a theologian believe God has chosen him to be President?"

"Well, Dan, the evidence of the past four years certainly bears this out, and in the context of your question, I find helpful the words of a 20th Century social commentator named Stuart Chase, who put it this way, 'For those who believe, no proof is necessary and for those who don't believe, no proof is possible.'"

"So as a trained theologian and as an evangelical Christian, are you willing then to go on record as saying God has actually called this President to the Oval Office?"

"Yes, I am willing to posit that. Again, Dan, the evidence—"

"But with all due respect, Chuck, how does such a perspective play with Americans who are not Christians, such as Jews, Muslims, Buddhists, Hindus and also with those who profess no religious faith?"

"Extraordinarily well. He's their President as well as the head of the Republican Party. And his policies are sound, and any fair-minded person would say he puts the interest of the American people first. But you see, Dan, there is no real conflict here when you consider God's will is always the right choice for America regardless of one's religious or theological persuasion. God's will is always good for us, both as individuals and also as a great and diverse nation of many faiths."

"So you have no problem with this President declaring that God has chosen him over his Democratic opponents in the previous two elections. Does that imply God approves of the Republican agenda more than what the Democrats offer?"

"Of course not. Read your Bible, Dan, and you will discover the recurring pattern throughout the whole of human history. God does *not* raise up political parties nor does God cobble together a particular political agenda. God raises up leaders, while the politics, or the machinations of power, are left entirely to us. Scripture also teaches—and here, I paraphrase—where there is no vision, the people perish. What fair-minded American can argue with the obvious? This President is a man of vision. And his vision is bold and right for this country."

Chuck removed the microphone from its stand, held it close to his mouth, and stood. "God has raised up this truly great man, and last month the majority of Americans voted for him a second time because they could see his character for what it is—impeccable—and his ability as exemplary, even unparalleled. Therefore, we the people very wisely, and by a wide majority, returned him to the Oval Office for another four years."

"Does God also love Democrats enough to raise one up as President every once in a while?"

Chuck Love smiled wide enough to be certain his recently bleached teeth glistened in the bright klieg lights.

The thought comforted him. "God loves all people!"

"Does God ever raise up women?"

"History is full of them. Joan of Arc, Deborah who was a judge in ancient Israel, and in our age many women have served their people well. Margaret Thatcher, Indira Gandhi, and Golda Meir are excellent examples, and several of this nation's state governors and most effective members of Congress are women."

"Do you think that God will ever raise up a woman to be President?"

"Dan, I'd best leave what God will or will not do entirely to God."

"Tell us about your wife. I understand she is overseas working as a missionary."

Chuck focused on preventing a scowl to appear on his handsome face and ruin the mood of this dream-come-true conversation. "Actually, Dan, she is in an undisclosed nation in the Central Americas.

"So you cannot tell us exactly where."

Pushing his smile once more toward a grin, he said, "You can certainly understand and the American people can appreciate the need for the utmost discretion here. There are unfriendly forces in that part of the world, so the need to protect her trumps everything else, including the public's right to know. I respect her and I admire her for what she does. She's the real Christian in our family. Me? I only preach the Gospel, but Jan actually goes into the world to live it out. And I couldn't be more proud or more blessed to have such a wonderful wife. She is truly, truly amazing."

"What kind of mission work does she do?"

"Primarily, she prays. And Dan, let me tell you something—that's the most important work there is."

"Will she return in time for the inauguration?"

"Very likely not. Her commitment is long-term, and I want to do everything in my power to support her."

"Will you go visit her?"

"As a matter of fact, I was down there last month visiting with her and I cannot tell you how very impressed I am with the important work she is doing. I wish I could boast more of her, but unfortunately I cannot do so without jeopardizing her ministry and even her life."

"Chuck, thank you for your time this morning."

"Thank you, Dan, and Merry Christmas."

"Merry Christmas to you, Chuck, and also to you, Mrs. Love, wherever you are this morning. This is Dan Slagle reporting live from Dallas and now back to you guys in New York."

The two men shook hands, and Dan stacked his papers before handing them to an assistant. He stood up and walked away from Chuck's desk.

Overhead the klieg lights went out. With his hands in his lap, Chuck sat still for a moment, as sound techs came forward to unhook wires and remove equipment. When the office was deserted, he wiped his brow and sighed.

CHAPTER FIFTY-THREE

Standing to peer through a gap separating St. Joseph's two big hanging doors, Royal spied Jan on her knees and deep in prayer before the butcher-block altar. "Janet," he said. He stepped into the chapel and spoke her name a second time but still she refused to turn about.

"Stay here," Royal said to the gaunt man. "I will go to her and find out what she wishes to do."

Dressed in what appeared to be a suit reduced to rags, the disheveled man nodded.

Royal crept on the warm dirt path down the narrow center aisle of the chapel until he arrived at the place where she knelt before a single lit candle. He sat on a splintery bench and waited for her to sense his presence.

I don't wish to startle her. How do I do this?

"Janet," he said.

She turned to him, blinking, and gave him a slight smile.

"Oh hello, Royal, how wonderful to see you. I didn't expect—"

"Janet, you have a visitor, a stranger dressed roughly who is sporting a two-day growth."

"Who is he?" She looked past the priest and toward the door. All she could make out was a tall thin shadow of a man she did not recognize.

"He didn't tell me his name, but he claims Juan Diego

sent him to this church to find you."

"Oh, how wonderful. Invite him in. But if you will, give me a minute or two to stand on these stiff legs and clear my head. I have no idea how long I've been here praying."

She stretched out her arms to balance herself against the railing as she struggled to her feet. "Never have I been so content, so very peaceful. I didn't know serenity was anything but a silly myth. God, what a miracle this whole thing has been. You can't imagine how I've suffered."

Royal returned to the door and nodded. The stranger followed the priest to the first row of benches. He smiled at the woman whose bright eyes burned with curiosity.

"I've seen you before. Oh my God, you're the man who was attacked by the bees. Are you okay? Whatever happened to you?"

He smiled. "I am fine, Mrs. Macdonald-Love, just a bit worse for wear, and a little weak from hunger."

"Why did you come down here?" said Royal.

The man held his smile in a way that only added to the priest's suspicions.

Jan trumped his question with one of her own. "Sir, by chance is your name Gregory?"

"May I sit?" said the gaunt man.

"Yes, of course," said Jan.

Easing down to straddle the narrow bench opposite her, he said, "My name is David Daemon. One of the President's men, a man named Buck Barrett, sent me. I came here to do evil."

"Exactly what kind of evil?" said Royal, jerking himself erect and tall.

"Barrett is the President's chief of staff and he paid me very well to see to it that you committed suicide."

Royal stepped toward the man.

"Why would you?" she said.

"Mrs. Macdonald-Love, you must understand that killing is my profession. I work for a syndicate back east and I make my living doing away with people for a very hefty fee. What you call a hit man."

"Why did this Mr. Barrett send you to kill me?"

"If I knew, I would tell you."

"Oh my God—"

Royal moved between them. "You've said enough, mister. Pablo will row you back to Texas. You've frightened her, and if that's what you came here to do, you've accomplished your purpose. Now get out of here!"

Jan threw her arms into the air. "Let him stay," she yelled. "He is not here to harm me or anyone else."

Clinching his fists, Royal said, "Then why are you here?"

"As you know, I was attacked by those bees several days ago. From here I managed to drive to Marathon where I happened upon a kid who, as it turns out, is a saint or an angel or something. I'm not sure what he is, but he's something other than ordinary."

"Oonie Garza," said Royal.

"Who is Oonie Garza?" said Jan.

The stranger smiled, "He's an instrument, ma'am. And he's also somewhat of a local sports phenomenon, but far more than that, he's God's instrument."

"I don't understand," she said.

"I don't either, ma'am, but I happened into him at the

Catholic Church in Marathon."

"That's Father O'Shea's church."

"I've also met the good father. By chance or fate or whatever, I happened into Oonie who took me to a woman's house. The woman is named Esperanza."

"Who is Esperanza?" Jan said.

"Esperanza is a *curandera*, a faith healer. And she healed me. And ma'am, to make what could easily be a long and most incredible story very brief, the only way I know to describe what happened is to say that my plan for killing you left with the fever she literally drew out of my body. Once I departed from that old woman's house, I knew I could no longer kill you or anyone else."

"How do we know this is not a trick?" said Royal as he straightened his broad shoulders.

"You don't. But after I watched this kid play basketball, which itself was something unforgettable, I somehow knew I had to return to Esperanza's house. Believe it or not, I asked her to take me out into the desert because I knew I was supposed to go there. Don't ask me how I knew, but the fact is I knew that going into the desert alone was what I was supposed to do."

Jan searched Royal's face for clues as to what she might do next. Finding none, she squatted on a pew and rested her head in her hands and stared at the dirt floor.

The man spoke again. "Of course, she was reluctant at first, but who could blame her? After she had healed me, I actually threatened her. But thankfully she agreed, and at straight up 8:00 two nights ago, she drove me into the desert very close to the spot where this kid Oonie is said to have met

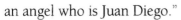

an angel who is Juan Diego."

Jan and Royal exchanged quick glances.

"The first day and night I did little but shiver and wait. Esperanza was supposed to pick me up at first light, but she failed to return which can mean only one thing."

Stepping toward the man, Jan said, "And what is that?"

"She has been arrested by the FBI."

Jan gasped. "Why what has she done?"

"Nothing except helped me. No doubt by now Barrett has put out an APB on me, and God only knows how, the FBI traced me to her house."

Daemon rose from the pew and raised his voice. "The second day, I lay down to hide in the brush. Above my head, helicopters circled all afternoon and even into the night shining their search lights."

"What are helicopters doing in the desert?" said Royal as he unclenched his fists to rub his tired eyes.

"They're searching for me," said Daemon.

"I don't get it, Daemon," said Jan. "What have you done?"

"It's what I've *not* done—and what I've not done is see to it that you, Dr. Chuck Love's wife, die by your own hands. And I can easily implicate the President's chief of staff in a conspiracy to commit murder, so I must be taken out to protect Barrett and this entire administration."

Royal stood on a bench to look down upon the man, "You're making this whole thing up. Our government doesn't do things like this. This is all your sick fantasy, and if not that, then a ruse."

"I only wish I were lying." The gaunt man stayed seated on the splintery bench as he gazed up into the pale blue eyes of the priest.

"You're paranoid, Mr. Daemon. Our government leaders are sworn to protect this nation's citizens. They don't go around putting contracts out on people. You must be out of your mind." Royal stepped off the bench and toward Jan. He gently took hold of her arm. "Jan, we've heard enough."

"Trust me, paranoia would be much easier to accept. What I am telling you is the truth. Mrs. Macdonald-Love is in danger, imminent danger."

"I don't believe you," said Royal.

"Mrs. Macdonald-Love, you must believe me, ma'am.

"Why did you come to us now?" said Jan.

"Because during the second night in the desert Juan Diego appeared to me and he spoke."

"What did he say?" she said.

"Nothing more than his name and that I was to travel to this village where I would find you on your knees in this little church. And he begged me to tell you that you are in danger. After that, he said nothing more as he led me for many miles until I reached the highway. Then he disappeared. About mid-afternoon two campers came by in a Jeep and took pity upon me, I suppose, and they drove me to the gravel parking lot where I happened upon you, Royal."

"How do we know we can trust you?" said Royal.

"You don't. But I have done what I was commanded to do. I have come to tell you, ma'am. You are in grave danger. This nation's government means to kill you. And since I'm no longer their go-to-guy, I can only tell you that someone else will be coming, much sooner than later. You must go into the mountains and hide and do it *now*. Night is less than an hour away and you must travel under the cover of darkness. There is no time to waste."

"But sir, I can't hide. I'm not done praying."

"What's in this for you?" said Royal, glowering at the man.

"I've asked myself that question, and the answer is nothing but the restoration of my soul. And what I have learned from Juan Diego is that the restoration of the soul is everything."

"But a man like you doesn't suddenly turn down money and put himself at risk for the sake of his soul. This just doesn't happen, not in the real world."

"My soul now means everything to me. And by being here and telling you what I know, I am jeopardizing not only my life but my son's life as well. He is incarcerated in a federal facility in Florida, facing capital murder charges in the wake of the alleged murder of an ATF officer."

"Did he kill the man?" said Royal.

"Only he and God know the truth about that. But he is charged with murder, and, if I fail with this hit, he will be found guilty and die very soon by lethal injection. So, to answer your question, my son's certain death is what's in this thing for me."

The gaunt man turned to Jan. "But I came here today because an angel who said his name was Juan Diego also told me where to find you. And he begged me to tell you that you are in danger. So that's why I'm here. That, and the truth that the state of my soul has become the most important thing in my life. But again, Mrs. Macdonald-Love, you must hide because men are coming to kill you, and are on their way as we speak. I have seen their helicopters, which means they cannot be far away."

Jan stepped toward the hanging front doors to peer into the dark sky. Royal doused the single altar candle and walked to where Jan stood at the door. He placed his hands upon her shoulders as together they searched a sky holding more stars than could be counted.

CHAPTER FIFTY-FOUR

Three commandoes dressed in black wet suits crawled on their bellies up the rocky path until they reached the front doors of St. Joseph's. They lay still in the moonless night.

Two other identically dressed men waited at the river's edge, holding fast to the nylon lines that secured three black inflatable rafts. Each was powered by a quiet electric motor.

As the leader of the three men inched toward the chapel door, he signaled his comrades to come no closer. Lying flat on his belly with his eyes peering out of the black rubber mask, he studied the scene before him. He smiled. The situation would make for an easier-than-expected shot.

Crawling back toward his comrades, who remained close to invisible, he whispered, "We fire the Azperone darts. This will knock them out instantly."

To the man on his right, he whispered, "The taller of the men is yours. He's the priest and he's the one presently standing."

To the man on his left, he said, "Daemon is sitting. It's a very easy shot. Remember, gentlemen, aim for the neck. Once they're out, grab them before they hit the floor and cuff them before you carry them to the rafts. I'll take the woman. Any questions?"

Without a sound, each man extricated a long air rifle from his backpack and, working in the pitch black with trained and nimble fingers, each inserted a small, feathered dart into the chamber. Then they sealed the dart into the weapon with the click of an aluminum bolt.

"Ready?" the leader said.

His two comrades nodded and the leader pivoted about on his belly a full one hundred-eighty degrees. Together they slithered like salamanders to the big hanging doors of St. Joseph's, where they waited as they watched. The priest relit the single altar candle, which then cast exaggerated shadows of the two men and the woman against the adobe wall.

As they lay at the boundary where the night shadows ended and the candle's meek light leaked through the big gap in the doors, the men studied the scene with trained eyes. Royal stepped a bit to the left while Daemon remained seated next to the woman with his head resting in his hands. Both elbows were braced against his knees.

When the taller man raised his voice, the leader in black considered it a bad sign. Years of training had taught him that declarations were always louder than conversation and often signaled the conclusion of a meeting. He and his men needed to act fast in order to keep this attack limited to as small a space as possible. His strong preference was to do what must be done in this primitive chapel rather than risk exposure outside.

From his prostrate position, he raised his hand to signal to his subordinates that they not move. They obeyed. From a distance, a dog barked once but no other sound came from the sleeping village.

The leader tapped both comrades on the shoulder. At his signal of three extended fingers, both men nodded.

The leader crept toward the door. He slipped through the big gap and into the chapel where he knelt behind the back pew. His men rose and followed him inside. All three aimed as their leader counted with his fingers. When the third digit appeared, they each fired the darts.

The whooshing sounds were so slight that not even a village dog stirred. Royal did turn his head toward the door and gasped, "What?" before the dart embedded in his neck took effect.

Within seconds, the three men scrambled under their dazed targets and hoisted them to their shoulders even before they could lose full consciousness. They lowered their unconscious prey to the floor, and then cuffed them with plastic bands. They lifted the two men and the woman to their shoulders and carried them to the river.

At the river's edge, the commando leader said, "The men go to Chopper One. They don't know it yet, but these fellows are going to exotic Guantanamo for quite a spell. They are to be detained indefinitely as terrorists and no one will miss them except maybe the people down here."

He pointed to the other helicopter. "The woman goes to Chopper Two, and she is off to what I understand will be a rather lengthy stay in our hospital. The docs there have a way of making their patients change their minds."

He shouldered his air rifle. "Let's get back across the river as quietly as we arrived. Gentlemen, we can't afford an international incident. The last thing I heard at the briefing this morning was that this had better not turn into another Bay of Pigs debacle."

The leader clapped one of the shooters on the back of the

shoulder. "Good job, men. Another good night's work for old Uncle Sam."

The three commandos loaded Daemon, Royal, and Jan into their respective rafts and then came together to fist bump before stepping into the rafts. Once the motors fired, the men then steered their sleek rafts toward the Texas side of the river. Three black vans, with engines running, awaited them.

Before a whippoorwill could conclude its nightly call to its mate, all three vans were swallowed by the blackness.

CHAPTER FIFTY-FIVE

"Six, five, four, three, two, one... Mr. President, you're on the air," said Stan Daly, director of White House Communications.

The President sat up straight at his desk and stared into the television camera. "Good evening, ladies and gentlemen. I come to you tonight from the Oval Office in the White House with an announcement that brings with it the highest hopes for the brightest future this world has ever known since the very beginning of civilization."

He focused on the red light, the way he'd been instructed. "Tomorrow morning when you awaken to go off to your work, place of business, or to school, or to begin your day on the farm, on the ranch, or in your home, you will step into the brightest day this nation, or for that matter, this world has ever known. This new day will mark the coming to full fruition of humankind's age-old dream of a new world forever free from armed conflict and blessed with the promise of a prosperity that only true liberty and the free enterprise system can deliver.

"Since my re-election in November I have invested a lion's share of my time meeting with members of my cabinet, with the leaders from both parties in both houses of Congress, with the heads of state of every NATO member nation, with the leadership of the United Nations, with the Joint Chiefs of Staff, and from these honest and frank discussions, I have come to the conclusion it is our nation's responsibility, but even more, our moral obligation as a free people, to put an end once and for all to every vestige of totalitarianism and its attendant oppression that has plagued humanity from the very beginning of time.

"The United States of America is this world's only remaining super-power, and as I and those who have advise me view it, our responsibility as a free people with unparalleled military might is to make certain totalitarianism can have no place in the 21ˢᵗ century. To that end, I have ordered a surgical air strike on Pyongyang North, Korea, at an hour of our choosing sometime tomorrow. Through a secret communication process, we have informed Chairman Kim Jong Un of our plans to destroy his government, and we have offered to accept his peaceful surrender and the full surrender of his army as the beginning of the long-overdue reunification of North Korea and South Korea. Not surprisingly, Chairman Kim Jong Un has treated our invitation with a deafening silence that can only be interpreted as a brutal and irresponsible defiance.

"Consequently, we will proceed with our plans and again at the time of our choosing, this ruthless tyrant and his government that has oppressed a people longing to be free for more than half a century will cease to exist. Because we are a people who love liberty, we will do our duty to liberate the long-suffering masses of the Korean Peninsula. From this time and forevermore, the people of North Korea will be free to be reunited to their brothers and sisters in the south, as together they become one of Asia's greatest and, in time, most industrious and prosperous democracies.

"Two additional points need to be made here: one, the device we will use is nuclear in nature but of such a low-yield that *only* the North Korean government will be destroyed. Civilian casualties will be minimum, if at all, and the radioactivity from this tactical device will dissipate in less than 48 hours. Two, this bomb, although humane and precise, is meant for Kim Jong Un, but in a very real sense it is also a shot across the bow of every totalitarian regime on the face of this planet. By the year's end we expect each dictator of every oppressed people the world over to have made significant strides in moving quickly toward full democratization of their respective countries, or they, too, will be notified they can expect the same fate as Kim Jong Un.

"Any decision of this nature is not easy and it, of course, bears risks, both political and military. However, as your President, I am convinced we owe it to our children and to their children to vouchsafe the safety of their future.

"As I have declared from this office before, I am the President of *all* of the American people regardless of race, ethnicity, creed or any other distinguishing factor. However, I am also a born-again Christian, and because of my deep faith in God and trust in God's sovereignty over all matters both large and small, I not only believe the path we the American people are taking tonight is right politically, I am also convinced that making this world free for democracy to flourish is precisely what our Lord had in mind when he spoke of blessings for those with the courage required to become peacemakers.

"The United States of America has been extraordinarily

blessed. Because we have, it is now incumbent on us to see to it that future generations the world over can know first-hand the great freedoms and the immense opportunities that come only from democracy.

"In making what has proven a difficult decision, I have been greatly helped and supported by a man who is no stranger to most Americans. Dr. Charles Love, or as he is more affectionately known Dr. Chuck Love, this nation's pastor and my new Secretary of National Spirituality, will now elaborate on the spiritual predicate for this bold new effort.

"I thank you for your support and please know I covet your prayers, and may God bless this bold new venture to bring freedom to all people everywhere and may God bless America.

"So I bid you goodnight. And now to you, Dr. Love."

Chuck gazed up into the eye of the camera and hoped he didn't seem too pale. "Good evening, ladies and gentlemen. My word tonight is to be brief and to the point.

"God is love and love's purpose is always the same, to liberate the oppressed. Six hundred years before the birth of Jesus, a Jerusalem prophet whose oracles bear the name Isaiah, wrote these holy and timeless words:

'Is this not the fast that I (God) choose:
to loose the bonds of injustice,
to undo the thongs of the yoke,
to let the oppressed go free,
and to break every yoke.'

"Our President has made the decision to break every yoke. This is not only the right decision for our times, but it is also even more what God would have us do in this hour.

"Without question, lives will necessarily be lost. But in Israel's early history when her people fled Pharaoh's pursuing army, Moses spoke these words: 'Do not be afraid, stand firm, and see the deliverance that the Lord will accomplish for you today; for the Egyptians whom you see today you shall never see again. The Lord will fight for you, and you have only to keep still.'

"This is God's word to us tonight on the eve of our liberation of a people too long oppressed.

God is speaking again through a voice that comes to us across the ages. His message is as clear and every bit as inspiring as when Moses first spoke these words: 'The Lord will fight for you, and you have only to keep still.'

"Thank you in advance for your prayers as together you and I and people of goodwill the world over enter into this bold new challenge of making our world finally and for all time safe for liberty and peace.

"Good night, and God bless you."

An assistant director waved at him. "You're off the air, sir"

The President wrapped his arm about Chuck's shoulder and said, "Great job, Chuck. Absolutely perfect! I'm so impressed. Who knew our friend could write such an impressive, biblically literate, and right to the point speech? Well, bully for him."

"Thank you, Mr. President. I had no idea Buck Barrett would actually write this excellent speech, but I must say he did a spectacular job."

"He did indeed, son, but now it's time I suspect to let you in on a state-secret. His name is not Buck. No, my goodness, that's only a nickname that's been around so long that everyone who knows him has all but forgotten what his mama actually named him. God rest her soul, the woman did have the good sense to name him something other than Buck."

"What is his real name?"

Smiling, the President said, "When that ornery little baby boy entered this world howling so many years ago back home in the piney woods of deep East Texas, his mama named him Gregory."

EPILOGUE

Your prophets have seen for you
false and deceptive visions;
they have exposed your iniquity
to restore your fortunes,
but have seen oracles for you
that are false and misleading.
Lamentations 2: 13

ABOUT THE AUTHOR

Bob Lively is a native Texan, raised and educated in the Dallas public schools. He is a graduate of Austin College and Austin Presbyterian Theological Seminary. The Presbyterian Church ordained him in 1973, and for the past four decades he has served the church as a pastor, community activist, teacher, certified pastoral counselor, campus minister, and recovery center chaplain.

He is the author of 9 books of non-fiction and is an award-winning short story writer. For 23 years he wrote a regular column in the *Austin American-Statesman*. **The Thin Place** is his first novel.

Today he is retired and lives with his wife, Mary Lynn, a retired university associate dean, on an acre in the Hill Country west of Austin. He has been named a distinguished alumnus of both Austin College and the Austin seminary.